FIRE AND ICE

This time she reached for the kiss. This time her arms
went around his neck and she pressed her breasts
against the strength of his chest. His mouth was hot
upon hers now, no less hungry than before, but this
time she matched him in ferocity, was his equal in
desire, as they clung together in the torrid night.
Arabella's mouth opened beneath his and his tongue
sought hers, exploring with maddening slowness the
silken softness of its inner contours.

At last the kiss ended and weakly she leaned against
him. The man who had been her enemy could now do
what he would with her; what she had feared, she could
fear no longer. For the moment she cared nothing
about power or escape, for to surrender to this man was
inevitable; to be his prisoner was her destiny. She felt
his touch as his fingers came up to very gently brush a
lock of hair from her cheek. His husky whisper was rich
and deep.

"Lady Arabella," he said as his hand fell away,
"someday, when you have grown old and gray and you
think back upon the days of your youth—perchance to
tell your grandchildren the tales of your wild folly—
remember that on this night you were kissed by the
man whom legend has deemed to call the Fox . . ."

SATIN FIRES

Rebecca Flanders

ZEBRA BOOKS
KENSINGTON PUBLISHING CORP.

ZEBRA BOOKS

are published by

Kensington Publishing Corp.
475 Park Avenue South
New York, NY 10016

First printing: July 1986

Printed in the United States of America

To Ginny, who was patient for a whole year

Chapter I

It was April. Wolfgang Amadeus Mozart was composing a memorable series of cantatas and quartets in Salzburg; Marie Antoinette was seventeen years old, had been married for three years to the *Dauphin* of France, and was still a virgin. Don Giovanni Jacapo Casanova was cutting a colorful path across the courts of Europe, and Catherine the Great was in the eleventh year of her reign.

The aristocracy of France was living out its last days, and the Austro-Hungarian empire was beginning to crumble with the collapse of the feudal system. King George III was on the throne of England and for five years had been engaged in a frustrating battle of wills with his unruly colonies. In the streets of Paris, Florence, Vienna, Warsaw, and Frankfurt, rumblings of discontent were beginning—a whisper that would gather force and, before the decade was out, shout a message that would shake the very foundations of Europe, and beyond.

This day, upon the streets of London, the fashionable shops were just opening. Vendors busily hawking their wares pushed carts laden with fish, fresh fruit, flowers, or baubles across the cobbles. Delivery wagons plodded through the traffic, their drivers immune to the stench of rotted fish, emptied chamber pots, and offal of every sort, which rose up from the gutters. Chimney sweeps and livery boys were halfway through another dreary day's work. Noble ladies wearing lace-trimmed eyeshades slept, with the aid of laudanum, upon eiderdown and muslin. Noble young gentlemen folded their final hands of cards with bored indifference and made for home or lingered over a last cup of wine while casting about for some new diversion or registered increasingly more outrageous bets in the book at White's. In the preceding hours, two duels had been fought over matters none of the participants recalled this morning, a curricle had been overturned in a race and its occupant left to bleed and die, and a serving girl, returning late from her duties, had been brutally raped and abandoned by three young members of the nobility who had grown tired of more respectable games.

In the fashionable districts of London, servants moved through elegantly appointed townhouses on silent feet, careful not to disturb the sleeping gentry. In one such house, Lord Reginald Winters, Earl of Chatley, had just come to a decision that would affect the lives of more people than he could now fathom, and he would have been less than pleased had he been able to foresee the ultimate consequences.

Lord Chatley linked his fingers together loosely upon his chest and eyed his sister grimly across the expanse of polished cherrywood desk that separated them. It was ten o'clock in the morning. At his elbow was a cup of cooling tea liberally laced with brandy and before him was the open copy of the latest edition of *Gentleman's Quarterly*. Less than a quarter of an hour ago the paper had been brought to him in bed, along with his customary tea and muffins. Three minutes later an ear-shattering roar had erupted, the breakfast tray had been flung across the room, and imperious, life-threatening commands had demanded the presence of Lady Arabella in his study without delay. In the moments of waiting for his sister's appearance, temper had turned into fury, fury into outrage, and outrage, at last, into cold determination. Now, as he surveyed the sibling who had caused him more discomfort over the past several years than he cared to remember, there was a hard glint reflecting from Chatley's eyes that warned of worse to come.

"Well, Missy," he pronounced at last, having prolonged the ominous silence as long as his deliberately controlled temper could reasonably tolerate, "what have you to say for yourself this time?"

Arabella had seen the paper. She stood before her brother in her dressing gown, her flame-colored hair an unbound mass of waves and curls about her face, her ice green eyes cool and remote. If her face was somewhat paler than usual, the effect could easily have been obscured by the composed lines into which her expression was set. The small lines around her tightly compressed lips might have betrayed stress, but the stubborn tilt of her chin revealed nothing but defiance. She was frightened but unapologetic, unnerved but determined. This time, she feared, she had gone too far, but not for all her life would she allow her brother to sense her unease. She said nothing.

Arabella had long since learned that the dignity of silence did nothing but provoke her quick-tempered brother, and Reginald did not disappoint her this time. His jowly face slowly took on a mottled color, his murky hazel eyes narrowed to their most furious level, and his fist clenched by degrees against the open paper, crumpling it. At last his carefully contained wrath could be restrained no longer and he exploded.

"Speak, woman! I *will* have an explanation for this . . . this . . . !" Words failed him, and he lifted his heavy fist and brought it down hard on the desk, rattling the teacup in its saucer. Now somewhat mollified, he regained a fraction of control and continued with tight-lipped forcefulness, "I had thought before that you had gone beyond the limit, but this . . . travesty"—again a contemptuous swipe at the newspaper—"is beyond all tolerance. Dressing in men's clothes!" He spat out the words, his color rising again. "Visiting a gaming house! And then, *publishing* an account of your misadventure in a paper for all the world to see! We are disgraced!" He was shouting again and both his fists were tightly clenched upon the desk as though to restrain himself forcefully from placing them about Arabella's neck. *"Disgraced,* do you hear me? And have you nothing to say?"

Arabella had a great deal to say, but she was wise enough, at this moment, to keep her counsel. None of this came as a surprise to her—although she *had* been promised anonymity for her article, and the betrayal of confidence irritated her—and she supposed some of Reginald's wrath was justified. She could not, however, by any stretch of the imagination, sympathize with the reasons for Reginald's outrage. In a society in which dancing bears performed at court, in which unspeakable atrocities were performed nightly upon willing and unwilling females in the notorious opium dens, in which ladies of quality kept handsome young men like pets, and in which perfectly respectable members of the peerage made no secret of illicit liaisons with members of their own or the opposite sex, Arabella hardly understood why such a fuss was being made over one small indiscretion at one insignificant gaming parlor. It was those very aberrations that she, through her writing, had been attempting to expose,

10

and she would not apologize for her actions now. She was, however, very, very sorry she had gotten caught.

Her chin lifted another fraction and she replied, "It occurs to me there is very little more to be said. I have disgraced you; it is not the first time. You are displeased; it is not the first time. What would you have me do?"

Reginald glared at her, his choked-back fury becoming an impotent force in the face of the cool, careless dismissal evident in her words. She had left him no reasonable rebuttal, but reason was not a method that seemed to apply to this situation—as it rarely did whenever his sister was involved.

"It's that Montagu woman," he spat at last, viciously. "She and her damnable crowd of high-thinking bluestockings! *She* has brought you to this ruin, and if her husband were half a man, I would call him out for this!"

The very thought of Reginald calling anyone out, much less the ancient and decrepit Mr. Montagu, almost caused Arabella to chuckle, but her momentary amusement was lost in an instant defense of her friend. If not for Elizabeth Montagu and her gentle salons of literary pursuit, Arabella surely would have gone mad these past few years. Only with Elizabeth had Arabella been able to find respite from the overbearing presence of her brother and the demanding conventions forced upon an unmarried woman in London society. Only within the stimulating atmosphere of intellect and wit that composed Elizabeth's salons had Arabella felt alive, purposeful, important, and accepted. True, it had been with Elizabeth's encouragement that Arabella had written the account of her adventure in a gentlemen's club, and it had been through Elizabeth's influence that the piece had made its way to the *Quarterly,* but it was hardly her fault that Arabella's name had been printed much less that the adventure had occurred in the first place.

Arabella's color surged and her eyes flashed a brief but dangerous warning. "I take credit for my own deeds, brother, and I will not have my friends besmirched because of it. It was *I* who had the wits and the courage to assume the masquerade, *I* who was clever enough to write of it, and *I* who wrote well enough to see it published." The last was declared upon a note of triumph, and now the tilt of her head displayed unmistakable pride. "Further, I am the first of my set to publish under her own name and I see not one whit of shame in that. I am not sorry, nor will I pretend to be."

"Your set!" Reginald practically choked out the words. His eyes were bulging and an engorged blue-purple vein protruded like a scar across his temple. "The same set that's brought you nothing but trouble for the past three seasons!" Then his eyes narrowed with shrewd perception. "Donner, I'll warrant! You had to get *entrée* into the club from someone, and who else but the selfsame scoundrel who ruined you last season and hadn't the honor to ask for your hand!"

Arabella's neck stiffened, but with a great effort she held her tongue. The scandal of last season's curricle race was still a sore point with everyone, and she could see no benefit in bringing it up again now.

It had been a dare, a wager between the Lords Donner and Smadely, two of the year's most reckless young bucks, to run the race from London to Bath with the added weight of a passenger. Arabella, always one for a lark, had willingly agreed to go with her old friend Donner, thereby giving him the advantage of her small size. It all should have been over and done with in a day. A broken wheel, however, had necessitated their passing the night in an inn along the wayside. Of course

12

her companion bespoke two rooms—Lord Donner, who had never thought of Arabella as anything other than a "right regular fellow," had no interest whatsoever in sullying her virtue—and they were well chaperoned at all times by both the innkeeper and his wife. Both had felt far more chagrined over forfeiting the wager than they had at any scandal the impropriety of their actions might have caused.

But their return to London the next morning put another light on the matter entirely. During the weeks that followed, poor Donner was brought to the point of a duel to defend Arabella's honor on more than one occasion. Finally, miserable and fumbling, he had blurted out a most ungracious offer of marriage, which Arabella merely laughed away.

Reginald had been like a caged bull for weeks, alternately threatening to call Donner out and to confine Arabella to a convent. In the end, the only reason he did not demand satisfaction from Donner— aside from his innate cowardice—was the fact that, when he considered all the eligible gentlemen in the marketplace, he realized that Lord Donner was one whose fortune placed him at the bottom of the list, and Reginald was determined to keep alive even a dim hope of making a profitable alliance through Arabella.

Arabella soon found the new hint of scandal that surrounded her more gratifying than distressing, and, for some very peculiar reason, being a "fallen woman" garnered her more respectability at Mrs. Montagu's salons. Further, her behavior had caused her name to be stricken from the list of marriageable young ladies acceptable by gentlemen of repute, a situation which Arabella found greatly to her liking.

Reginald had never forgiven her the transgression, which, for all intents, had cost him a fortune in a marriage settlement, and he was still on uneasy terms with Lord Donner, despite all Arabella's assurances of his innocence. As a matter of fact, Arabella mused, a subtle play upon her old friend's guilt over last year's adventure was all it had taken to assure Lord Donner's cooperation in her attempt to gain admittance to the club—as well as in obtaining a very nice suit of breeches and coat for the disguise—though Arabella thought it would be ill-advised to admit as much to her brother. On Donner's part, it had been no more than a lark, and she did not wish to bring more trouble down upon her friend's head.

Reginald's thin lips curled into a sneer that wrinkled the loose flesh of his face and suddenly made him very ugly indeed. "At least I needn't ask how you got the trousers. If the truth be known, you haven't been *out* of Donner's breeches since last spring, have you?"

Arabella's color flamed; her eyes glittered. "I will not stay and be insulted," she said shortly and turned with a flutter of her lace-trimmed skirt to exit.

"You will stay."

Reginald's voice was cold, each word clipped and distinct, and Arabella, though not temperate by nature, knew when to heed it. There was a cruel streak in her brother that was carefully disguised beneath his soft, excessively self-indulgent nature, something as hard and as unexpected as a knife blade hidden beneath a fold of silk—and just as deadly. He was known to beat his servants without provocation and cold-bloodedly shoot the hound who lost the chase. More than once Arabella had accidentally overheard some of her male friends refer, in undertones of distaste, to the deviant manner in which Lord Chatley treated his whores. There was no love of women in Reginald's nature, and of all the females within his sphere, Arabella was, at the moment, his least favorite. She had never known the depths to which her brother could be pushed; she was not, at this point in time, particularly anxious to find out.

Arabella turned slowly, her head high, her hands folded with simple dignity before her, and she waited.

"You have done your best to ruin me," he pronounced at last. Each word was cold and measured. "You have been disobedient, disrespectful and ungovernable since the day of your birth. You have given your honor to a man not worth the spit on my boots and you have no shame." Again Arabella bit her tongue. "You have ruined any chance you might have had for making a match with any decent man in the kingdom or abroad, and you do not even appear to be concerned by it."

Lifting her chin another fraction, Arabella said, "I have no need for men. I am content in my state the way it is."

"As well you should be!" barked Reginald. "Dressing in breeches! What man would want a woman who prefers to be a man?"

Arabella's temper flared. "Why shouldn't I prefer to be a man?" she shot back, a flush of angry color suffusing her cheeks. "Men are the only ones who have any fun—or power, Lord knows why! And I make a far better man," she spat disdainfully, "than any of the mincing, sniveling idiots of your set, I dare say!"

"And the much-esteemed Greeks of your set are so much better, I suppose! So much talk of 'intellectual stimulation'—I shouldn't be at all surprised if it weren't more than the intellect that's being stimulated in Mayfair! Blessed Jesus only knows what sort of abominations go on in that woman's salon. Is that where you learned to wear men's clothing, Arabella?" he sneered. "And do the gentlemen also enjoy dressing up in skirts and petticoats?"

Arabella caught her breath. That he should dare,

15

with his depraved personal preferences which were, from all accounts, the talk of London, cast aspersions upon the one decent gathering society had to offer . . . ! She held her temper and said tightly, "I will thank you to keep a civil tongue in your head where my choice of companions is concerned, Reginald. The fine ladies and gentlemen to whom you refer would not be flattered by your descriptions of them, and more than one, I wager, would be happy to face you at twenty paces on the sunrise. Furthermore, my friends have been far more family to me than you have ever been, and they have certainly done more for me—"

Reginald interrupted coolly, "I have done something for you now." He slid open a drawer of his desk and withdrew from it a folded sheet of paper. As he held it lightly between the fingers of two hands, like a weapon handled carelessly, he projected a confidence that Arabella had rarely before witnessed. He relaxed in his chair and his eyes took on a peculiar, deceptively calm glow while his small mouth curved into a benign smile. He was the lord of the manor, content in his power and about to exercise it. There was a malevolence about his countenance now to which Arabella responded with an almost imperceptible shiver of unease, but she was also fascinated into alertness. She knew that whatever was about to occur, it would be Reginald's *coup de grace*.

Reginald would have preferred, of course, to have used Arabella's marriageability to further his own interests, financially and otherwise, and for the first few years he had set about arranging matches for her with precisely that intention. By her third season he had become desperate, and he had begun to explore other options. Over the past winter he had grown to realize that making a profitable marriage was no longer worth the trouble to consider; it would be enough to simply have her off his hands. And this final escapade was just the prompting he needed to dispense with the matter in the only way left to him. It seemed a shame to waste such promising goods in what amounted to little more than a sacrificial sale, but she had left him no choice. He had had his fill.

"This time, my dear young sister," he pronounced implacably, "I'm afraid you have gone beyond the limit. For years I have tolerated your disobedience, your irascible behavior, your insistence upon disgracing the family name in every way that occurs to you, and your refusal even to consider the many perfectly proper offers for your hand. Surely you see that this cannot continue. You are long since past the time to be wedded and bedded, and I have taken the liberty of arranging the matter for you."

Arabella felt the breath leave her body in an inaudible gasp of outrage even as a flare of hot denial flamed to her cheeks. But before she could even open her mouth for the expected protest, Reginald continued calmly, "During the past winter I have been in correspondence with an old friend of mine—of yours, too, if I am not mistaken. In a fortnight's time we will depart for the colony of Virginia, where we will spend some time as guests of Shadowood Plantation. Phillip Everett has graciously consented to accept you as his bride, and I suggest we waste no more time in accepting his offer. I have here the papers for a proxy marriage, which can be executed even before we sail, and before, God willing"—his meaty hand brushed distastefully at the open newspaper on his desk—"news of this latest . . . debacle . . . reaches Virginia."

Phillip Everett, she mused silently. The name, and the memories it evoked rang like an echo through her mind, subduing all else in its wake. The street sounds, the damp and foul-smelling London air, the movements in the household about her all faded into a

17

distant background as Arabella stared at her brother. Had he said Phillip Everett?

Reginald assumed her shock presaged a protest and he continued smoothly, "But I am not an unreasonable man. I would prefer, for the sake of the family name, that your womanhood be put to the use for which it was intended, but should you feel otherwise"—that frightening, ugly smile graced his lips again—"I can be generous. I have here another paper"—with his left hand he reached into the drawer—"which endows the good sisters of St. Augustus for your keeping. It is your choice which of the two contracts you will sign." His tone, and his eyes, sharpened noticeably. "You will not have your life strewn all over the papers for all the world to see and mock. I have had done with it. Before this season is out you *will* be married, dear sister, and that is a promise. It matters little to me whether your alliance is made with the estimable Phillip Everett or with our Blessed Saviour, but it will be done."

Still, Arabella could say nothing. It occurred to her dimly that yes, this time Reginald was serious. He would have to be very serious indeed to consider donating her dowry to a convent, with no promise of return on his investment. He even had the papers ready to sign.

But the thought of the nunnery registered with Arabella and passed by without a shiver of dread or a moment's consideration. Virginia, he had said. *Virginia*.

Arabella, who had lived the entirety of her youth for adventure, was now faced with the promise of the grandest adventure of all. In fact, it seemed that all the years that had gone before had merely been preparing her for this, and she could hardly believe her good fortune. She had thought it a magnificent *coup* to be the first lady of her set to publish under her own name, but how many women of her age were presented with the opportunity to travel across an ocean to the rugged outposts of the Colonies and to make new lives for themselves there?

Her mind raced and was filled with so many possibilities that she could scarcely examine them all. All his life Papa had wanted to go to the Colonies, the land of adventure, he had said, where men were men and life was a challenge . . . and yet it was his own daughter who would have the chance to fulfill his dream. How proud he would be, and how envious. And what tales she had heard! The opportunities for discovery, for excitement, in a world filled with the unfamiliar, a world to be explored . . . These thoughts provided unending fodder for Arabella's active imagination.

Of course it meant marriage, a state which Arabella had heretofore deplored and most certainly would not under any other circumstances, have allowed—especially by proxy. But if Elizabeth Montagu had taught Arabella anything, it was the value of practicality, and despite the rush of girlish enthusiasm and the visions of fantastic possibilities that filled her now, Arabella was no fool. She knew Reginald meant what he said, and if there was anything to wonder over, it was only that he had waited this long to execute the threats he had made last season. He would waste no time before seeing his troublesome sister safely tucked away in a convent if she refused this marriage, and Arabella had no intention of spending the rest of her life with the good sisters at St. Augustus.

Either way, in the nunnery or in Virginia, she would have to bid *adieu* to her friends and the literary society she loved so well, and against that separation she momentarily rebelled, but finally she told herself once again that she must be practical. She had never deceived herself into thinking she could rightly spend the rest of her life unmarried, for an unmarried woman, even from the wealthiest of families, had neither power nor position and was very often left without any means of her own at all. Arabella had only wished to postpone the awful inevitability as long as possible, hoping to find someone, like Mr. Montagu, who was rich and old and rarely underfoot. But Phillip Everett . . . that was a different matter altogether.

Eight years had passed since she had seen him, and, in truth, she remembered him hardly at all. But what she did remember was shaded in a rosy haze of girlish romanticism that she found, even now, impossible to shake. He was seven years older than she, and her earliest memories were of the tawny-haired young man who, to Arabella's girlish imagination, had been the most splendid thing ever to walk the earth. Strong, brave, gallant, and dreadfully good-looking, he had always had time for the little girl in short skirts and braids, and Arabella had worshiped him unabashedly from the moment she had first laid eyes on him.

Phillip was the youngest son of a baronet and, as such, untitled. In the years of his reckless youth, Arabella now recalled, there had been rumors that he had fallen in with a bad set and had developed quite a wild reputation. There had been a scandal at court of some sort and then a duel . . . In better circumstances, he would have been quite low on Reginald's list of suitable matches for his very eligible young sister, but now, ironically, the matters that Reginald counted as disadvantages, Arabella considered advantages. Rank meant little to her, and Phillip's reputation had never frightened her. In fact, she had always found herself titillated by the half-believable stories that drifted down about her girlhood companion, for she had been drawn then as always, to the drama of the unexpected.

The fact that he was frowned upon by society only made him more exciting; the mystique of his reputation as a rakehell was only one of his many allures. Besides, Arabella knew the boy from which the man had grown, and she was certain that nothing about him could be truly bad.

As the years had progressed, the difference in their ages had kept them a great deal apart, but even as an impetuous adolescent, Arabella had never lost her fascination for the dashing Phillip Everett. The last summer he had been home—she realized now it had been the summer he had had the falling-out with his father and had been sent to supervise the family holdings in the Colonies—she had been stricken with such unaccustomed shyness that she could do no more than gaze at him rapturously from a distance. She had been twelve; he had been nineteen, a full man. Doubtless, he would not have noticed the gangly, blotch-faced girl she had been then even if she had made herself visible. But she noticed him—a great deal.

Of course, Arabella knew the childhood infatuation exactly for what it was—unreciprocated and barely worth mentioning. If she could hardly remember what Phillip looked like, she knew he would have no cause whatsoever to remember her. A case of youthful hero worship was hardly sufficient cause for Lady Arabella Winters, twenty years of age, level headed, independent, and as fully in charge of her life as any woman could reasonably expect to be, to agree to an impulsive marriage in a faraway land.

Yet somehow it seemed as though the hand of fate in its subtle, ever-mysterious motions, had reached out from afar to embrace her. *Virginia.* Even the sound of it was mystical, exotic, unbearably compelling. It lay an ocean away in a rough, untamed land where adventure was in the very air and a new life was hers for the

21

asking . . . a new life, a world away from Reginald and all the painted and powdered fools like him, away from the courtly ballrooms and the corrupt affectations of this ridiculous society. It seemed an unknown filled with possibilities, and the lure of the "Grand Adventure" was one Arabella had no intention of resisting.

Impetuosity was a trait for which Arabella was well renowned. It had landed her into scrape after disgraceful scrape, had brought her to the point of ruin and back again, and had driven Reginald to the consumption of vast quantities of brandy with his morning tea. But even he was not prepared for what she did next.

Arabella gave her brother a small, enigmatic smile as she reached for the door. "This is one thing, dear brother," she announced softly, "that does not displease me at all. I will begin packing today."

Reginald could only gape at her as she disappeared through the doorway. Then, after a long period of helpless, astonished silence that was almost anticlimactic, he rummaged in the desk for his private store of whiskey. He poured a full glass and downed it in almost one gulp. But even as a smug smile found its way to his lips, he could not completely dismiss an uneasy feeling that his self-congratulations might be somewhat premature.

The morning fog was just beginning to break by the time the heavy draperies were drawn back in the royal chamber at Buckingham Palace. The King, who had awakened in an exceptionally foul mood, had sent his attendants away and now sat propped up in the enormous dais bed sipping chocolate and glancing through his morning dispatches. The topmost of these was from Lord Dunmore of Virginia, and the King broke the seal with particular impatience. The contents

22

of the governor's missive brought another crease to His Majesty's scowling face. His eyes darkened and after a moment his hand tightened around the heavy parchment, crushing it, twisting it, and at last flinging it with a vicious motion into the grate, where he watched it catch and burn with grim pleasure.

But, as His Majesty surely must have known, the source of his problems would not be so easily disposed of.

Off the coast of Virginia, dawn was barely breaking and a band of anonymous men rowed silently through the fog, away from a customs schooner that awaited daybreak and admittance to the harbor. They were less than a hundred yards from shore when the first shouts rose up. An instant later a tendril of flame and the smell of smoke invaded the morning air. The small boat paused in the water, and heads turned to watch in silent satisfaction as the fog parted to reveal the artificial dawn of the burning schooner, the crackle of fire, the aureole of red-yellow brilliance, the shouts, and the splashes of the crew jumping overboard and swimming for shore.

The year was 1773, and the troubles of Good King George had only just begun.

Chapter II

17 May, 1773

The Voyage to Virginia has been more dreary than I imagin'd. E'en at this Season, the North Atlantic is gray and stormy, and our Ship is buffeted by great Swells and Waves, confining us to our Quarters below. Reginald at first made a great Fuss over his Mal de Mer, but as soon as He found Companions for the Card Table, He recover'd quyte suddenly . . .

As for Myself, I have spent much Tyme alone, reading and writing in my Journal. The first Nyte out I was introduced to two Ladies from Winchester, a Mother and a Daughter, but when They learnt that I was the Lady Arabella Winters of the by-now Infamous Article, They cut Me stone dead the next Day. I found it all quyte amusing.

E'en though the Proxy has been done and I am now in the Marri'd State, I scarce feel wed at all . . . Sometymes there are Moments of Dreade, which I suppose are only natural when I think of how abruptly I have left All I know Behind, but

then It comes to Me, the Excitement and the
Wonder of this Place to which I journey, and I can
hardly contain my Eagerness. It is a Coming of
Age, a Beginning Anew, a Life that will at last be
my Owne . . . And Phillip to welcome Me. . . .

Wedged in the corner of her bunk in order to be braced against the roll and pitch of the ship on the heavy seas, Arabella put down her pen and paused in her writing. In another woman the long solitude might have given way to dejection and regret, or, at the very least, sober reflection on the rashness of her decision. But with Arabella the effect was just the opposite. Daydream had spun out into daydream and with each passing day the Phillip of her imaginings grew larger than life. He would be even handsomer than she remembered him, and stronger, and as kind and as noble as she recalled from her girlish adoration. Sometimes she could almost hear the gentle sound of his laughter and see his dancing gray eyes . . .

That the twenty-seven-year-old Phillip of real life might be somewhat different from the enhanced nineteen-year-old Phillip of her reveries was certainly a possibility that occurred to Arabella's rational side, but it mattered little. For now, he was a fantasy she enjoyed to pass the time, and it was her prerogative to make him into a brave, dashing hero of storybook proportions: handsome, strong, honorable, and capable—the perfect antithesis of all the young swains she had left behind in England.

Arabella was accustomed to change, even upheaval, and the prospect of something new did not frighten her as much as it challenged her. This was perhaps the most important legacy given her by her generous and adventurous father.

There had been no doubt in anyone's mind that the

fun-loving, red-haired Earl of Chatley had adored his daughter and had lavished upon her every attention that could be desired. Arabella had come to him late in life, and when his frail wife died of childbirth fever only months later, the Earl had turned all his attention to the infant left in his charge. He had taught her to ride long before she was tall enough to reach the stirrup; he had taught her to shoot as soon as she could lift a pistol, and before she was twelve, Arabella had begun accompanying her father on the hunt. At Lord Chatley's knee she had learned to keep the accounts, to know and appreciate fine horseflesh, and to play whist and chess—all the necessary accomplishments of any well-bred gentleman.

The Earl had made certain that no aspect of Arabella's education would be neglected. Unlike many fathers of the time, Lord Chatley had encouraged intellectual pursuits, even to the extent of importing a tutor to teach her to read in Latin and Greek, to speak French, and to write and cipher fluently.

Arabella had begun to keep her journal then and had even written poems and little stories, which she read aloud to her father. He would beam at her accomplishments and would often instigate intellectual debates that spurred her on to further essays and written dissertations. This period she recalled as the happiest of her life.

As she grew older, a Mistress was brought in to teach Arabella the proper deportment for a highborn lady, household management, ballroom dancing, and needlework. These domestic pursuits were less to Arabella's liking than others she had learned, but she managed them with accomplishment and her father was proud of her.

"You'll make some man a fine wife one day, daughter," he had often told her, "though I'll miss you sorely as my companion." And then Arabella would laugh and tease that she would never leave him, that he would be cursed with her the rest of his life.

They had come in from hunting one fine autumn day, faces rosy with the wind, laughing, and exchanging quick-witted repartee as they always did. And four hours later her beloved father lay dead, taken by a sudden and unexpected seizure. Arabella's life would never be the same, and Reginald was Earl of Chatley.

Reginald's only concern regarding the precocious young sister he had never known was that he be bothered with her as little as possible. He managed to ignore the reports of relatively harmless escapades at Chatley Hall, resolving only to bring her out as quickly as possible and have her off his hands.

Arabella had made her debut into society at age sixteen, and from there disaster followed disaster. She was comely and personable, and her striking good looks attracted the eye of more than one eligible bachelor that season, though her quick tongue and scathing wit just as soon discouraged them. The subsequent seasons were equally tumultuous and as fruitless, for Arabella despised the endless rounds of parties and galas, the only aim of which was to introduce marriageable young ladies into the market. She rebelled, proclaiming often and loudly to her determined brother that she would not be handled like a horse brought to auction. She found much more pleasure in the group of literary ladies she met through her long-time friend, Lord Donner, and especially in Mrs. Elizabeth Montagu of Mayfair, whom Dr. Samuel Johnson himself had dubbed "queen of the bluestockings."

The culminating disgrace of last year's scandal with the curricle race would have persuaded a less stubborn, more sensitive man than Reginald to abandon all hope of a marriage, but he had insisted upon bringing Arabella to London one more time. Arabella ignored what invitations were offered her and found refuge again with Elizabeth Montagu.

Mr. Montagu, the grandson of the Earl of Sandwich, was well over eighty, never seen, and seldom heard, which allowed his wife the freedom to indulge her passions for literature and good conversation. No card games were allowed in her salons, and alcoholic beverages were forbidden. Many soon-to-be acclaimed literary giants, such as Laurence Stern, Samuel Johnson, Fanny Burney, Oliver Goldsmith, Horace Walpole, gathered there to discuss the pertinent issues of the day.

Arabella was much on the periphery, but she was bright and clever and had a quick tongue, and the eccentric Elizabeth Montagu saw something of herself in the rebellious, daring young girl. She encouraged Arabella's attempts at writing, and it was through her aegis that the story of the visit to the gaming house had been accepted by the editor of the *Quarterly* and a promise had been made by him that Lady Arabella's name would not be used. For the editor's blatant abuse of their friendship, Mrs. Montagu had permanently struck his name from the list of those who were invited to her salons.

Elizabeth Montagu had been as pragmatic about Arabella's marriage as she was about her own. She had found the married state no impediment to doing exactly as she wished. In fact, her husband's considerable funds made possible her generosity to striving young authors. Arabella had gone to her mentor with some trepidation, expecting disapproval and dismay over her hasty decision, but she found instead a cool common sense that was to do much to fortify her throughout the voyage.

29

"Very wise of you, my dear," announced Mrs. Montagu with a curt nod. "The man is wealthy, is he not? So much the better, for a woman's wits will carry her only so far in this world; in the end it is gold that will see you rise above the masses. There is much to discover in the Colonies, I am told, and you have a chance few of us ever see—to make your own place in a new world. . . ."

A New World, Arabella wrote now, and with these words the heavy reflections of the past moments gave way to thoughts that brought bright-eyed excitement to her face. *Adventure and Promise such as I never dreamt . . . And All of It for myne Owne . . .*

Chapter III

Surely no queen of antiquity ever appeared as regal as Lady Charlotte Parkington as her barge approached the landing at Shadowood Plantation. She was surrounded by a retinue of black servants, three of whom waved wide palmetto leaf fans across the lady's chaise while another stood in readiness beyond a white-clothed table that displayed dishes of sweetmeats and sugared fruit. Yet another servant applied cloths dampened with lemon water to the lady's forehead and wrists, both to guard against whatever stray rays of sun might penetrate the protective awning above Lady Charlotte's head and to spare her delicate nostrils from encountering the odors of the river, which she found exceptionally disagreeable.

She was elegance personified as she glided through the shadows and sun on the James River, and she was confident that the gentleman upon whom she was about to call, above all others, would be appreciative of the fact. Her gown was of the very finest silk in amber and blue, trimmed with a fall of taupe lace at the shoulders and elbows. The bodice was cut rather low for this hour of the morning, but it accented her voluptuous bosom to its very best advantage, and Lady

31

Charlotte was one to seize any opportunity to capitalize upon her most alluring features.

She was careful, however, to shade her exposed bosom and shoulders with a peach-colored shawl of delicate lace, and to sheath her small, plump hands in gloves of soft kid. Nothing was more abhorrent to her then the thought of freckles marring her perfect skin, and she was careful to guard against such a prospect with every device known to her.

Though well protected by a canopy of bright green and gold panels, the Lady Parkington wore a large hat of pale straw, the crown of which was bordered with flowers. Its broad brim shaded her face from the few rays of sun that managed to skirt the canopy. Her jet black hair was fashioned into a knot at the back of her head, which allowed an alluring clump of fat ringlets to fall over her left shoulder, contrasting strikingly with the magnolia creaminess of her skin.

Being on the far side of thirty, Charlotte Parkington took particular care with her complexion, well aware that it was one of her strongest features. The faintest trace of worry or exposure to the sun's glare could cause those telltale signs of aging, which even her expensive potions and baths of mare's milk could not erase. She often bemoaned the fact that fate had brought her to spend her years of beauty upon shores that could so easily destroy it, for the sun of Tidewater Virginia could be merciless and was her greatest foe.

She sighed and raised a finger to smooth away an imaginary line. Only the most extreme urgency would have drawn her out on a day like today, when the sun beat down so brightly on the waters of the James and was reflected back a hundredfold. But, she mused silently, when Phillip Everett had refused to answer her summons . . . well, there remained nothing for her to do but to go to him herself.

Charlotte had sent a servant with a message that she would arrive mid-morning, and she fully expected Phillip to be waiting at the landing with a closed carriage to drive her the short distance to his house. He would have tea prepared and perhaps some of those luscious little cakes his cook was so adept at whipping up. Whatever else could be said for him, Phillip Everett was an enviable epicurean, and only the best was served at his home. Her mouth began to water in anticipation of his repast, and she stretched out a languid hand for a sugared grape from her own table. She was not in the least worried about her figure, for Phillip liked full-bodied women. Or at least he had . . .

Though over the past weeks he had sent various excuses for his failure to visit her at Parkland Manor, Charlotte knew that Phillip was too much of a gentleman to refuse to receive her at his own home. Obviously, he knew what she wanted to discuss with him, and just as obviously he wished to avoid it and, like a naughty boy, hid himself from her censure.

Charlotte's heavy-lidded eyes narrowed slightly as she formed the hint of an indulgent smile, then she quickly erased the gesture against the possibility of its wrinkle-inducing tendencies. Phillip was a darling— *her* darling—and despite their recent differences, she would ever hold him in fondness. Ex-lovers, she paused to reflect now, were almost more pleasurable than present ones, though not quite, for the poor dears were so much more manipulable when one was not dependent upon them for one's own gratification. Phillip, of course, was more of a puzzle than most, but that was precisely why she had such affection for him. And she would greatly enjoy taking him to task for his latest little transgression.

Lazy green banks swathed in willows and moss drifted by as the six hefty oarsmen applied themselves to their strokes, keeping time with a low, musical chant. Charlotte found the gleam of sweat upon naked black backs and shoulders faintly erotic, and her thoughts drifted as she lay back in the chaise, chewing upon a dried apricot. The rhythm of the water and the silence overlaid with the lulling music of Negro voices was soothing.

The dogwoods were in brilliant bloom and the pink and white blossoms were colorfully interspersed against the verdant green hardwoods. Stately poplar and red cedars lined the shoreline, their branches trembling with the gay play of red and brown squirrels. A blackbird outlined itself against the cerulean sky, darting over the treetops. Occasionally a cow, grazing in the fat marshlands, would look up lazily to observe the passing barge, then return to its feasting.

Mockingbirds called and bluejays squawked, and once a large marsh hawk was startled by the movement of the barge and fluttered upward toward the sky, gazing down once in disdain before retracting its talons and sailing away. Near the grassy shoreline a water snake left a ripple in the water, and before the barge a shiny fish jumped and splashed. The land was fat and lush with the coming of spring, and privileged indeed were those who lived off its bounty.

As the barge rounded the last wooded point of land, Charlotte saw him waiting for her at Shadowood's landing, and just to the right was the carriage—closed, as she had expected. Charlotte smiled, not caring for the moment that the expression caused tiny lines to form around her eyes.

To the right lay the warehouses, the wharves, and deeper waters where larger ships and barges weighed anchor. A tobacco plantation was a self-sufficient enterprise and the waterways of Tidewater Virginia its lifeline. Phillip Everett, like the other successful planters along the James, shipped his goods directly from his own warehouses up the river.

Occasionally a stop was made in a colonial port to transfer the cargo from barges onto larger ships, but if the distance was short—to another colony, perhaps, or to the Indies—clever planters like Phillip equipped their own lightweight ships to sail from the docks of their plantations into the open sea. Before the days of the new trade laws this had been the most expedient way to do business, but with recent tightening of customs' regulations, the profit in running one's own ship had been greatly reduced. Trade between the Colonies was limited, and trade to the Indies illegal, and the privately owned ships in Virginia lay in dry dock awaiting better times.

The riverfront, as always, was bustling with activity. A brigade of slaves was transferring hogsheads of dried tobacco from the warehouses onto a waiting barge, where they would be transported to Williamsburg to be sold for credit against imported goods. Inside the warehouses hanging sheaves of drying tobacco were being checked and packed under the astute eye of William Hampton, Phillip's overseer, and the sounds of shouted orders and brisk movements carried musically on the clear morning.

The barge scraped the sandy beach near the shade of an avenue of willows, and Charlotte alighted gracefully with the aid of two footmen. She held a cool smile, which caused no stress on the muscles of her face, and made certain that Phillip was treated to a flash of smooth ankle and the best profile of tiny waist and lush bosom as she stepped onto the grassy shore. Her skirts rustled and whirled enticingly around her as she settled herself into an attractive pose and waited for Phillip to reach her.

"My dear, dear Charlotte." An elegantly clad Phillip

Everett strode across the wooden landing to offer his arm to her. "What a vision you make arriving upon my shores like the Queen of the Nile. It is fair enough to set the head spinning at such an hour of the morn."

He took her hand, turning it upward, and placed a kiss upon her gloved palm. Charlotte spared him one of her rare dimples, for, in truth, she could not help it. He was a beautiful one, her Phillip, well formed and young, and she did miss him.

With an artistic pout, Charlotte retrieved her hand. "Fie on you, Phillip, with your pretty words! You know how I hate to travel, and it is your fault that I've made this hideous journey in the heat of the day. Soon I shall be a wrinkled old prune and then you will regret your rudeness!"

Phillip looked contrite. "Rude, madame? I? I am cut to the quick to be so accused and will dispose this minute to atone for whatever transgression of mine has caused you such discomfort. But first, we must get you out of this sun immediately. What a deucedly hot day it's turned into already."

Charlotte's expression softened into indulgent affection as she rested her gloved fingers atop Phillip's arm for the short walk to the carriage. "Phillip, dearest, what a foolish popinjay you are," she chided lazily. "Prattling on about transgressions and atonements when you haven't even bothered to remark on my new gown, and you know I had it done up especially for you."

"My most gracious lady," he declared, helping her into the carriage, "I would never dream of insulting you by offering my most humble opinion on the work of art that graces your lovely form. However"—he paused to observe her as she settled her wide skirts about her with much pomp and circumstance, fully covering the seat of the carriage—"were I to be asked, I could only remark—" He stopped to kiss his fingers to the air in a delightfully French gesture that gratified Charlotte enormously. "Your exquisite taste is outdone only by your own beauty. The gown is sheer confection, my dear. And how I do envy your dressmaker, to have such a model as you to adorn."

Charlotte reached forward and patted his cheek as he settled in the seat opposite her, her expression pleased. "What a sweet boy you are, Phillip." She let her fingers trail into a caress along the side of his cheek as her tone softened. "And how very, very handsome."

Phillip's own expression remained polite and remote as he took her hand and barely brushed it with his lips. "And what a flatterer you are, dear lady, as ever. One day you shall break my heart." Charlotte laughed and withdrew her hand, settling back to enjoy the remainder of the journey in comfort.

The ride along the oak-lined avenue was not long, one that Phillip had made by foot in less than five minutes. But he knew from experience that Charlotte would certainly not walk, especially in this heat.

.The wide lawn of Shadowood came into view behind a slight dip in the drive. It was lush with blooming rhododendron and stately beds of shrubs and spring tulips. Three gardeners were employed at all times to attend the pruning and cultivation of Shadowood's gardens, and in the west corner a small boy kept herd over the sheep who were responsible for the well-cropped expanse of lawn. Brightly colored peacocks strutted about, and a small, central pond supported a family of graceful ducks.

The house was rose-colored brick towering three stately stories above the ground and was surrounded by a wide veranda. A multitude of wide windows lined its front, each one thrown open now to admit the spring air. When they arrived before the broad front door,

Phillip alighted first and then, with a graceful bow, gestured toward the formal gardens at the side of the house.

"Shall we retire to the gardens? My roses are simply lovely this time of year."

"Phillip! In this heat?" Charlotte set her small foot on the velvet-covered coach step offered by the footman and extended a languid hand to Phillip. "Surely you mistake me."

Charlotte was sweltering under the weight of her clothes, almost thirty pounds of corsets, stays, hoops, petticoats and the heavy materials of her gown, and she cared much less for the aesthetics of the rose garden than for her own comfort. "What I crave now, dear boy, are the cool recesses of your parlor and an iced drink. Surely your ice house is still filled?"

Phillip smiled as he tucked her hand through the crook of his arm. "I have anticipated your wish, my dear. All should be in readiness in the parlor momentarily."

Minutes later, settled upon a small, dove-colored velvet settee in the morning parlor with an icy lemonade in one hand and a plate of lacy cakes at her elbow, Charlotte Parkington favored Phillip with a long, assessing glance. The time for flirtation between them was gone, and she was always one to come to the point of a matter when doing otherwise served no personal advantage.

"And now, you naughty boy," she declared with purpose, "you will tell me the truth of these nasty rumors I've heard about you and your so-called marriage."

"Rumors?" Phillip feigned amazement lazily. "Has some blackguard dared to smudge my name in idle talk, or that of my bride? I shall have him at sword point!"

Charlotte inclined her head in a satisfied nod. "So, there *is* a bride!"

"But of course." Phillip sipped his lemonade, his eyebrow quirking quizzically. "But I felt certain I had dispatched notice to you of the fact."

"You did not," responded Charlotte somewhat huffily. "Otherwise, why would I be here?"

"An oversight, my dear, for which I beg your forgiveness."

The murmured apology, far from heartfelt, brought little satisfaction to Charlotte, and she was hard put not to scowl. Only the remembrance of her rapidly aging skin kept her expression bland. "Well, now that I am here," she suggested irritably, "perhaps you would be good enough to satisfy my curiosity. Who *is* this person?"

"Lady Arabella Winters, daughter of Lord Chatley of Devon."

Charlotte was impressed and hid it well. She knew the name. Phillip had made quite a match for himself, and here, in the outposts of nowhere. She wondered how he had managed it.

"I knew her in Devon when she was a child," Phillip added carelessly as he stood and crossed to the mantelpiece, sipping his lemonade and lounging against the mantel in a way that displayed his long, well-shaped legs to their best advantage.

Charlotte admired his masculine attributes with an automatic, barely noticed appreciation, then she returned her gaze to his face. "And is she a child still?" she inquired with arch superiority. Being greatly conscious of her own age, she could not find any charity in her soul for the nubile young girls who caught the fancies of most of her ex-lovers.

She was somewhat relieved when Phillip responded offhandedly, "She has attained the age of twenty,

39

I believe."

Charlotte regarded him thoughtfully. "Well past the age to be wed," she acknowledged. "I wonder what is wrong with her?"

There was no way a gentleman could respond to her remark, and Phillip remained silent, as Charlotte had known he would. Somewhat satisfied with her small victory, Charlotte pulled out a fan from the small reticule she carried and began to whip it about in the still, hot air. "When you broke our liaison," she pointed out with charming sullenness, "you swore you would never marry. And suddenly I hear—and not from you—of this . . . this debacle!"

Her eyes widened and she let the fan fall still in her lap. "A proxy marriage, of all things! Why, it is barely decent. For all you know, that ship's captain might have married you to a blackmoor or a woman already great with child, and what," she demanded with vengeful pleasure, "would you have to say to that, my fine friend?"

Phillip's expression was impassive. His even temperament was one of his most frustrating—and challenging—traits. "I'm afraid I should be much put out, my lady."

Charlotte took up her fan again, sparing him a brief withering look. "And it may have occurred to you, sir, that I am much put out with you!"

"For that I am most truly sorry."

Charlotte reached for a cake and nibbled upon it thoughtfully. It was difficult to keep the pique in her expression with such a delightful concoction soothing her senses, but she managed it. She glanced at Phillip beneath slanted lashes. "She is wealthy, I imagine."

"Comfortable, I believe. But her fortune is not excessive."

Charlotte was at the end of her patience. It was not

that she had any jealousy for Phillip—at least not in a romantic sense—but her curiosity was a driving force. And she was more than a little miffed that everyone in the county had known of this arrangement of Phillip's before she had—she, who was his oldest and dearest friend.

"Then what is it, Phillip?" she demanded plainly, now casting all pretenses aside. "I know you have a reason for marrying the little wench—probably a devious one. You and I were ever alike in that respect."

For a moment his eyes glinted with amusement and brief admiration, and he directed at her a lazy bow. "That we were, my lady. That we were."

There was in that moment a flash of the old Phillip, in his stance, in his eyes, in the cynical curve of his smile. Involuntarily Charlotte felt a stab of wistfulness for things past and wondered idly if the new Mistress Everett would give her much fight for Phillip should Charlotte be inclined to so engage her. Almost immediately, however, the notion was dismissed. Charlotte's interest in Phillip as a lover had long since waned, although occasionally she felt a twinge of resentment that he had been the one to do the spurning, not she. He was the first—the only—gentleman who had dared make the first move to dissolve a relationship with her. This was probably the reason she still held him in such special esteem. He was a puzzle, in more ways than one.

He had not been the most exciting lover she had ever had, though he had come to her well-schooled in the ways of passion and almost as much of a connoisseur of physical pleasure as she was herself. Charlotte's taste, however, sometimes ran to the savage, and unfortunately, Phillip had no stomach for such. Moreover, he had refused to be manipulated beyond a certain point, much to Charlotte's regret.

41

He was skilled, imaginative, and oh, so very well made, but Charlotte had had lithe young men before. What fascinated her about Phillip was that he had never allowed himself to become her slave, as so many had before him. He kept a part of himself remote from her and always in control, as though she amused him as much as he amused her. Their liaison had been greatly satisfying to both, for they met in cynicism and wit and related as equals. Yet, though Charlotte had been closer to Phillip than any woman since his arrival in the Colonies, she was reminded more and more each day that she did not know him at all. That did not trouble her, however, it merely entertained her.

She should have married him, she mused now. What a perfect husband he would have been. Handsome and impeccably groomed, sweet smelling and charmingly mannered, he had the advantages of being well connected and wealthy. They enjoyed the same amusements, and he was of a temperament to overlook her occasional indiscretions. And in her old age it would have been comforting to have a strong young bedpartner. She wondered for a moment why the thought of marriage had not struck her sooner, and the answer, when it came, was both discomfiting and mildly amusing. It was that Phillip simply had not been interested. And, if the point be made, neither had she. Charlotte had no need of wealth or protection, and she would have made a greatly discontented wife, even to one as entertaining as Phillip. She much preferred to keep him as her most cherished pet.

She turned her attention back to the matter at hand, for Phillip's reticence was beginning to border on the vexatious. "Tell me, then," she commanded, reaching for another cake, "what low motive has brought you, at this point in life, to the state of marriage with a chit you haven't seen since she was an infant?"

42

Phillip crossed the room and sank gracefully into the chair opposite her. He delicately arranged a cake on a saucer and balanced it upon his knee, regarding her with lazy, heavy-lidded eyes. "Shall I speak of love, Charlotte dear?" he drawled indifferently. "Do you not believe in the magic of Cupid's bow?"

Charlotte made a derisive sound in the back of her throat and dismissed the notion with a snap of her fan. "Phillip Everett, you are no more capable of love than I am. That"—she fixed him with a limpid stare—"is why I once was so foolish as to think you and I might be special to each other."

"But you are special to me, Charlotte dearest," he asserted without energy. "And so shall you always be."

She shook her head, releasing a sigh that was only half feigned. "No, things have changed between us, Phillip, and not entirely, I think, for the better. You have changed . . ."

"And not for the better?" The faintest lift of an eyebrow betrayed his amusement, and he shrugged a disinterested shoulder. "Well, one cannot always be the *gauche emigré,* can one? And I am pleased to say my association with you, dearest heart, has much improved my view of life and my position in it. Now that Shadowood is a successful enterprise, should I not dress and act the part?"

Charlotte regarded him thoughtfully. "You are always the consummate actor."

He smiled and inclined his head modestly. "No more than are you, my dear lady."

Their eyes met then in a spark of recognition and mutual admiration, for though much had changed between them, this much had not. Neither held any illusions about the other, nor would either have wished to do so.

Charlotte turned her attention to the cake, slicing a

delicate bit with her fork before transferring it to her lips, and in a moment Phillip did the same. "What a treasure you have in your cook, Phillip," Charlotte murmured, dabbing her lips with a floral-scented pink napkin. "I daresay none could make her match on the Continent."

"Indeed," Phillip agreed modestly. "I do endeavor to bring the finest of gracious living to my table, despite the restrictions of this dreadful Colonial life, which does so try the patience. When my bride arrives," he continued grandly, "I will give a *fete* to introduce her to Virginia society. It will be the most stunning affair this season, and your name, of course"—he inclined his head toward her graciously—"will be at the top of my list."

"And I, my love, shall be happy to attend." Charlotte smiled sweetly. In truth, she had no plans at all to attend a party where she would not be the center of attention, especially one at which she would be competing with a woman ten years younger than she. When the time came for the event, she would be conveniently indisposed, and then later she would meet the chit—on her own terms. Lady Charlotte Parkington disliked sharing the spotlight with anyone else. All her life she had known accolades and admiration, and she had no intention of stepping offstage at this point in her career.

She had caused an enormous stir in London when she had married the aging Lord Ferdie Parkington. All sorts of rumors circulated about Charlotte, and she, with her sense of the dramatic, did nothing to discourage them. Some said that Parkington had met her in Paris where she had been an artist's model, and others claimed that he had met her when she had been touring in West Britain with an acting troupe. Still others whispered that she had not been Charlotte at all,

44

but Carlotta, and that her father had been Italian or, even worse, a Spaniard, for even after three hundred years the British still remembered their Spanish enemies during the time of Good Queen Bess.

While society gossiped on and Lord Parkington's children by his first wife refused to receive Charlotte, she and Parkington cared not a fig. They had a wonderful time and it was with a great sense of adventure that they sailed for the new world and his estates in Virginia. If nothing else, it could be said of Charlotte that she made Ferdie's last days his most lively, and it was often bandied about that Lord Parkington had died with a smile on his face.

No one in the colony had faulted Charlotte's behavior while her husband was alive, for he had made her a wealthy woman and she had exhibited intense loyalty to the old dear. She had been a devoted and caring wife, but once he was dead, once the funeral was over and the period of mourning had passed, Lady Charlotte Parkington came into her own.

She loved life, and always had. She loved to dance, to play at cards, to attend balls and hunts and *soirees*. And most of all she loved men—not just young men, slim and strong, though she had those in quantity, but even those who were portly and sedate. The masculine sex was an endless delight to her, for all had something to offer in their own way. She had no one in the world but herself to please, and she set about pleasing herself with unrestrained enthusiasm.

She glanced at Phillip now, speculatively. "You know, my dear, I worry for you. You may not find yourself entirely content with your married state, for all else aside, virgins can be such tiresome creatures."

He met her gaze with no evidence of interest at all. "Can they?"

"Indeed." Charlotte smiled at him, not a whit

serious, wanting as ever merely to toy with him, to make certain he did not forget how very pleasant their time together had been. "And when you discover this for yourself, perhaps you will not hesitate to call upon an old friend?"

Phillip's brow lifted graciously, but a corner of his lips betrayed the wonderful, familiar cynicism. "Ah, my lady, you are as charming as ever and such a flatterer, but I'm afraid I shall have to decline."

She widened her eyes purposefully. "And have your tastes changed that much, then?" She dimpled charmingly. "Perhaps you've now developed a fancy for young boys?"

"How indelicate, my dear. You make me blush." He got to his feet politely as Charlotte gathered up her fan and reticule and prepared to depart.

He suffered her to lean close and brush her breasts against his waistcoat, then pat his cheek affectionately, once again, with her fingers. Her eyes twinkled. "You are a darling, Phillip, but you forget that I know you too well. You may pull the wool over the eyes of others, but you shall never deceive me."

"Most gracious lady"—he bowed low over her hand—"it has never been my intention to do so."

Regarding him with secret amusement, Charlotte allowed him to take her arm and escort her outside. Not being of a strongly analytical nature, she had never expended a great deal of thought on the changes that had overtaken Phillip in the past few years, nor did she care overmuch about the reasons. She had never really been able to pin down the exact moment those changes had begun, and now she found herself seriously questioning them for the first time. Suddenly she longed to put together the pieces of the puzzle that comprised her favorite swain.

The ending of their liaison had been amiable, for it

would have been outside the bounds of their relationship for it to have been otherwise. Yet there had been a coolness in Phillip's turning away from her, and it had provoked her then.

Of course, when the gossip had started, Phillip, gentleman that he was, had let it be known that it was she who had tired of him, not the other way around. Charlotte had been grateful for that, as any woman in her position would have been. He had thoughtfully maintained her reputation for those who came after him, which was only evidence of his considerate nature.

Yet what of her reputation now that he had chosen someone younger, much younger than she? That irked. It was not that she particularly wanted Phillip—not the Phillip he had become, though it *would* have been pleasant to have known she could have had him—but that she greatly disliked losing him to this Arabella Winters. The entire notion was far more upsetting than she had let on, and she could not let it rest.

She cast him a glance from beneath lowered lashes as he helped her into the carriage for the return trip to the landing. "Do you know, Phillip," she began, "I have often pondered the matter of your decision to . . . ah . . . seek your pleasures elsewhere. Not that it matters a whit to me now"—she twitched her skirts provocatively as she preceded him into the carriage—"but I do so dislike mysteries. You have ever found in me a satisfactory"—she emphasized the word slightly as she met his eyes again—"*companion,* have you not?"

He smiled, revealing faint, dry amusement. "Satisfactory to be sure, my dear. If not always entirely loyal."

"Aha," she declared, delighted. "You were jealous! Though," she added thoughtfully, "I wouldn't have thought it of you."

His eyes twinkled as he arranged his long legs across

47

from her, and his voice was smooth. "Then you would have thought correctly, for I haven't a jealous bone in my body, as you well know. Your varied tastes have always been among the most stimulating of your many charms," he added with a complimentary bow of his head.

Charlotte reflected upon that. "So I've always thought," she agreed frankly. "But how else do you explain your peculiar cooling toward me when the Lord Governor and I became . . . ah . . . special friends?"

She thought she saw a slight tensing of his face and believed that at last she had hit upon it, though she still found his motives most perplexing. Phillip was in exceptionally good favor with Governor Dunmore and counted him among his closest friends. He had never before displayed signs of possessiveness or jealousy, yet when she began to include Lord Dunmore among her admirers, Phillip had turned from her. It made no sense.

His smile was lazy and his tone light. "Ah, our beloved governor. Smashing good fellow and a fine sport at the hunt. You should do well with him, my dear, as long as you do not awaken one morning to find yourself on the wrong side of his hounds." Here she caught a glimpse again of something in his eyes—was it hard cynicism, or merely amusement?

Charlotte frowned irritably. Phillip's propensity for speaking in riddles was not one of his most endearing traits, and he had taken to it far too often lately for her liking. "Whatever are you chattering about, Phillip? Will you make yourself clear for once?"

Phillip shrugged, displaying quickly waning attention. "Only that in these uncertain times, our good friend, if I know him well, is as apt to use as to be used."

Charlotte's attention sharpened in perplexity tempered by annoyance. "Whatever in the world could you mean, Phillip? What could Lord Dunmore gain from me—or you, for that matter!"

Phillip's smile was sweet and fatuous as the carriage rolled to a stop at the landing and the footman came to the door. "Why," he declared, alighting, "I shouldn't be in the least surprised if the villain were after the secret of my magnificent roses, come to think of it, for it is well known that I grow the finest in all the Colonies and Lord Dunmore, upstanding gentleman that he is, does have a fiendish streak about him when it comes to being outdone. So do be careful, my dear," he implored, extending his hand to her.

Charlotte's mouth formed a pretty bow of tolerant reprimand as she placed her hand in his and stepped down. She had never been able to tell when Phillip was serious—that had always been one of his most fascinating qualities—and for just a moment he had almost taken her in. "You are as impossible as ever," she declared with a pout, but her features were quickly transformed by a smile as he brought her fingers to his lips for a farewell kiss.

"And you, my dearest Charlotte, are ever more delightful to amuse." He held her hand at a distance as he guided her toward the waiting barge. "Do call again soon," he advised, smiling innocently as he added, "and make my bride welcome."

Charlotte paused before stepping onto the barge, looking at him with a mixture of despair and affection in her expression. His sincerity left much to be desired, and well she knew it. He was being Phillip again, acting a role, playing a part. And who better to judge another actor than she? If only she could determine his game.

She curtsied deeply to him, then blew a kiss from her fingers before swinging her skirts around to step onto the barge. Within moments of settling down in her chaise she had forgotten about Phillip, the governor, Phillip's riddled innuendos and his bothersome bride, absorbed as she became in her much more pressing concern over what the cruel sun was doing to her complexion.

Phillip, however, had not forgotten. He stood on the shore for a long time, and as he watched the barge grow smaller in his vision, a preoccupied frown marred his handsome features. Finally he turned, slowly, and walked back to the house.

Chapter IV

The Norfolk Harbor was excessively busy on the bright June day in 1773 when the ship finally made port and Arabella strained to take it all in. She stood on the deck like a child released from a winter's confinement on the first day of spring, turning this way and that, eager eyes scanning the scene below, trying to see everything at once, and, failing that, trying to see everything at least twice.

The interminable voyage was over, and she felt as a prisoner might, breathing his first breath of air after long, dark years in a dungeon. Free. And home. She could hardly believe it. After all this time, it was finally happening.

"Don't dawdle, girl," Reginald barked behind her, grunting and huffing as he approached, dragging his gouty left leg behind him. "Somewhere down there, Everett is waiting for us. Let's get on with it."

Black men, stripped to the waist, and with sweat streaming down their backs, unloaded cargo of molasses, cloth, and rum from the ships at anchor in the harbor while other slaves loaded into waiting vessels bales and barrels of tobacco, indigo, rice, and hemp. Newly arrived slaves, mute with awe and terror and headed for the auction block, were chained together in a shuffling single file as they were herded along the dock. Horses and carriages crowded the street below, voices called out, dogs barked, and children cried in an ever-shifting panorama of color and sound. The scene was so filled with energy, movement, and life that Arabella felt giddy as she tried to drink it all in at once. This was Virginia, the New World, and nothing she had ever imagined had been quite this fresh, this brilliant, this exciting.

Arabella, on not-quite-steady sea legs, followed Reginald down the ramp and into the midst of this teeming humanity. Porters followed, burdened by the trunks and valises she had brought with her. Most of her belongings had arrived on a previous ship, but there simply had not been time to pack everything in advance. Repeatedly, Arabella's eyes scanned the jostling crowd around her, seeking the one man who might be Phillip.

Could that be he, there, she wondered, broad shouldered and tall, rising up on a carriage step to wave to someone . . . But no, a short, bald man answered the other's beckon, and Arabella searched anew. Perhaps there, that magnificent young man with the light brown hair tied into a simple queue, his full-sleeved lawn shirt draped across the heavy musculature of his strong arms and bare throat . . . But she was disappointed again when the man lifted a small, laughing boy to his shoulder and turned to walk the other way.

Reginald stood still, peering through the throng in undisguised irritation. "Damn it. I thought that at least he'd meet his bride. Perhaps he's not so eager after all, not that I could blame him . . ."

Arabella found it easy to ignore Reginald's foul mood. She was far too fascinated by all that was going on about her. But she did wonder where Phillip was.

A large black man, clean shaven and neatly dressed in blue trousers and a gray jacket suddenly materialized at their side. "Lord Winters and Miss Arabella." He bent his head in polite acknowledgment. "My name is Sam. I'm sent from Master Phillip to take you home."

Home! What a wonderful sound that had, Arabella reflected. Eagerly, she stepped forward to follow the path the huge man was clearing in the crowd.

Voices—this time voices raised in anger—penetrated the usual crowd noises that surrounded them. Sam stopped, cast a concerned glance over his shoulder at his charges, then changed direction, but not before Arabella had caught a glimpse of the scene from which he was trying to protect her.

A man—an old man—was being dragged by an angry mob along the street that skirted the docks. Around his neck was a rope, pulled taut. His clothes were torn and his face showed a series of marks and bruises. As Arabella watched, he stumbled and almost fell, only to be jerked cruelly to his feet again while a jeering crowd of dockside rabble threw taunts and fruit at him and snatched at his clothing with dirty, vicious fingers.

"Move along, Arabella. Don't stand there staring like some common street urchin," Reginald snarled at her. But Arabella stood firm. What was happening? What crime had this man committed that he was being hauled through the streets like an animal on a chain? She opened her mouth to inquire as Sam loomed beside her.

His face was grim and his tone terse. "This is not for your eyes, Miss Arabella. Come to the carriage." But even as he spoke, Sam's own eyes, intent and searching, traveled back toward the scene.

"What is it?" she demanded. Her face was flushed

53

and her eyes glinted emerald sparks. "What are they doing to that poor man? What is his offense? Do you know him?"

A look of annoyance flickered across Sam's face so quickly that Arabella thought she might have imagined it as reluctantly his eyes moved back to her and his face resumed its mask of servility. He said nothing.

From inside the coach Reginald called out in irritation, "Get in this coach, Missy, and at once. Get in and let us be away from this abominable place!"

But Arabella stood her ground, waiting for Sam's reply.

She saw the muscle of his jaw tighten, and something very close to anger momentarily sparked in his dark eyes. "I'm sorry you had to see that, Mistress," he said in a moment. "It's not the best way to start your first day in Virginia."

The sound of Sam's voice, so beautifully accented and culturally softened, fascinated Arabella, as did his impeccable form of address—as did, in fact, everything about him. He bore himself like a man used to controlling his own destiny, he spoke like a man well educated and well born, yet he was a slave. Arabella knew little about the institution of slavery, but she had been led to expect barely civilized replicas of humanity in chains and loincloths, or, at the very most, poorly trained servants of the lowest class. Nothing had prepared her for a man such as Sam, and she was curious about him. But at the moment she was a great deal more curious about what had just transpired in the street.

"What was his crime?" she insisted with what she hoped did not sound like too avid a display of morbid inquisitiveness. It was simply that she wanted to know and absorb every detail of the strange new life in which she found herself, and never in her life had Arabella tolerated her questions going unanswered.

She could sense his inner debate, for it was reflected in his eyes, but she could not know that the intelligence with which she had instinctively credited him would soon register her, his new mistress, as a force to be reckoned with. "He was a shopkeeper," Sam said, his words quick and clipped. "Arrested for selling tea."

Arabella stared. "Tea? Why, that is absurd! What—"

"Dutch tea," Sam replied in hurried, almost disdainful tones. "Smuggled tea. Only British tea is allowed to be sold in the Colonies. The man was a criminal who tried to avoid the taxes."

Arabella's eyes widened in unabashed fascination. What an extraordinary country this was; where a man could be dragged through the streets for selling tea! "Will he be imprisoned?" she insisted, then her tone dropped with a note of dread. "Or even hanged . . . ?"

Reginald's florid, overheated face appeared at the coach door. "Serves him right, by God, if you ask me. Damned smashing show, too. Now will you get in this coach and let us be away? I don't plan to spend all day in this inferno!"

Sam, whose face was now completely expressionless, helped Arabella into the coach, and she was too thoughtful to protest. The sight of that poor old man haunted her, and she could not help but think that the punishment far outweighed the crime, but what did she know of colonial life or politics? This was indeed a most peculiar land . . .

28 June, 1773

The Ryde from the Harbour was tiring and abominably hot & dusty, but my Fatigue fell away when I saw Shadowood glowing like a

Cathedral in the Setting Sun. What a Surprise to find such Grace & Civility in so rugged a Place . . . and what Manner of Man must be my Husbande to have made it so! I confess I scarce can contain my Eagerness to meet him, for already I feel I have come Home . . .

What a strange and beautiful Place this is. The Fields are lush and green and stretch into Forever as God first made Them—the River, broad and sweet, the yellow Flatlands that seeme so wilde . . . The Lande Itself appeares peaceful and content, yet there is Much I find disturbing . . .

Today We scarce had Reach'd our Carriage when We were Halt'd by a Mob of jeering Ruffians who dragg'd a Man of quyte advanced Years through the Streets with a Rope around his Neck . . . Phillip's manservant, Sam, explain'd the poore Fellow had been arrest'd for selling Tea upon which no Duty had been pay'd. Is this not extraordinary, that a Man can be punish'd for selling Tea?

Yet is it any more extraordinary, I wonder, than a Bride coming to her Groome with no Knowledge of Him beyonde the dim & fading Memories of the Past? Were not those Memories so strong, I have Doubt that I should be here . . . Oh, Phillip, my Heart beats with the Minutes until We shall be together once again, for I know I shall be happy Here . . .

The big black man flitted like a shadow through the dusky pines that deepened the forest, moving with inexorable stealth toward a lighter clump of shadows beneath a gnarled oak tree. The murmurs of low conversation ceased with a snap as his foot broke a

56

twig, and stealthy hands moved, without appearing to move at all, toward belted pistols and nearby muskets. A collective breath was released as Sam made himself known to them.

"You've been a long time getting back," commented one man who was again propping his musket against the trunk of the tree.

Sam nodded curtly. "We made more stops than I had thought. The brother-in-law has gout." And then he couldn't resist the slight half curve of a rueful grin. "I don't envy the good Master Phillip his choice of family, that I'll tell you."

There were some subdued chuckles and grins, and one man queried, "But what of his choice of a bride? That's what we want to hear! Ugly as a horse, eh?"

This was followed by more soft laughter and some nudges, but Sam sobered a fraction. "No," he said thoughtfully. "Comely enough, I wager, but . . ."

He did not finish, and another man, sturdy and plain in build, insisted sharply, "But what?"

Sam, for all his size and position of authority, looked momentarily uncertain. "I cannot be sure, but there is something about her I do not quite trust. She is bright. And too curious, I think."

Their subsequent laughter was muffled by the forest sounds and the encroaching night. Finally, someone commented, "A fitting match for Everett, eh? This will give the womenfolk food for gossip for a time!"

There were almost a dozen of them gathered there in the deepening forest twilight, farmers and tradesmen, indentured and free, common and privileged. They dressed in homespun and muslin, spoke in accents of education and deprivation; had they been assembled in a tavern or upon a street corner no one would have glanced at them twice. But here, in their element, a strand of something indeterminate wove them together

57

and proclaimed the fact that these were no ordinary men. It was an alertness, a discreet, well-disguised toughness, a subtle sense of danger that bespoke men who had faced death and would not surrender to it easily.

One man kept himself more in the shadows than the others, yet it was his presence that seemed to project, to control the responses of all the others. He wore a dark traveling cloak and high boots, and upon his face there was a woolen mask that had been fashioned to cover his features from brow to mouth. No one knew why he wore the mask. Some said it was because of a hideous disfigurement earned in some daring feat of rebellion early on; some said it was because he was, in fact, a member of European royalty in exile; others said it was because of crimes committed outside the Colonies. No one asked; no one, in fact, cared. He had earned their loyalty and respect without question; his authority was absolute.

When he spoke, everyone listened. "We are not women," he said, his voice low and smooth and husky, "and will leave this discussion to another time." He turned to Sam, his tone this time carrying the sharpness of a command. "How did you find the situation in Norfolk?"

Sam turned to look at his leader, and if there was a momentary disorientation due to the duality of his role, not a flicker of it showed in his eyes. He had been sent to Norfolk on an errand for Phillip Everett; he had gone to Norfolk on a mission for this man. Others might have wondered how Sam made such a division of loyalty between his master, one of the wealthiest and most vocal Loyalists in the county, and this man, who daily fought against all that Everett and his kind stood for. But for Sam there had never been a question. Phillip Everett had given him his freedom, but this masked man had taught him the meaning of the word. He owed each of them his life.

Sam had been born a slave but had been sold at an early age to a progressive teacher at William and Mary, who considered it quite an accomplishment to teach his house servants to read, write, and cipher along with their rudimentary chores. Being won by Phillip Everett in a card game had been for Sam nothing short of good fortune. Everett had freed him almost immediately, and the huge library at Shadowood had allowed him to continue his passion for knowledge. Sam had stayed with Phillip Everett as his valet for the best of all possible reasons: because it had suited him. And he had come here to the forest this night because he, as much as anyone present, valued all they were fighting for.

His mind fully back to business once more, Sam reported, "He was being taken to the garrison as we departed the dock." A small, almost imperceptible grimace crossed his face at the memory of the sight. "The crowd seemed more intent upon tormenting the poor fellow with rotten fruit and jeers than in doing him any real harm, and his guard was light. We should have no trouble getting to him before the trial."

The masked leader nodded, thoughtfully. "He will no doubt be taken to the public square at dawn for trial"—his lips curved into a vague hint of a smile— "which, by good fortune, happens to be the time of day we do our best work."

Reciprocal grins and nods from the gathered men acknowledged that they were ready and eager for the adventure. "Very well then." The masked man spoke briskly and moved toward his horse. "Sam will notify you of the day. We will need six men this time, including myself. Cast lots for duty and give your numbers to Sam."

The men who remained waited until the sound of his

retreating hoofbeats grew dimmer and finally disappeared, then they moved quickly to toss for position. The hunt was on once again.

Arabella closed her journal, for the supper hour was near, and she placed it carefully in the drawer of the fruitwood *escritoire* in her new chambers. She looked around once again at her surroundings, allowing pleasure and contentment to fill her.

The walls were papered in a pattern of pale pink roses, and the counterpane and curtains that covered the ornately carved bed repeated the design. The windows that opened on two sides were shaded by heavy brocade draperies of dusky rose lined with gold. Arabella found herself wondering with breathless excitement what the view would be like from those windows in the mornings. The looped rug in the center of the floor was woven with the pattern of a single huge rose, and Arabella noted that a vase of the same fresh-cut flowers she had seen in abundance in the foyer decorated her bureau. She mused with a secret smile that her new husband, or someone in his household, must be exceptionally fond of roses.

There was a small dressing room, where the gowns that had been shipped ahead of her had been unpacked, pressed and brushed, and hung neatly from hooks around the room. Coordinating slippers and under-clothes were arranged on shelves beneath them, and hats and gloves above. Every detail in preparation for the new mistress's arrival had been seen to, and welcome had seemed to exude from the house the moment Arabella had set foot in it. Had Phillip overseen these details himself? Arabella wondered. Had he been just as excited about her arrival as Arabella herself had been?

A hot, perfumed bath had soothed Arabella's exhausted body, but her mind had remained full to bursting with all the newness and excitement she had encountered today. And the greatest adventure was yet to come. Phillip. In only a matter of minutes now she would see him, and as anticipation was heightened, nervousness grew. Would he remember her at all? Would she be a disappointment to him? If only he had written her or in some way had communicated to her that this marriage was as much to his liking as it had been to hers . . . But there had been very little time, she reprimanded herself sternly. They had been on the ship for Norfolk before any missive of Phillip's could have reached her. Of course the marriage pleased him. Phillip was not the type of man who would agree to any undertaking against his will, not for any reason. He was far too strong minded for that.

Arabella could stay alone in her chamber no longer, and she paused for one last, nervous look in the full-length pier glass before descending to greet her husband. She had chosen for this first night in her new home a taupe brocade gown, and she was pleased with her selection. Its low neck cut a provocative heart-shaped dip over her creamy breasts, which were pushed high and full by her corset and barely concealed by her lace cape. Its full folds were gathered tightly away from the stomacher and flowed regally in back, accenting her figure to perfection. Arabella had never been much concerned with her womanly curves, but tonight she took full stock of her assets and was not displeased. The color of the gown, too, was flattering, turning her skin to ivory and enhancing the golden highlights in her hair.

Her maid had frowned reprovingly when Arabella had refused to powder her hair, but it was an affection Arabella had stubbornly decided to abandon the moment she stepped off English soil. Tonight her hair was brushed across a small wire frame atop her head in a simple but elegant style and, with the aid of the gown's rich hue, took on a soft, glowing color that to her seemed not at all objectionable. A topaz necklace, lying like a small string of gold around her neck, was her only adornment. Yes, she looked exactly as she would wish Phillip to see her for the first time—composed, confident, and completely natural, as she intended to be for the rest of her life.

Arabella heard the voices and stopped halfway down the stairs with her hand resting lightly on the polished banister. She could see into the open door of the room across the hallway below her. Reginald was standing beside the painted marble of the fireplace and beside him stood another figure, elaborately wigged and grandly attired in velvet, and speaking in the over-bred, aristocratic drawl of a British dandy. For a moment irritation clouded with disappointment flashed in her eyes. She had hoped that on this first night there would be no other guests at Shadowood—that for their first meeting, at least, she and Phillip could be alone.

Resolutely squaring her shoulders and forcing a smile, she continued her descent. There would be plenty of time for her and Phillip to be alone, she told herself, and all that mattered now was that, at last, she would meet him.

Reginald noticed her first as she paused in the doorway, and when he greeted her with a benevolent wave of the hand that held his wine glass, Arabella relaxed, relieved to see that her brother seemed in much better spirits. But where was Phillip? she wondered.

The room was empty except for the man who turned at Reginald's greeting and came toward her. For an awful moment, Arabella experienced a sense of *déjà vu* as she looked at him, and it was almost as if she were back in one of the stuffy drawing rooms of London. The apparition approaching her was the last possible thing Arabella had ever expected to encounter on this remote tidewater plantation.

He was of more than average height, but the swirls and puffs of his elaborately designed powdered wig made him seem even taller. His face was powdered, too, and his lips and cheeks brightly rouged. An ingratiating little smile hovered about the corners of those cherry-colored lips, emphasizing the dark speck of a beauty mark that artistically adorned the line of his cheekbone. It was the kind of smile Arabella was used to encountering upon the countenances of her London swains. It offered only the merest hint of an expression, for anything more might cause the heavily painted face to crack into most unbecoming lines.

This gentleman, spectacle that he was, had spared no expense on fashion. The peach-colored velvet coat, which fit his shoulders to perfection, featured a darker satin lining and was cut away to show a waistcoat heavily embroidered in gold, bright reds, and green. Its pearl buttons glowed softly in the candlelight. Pale fawn breeches clung tightly to muscled thighs and white silk stockings hugged his well-formed calves. His knee buckles were jeweled as were the buckles on his high-heeled slippers. He looked like nothing more than a strutting peacock, and for one wild moment Arabella was hard put to suppress a sudden and most impolite urge to burst into laughter.

His steps were a practiced mince that caused the jeweled heels of his slippers to click out a predesigned rhythm on the hardwood floor. It was a walk perfected by the finest dandies of London and was usually at its most effective with the counterrhythm of a walking stick, but this young fop, obviously well tutored, made quite a good show of it with the aid of nothing but one gracefully trailing hand. The ever-present, languishing half-smile did not fade.

With a perfectly executed court bow, he extended a limp-wristed hand to her that, Arabella noticed with some distaste, was also powdered as well as being adorned by gleaming stones set in heavy gold. Arabella made her curtsy and allowed him to clasp the tips of her fingers between the cool, dry touch of his own. A wave of heavy perfume engulfed her as he bent close to draw her fingers to his lips.

"My dearest Lady Arabella. *Enchanté, enchanté,* I'm sure." His drawl was languidly affected. "Welcome to Shadowood. And please accept my apologies that I was not here to greet you sooner."

A horrible premonition gripped Arabella as she straightened from her curtsy and looked up into the strangely, and somehow horribly, familiar gray eyes of the man who held her hand. Desperate for reassurance, she jerked her eyes toward her brother, who seemed at this moment to be witnessing the most entertaining event of his life.

Unable to keep the secret any longer, Reginald gave a hoot of laughter that turned his face a deeper shade of red. "Ah, so you don't know him, girlie. It's been a long time, I warrant." He choked on his laughter, coughed and wheezed, and then finally took control of himself. All the while Arabella could only stare dumbly, knowing what was about to come but hoping it would not be so—praying that it would not be so.

"It's Phillip Everett, Arabella," Reginald said, dabbing at his mirthfully damp eyes with the back of his hand while never once taking his gaze from the dumbfounded Arabella. "It's your husband come at last to welcome his bride."

Chapter V

It could have been an eternity that Arabella stood there staring dumbly into the face of the man before her, but in truth it was no more than a second or two. He released her hand and took a tiny step backward, raising a quizzing glass to his eye as his bright lips formed a lazy *moue,* which could have indicated either pleasure or bored indifference.

"Dear me, dear me," he clucked, surveying her up and down through the monocled, fishlike eye. "What a fetching gown m'dear—most becoming. Do tell, is it from Paris? I understand they are doing the most *daring* things with lace these days." He circled her once, craning his neck to take in the tips of her slippers, nodding with approval as he murmured, "Lovely, quite lovely. Who is your dressmaker, dear child? Anyone I know?"

Without giving her a chance to respond, he came full circle again and stopped to stand directly before her. He paused in the process of dropping his glass and an expression of distaste and perhaps even a shade of politely controlled alarm crossed his face.

"But my dear Lady Arabella," he exclaimed with as much animation as the tight fit of his coat allowed, "your hair! Can this be true? Is powdering out? And my wig maker assured me only last month that this wig was the very latest thing! The doddering old fool! How very distressing! But I am so dreadfully out of step locked away in these wretched provinces, you understand . . . *Mon dieu!*"

With his lightning-quick change of subject, his eyes grew round with horror and he let the quizzing glass fall to the length of its satin ribbon against his waistcoat. "This puts me in mind of the most disturbing rumor! The *Gazette* prints that lace is out in favor of a more simply tied stock, but I persist that it cannot be. Tell me true, what do you think?" He struck a pose before her with his head profiled, his knee bent, and his waist turned, to allow the full effect of his extravagantly tiered lace neckcloth to penetrate. "Am I overdone? Hmmm?"

In the background Arabella was aware of Reginald threatening to choke again on another great guffaw. The man who called himself Phillip appeared to be awaiting some sort of reply from her, and without even recognizing the sound of her own voice, Arabella managed a strangulated, "I . . . I'm sure I don't know, sir . . ."

He turned his gaze on her again, peering at her speculatively. "Why, my dear Lady Arabella, you look quite *fatigué!* What a dreadful host I am! You must be famished. Let us go in, shall we, and you will relate the news from the London set. How perfectly splendid it is to have you here to tell me the latest . . ."

It cannot be true; it cannot be true, Arabella thought in desperation. *It is some dreadful jest of Reginald's to repay me for all the distress I've caused him, or some great misunderstanding . . . It simply cannot be true . . .*

Her fingers were somehow resting lightly atop the

velvet-clad arm of the prattling Phillip. They were moving toward the dining room and she kept thinking, *Soon I will awake and this will be over. It is some horrible dream induced by spoiled wine and the motion of the coach* . . . Surely this could not be real.

The dining room was papered in a delicate etching of forest green and the overhead chandelier displayed the light of a dozen dancing tapers. The huge oval table was covered in a lace cloth and set with gleaming crystal, china, and ornate silver. In the center was a heavy glass vase filled with more of the deep-hued roses.

Phillip took Arabella to her seat, then paused to snap a blossom from the centerpiece. He brought it to his nostrils and inhaled deeply before presenting it to Arabella. "Ah, even the beauty of my darlings pales before your own, Lady Arabella." He made an extravagant bow as he offered her the rose. "With my deepest compliments."

Arabella accepted the rose with cold fingers, looking once more into his face. What she saw there only filled her further with despair. Beneath the powder and rouge, the shape of the jaw and the line of the cheek were disturbingly familiar. The grotesquely painted mouth was an effective disguise for the full, masculine lips she remembered. But it was only a disguise, wasn't it?

It was Phillip. It was no jest.

"And do you grow the roses yourself, my boy?" Reginald was saying with a fair imitation of grave interest.

"Indeed, my lord. Yes, my greatest pleasure." Phillip settled himself into the head chair and unfolded his napkin with a graceful snap of his wrist. "Such a relaxing pastime, to be cloistered from the cares of the world, alone with my little beauties. Now, Lady

Arabella, we truly must discuss this matter of coiffure."
He turned to her with a renewed expression of
delicately outraged civility. "I cannot believe that
powdering and wiggery will no longer be in fashion. I
am not at all certain how one is suspected to survive
without one's wig, don't you know. Why, I have always
held that the strength of blessed England lies within her
wig makers . . ."

And so it progressed. Conversation with Phillip
Everett did not require either participation or attention, which was fortunate because Arabella was
capable of giving neither. There was Reginald, sitting
across from her, looking as though he were enjoying
the greatest sport of his life as she observed him
through the gaily dancing candle flame. There were the
platters of succulent dishes that were brought in from
the warming kitchen—turtle soup and fresh broccoli,
battered eggs and pheasant stuffed with chestnuts,
strawberry trifle thick with cream—few of which
Arabella tried, and those she barely tasted. There was a
sweet evening breeze that fluttered through the half-
open window, and sumptuous aromas and silent-
footed black servants. And there was Phillip.

Was it possible? Was it truly possible? Could he have
changed so much? Had she ever really known
him . . . or had she simply remembered what she had
dreamed him to be?

Her mind went racing back across the years and the
windswept fields of Devon to a ten-year-old girl with
tangled braids and starry eyes and a handsome young
man with tawny hair and strong shoulders, whose
laughter was as rich as the wind, whose sparkling eyes
were as playful as a colt's, and whose nature was as
generous as all the world. Phillip had just come down
from Eton, and his father had presented him with a new
stallion.

It was a magnificent creature, midnight black and fiery tempered, and astride it Phillip looked as tall as a god. And oh, how he rode! Simply watching him race across the fields in a cloud of flying turf was enough to send Arabella's childish imagination into a torment of ecstasy and envy.

But even at that tender age, Arabella had not been one to be an idle spectator. Only a few days had passed before she determined to no longer resist the urge to emulate her idol, and she had availed herself of the one horse on the estate that she was not allowed to ride—her father's championship Arabian.

The animal, high-spirited at best and unused to the strange rider, had immediately bolted. Even though Arabella was a good rider, she had found herself clinging in terror to the mane of the fierce animal as he plunged over hills and leapt fences, tearing across the meadows completely out of control. Arabella had thought she would surely die and her own fear had been communicated to her mount, who had raced at a crazed pace toward a looming copse, from which neither of them could possibly have emerged unscathed.

And then, as though her own desperate imaginings had conjured him up, Phillip had been there, the pounding hooves of his black stallion gaining ground and coming abreast of her, his strong arm reaching for her, sweeping her off her mount and into his own saddle, where she had been cradled, safe and secure, against his broad chest. Arabella had loved him then, with the pure and unquestioning adoration of a child. He had been a hero in the only true sense of the word, and, in the way of heroes, completely unflawed, unchanging—perfect.

And that was what she had held in her mind all these years, Arabella realized now as she turned a somewhat dazed gaze upon the painted and furbelowed man who sat beside her—the image of a hero, too perfect to be real. Had he changed, or had she never really seen him for what he was? It mattered little now, for the truth was she could not—she simply could *not*—consent to spend the rest of her life as this man's wife.

Oh, Papa, she thought in deep despair, *I was not meant for this. Not for this.*

There was simply no possibility of it. Her chin lifted slightly at the reassurance of this decision. The entire matter was beyond imagining, and she would not have it. Reginald could book passage for the two of them on the return voyage to London, for she had no intention of staying a moment longer than necessary in the company of this—this blathering popinjay. Fate was indeed a cruel jokester, but Arabella Katherine Sarah Winters, mistress of her own destiny, would not be its victim—not this time.

A discreet sound at the doorway interrupted Phillip's incessant babbling, and he turned his head with an irritated frown to see Sam standing there. "Slay me, man! Must you people always be creeping up on a fellow?" he exclaimed. The nasal intonation of his barely enunciated drawl grated on Arabella's nerves. "You've quite caused me to lose my train of thought just as I was getting to the most entertaining part of the tale! What is it now, and be quick about it."

Sam inclined his head apologetically. "Pardon, sir, but there is a small disturbance in the stable yard that requires your attention. I believe some of the men have"—he cleared his throat discreetly—"overtaxed their weekly allotment of rum."

"Oh, bother!" Phillip flung down his napkin in annoyance and drained the last of his wine. "Yes, yes, I suppose there is nothing to do but to attend to the matter personally." He gave a great martyred sigh as he rose. "Count yourself blessed, Reggie, old boy, that you have not the command of three hundred ninnies on your conscience. How dreadfully fatiguing it can all be." He turned to Arabella with a bow. "A thousand pardons, my lady. I shall return with the greatest possible speed."

Arabella held her breath until he was out of the room and she heard the wide double door close behind him. Then she crumpled her napkin on the table in an abrupt movement. Her knuckles, clenched around the napkin, were white and her eyes were dark with shock, but with a very great effort she kept her voice steady. "Reginald, this is preposterous! I won't take another moment of it! You will call off this absurd marriage the instant he returns, and there will be no further discussion of the matter."

Reginald calmly helped himself to the decanter of wine before his plate and did not quite succeed in keeping a small smile from toying with the corner of his lips. "What is this, my dear? Can it be you find your husband . . . somewhat less than to your liking?"

Arabella did not trouble to calm her temper before she spoke. Her color heightened and her fists clenched. "You know perfectly well what I think of my . . . *husband!*" She practically spat the word. "I did not cross an ocean to escape from the absurdities and falseness of London society only to be confronted with . . . with"— words failed her and she made a vicious, all-encompassing gesture with her wrist—"with *this!*"

Reginald leaned back in his chair and inhaled the bouquet of the wine, completely absorbing himself in the pleasure of it. Arabella took a calming breath. She counted to ten, then to twenty. She mentally began to recite the Greek alphabet. When she thought she could keep the tone of her voice at a rational level, she said, "I see that you find the situation quite entertaining,

Reginald, and I do not begrudge you that. But you must also see that it is quite out of the question. We shall thank Mr. Everett for his hospitality and return to England. And that," she finished simply and rose, "is that."

But as she swept past Reginald's chair, his hand abruptly shot out to clasp her wrist in a surprisingly vicious grip. Arabella turned in some shock to meet eyes that were coal dark and iron hard in a face that was suffused with an ugly, dangerous color. Every curve of his corpulent body suddenly seemed galvanized into deadly serious intent, and a coldness ran through Arabella at the expression contorting her brother's features.

"Not this time, Missy," he growled low in his throat. "None of your tears and tantrums and grand schemes will get you your way now. I've ruled you with a slack hand for far too long and see what it's gotten me. Well, no more!" He gave her wrist a sharp jerk and his fleshy fingers bit into her bones. "I've finally found a man, or almost a man"—with this he sniggered mirthlessly— "who'll have you, and, by God, have you he will!" He released her wrist with a jerk, and Arabella's other hand unconsciously went to rub her injured flesh as he turned back to his wine. "Make of that what you will," he declared in grim satisfaction.

Arabella tossed her head as a glitter came into her eyes. "I will tell you precisely what I shall make of it," she returned. "Neither you nor anyone else can force me to stay here with that—that bag of feathers and curls against my will! I will return to England, explanations or no!"

Reginald looked at her with a peculiar, almost malicious gleam in his eye. His voice was deceptively soft. "Surely you realize, my dear," he said smoothly, "that nothing short of an act of Parliament—and a

72

great deal more pocket money than you presently have to spare—will grant you a divorce. I'm afraid I see no hope for your case." He shook his head in mock sympathy. "None at all."

Divorce. It was an ugly word that caused even Arabella to shrink from it momentarily. The reality of the situation was beginning to close in on her with horrible finality, yet she had to insist, "You have influence at Parliament . . . we have funds . . ."

"We?" Reginald's smile was cool and sarcastic. "Think again, Missy. The Chatley estate is entailed entirely to me; you have benefited from the family fortune solely through my generosity, but now that the marriage papers have been signed and I have delivered you safely to your husband, my responsibility is ended. From this moment onward, every morsel of food that passes your lips, the clothes upon your back, even the quills with which you do your damnable scribblings will belong to Phillip Everett. In short, dear sister, you haven't a farthing."

Arabella stared at him, and at last the shock of what she had done—what had been done to her—penetrated the layers of her consciousness and made itself known. She had given herself completely into the keeping of a man she did not know. She had nowhere to go and no one to whom to turn. This was not England, and she was no longer Lady Arabella Winters, who was accustomed, with the slightest crook of her finger, to obtaining her every wish. She was Mistress Phillip Everett, powerless and penniless, and totally dependent for her very existence upon the largesse of her husband.

But still she could not accept it, not completely. Determinedly she kept her gaze upon her brother. "I have my dowry," she insisted coolly. "I will write and dispose of it—"

"Your dower house and all it entails is now the property of your husband, foolish girl," Reginald drawled in a bored tone. He sipped his wine, then added, "What else do you imagine dowries are for?"

Arabella's hand went instinctively to the topaz necklace at her throat. Reginald caught the movement and sneered. "Your jewels are pretty but hardly enough to finance a return to England and a divorce—a divorce in which your husband does not wish to participate. I doubt that Parliament would even act."

Defiantly, Arabella lifted her chin. "I am not without friends in England," she told him. "If I contacted them . . ."

Reginald gave a snort of laughter and drained his glass. "Ah, the inestimable Mistress Montagu and her lot. You were nothing but a plaything to them, Arabella, a pretty toy. Do you really think any of them would be out of pocket for you? Certainly not the great lady herself. Why, she's been married to old Montagu for thirty years with ne'er a complaint." The sidelong look he cast her as he refilled her glass was narrow and malevolent. "Best take a leaf from her book, my dear, for there's no escape for you now."

Even as he spoke Arabella realized that the hope of receiving aid from England was more bluster than possibility. She would never write. How could she go to her friends and beg like a common street urchin? How could she admit failure to those whose respect she coveted more than anything in the world? No, there was no hope for her from that quarter.

And for the final time in her life Arabella had to face the truth of her brother's feelings for her. She had been an impediment to him, no more than a nuisance to be rid of. He cared nothing for her and never had. Whether or not she was happy in her marriage—indeed, whether she lived or died—meant nothing to him. Arabella was completely alone. And, being alone, she had no one to rely upon but herself.

Her chin lifted marginally with a resurgence of strength and confidence. Very well, then, she resolved, rely upon herself she would. She could not keep the bitterness out of her voice as she said. "Thank you so much for understanding my plight, brother"—her own lips curled into a gentle semblance of a sneer as she finished—"but as you so wisely pointed out, *you* are no longer in charge of my destiny. Good night."

Arabella swept up her skirts and exited the room to the sound of Reginald's self-indulgent chuckles. She moved toward the stairs, her head held high, her skirts billowing behind her, and almost missed the entrance of Phillip Everett from a door at the rear of the hall. His high-pitched, gratingly solicitous voice stopped her.

"Lady Arabella! You look quite distraught! Is there a problem? Supper not to your liking? A wee bit of biliousness, perhaps . . ."

Arabella turned slowly, drawing in her breath. Very well, she decided silently. This was best. Fie on Reginald and all his grand schemes. She would take care of this matter on her own.

"I fear I have rather unhappy news, sir," she said. She determinedly kept her voice formal, carefully couching her sentiments in a civility she was far from feeling. Yet she minced no words. "I regret to inform you that this contract is terminated. I . . . I cannot agree to this marriage."

Only the faintest flicker of an eyelid, the slightest tightening of a muscle, betrayed Phillip's surprise. But immediately whatever chagrin he had experienced was smoothed over and his words gushed out, conciliatory, soothing. "My dear, dear Lady Arabella, I'm quite taken aback. Surely you speak in haste . . ."

Arabella shook her head and tried to control the

75

hysteria that had been building since she had first laid eyes on Phillip Everett. But at least it would go no further. This charade would be ended at once, and all would be better for it.

She gentled her voice somewhat. "You must realize also, sir, how ill-matched we are. I am not the wife for you. It will be better for us both if I return to England."

Phillip's face was perfectly bland. "But, my dear girl, we *are* married! There is no going back. How silly you are!"

Her voice rising, Arabella strove for control. "Can't you see how foolish we both were to sign that contract? A childhood acquaintance—it was nothing more." With these words and a turn of her wrist she deftly dismissed all those years of longing for him. "That surely is no basis for a marriage. You must realize that, sir." And, when absolutely no sign of acquiescence, understanding, or even acknowledgment of her words registered on his face, she felt desperation begin to rise. "You *must* realize that."

His lazy gray eyes were measuring, thoughtful. "I realize one thing only," he replied after a lengthy pause, and Arabella began to breathe a sigh of relief. At least he had heard her. But with his next words her spirits sank abruptly. "You are exhausted with nerves and travel," he pronounced, pleased to have deduced the fact so easily. "Quite beside yourself, in fact. How rude of me to tire you so with my greed for news of London. You need to rest and you shall do so at once." He clapped his hands once, twice, and in an instant Sam materialized.

"Sam, have Lady Arabella's woman prepare some tea for her at once . . . chamomile, I believe." He smiled ingratiatingly at Arabella. "You will find it so relaxing. In only a moment all of those dreadful nervous anxieties will be borne away like"—he cast a

76

hand into the air, as though searching for the right metaphor—"like the morning mist by the sun."

Arabella stared at him. Hadn't he heard her, after all? She had just demanded an end to their marriage! "But I—"

"No buts, m'dear. I can tell you are quite ready to swoon. We must get you to your room at once, and I shall disturb you no more tonight." His hand was beneath her arm and solicitously he began guiding her up the stairs.

Arabella, who had never swooned in her life, tried to protest, but her words were lost beneath Phillip's grandiose praises of the efficacies of chamomile tea. "And if that doesn't work, my lady, then I will have Sam prepare a sleeping draught. When you awaken in the morning you will have quite forgotten that this foolish conversation ever transpired. All this talk of ending our blissful union! I should die of mortification to even consider such a thing! Now, what we must concern ourselves with is your health."

They had arrived at the door to her room. Arabella opened her mouth for one final, firm protest but closed it again in dismay. Phillip was still droning on about illness of the nerves and the curative powers of various teas, and she knew without a doubt that anything more she could say would be only so much wasted breath. Talking to Phillip was like swiping at the morning mist to which he had alluded. All rational thought dissipated beneath the incessant flow of his meaningless chatter. Trying to make herself clear to him was hopeless.

"And so good night, Lady Arabella." He bowed over her hand. "May flights of angels—or my very excellent tea—sing thee to thy rest."

Arabella turned without replying and swept into her room. She closed the door behind her, and, on second thought, bolted it. Then she could only lean against it, eyes closed, breathing deeply, trying to fight off the despair that was threatening to engulf her.

How could such a good thing go so bad? How had all her dreams, her eager hopes, her clear-eyed certainty of happiness in this new life have turned so abruptly and unpredictably sour?

Twenty minutes later the promised tea sat cooling upon a silver tray at her bedside, and Arabella lay stomach-down upon the bed, careless of the rumpled brocade gown, confiding her despair to her journal.

> *How foolish I have been to have rushed so impetuously into this Marriage! The Daring and the Recklessness which Elizabeth so admires has brought me to Nothing but Ruin and I am helpless in the Hands of a Man who is at best ineffectual, at worst perhaps a little mad . . . Oh, Phillip, Phillip, how could this have happened? How could You have been so different from my Imaginings? How could All my Hopes and Dreams of Happiness disappear so unforewarned . . . ? How can I be doom'd to this Marriage yet how shall I escape without Funds, and at any Rate I have no other Place to go . . . I am trapp'd in this unfamiliar Place with a Husbande who, for bizarre Reasons of His Owne, no more wishes Me to leave than Reg—*

In the middle of the word, Arabella put down her quill and tossed the diary aside. For once she found no comfort in her writing, no solace in pouring out her heart to the familiar parchment pages. She stood up and began to pace, a caged animal all too aware of her captor's power over her. There must be a way; there must be a way out, her mind cried.

She moved to the window and looked out across the

78

lawn. In the shadowy darkness the river shone in the moonlight, as wide as an ocean and just as unbreachable. To the north she could see only the shapes of pine, a dense thicket of trees, a seemingly impenetrable forest. Arabella sighed. This land was not like the neatly manicured, well-kept meadows of Devon. There was danger here—she could feel it—and she knew that any thought of escape was not only foolhardy but self-defeating.

She was virtually alone and without funds in a strange, inhospitable land. Even one so impetuous as she would not dare to run into the Virginia wilderness without a guide or preparation for the journey. Arabella gave a little shiver of premonitory dread as she turned away from the window. There was no hope for it. She could not leave this place; she must instead somehow find a way to resign herself to her fate.

The late summer air hung hot and heavy. In the slave quarters, the Negroes left their cabins and lay on pallets dragged out beneath the stars, hoping for a whisper of wind from the river. The hounds stirred in their kennels, rose, and dug into the hard, dry soil, seeking the cooler layers of earth beneath. Cattle stood knee deep in their ponds, lowing mournfully into the hot, airless night.

Arabella tossed restlessly on the sheets, which were damp with perspiration. Even in her large, high-ceilinged room the heat at midnight was oppressive. As she turned and twisted, fighting the clinging material of her nightdress, she was aware that her body burned with more than the heat of the summer night. It burned with resentment at her situation and flamed with anger at the trick her brother had played on her.

Finally she gave up the struggle to sleep and poured a

glass of water from the pitcher by her bed. The tepid drink helped soothe her parched throat, yet it could not cool the feverish anxiety that consumed her.

With an impatient gesture, Arabella pulled off her nightcap and tossed it on the floor. The silly convention had no place in the summer heat and she vowed she would not wear it again. Barefoot, she slipped out of bed and padded to the window. The draperies were open to allow a breeze, but nothing stirred outside. The leaves of the crepe myrtle hung dry and lifeless in the sweltering air, and not even the cry of a night bird broke the stillness.

Arabella lifted her heavy hair from her shoulders, letting the damp tendrils sift through her fingers. She considered quite seriously removing her nightdress just as she had tossed aside her cap. All her life she had been warned of the dangers of sleeping unclothed, but then her very respectable nannies had never endured the heat of a Virginia summer.

She made up her mind and was reaching for the hem of her gown when she caught a glimmer of the James lying like a satin ribbon in the moonlight. It looked wide and endless and infinitely cool, and, as if it were a magnet, it drew her to it.

Without pausing for thought, Arabella moved to the door and slipped the bolt. Ever so slowly, she opened the door. She padded across the hall and down the stairs, fleeing not the heat but the oppression of the house that was now her prison.

The front door was heavy, and when she threw the bolt she held her breath, waiting for an alarm to be sounded, but the house slumbered on. Once outside, Arabella raised her arms to the moon as if in tribute, then, feeling the dampness of the dew upon her feet and drinking in the sweetness of a summer night, she ran across the grass toward the river.

When the sloping lawn gave way to the scrubby, tangled bank of the river, she turned and looked back at the solid mass of the house framed against the starlit sky. No, she could not live there. She would not live there. As yet Arabella had not given way to tears. Tears were for babies, for women who swooned over spoiled gowns and crushed feathers, for silly slips of girls. But standing in the moonlight, feeling more alone than she had ever felt in her life, she let the tears fall. They glistened on her face only to be wiped away by the sleeve of her gown and then to fall again. She did not cry only for her brother's betrayal or her disappointment over her groom. She cried for the loveless years that stretched before her, years without children, without a husband to care for her, for never, ever, would she allow Phillip Everett to share her bed.

She moved closer to the edge of the river and looked down at her reflection shimmering on the placid surface. She saw a ghostly figure in thin white lawn surrounded by a tangled aureole of auburn hair, yet she was completely unaware of what a desperate, despairing figure she made as she hovered so near the edge. "I shall die first," she murmured out loud, shuddering as the thought of Phillip Everett's clammy, powdered hands touching her body loomed close in her vision. "As God is my witness, I shall die . . ."

It was no more than a whisper, the sound behind her, as soft as the fluttering of a bird's wings, as silent as the footpads of a cougar. But the arm that grabbed her waist was strong and sinewy and the chest against which she was pressed was hard, and Arabella, with a startled, terrified cry, began to struggle, twisting and raking at his face with her nails but coming away with nothing but handfuls of wool from her feverish assault.

He dragged her back from the river and Arabella felt feather light in his grasp, powerless, and she was at first

81

enraged to feel such helplessness. A multitude of thoughts careened wildly through her mind then the truth came swirling to meet her in great, swimming gulps. Nausea rose and fell, and for a moment she felt that she might truly faint.

The sickness abated but the relentless truth did not. Had she not been warned, before ever leaving England, of the ruthless renegades, the outlaws and savages that roamed the wilds of Virginia? Had she thought herself safe merely because she was on her husband's estate? The land was vast and cutthroats were everywhere . . .

He will kill me, she thought. *He will rape me first and then kill me—and all within sight of Shadowood.*

At last, thought gave way to action and paralyzing fear to the desperate need for survival. She opened her mouth to scream, and a warm hand clamped down upon it. Quickly, without thinking about it once, she bit down hard upon that hand. She heard his surprised "Damn!" and immediately his hand jerked away, but it seemed more reflex than anything else because before she could even draw another breath his hand had smothered her mouth again, harder this time and without allowing her a vantage point for her teeth.

"Vicious little vixen!" he muttered, holding her firm as she began to struggle again, more wildly now. "Bite the man who would save your skin, will you?" And then, as she struck out frantically with her feet, trying to kick him, there seemed to be a note of amusement in his voice as he commanded, "Be still, confound you, or we'll both end up with a dunking!"

Arabella barely heard nor gave notice to the meaning of his words. She was fighting for her life, but it was becoming more and more apparent that her struggle was in vain. His strong hand was crushing her mouth, holding her head motionless; one arm held her tightly beneath her straining breasts. She could feel

82

his hand burning into her waist through the thin fabric of her nightdress and her hands were pinned uselessly at her sides. His chest was hard against her fragile spine and his thighs had somehow managed to pin hers with their muscular strength. No matter how she turned and bucked, she could not break away.

Her strength was beginning to ebb; despair was overtaking her. As her twisting and writhing within his embrace increased in one final, desperate effort, her captor gave a low laugh. "You shall not get away from me, Lady Arabella, no matter how you struggle. In fact, I find our little tussle somewhat pleasurable and I should be happy to continue awhile, but I sense you are growing tired. Perhaps you would be wise to cease your efforts now, before the consequences of this stimulating little game become more than you wish to deal with."

Arabella, abruptly drained, stood still, though the shock that coursed through her was not so much from the explicit nature of his warning as from the words in which it was couched. *Lady Arabella.* He knew her. His voice was a husky whisper, an airy mixture of deep tone and smooth hoarseness, and he used the words of an educated man. He knew her. He had been watching her, waiting for her . . .

Her mind was racing in frantic tune to the rhythm of her pounding heart. He had not, after all, tried to rape her or kill her. If that was his intent, would he not have dispatched the matter by now? Instead, as the strength went out of her body, he only held her lightly, supporting rather than restraining her. What had he said earlier . . . that he had only tried to save her skin? Who *was* this man, and what did he intend to do with her?

The low voice whispered in her ear again. "You could scream, you know, but it is doubtful anyone would hear. Even if someone did, your husband has not a great reputation for courage or skill, and I'm afraid I might be forced to dispatch him into the river and I think you might not want that on your conscience. I will take my hand away now, but first I need your promise that you won't scream, for I've had a long night and don't need any more unpleasantness. Nod your head if you promise."

Arabella, who saw no choice in it, nodded.

The hand was removed from her mouth and she took in great gulps of the sweet night air. She felt his arm loosen around her waist. "Very good, Lady Arabella." There was a hint of mockery in his tone. "I thought you were a woman of common sense."

Arabella took a quick step away from him only to find her arm held once more in his grasp. "Not so soon, my lady. Our interview is not yet ended."

Arabella turned then for the first time to look into the face of the man who had sent her to the brink of terror. Her heart was pounding so loudly that she was certain he could hear it. Still she held her head high and lifted her chin to glare up at him in a manner suitable to the station of Lady Arabella Winters. Any words she might have uttered, however, were cut short by a gasp of fear as she looked at his face. Her hand flew to her mouth to stifle a cry, because for a moment—a horrible, heart-stopping moment—she thought he had no face at all. But no, she saw it was a dark mask he wore to cover his features—a mask of highwaymen and cutthroats—and nothing was visible to her except the two slits of his dark, shadowy eyes.

Her situation was indeed dire. There was no doubt that this man was here for no good intent, and she must escape as best she could. She could not overpower him or outrun him; her only choice was to reason with him. "What . . . what do you want of me?" she managed to choke out. "I have no money, but my husband is a wealthy man if it's robbery you have on your mind . . ."

He shook his head. There seemed to be a glint of amusement in his eyes. "I have no need of your husband's money—at least, not at present—nor of yours. And I want nothing of you except to save you from a watery grave. You were standing dangerously close to the river's edge."

Arabella was nonplussed. Could this be true? Could he have come upon her, thought that she meant to throw herself into the river, and intended only to save her from her own destruction? Not that it mattered, for the man was certainly a criminal and was yet capable of doing her harm. Indeed, she thought, dressed as he was in mask and woolen cape, and trespassing upon the property of Phillip Everett, it was obvious that saving a lady's life had not been his primary business of the evening. Perhaps he had come here with the intent to rob, or perhaps he had already done his dirty deeds and left his victims helpless upon the highway, and perhaps, in fact, he had chanced to see her and had thought her in danger . . . But it did not matter. Arabella knew she must take her chance for escape now and go back to the house, to warn them of the intruder.

Just as calmly as she might address an underling who had chanced to do her some minor service, Arabella said, "I was quite sure of my footing, sir, and can assure you I was in no need of saving. And now, if you will kindly step aside and let me pass . . ."

He did not move. The dark shadowy figure remained where it was, effectively blocking her return to the house. The eyes, like flecks of slate in the moonlight, swept up and down her form and came at last to rest upon her face. "Is it your custom, my lady, to stroll by the river at midnight clad only in your nightdress?"

Because of the swiftness of the encounter, Arabella

had forgotten her attire, forgotten that she had slipped out of the house wearing nothing but the thin white gown. The low neck exposed the creaminess of her skin and the material stretched softly across her full breasts. During the struggle, perspiration had dampened the material so that it now clung to her contours and outlined her shadowed nipples most explicitly.

A wave of embarrassment flooded her, but she would not yield to it in front of this brigand. Her chin lifted haughtily. "How I stroll or where I stroll is no business of yours," she snapped, making ready to move past him. "Now let me pass."

"Oh, no, Lady Arabella. Not yet." His hands grasped her shoulders and held her before him. "I expected more of English manners," he teased. "I expected more of Lady Arabella."

She tried to jerk away but he held her tightly. Frantically she tried to keep her wits, to think of a way to distract him. "You seem to know much of me, sir, but I have not yet had the honor of an introduction."

He laughed again then, and it was a deep and rumbling sound. "Ah, you're a spirited one, my lady." He moved one hand and held her face so that he could look down into it. "Everyone knows of the notorious Lady Arabella—even on this side of the ocean. And the bets are that you will lead Everett a merry chase—which is no doubt more of an amusement than the weakling deserves."

Arabella tried to jerk her head away but his hand held it firm. "You'll not get away so easily, Arabella. Not until you've given me a boon for saving your life."

Fire sputtered in her eyes. "You oaf! You did not save my life! The day will never come when I would fling myself into the river over a fool such as—" She broke off, horrified by the declaration she had almost made to this stranger.

86

"So already the marriage bed pales." There seemed to be satisfaction in his husky tone. "Ah, that is a great shame, for if ever there was a woman made for loving . . ."

And as Arabella watched, suddenly breathless and suspended, his face moved closer, and closer, until she could feel his breath on her cheek. He turned his mouth to hers.

So many sensations and perceptions assaulted her at once that Arabella could not possibly absorb them all. There was the warmth of his hands cupping her neck, the point of his thumbs against the edge of her jaw, touching her in such a bold yet gentle manner. The rough wool of his mask was against her face, yet she felt the soft-coarse texture of the man's face below the wool, brushing against her own. His scent, leather and clean perspiration combined with a faint hint of something she could only define as distinctly masculine, mingled with the earthy quality of the night air that surrounded them and became a part of it; it engulfed her. And his lips, strangely soft, moist, warm, peculiarly tender, by the very nature of their touch caused her heart to rush a flood of crazed, helpless sensations throughout her bloodstream and into every part of her body.

She felt incredulity, wonder, excitement, anticipation, and perhaps even fear—though now of the newness of it all, not of the man. She was being kissed in the night by a masked stranger with her husband sleeping complacently only a few hundred yards away. She knew the feel of a man's lips upon hers, a man's body close to hers, the warmth and the power and the presence of him, and she reveled in the odd, inexplicable things that were happening to her body from what she told herself was no more than the novelty of it. She had expected him to be rough; he was not. She had

87

expected to be terrified; she was not. She had never known a man's lips could be so soft, nor had she imagined that slightly salty, slightly musky taste they would have.

And then, so slowly she hardly noticed the change, his hands slipped down the course of her back to her waist. A slight pressure brought her against him and she could feel his thighs, hard and strong, pressing through the thin fabric of her nightdress. The intimacy made her heart lurch just as his lips became bolder and his hands on her waist stronger; his mouth opened and in so doing parted hers so that he seemed to be drinking from the inside of her, hungrily, thoroughly, with a barely restrained ferocity of which she was only dimly aware.

Her body, untutored in such sensations, reacted wildly and uncontrollably. A hot weakness went through her, an uncomfortable, aching warmth blossomed in her lower regions, her stomach grew weak, her pulses roared. She felt dizzy. She could feel the beat of his heart, the strange aching in her breasts, yet all of this was disassociated from her reason, for she felt at that moment as though her very mind was being stripped from her, drawn in great, eager waves into the will of this man.

And then, slowly, he released her. A tightening of his muscles was the signal, an uneven breath, a gentle clasping of her lips, and then another, and she was standing, trembling in waves of shallow breath and liquid pulses, gazing numbly into the shadowed face of the man who held her still.

They seemed suspended in time and space, two figures apart from the rest of the world, locked in their own reality where nothing else could enter. Gone was her fear, her shock, her need to escape. It no longer mattered that he wore the mask of a criminal or that moments ago she had struggled for her life against the confinement of his arms. He had touched her in a way no man had dared before, he had made her feel things she had never even dreamt of, and her entire being was suffused with the mystery of it.

Slowly he lifted his hand and touched her face, her cheek, the line of her mouth. She closed her eyes, drifting with the pattern of his fingers that seemed not quite real yet at the same time the only real thing that had ever happened in her life. His hand drifted down, along the line of her neck and the fluted division of her collarbone. She felt her breath catch in her throat and her heart contract as if it would explode.

Then his hand found her breast and cupped it gently. Arabella let out a low, unpreventable moan of pleasure, for even with the shock of his touch where no one had ever touched her before there was wonder, the temptation of a great exploration, the promise of some intensely pleasurable secret yet to be discovered. He held her then, one arm strong around her waist, while his hand, his magical hand, traced the contour of her breast. She could feel his breath, warm and low and not entirely steady, against her ear. His palm lightly rubbed against her swollen nipple and each time she felt that grazing touch a trembling rose deep within her, a sensation like waves rising to a crest, receding, and rising higher still.

This time she reached for the kiss. This time her arms went around his neck and she pressed her breasts against the strength of his chest. His mouth was hot upon hers now, no less hungry than before, but this time she matched him in ferocity, was his equal in desire, as they clung together in the torrid night. Her mouth opened beneath his and his tongue sought hers, exploring with maddening slowness the silken softness of its inner contours.

At last the kiss ended and weakly she leaned against him. The man who had been her enemy could now do what he would with her; what she had feared, she could fear no longer. For the moment she cared nothing about power or escape, for to surrender to this man was inevitable, to be his prisoner was her destiny.

But then his hands came away from her, and though she wanted to reach for him, to hold him again, some instinct, deep and unreasoning, stayed her. She simply stared and felt his eyes going over her face, searching and almost hungry, and she heard his uneven breath and felt his touch as his fingers came up to very gently brush a lock of hair from her cheek. His husky whisper was rich and deep.

"Lady Arabella," he said as his hand fell away, "someday, when you have grown old and gray and you think back upon the days of your youth—perchance to tell your grandchildren the tales of your wild folly—remember that upon this night you were kissed by the man whom legend has deemed to call the Fox."

She felt his breath upon her cheek and the brush of his lips. Then he turned and was gone.

Chapter VI

Across the shaded lawns of Shadowood drifted the sounds of male laughter, the scents of rich cigars, and the last rays of sunshine from a day well spent. There had been a good hunt, fine companionship, and the best Madeira in the Colonies—everyone enjoyed a day spent at Shadowood, for whatever else he was, Phillip Everett was an unsurpassed host.

Because of the distances involved in travel, colonial parties often lasted several days, beginning in the early afternoon, lasting through an evening reception and ball that would often continue into the early hours of dawn, progressing to an afternoon of late rising, whist, and yard games, and followed by a late supper and perhaps an impromptu musicale. The guests attending Phillip Everett's reception in honor of his bride had begun to arrive hours ago, when the men had been treated to a late hunt and the ladies a lawn party. Now the gentlemen relaxed with rum punch on the veranda and in the study, telling tales and catching up on all the latest news; the ladies rested upstairs while their maids busily prepared their finery for the gala supper ball that would soon begin.

Away from the party of men who lingered on the

veranda, two walked alone over the parklike meadow of neatly shorn grass that flanked both sides of the wide, marble-chip drive. One of the pair, elegantly coiffed and clad in rich butternut accented with the spotless lace of a discreet jabot and cuffs, highly polished boots of Russian leather that looked as though they had not seen a stirrup since the boot-maker, and a perfectly turned hat placed at a precise cocked angle atop his heavily powdered wig, was greatly concerned with a small scratch he had discovered in the carved handle of his riding crop. The other, wearing coarse homespun and a loose-fitting jacket, was trying, and repeatedly failing, to contain his mirth.

"My dear man," he said at last, giving up the effort and planting his feet apart, arms akimbo, to regard his friend with outrageously snapping blue eyes. "You cannot be serious! Come, call off the jest before it goes too far!"

The other man frowned impatiently over his attempts to scrub away the scratch on the crop with a lace kerchief. "Of course I'm serious. Why shouldn't I be serious? It's a serious matter. Damn me, William, I think it's ruined!" And he flung away the scarred crop in disgust. "It spoils the whole effect, don't you see? Blasted brambles!"

"Will you leave the crop?" Amusement faded into exasperation in William's eyes, tinged with a slight measure of genuine concern. "A bride, Phillip? Are you insane?"

"Oh, that." With a careless wave of his fluttering wrist, Phillip took from his pocket a small enameled snuff box. His expression grew bored. "Yes indeed, and why shouldn't I take a bride? Quite a good idea at that, I thought . . . will you?" He offered the snuff box to William, who refused with a grimace, and then he indulged himself with a delicate pinch for each nostril.

William Hampton, the overseer of Shadowood, was the only man at the gathering today who was close enough to Phillip Everett to speak so frankly, though he only voiced the silent opinions of all others present. The county had been at first shocked, then amused, then curiously titillated by the news that Phillip Everett of Shadowood was taking a bride. In this close-knit community in which everyone knew the business of everyone else, this was the last thing any of them had expected.

Little about Phillip Everett was known to the populace in general. Because he had come late to a colony in which most of the wealthy planters were second or third generation, it was natural that he should have some difficulty adjusting to the way of life there and that he should be the object of great speculation and curiosity. Phillip had not made matters any easier by keeping so greatly to himself during the first years after his arrival that all his new neighbors had by which to judge him were rumors and idle speculation.

It was known that he came from a wealthy, titled British family, second son to a Baron or Baronet—no one was ever quite certain which—and had been all but disinherited after a duel over some gaming loss. Those who claimed to have known the family before Phillip's arrival gossiped that he was the black sheep of the family, a hotheaded youth, as frivolous, reckless, and incorrigible as any of the young rakes of the day. It was a great wonder that, after the scandal of the duel, his father had not cut him off completely. Instead he had sent him to the Colonies—banished, some said—to manage Shadowood, his only inheritance.

The planters of Virginia had shaken their heads sadly over this turn of events. Shadowood, once one of the great plantations of the James River, had fallen into sad condition during the years of the absentee landlord, and it had seemed doubtful that the young Everett would be able to do much to mend matters. And though it was true that within only two years Shadowood had regained and surpassed its former glory as the tobacco empire of the James, that success was generally attributed to young Everett's choice of overseer, not to any particular brilliance or talent for agricultural pursuits on the part of the owner himself.

Personally, Everett was still considered by the members of the planting society a "damned peculiar bird," but they all enjoyed his hospitality and reciprocated as was the custom of the community. When, seven years after his first appearance in the Colonies, Phillip was elected to a seat in the House of Burgesses, only the most ill-bred publicly questioned his effectiveness, though there was a great deal of snickering in private.

Phillip Everett was a loyal subject of the king's, a close friend of the Lord Governor's, and powerfully connected by wealth and class throughout the Colonies. It was a damned pity, claimed most of those who knew him, that he was such a fool.

"Phillip"—William's tone was unmistakably sober now, and so was his expression—"you cannot have thought. Have you considered—"

"Oh, yes, yes, indeed, I have considered a great many things." With much graceful fluttering of lace and two precise and elaborate sniffs, Phillip returned the snuff box to his pocket and tucked the lace kerchief into his cuff, carefully arranging each fold so that the view of lace was seen to its best effect. "One could do worse, don't you know, than to marry a comely girl of wealth and position . . . whose brother, quite incidentally, holds an important seat in the House of Lords . . . and is a confidant of both Lord North and the King."

"You've no need for wealth," William scoffed impatiently, "nor position either. As for—" But suddenly he stopped as slow understanding dawned, and he simply looked at his friend.

But Phillip had bent to retrieve the discarded crop, ever mindful as he did so to present a graceful turn of the calf, and he murmured worriedly, "Perhaps something can be done to save it after all. Waste of good leather, that. I will take it to Sam." And his boyish, heavily rouged face broke into a delighted grin at a problem well solved. "Yes, that is what I will do. Sam will mend it." Pleased with himself, he picked up the pace of their walk again.

William hesitated in a mixed paralysis of disgust, amusement, and exasperation for a pace or two, then hurried to catch up. "Phillip," he demanded patiently, "the matter at hand?"

A small, perplexed frown troubled the other man's brow for a moment, then was quickly dismissed as remembrance dawned. "Ah, the wench. Indeed, friend, one must be practical about these matters. It is the brother we need, *n'est pas,* not the girl, and we mustn't belabor inconsequentials. Besides, there seems to be a growing wind of vicious gossip whirling through this damnably provincial society as to the cause of my perpetual state of bachelorhood," he drawled, completely unconcerned. "A woman about the place can't help but mend that. One must keep up appearances, don't you know."

William stopped walking and fixed a gaze upon his friend that was long and solemn. "This is not a matter to be dealt with lightly, Phillip," he said. "There surely must have been a less . . . permanent method of securing our ends than marriage. You may find you have bought more trouble than you've dispensed with, in the end."

Still greatly concerned with the state of his spoiled riding crop, Phillip shrugged off his companion's words carelessly. "She was going cheap. Besides, insipid socialites bore me. Lady Arabella will be entertaining, if nothing else. And perhaps," he added lightly, "when she has served her purpose, she can be pensioned off to that dreadful dower cottage in Devon of hers—*comme si, comme ça, eh?* We shall keep her as long as needed, then be rid of her. Not to fret."

William looked at his friend long and hard. "Sometimes," he said quietly, "I think you are quite heartless."

Phillip's gaze briefly distant grew and strangely thoughtful. "I knew her once in Devon," he remembered. "A child, but even then . . . interesting." The peculiar reflectiveness in his eyes was gone in the flash of a brilliant, vacant smile, and he declared, "How wondrous are the workings of Fate, that we should come together again as man and wife. I think I shall write a poem."

William's steady gaze did not waver. "This could be dangerous," he said. Then, taking another tack, he continued, "You did well to break off with the Parkington woman. Her ties to the governor were much too close. But now you do this damned foolish thing . . ."

Phillip only gave him one of his high, slightly crazed little laughs, and flung a companionable arm around his friend's shoulders. "Now," he declared, leading William back toward the house, "let us abandon this subject, for I find I grow rather bored and there is a quite pressing matter upon which I need your advice. What do you think of my blue velvet? The one with the silver threads? Do you think it's quite grand enough for the reception tonight? I do so want to look my most

96

stunning. Lord Dunmore is due to arrive and he always takes such great pleasure in my sense of fashion. Tell me true now, do you think it makes me look a little sallow? What about the fit of the jacket? The lace might be a bit overdone, I think . . ."

The room was stifling in the heat of the summer night. The cloying scent of Phillip's prize roses was thick in the air and mingled with the odor of burning candles, the flames of which only added to the intense heat. The reception had begun in full over an hour before, and every room in the house was overflowed with the press of elegantly clad bodies. The air seemed alive with laughter and voices and the courtly music that preceded supper. Under other circumstances the gay, brightly lit atmosphere would have seemed exciting, exhilarating, to Arabella. Tonight she found it almost unbearably confining.

Arabella, unused to summers of such uncomfortable temperatures, stepped out onto the wide veranda, seeking its welcoming coolness. If she could not escape the noise, she could at least escape the heat. A faint breeze stirred off the river, bringing with it memories of the man who called himself the Fox, though in truth he had scarcely been out of her thoughts since they had met. Sometimes she could almost believe it had been a dream, a figment of her imagination, to be held in his arms, to feel his lips upon hers. But no, he had been real, flesh and blood, and even now as she thought of him her face flamed with the wantonness of her behavior the night before, her heart pounded with excitement, her flesh tingled with the remembrance of his touch. The dashing stranger had become more real to her than her mannequin of a husband.

Phillip. How could he insist that they continue with

this farce of a union? Arabella was more determined than ever that theirs be a marriage in name only. Even though she knew she could not fight the implacable bonds that tied her to her husband or break the powerful hold that Phillip and Reginald maintained over her, she could protest. Phillip Everett would rue the day he had ever taken Lady Arabella Winters to wife. She could not leave him—at least not yet—but she could humiliate him and make more than rumor the exploits of Lady Arabella Winters that drifted across the Atlantic. She doubted her husband would be speaking to her by the end of the evening, and she would be quite free to live her life exactly as she pleased, just as Elizabeth Montagu did.

Her lips curved in a slow smile. Even *he* had heard of her. Even the Fox knew that she was Lady Arabella. But she knew nothing of him except the feel of his arms and the warmth of his lips. She dared not ask anyone about him, for she had vowed to keep her wonderful adventure to herself, yet she ached to know more of him. Surely at a party as large as this, she mused, there would be those who would speak of the Fox, never knowing that she, Lady Arabella, wife of Phillip Everett, had been held in his arms. It was a wonderful joke on everyone, but most especially on Phillip.

Lost in her dreams of the Fox, Arabella was suddenly brought back to the present when she heard her own name mentioned. She could not help but stand quietly and listen.

"Her gown is lovely," one sugar-sweet voice intoned. "It must have cost dearly."

"They obviously have money," a second joined in, "but, my dear, that color! Deep rose with her hair? Why, the bodice is all but scandalous! Most of her bosom is exposed without an ounce of shame. And not to wear a wig, or at least powder! I find it most outrageous."

Arabella recognized the next voice. She remembered Caroline Hampton, whom Phillip had introduced as the wife of his overseer, for she had seemed so different from the rest of the bejeweled and elaborately coiffed women. She was a young woman, round and plump and rather plain looking, with wide, kind brown eyes. She was dressed simply in dove gray silk.

"I think the color is quite lovely on her," spoke up Caroline mildly, "and her hair is most enchanting. I don't recall ever having seen that shade before, and if it were mine, I daresay I wouldn't powder it either." Caroline's voice was low and soft, with the slurring intonation of the Tidewater Virginia accent that Arabella found so intriguing.

"Oh, Caroline, you're much too kind—and absolutely no fun to gossip with, though Lady Arabella makes gossiping wonderfully easy. Have you seen the way she flirts with every man in sight? That may be the fashion on the Continent, but I tell you true, it won't be tolerated a minute here! She's gone after every man present!"

"Including your husband, my dear." That was the first voice again. Arabella stood perfectly still, not daring even to breathe as the women continued their discussion. She could hear the click of their fans as they snapped them open and vigorously began moving the torpid air.

So, Arabella thought to herself in satisfaction, the painted hens had noticed her behavior. So, then, must have her husband. All was going precisely as she had planned.

The second woman, with a high, nasal voice that completely obliterated the beauty Arabella had previously found in the Virginia dialect, defended her mate testily. "It's not only my husband, but everyone else's— including poor Colonel Masterson, who must be near eighty! Even," she pointed out slightly, "your own

99

William, dear Caroline."

There was a slight pause before Caroline answered. "Everyone seems to be quite charmed with her. Perhaps she is only being friendly. Or she may be nervous and unused to our ways . . ."

"But her rudeness, my dear, can hardly be excused! She all but cut me dead and immediately set out after my own Gregory . . ."

For the first time Arabella was stricken with a slight twinge of conscience for her determinedly outrageous behavior throughout the reception. Caroline Hampton was a kind soul and she had not meant to offend her. She had not meant to offend anyone but the dandified, strictly convention-bound Phillip, who would rather die than suffer the embarrassment of social disapproval.

But the next voice erased whatever qualms Arabella might have begun to experience, and her chin came up defiantly again. "Nervous! That one?" The other women broke into tittering laughter. "The one who should be nervous is poor Phillip Everett. I've never held the poor man in much esteem, but I confess to feeling a bit of pity for him on this night." She lowered her voice slightly and confided, "It is commonly known, understand, that she had been undeniably compromised before her marriage, and by more than one young man . . ."

The shocked silence barely had time to die away before someone else declared triumphantly, "And she *writes,* I hear, heaven knows what filthy stuff . . ."

And another added, "Why, I've heard a tale—"

"Ladies, please!" Caroline's voice, brimming with indignation, rose in defense of her hostess. "Have you no shame? She is Phillip Everett's bride, after all—"

"And he deserves what he gets, I'll warrant," someone snorted.

There was another burst of girlish giggles, then the second woman added, "But you and William know him best, Caroline. Do tell, what can Phillip Everett want with a bride? And what can she possibly see in him?"

"Phillip is a fine man," responded Caroline evenly. Her voice had grown somewhat tight, though whether with anger or embarrassment Arabella did not know. "He has been a good friend and a generous employer, and I will not hear him slighted in his own house. You ladies should be ashamed. Phillip Everett is one of the most"—she obviously had to search for an appropriate word—"honored men in the county. He is a member of the Burgesses and a successful planter—"

The first speaker dismissed Caroline's defense of their host with a low laugh. "And all for naught, Caroline, if he's worth little in the bedroom. That is all that concerns the lovely Lady Arabella—as it would, I'm sure, any thinking woman in her position!"

"Perhaps it is in dread of the answer that she goes after our men!" added the second voice and the burst of laughter that followed revealed new participants in the discussion. "After all, he could not satisfy the Italian woman."

"That is only gossip and one side of the story," Caroline began.

"Where there's smoke . . ."

Arabella's face flamed as she moved away from the door. They were laughing at her, all of them, and she could not blame them. But this was what she wanted, was it not? To be the center of gossip, speculation, and disapproval—the very things that a man like Phillip Everett would find most abhorrent. She knew his type, for they all were of a mold. Though he fancied himself a model for others, he would not make a move without the approval of his set; though he affected a jaded apathy toward all around him, in fact he was guided by

101

nothing other than the opinions of those he seemed to ignore. Nothing would distress him more than a wife who brought notoriety upon herself, who behaved improperly, alienated his guests, and put herself in the center of controversy. And nothing would please Arabella more than to cause Phillip as much heartache as he had caused her.

Arabella took a deep breath, straightened her bodice—pulling the neckline still lower over her greatly exposed breasts—and with her head held high she stepped back into the parlor. She looked neither right nor left. Whoever the gossiping women were, she did not want to know. It meant nothing to her.

She stopped a passing steward and took another cup of punch from his silver tray. With a bright smile and vacant eyes, she looked across the room. She had not seen Phillip in hours. After the reception line, he had disappeared with half a dozen other men into the game room for billiards and whist. She could still hear his stilted giggle now and again, or catch a glimpse of his high-puffed wig as he made an appearance among the other guests. He had seen her flirtations—the gossips had been right; there had been many—and Arabella knew that her behavior would be working its insidious effect upon him. But being the perfect host required that Phillip turn a blind eye to the disgraceful antics of the guest of honor—even if she was his wife.

She could see him now, standing across the room in a peacock blue coat and bright apricot breeches, his silk stockings elaborately clocked and stitched, and for a moment she was disoriented. It was as if she were back in a stuffy drawing room in London, with all the pretense and affectations she had always held in such contempt. Why, Phillip Everett was no better than the macaronis, she realized, the most effete and laughable of the London aristocrats, who sought to outdo one

102

another in extremes of fashion. But they had an excuse of sorts. They were mindless ne'er-do-wells with too much money and no responsibility. She had expected more from the master of a great plantation and a leader in government. She had expected more from this new country.

But the disease of duplicity knew no geographic boundaries, she was beginning to understand, and nothing was ever quite what it seemed. In London the titled and the privileged doused unwashed bodies in expensive perfumes and disguised pockmarked faces with paint and beauty marks; they hid their infidelities and indiscretions under a veneer of breeding and manners. The macaronis masked cruelty and violence with waist-length curls and lace cuffs, and Phillip Everett smothered whatever man he once might have been with social ambition and assumed postures. Nothing had changed for Arabella, for Phillip was the embodiment of all she had wanted to escape.

For a moment Arabella felt very alone standing in the midst of the swirling crowd. The mirrors reflected the wigs and brocaded coats of the gentlemen, the powdered faces and glittering jewels of the ladies, and her own face, with eyes much too bright, cheeks flaming, mouth set in a false smile. Suddenly another face appeared beside hers in the mirror, Caroline Hampton's. Arabella's frozen smile relaxed into one of genuine warmth. Caroline had defended her, and Arabella was grateful. Loyalty was not a commodity Arabella could afford to take lightly.

"William and I are so pleased that you and Phillip have married," said Caroline in a low, dulcet tone. Her eyes held the truth of the sentiment. "He is a fine man, Lady Arabella."

For a moment Arabella did not know to whom the other woman was referring, then realized with a slight

103

jolt that she meant Phillip. "Yes," she responded with a slightly choked voice. "But call me Arabella, please," she offered without knowing precisely why. There was no point in allowing herself to become fond of Caroline, for their ways would soon part.

Caroline's smile deepened in response to Arabella's warmth, and she impulsively took Arabella's hands in her small gloved ones. "Life can be so lonely on a plantation. How nice it will be to have another woman close by. Phillip and William are such good friends; I hope that we can be too."

"Your kindness is most welcome," Arabella said, and she meant it. She wondered again over William's extraordinary character, that he could claim to be a close friend of Phillip Everett's. Never had she met two men who seemed so diverse.

Yet it was an eclectic gathering, she realized. The lord governor had come from Williamsburg, along with his retinue and hangers on, to celebrate the marriage of his good friend and loyal supporter. Inside the house landed aristocracy mixed with common farmers in a manner that never would have been possible in England, and outside, under the light of paper lanterns, yeomen and craftsmen from all over the county celebrated in their own, more boisterous way, the occasion of festivity. Perhaps it was simply that in this vast and sometimes threatening land, all men, whether great or common, had learned to band together for survival. That was only another aspect of Virginia life that Arabella found intriguing—and somewhat appealing.

The crowd of elegantly attired guests began to move apart, stepping aside for the approaching figure. "The governor," Caroline said with a nervous smile. Arabella got the brief impression, for no distinct reason, that the gentle woman did not hold the representative

104

of the king in much esteem. "I'm sure he wants to escort you to supper. You've made a great impression." There was nothing but kindness in the words and in her smile as she took her leave before the governor reached Arabella's side.

Arabella was left the center of all attention as the governor bent low over her hand, bringing it near his lips but politely not touching. When he straightened, he was scarcely taller than she. A short, squat man, he was nonetheless muscular and carried himself well as befitted his military status. John Murray, Lord Dunmore, had arrived in Virginia two years before, replacing the greatly respected Lord Botetourt. Many of the Williamsburg wits had compared him unfavorably to his huge brown and white bulldog, Glasgow, but he had a courtly manner that could charm many a female heart. His wit, sportsmanship, and affability had won him friends among the Virginia aristocrats as well. George Washington of Mount Vernon Plantation dined frequently at the governor's palace, as did other influential members of the Burgesses, among them Benjamin Harris, Peyton Randolph, and Phillip Everett.

Tonight the governor's charm radiated toward the young Englishwoman who stood before him. "My dear Lady Arabella, I have been desolate. You have hidden yourself away from me for the best part of an hour, neglecting me most sorely."

Arabella tapped her ivory fan against the low *décolletage* of her gown before she snapped it open with a graceful motion. She noted with satisfaction that the governor's eyes followed the motion to the swell of her breasts and the smoothness of her skin and lingered there.

She lowered her darkened lashes modestly as a smile curved her lips. "I have been quite disconsolate too, my

105

lord. You cannot imagine how dreary this company is. You are by far the only man of any refinement here." She opened her eyes wide now and tilted her head to give him an enticing view of her long, smooth throat.

"I can tell that life in the Colonies will be much enhanced by your presence, Lady Arabella. And may I hope that you will be a frequent visitor at the palace?"

"If I am beckoned, then I shall heed your call, my lord," she responded coquettishly. "Of that you may be sure." She extended her hand and when their fingers touched, she sank into a deep curtsy.

Dunmore's eyes glowed with pleasure. He had come to Virginia without his wife or children, and he was not the kind of man to be long without female companionship. He had soon become bored with the provincial wives of Williamsburg, but this young vixen seemed ready to play his game. Dunmore had no reason to fear Everett—indeed, what man had?—and Arabella was simply too delicate a morsel to resist. She was as fresh as a peach ready to be plucked, and Dunmore could hardly await the harvest. He could barely restrain an inward chuckle as he thought that, indeed, he would be doing the young bride—and Everett—a great service by supplying for her what her husband could not.

They swept into dinner, Arabella on the governor's arm, Phillip walking two steps behind. She sat on Dunmore's right with Phillip across from her and Reginald next to him. On her right was a French essayist who had somehow attached himself to the governor's retinue. All in all, Arabella had managed to surround herself with most amusing company, which she surely would have enjoyed had the circumstances been different. Phillip, for all his irritating mannerisms, was without a doubt entertaining; the Frenchman was articulate and well read, and the governor . . . Arabella could not prevent a brief smile of satisfaction at her thoughts, for the governor seemed quite infatuated with her.

There was hardly a break in the animated conversation as the servants, wigged and liveried for the occasion, brought in the huge, heavily laden silver platters of food. Unlike the supper parties in England, with their polite repartee and the discreet clinking of silver and crystal, this gathering was enthusiastic, even boisterous; yet none were ill-mannered but only lively with the enjoyment of one another's company. Arabella found that she quite preferred it this way.

With all that was going on around her, it was very difficult for Arabella to call attention to herself in the manner in which she had planned. But when she noticed a group of men at the center of the long table involved in a low, intense, and apparently private conversation, she grasped the opportunity to make a display of, if not bad manners, then at least the type of outspokenness of which Phillip could not possibly approve.

"Pray gentlemen," she called out, lifting her wine glass with a brilliant, inviting smile, "share with the rest of us what you find so engrossing. Surely there are no secrets at our table."

They moved uneasily, looking at one another and then at their hostess with deprecating smiles. "'Tis nothing, ma'am," one of them replied, "to concern the delicate ears of one as beautiful as you."

Dismissing the matter, they turned back to their meal, but Arabella did not intend to allow such a grand opportunity for devilment to slip by. "Come, come, good sirs," she coaxed, laughing lightly, "your secrets are only more intriguing when you try to conceal them from me. Do tell. Some affair of the heart? Some grand liaison amongst our company? You cannot be so cruel as to keep us all in suspense!"

107

"Indeed, gentlemen," agreed the governor boisterously, joining in the spirit of Arabella's game. "You cannot offend your hostess in such a manner! Do share your gossip so we can all be enlightened."

Arabella had succeeded in capturing the attention of the entire table, and the hapless men to whom she had first directed herself shared an abashed look while those around them waited in embarrassed silence for their reply. There, Arabella thought with some satisfaction. Let Master Phillip Everett see now what kind of woman he has engaged as hostess. His precious supper party is well on its way to being spoiled, and I have not yet even begun my campaign.

One of the men cleared his throat uncomfortably and addressed himself to the benignly waiting Arabella. "It is only," he explained reluctantly, "a matter of some distress to the colonists hereabouts, regarding the latest raid by a band of renegade rebels."

"Rebels?" Arabella insisted with an exaggerated widening of her eyes. "Rebels against what? Do tell!"

"But it is the most fascinating thing, Lady Arabella," supplied the Frenchman, his avidity growing in his eyes to be of help in enlightening his vivacious hostess, whose attention, to this point, had been almost completely captured by the governor. "These colonists rebel against everything—shipping, taxes, trade, customs—even tea!"

An uneasy round of laughter went about the table, though Arabella noticed that some of the smiles were strained. Unaccountably, she remembered the poor man she had seen dragged through the streets of Norfolk, and she was hard put to maintain the sparkle of her own laughter.

"Dear me!" she exclaimed. "How very silly they all sound!"

"Indeed, madame," assured the essayist, "a most

108

discontented lot! Why one would think they are out to rule themselves! They have no regard at all for the law."

"Stuff and nonsense," dismissed the governor imperiously. "You credit this sorry lot with far more than they deserve. To good King George, these bothersome rebels are of no more consequence than a gnat on a horse."

A voice from the other end of the table spoke up dryly, "Ah, but they have caused a mite of inconvenience to His Majesty's troops hereabouts in the past year, and they seem to be busier than ever."

From the corner of her eye, Arabella noticed the governor's hand tighten around the stem of his wine glass, and she knew she had stumbled upon a topic of conversation that could be built to quite incendiary proportions if she handled it correctly. Furthermore, she found the subject fascinating in itself. Just as she opened her mouth to encourage the trend of talk, Phillip's high-pitched, lazily droning voice interrupted.

"Dear, dear," he clucked with a languid wave of his lace handkerchief. "Sedition—what an abominably boring topic of conversation for the supper table. Surely we can find something more entertaining to discuss than the antics of a group of uncivilized rabble-rousers."

The governor's grunt seemed to signify approval, but Arabella was not about to let Phillip divert disaster so easily. "But I am quite intrigued, sir," she insisted to her husband sweetly. "I find colonial politics most stimulating."

"Politics?" scoffed Phillip with a delicate sniff. *"Mon dieu,* these are nothing more than plebians and peasants. Why, this Patrick Henry fellow who caused such a stir a few years back is no more than an uneducated shopkeeper who decided to declare himself a barrister. He can scarcely speak the King's English!"

The governor nodded vigorously and inserted gruffly, "Hotheaded young traitor. Would've been hung if I'd been governing then."

"I find the entire subject most distasteful and quite likely to spoil my digestion," drawled Phillip. "Certainly the activities of these ne'er-do-wells are not worth the time of our discussion."

Determined to play devil's advocate, Arabella contradicted sweetly, "Oh, I can't agree, Phillip. Perhaps there are two sides to this story. I wager there is not one of us present would not rise up and fight if pushed too far." And though she smiled prettily at Phillip, her eyes moved down the table to her brother and flashed a dangerous message there.

If Reginald understood her double meaning, he gave no verbal response, but his eyes gleamed darkly from his ruddy, swollen face. Arabella defiantly held his gaze for a moment, then turned her fatuous smile back to Phillip.

The ingratiating little smirk was still on Phillip's features, and he gave a high-pitched giggle of approval. "Slay me, m'lady, what a sketch you are, jigging us about these rebels! I've always liked a girl with wit!" Then, to the company at large he remarked, "This trout was freshly caught this morning and simply melts on the tongue, *n'est-ce pas?*"

With an almost audible sigh of relief, those at the table turned to resume their meals and more innocuous topics of conversation, but Arabella had no intention of being diverted. "Why, sir," she countered pleasantly, "I do believe you are trying to distract me! And I find talking about politics so much more refreshing than talking about fish."

There were some spontaneous chuckles and grins across the table that seemed an unspoken acknowledgment that this woman would be a handful for any man and that Phillip Everett would not stand a chance.

Reginald, however, did not share in the frivolity. His face showed plainly that his sister had overstepped her bounds. Yet short of standing up and ordering her from the table, he was helpless. Uncomfortably, his eyes shifted to Phillip, who, it was plain at the moment, was giving serious second thought to the wisdom of accepting a bride sight unseen.

Arabella felt a stab of satisfaction as she saw her husband's long fingers tighten upon his wine glass and his lips curve stiffly into a forced smile. Phillip was not only embarrassed but very close to being angry, and Arabella reveled in the knowledge, as well as in the security of the fact that Phillip's good breeding and good manners rendered him utterly helpless in the face of these or any other machinations she might conceive.

The governor had been hard pressed during these past few moments to keep the discussion civil. He had endured the humiliation of being outwitted by these rebels for far too long to find it an enjoyable topic of table conversation, and to suffer such embarrassment in the home of one of his most trusted friends seemed almost too much. "I wonder, Lady Arabella," he said stiffly, "what your interest can be? Surely you have no sympathy for these renegades?"

She laughed lightly. "To be sure, sir, it is of little consequence to me at all! I merely find your difficulties amusing and wonder why the might of England cannot control this plague of rabble that seems to be menacing your shores." The governor started to bluster a reply, but Arabella did not give him a chance. "Perhaps," she suggested innocently, "if you only ignored them and let them live their lives the way they pleased, they would go about their business quite peacefully and you would not have to worry yourself."

His mounting temper soothed by her naive grasp of

111

the ways of government, the governor teased her indulgently. "Ha! Would you have the cutthroats and criminals of Newgate Prison set free to roam the streets as well? All they want, I'm sure, is to lead their lives in the way they please!"

A hearty round of laughter rewarded this witticism. The governor looked pleased with himself and Arabella could do nothing but smile graciously. When the good-natured joking had died down, however, she could not help pushing the matter one step further. "But are these rebels such desperate criminals, my lord?" she insisted, widening her eyes in feigned dread.

"Indeed it would appear so," joined in William, who thus far had been a silent though secretly entertained listener to the repartee, " judging from their actions of last week."

"Indeed?" encouraged Arabella breathlessly. "What did they do?"

"Why, they waylaid a shipment of military supplies bound for the garrison, trussed up the guards like Christmas turkeys, and made off with a wagon of muskets."

"My goodness! Were they ever captured? Who are these people?"

"No one knows." William shrugged and continued, "But it seems that it is the same group as before. They have established a definite pattern of operation over the past year and are more irritating than harmful, always attacking properties of the king or his representatives—burning wagonloads of foodstuffs, stripping warehouses, stealing munitions. Their leader must be a deucedly clever fellow. They always enter under the cover of darkness, make the raid, then blend into the night and the forest."

"Le Renard," said the Frenchman with a laugh. "His name is well chosen."

"But a fox quickly brought to the ground," promised the governor grimly.

A pall fell over the supper table then that even the most gracious host—and Phillip was indeed that—could not have lifted, but Arabella was oblivious to it all. *Le Renard*. The Fox. *Her* Fox—the very man who had held her in his arms only last night . . . Her heart missed several beats and then resumed its rhythm again, wildly. His name rang in her head and sang through her veins. The man who had pressed his lips to hers so passionately, who had molded her body with his hands and had awakened such insane stirrings within her was a notorious renegade, a man of adventure and romance—a hero, even, to some. He could have done her harm—surely he had that capability—but he had not used his strength against her. Instead he had been remarkably gentle, almost tender.

Whoever this Fox might be to the rest of Virginia—terrorist, rebel, traitor—to her he was the man whose kiss warmed her heart and made this new world less lonely. If she had any reason for being in this strange land, it was the Fox. Had not Fate brought her to him? Had not the hand of the Almighty been at work, even tonight, as her dinner guests sat about her table discussing the very man whose secret destiny it was hers to be?

She was more determined than ever that Phillip dislike her as much as she despised him. She had found her purpose in the New World, and her only intent now was to make certain that her husband leave her free to pursue it.

Chapter VII

While the guests were partaking of the sumptuous supper, the floors were being cleared for dancing, and in a corner of the great parlor an orchestra reassembled, a collection of Negro musicians bedecked in red velvet and white wigs, who were accomplished with the music of the day on viola, violin, spinet, and harpsichord.

As she led her guests from the table, Arabella's head was spinning with her new knowledge of Le Renard and she decided to cast caution to the wind. Reginald was furious, Phillip was embarrassed, and the Lord Governor—she almost giggled at the thought—was in the palm of her hand. All in all, Arabella was quite pleased with herself. Her color was high and her eyes shot sparks of emerald fire as she opened the first set with John Murray, Lord Dunmore, as her partner.

Although it was a skill she rarely used, Arabella knew how to play the seductress and she now summoned every talent she possessed to achieve her end this night. She entranced the young would-be swains of Virginia who gathered around her, showering them with flirtatious laughter and outrageous promises, while earning barbed glances from the outraged ladies. In groups of twos and threes they gathered to discuss her; words like "shameful!" and "inexcusable!" reached Arabella's ears and only made her spirits soar. She had set out tonight to live up to every scandalous word of the reputation that had followed her from London, and thanks to the governor and the mysterious Fox, she was succeeding beyond her wildest expectations.

Phillip did not disappear into the card room again. He stayed in the midst of the company, soothing the ruffled tempers of the ladies with extravagant compliments, seeking to draw the attention of the gentlemen away from Arabella with his own exuberant story-telling and jokes, and always keeping a close eye on Arabella, obviously in dread of what she would do next.

Phillip no longer made any effort to hide the distress he was feeling or the disapproval. This was not at all what he had planned. The impressive company he had assembled to inspect his bride would go away remembering a shameless flirt, a mannerless, out-spoken troublemaker, and a hopeless misfit. She was making a mockery of him and he was helpless to prevent it.

On several occasions Phillip tried to get her alone using the pretext of a dance, but Arabella always refused with a dismissing laugh and an insult that she made certain would ring through the room. She would announce, "Good heavens, sir, why should I wish to dance with you when I can have this pretty, pretty boy here . . . who has not asked me yet but will take very little persuasion?" or "Dear me, how dreadfully boring! We have years and years to dance together and I have much more interesting things to do tonight!" Then she would watch the heads turn, see Phillip's color rise, and observe his struggle to maintain his appearance of politeness. And she loved every moment of it.

From time to time Arabella would notice that Phillip was being drawn into private conversation, once with William and other times with other well-meaning friends who were obviously commiserating with Phillip over the folly of his marriage. But at last, Arabella saw what she had been waiting for. Phillip had taken Reginald aside and the meaningful glances they were casting her way left no doubt in Arabella's mind as to the subject of their intense discussion. Already Phillip Everett was regretting his marriage to the hotheaded and indiscreet Lady Arabella and was perhaps this very moment setting in motion the mechanisms to end it. She had won.

Late in the evening the reels began. As Arabella waited for her partner to return with a cup of punch, she saw Phillip approaching and anticipated the coming confrontation with relish. She tapped her toe and swayed her hips in time to the music, sweeping her husband a deep curtsy when he reached her.

Phillip's face was perfectly composed as he returned her bow. "Lady Arabella, the honor of this dance?"

"I'm so sorry, sir," she replied brightly, "but I am already partnered with the Lord Governor."

His bland smile remained undisturbed and his lazy drawl unconcerned. "But I am crushed! You have not danced with me all evening, and this is the last set."

Arabella laughed gaily and fluttered her fan at him. "Don't be absurd, dear boy. I am quite prepared to dance the night away! I have only just begun!"

One corner of his lips twisted upward into a dry smile. "No, m'dear, I fear you are quite finished. This evening has gone on long enough, and the orchestra will play no more. Do enjoy your dance." With another short bow, he departed.

Arabella laughed out loud in delight. She could have

asked for no greater pleasure that evening than to see the look of stung sensibilities on Phillip's face as he walked away.

During the rousing dance, the last of Arabella's inhibitions flew away. She turned and spun, and her skirts flew out around her, exposing silken stockings and delicate ankles. Her laughter was loud, her stance tipsy, her conversation verging on the ribald. Those who did not dance gathered in groups to look askance, and Phillip, who partnered Caroline, never took his eyes from her. Arabella had never been more confident of her success, and the thrill was heady.

True to his word, Phillip had instructed the orchestra to cease, and there was no more dancing. Caroline and William were the first to leave, and the pained, embarrassed glance Caroline cast her as she said good night caused a real pang in Arabella's conscience. If things had been different at Shadowood, she reflected, and if Phillip . . . But Arabella determinedly shut those regrets from her mind. Daydreams and fantasies had led her to this hideous situation and she would encourage them no more.

Slowly, in groups of twos and threes, the guests who lived within driving distance called for their carriages, and those who were staying the night drifted in separate directions—the women upstairs to their beds and the gentlemen to cards or billiards in the game room.

As Arabella prepared to go upstairs, she saw that the governor, who was planning to depart early in the morning, was making long, effusive farewells, inviting Phillip to bring his lovely bride often to the palace in Williamsburg. Phillip bowed and said all the polite things, yet he seemed relieved when another guest pulled him away. For a moment Arabella and the governor stood alone.

Lord Dunmore smiled intimately at her. "I can show you much of Williamsburg, Lady Arabella," he said softly. A feather-light finger trailed along her bare forearm, and his eyes gleamed with explicit suggestion. "Perhaps if your husband is ever indisposed . . ."

Phillip was beside them again before Arabella could reply, clapping the governor on the shoulder with an excessive display of exuberance. "We're beginning a game of cards, Your Lordship. If you'd like to join me after I see the lady to her room . . ."

"Of course, of course. You know I wouldn't miss a chance to even the score between us!" Lord Dunmore's response was enthusiastic, but his eyes were only for Arabella. She curtsied modestly and turned to take her husband's arm.

Phillip was silent as he escorted her past the lingering guests and up the broad and curving staircase. Arabella's heart began to pound in anticipation of the scene she knew was approaching.

At the top of the stairs, he stopped. "A word with you, if I may, Lady Arabella."

She turned, restraining a smile of victory, but she could not resist playing him out a bit longer. She molded her mouth into a little *moue* of regret, touched her fan to her temple, and said, "Perhaps on the morrow, sir. I find myself quite fatigued . . ."

She started to proceed to her room, but Phillip's hand stayed her before she had taken her first step.

"We need to talk, Lady Arabella," he said, "about your behavior this evening. It has been most unsettling to both your brother and myself."

She turned to meet his eyes, barely able to conceal her triumph. "Indeed, sir? And what in my behavior could you have found disturbing?" Her voice was ingenuous, her eyes innocent.

"It was quite an entertainment," Phillip admitted,

119

"—the flirtation, the dancing, the abominable lack of manners—but one hardly suited to the woman who is the new mistress of Shadowood. One quite unsuited to my wife."

With a jerk, Arabella withdrew her arm from his grasp. "Your wife!" She spat the word in derision. "I have made it clear that no matter how long I live in this house, I shall never be your wife."

Beneath the rouge his mouth closed in a hard line and barely repressed anger glittered in his eyes. "But you are my wife, dear lady, and therefore subservient to your husband in all matters matrimonial."

Until this night, Phillip had made no attempt to breach the privacy of her chamber, but with the word, "matrimonial," a gleam of avaricious lust had come into his eyes and the word reverberated in Arabella's head. Matrimonial . . . marriage to this man, and all it implied . . .

He lifted a hand as though to touch her face, and swiftly Arabella shrank from him. She remembered other hands—strong, warm, caressing hands—and the thought of Phillip's cool, powdered fingers touching her skin caused a wave of revulsion to sweep over her. "Stay away from me!" she hissed. "Don't come near me!"

The light of lust she thought she had seen in Phillip's eyes changed into something harder, then swiftly disappeared. His eyes, like his face, were once more only a smooth blank.

He looked at her, and a cynical, half-amused smile curved one corner of his polished lips upward, though it never touched his eyes. "Lay your maidenly pretenses to rest, Lady Arabella," he drawled smoothly, "for the sanctity of your bridal chamber will not be violated this night—or any other."

At the look of undisguised relief upon her face, he

went on coolly, "I don't wish to offend, m'dear, but as it happens . . ." He paused to take her slender hand, turn it in his, and kiss her palm with dry, cool lips. As he straightened, his eyes traveled along her figure with a disdain that enraged her blood and he concluded, "I have little interest in damaged goods. The fortress has been breached far too often for its treasure to be of value to me."

There was no mistaking the mocking curl of his lips or the tinge of contempt in his gaze, and for a moment Arabella could do nothing but battle the conflicting emotions of outrage, relief, furious indignation, and even hurt, until at last, the whole was swallowed in an overwhelming sense of release. This, after all, was what she had wanted, was it not—a marriage of convenience with all the privileges but none of the obligations . . . ?

Yes, this was exactly what she had wanted. Like Lady Elizabeth, she would be a married woman secure in her position but unencumbered by the demands of a husband, free to live her life the way she chose. She could not have asked for more.

Phillip bowed once, smartly, over her hand, clicked his heels together in salute, and turned to descend the stairs. Arabella watched him go, congratulating herself on her smooth victory, trying to dredge up some feeling of triumph, but, as she turned to make her way slowly to her solitary chamber, she found it strangely missing.

The hour was late, and most of the guests had long since gone to their beds to rest before beginning the revelry anew on the morrow. Reginald, having sunk heavily into a comfortable chair, looked up over his glass of brandy as Phillip entered the library. "So soon from the nuptial bed, Everett?"

Phillip strolled casually to the side table and poured

a measure of brandy into a bell-shaped snifter. He inhaled the aroma, admired the color, and brought it appreciatively to his lips. His voice was low and smooth when at last he answered without turning. "I've more important matters on my mind this evening than bedding a wife, Chatley. There is a bit of business to be discussed between us, I believe."

Reginald's eyes sharpened alertly on the graceful figure across from him, but he kept his manner as matter-of-fact as Phillip's had been. "Business? Indeed? I can't imagine what business the two of us would have in common."

Phillip turned slowly with the glass held negligently in his long fingers, and his face was a study in bored disdain. "Why surely, my good sir," he drawled, "you did not expect me to take your damaged goods off your hands for nothing. I find this wife you've foisted upon me to have far more to her discredit than a slightly fouled reputation." From his coat he pulled a copy of a newspaper opened to the familiar, incriminating article, and tossed it carelessly on the desk. His smile was cold, and almost reptilian. "The captain of the ship upon which you made your voyage is a friend. He often brings me much-needed news from home."

Reginald stiffened with his glass half-way to his lips; he swallowed hard, but there was nothing on his face but a semblance of dignified hostility. "The marriage settlement was more than respectable, sir," he pronounced flatly, "as you yourself agreed. And if you think that at this late date—"

Phillip laughed lazily and sank into a chair across from Reginald. He plumped a pillow behind his back, arranged his feet upon a *petit-point* stool, and lounged back comfortably in the chair. He appeared to be watching Reginald carefully from above the snifter of brandy, but with the shadows obscuring most of his

122

face, it was difficult to tell. "There are things of more import in these troubled times," he said casually, "than gold and stocks. And what would I do with a dower cottage in Devon?" A wave of his arm fluttered the cascading lace of his sleeve and imperiously dismissed what Reginald had always considered a dowry far more generous than his wretched sister deserved.

Reginald's fury built, as did his uneasiness. "The settlement seemed rich enough when you signed it," he replied shortly. "And I must protest your behavior in this matter, Everett. I had thought you a gentleman."

This time the laugh that floated from the shadows had an edge to it. "Only when it suits my purpose. And tonight it does not. Tonight my purpose is to discuss pursuits rarely associated with gentlemen—which, of course, is why you have been invited to join the discussion." Phillip lifted his glass magnanimously.

Reginald started from his chair, his full lips quivering with outrage, his face growing mottled. Fortunately, he was not to be called upon to defend against the insult, for before he had half-risen, Phillip concluded easily, "Pursuits which, while they are not generally considered gentlemanly, could greatly enrich the coffers of the house of Everett . . . and of Chatley."

Phillip had been studying the candlelit liquid in his glass, but now he raised enigmatic eyes to Reginald's own. Reginald sank back carefully, a measure of qualified relief seeping through him. Something was very strange here, he mused, but not as alarming as he had imagined. First Everett talked of dissatisfaction with the marriage contract, and now he spoke of mutual profit . . . It was doubtful that even the most avaricious man would put much faith in any schemes hatched by the harebrained Everett, but still—Reginald's eyes narrowed thoughtfully—still, the man had kept his fortune somehow, and it would do no harm to

123

listen . . . "It might be amusing to hear your ideas," he replied generously, relaxing. "Pray continue."

Phillip smiled in the darkness. He had just baited the hook. Now all he would have to do was wait for his catch to take the bait. "You are aware, no doubt, that I have an interest in a ship."

Reginald nodded.

"You know also that colonial ships are forbidden by law to trade with any country other than Mother England."

Again, Reginald nodded. If he was surprised by Phillip's concern with, or even his knowledge of, such complicated things as law, he gave no sign, as he remarked, "Those laws were passed by our Parliament, supported by Lord North and the King . . . and myself, I might add"—there was a touch of pride in his voice for his own small part in passing such monumental legislation—"and well supported by the citizens of England. What has this to do with—"

Impatiently, Phillip brushed Reginald's pontifications aside. "I am not here to argue the rightness of the law. What I wish to discuss is how we might bend those laws in a way profitable to both of us."

Reginald stared. What Everett alluded to was dangerous as well as unlawful, but very worthwhile to those with the daring and luck to brazen it out. What amazed him—indeed, flabbergasted him—was that Everett had the cunning to perceive this, to say nothing of the courage to suggest it. Something was wrong here. Very wrong.

Reginald shook his head, curving his lips down into his ponderous chin in an expression of distaste. "You are mad, man. You're talking smuggling. That's treasonable. I should depart this room this minute and leave you to your insane ruminations and improbable schemes."

But he did not; neither did Phillip expect him to. The air between them was heavy with expectation as Phillip took a leisurely sip of his brandy. Reginald could feel the other man's eyes upon him but could not see them. It was most unsettling.

"Smuggling is becoming far too hazardous a game, Chatley," Phillip replied at length, lifting one shoulder in lazy dismissal, "not to mention expensive. All those bribes to port officials do tend to eat away at the profit. And indeed, there is the small matter of treason. I'm sure that as an obedient subject of the crown, you would be certain to discourage such risky business."

Unaccountably, Reginald was reminded of some of the tales he had heard about Everett as a youth. A veritable rakehell he was, always into one scrape or another, a member, rumor had it, of one of the notorious Hellfire clubs of London, whose activities, in the years before Everett had been sent abroad, had become so scandalous they were not even whispered about in respectable drawing rooms. And then there was that matter of a duel . . .

Reginald's mind was racing furiously even as it could not escape the obvious truth: Phillip Everett was serious, and Reginald Winters, Lord Chatley, had vastly underestimated his opponent.

"But you do speak true," Phillip continued easily, sipping his brandy. "British customs ships ply the waters of Virginia with some regularity and board colonial ships at will. If I were arrested, it might prove quite embarrassing to you. How would that appear, I wonder," he mused, thoughtfully swirling the liquid in his glass, "—the brother-in-law of a member of the House of Lords arrested for smuggling?"

Reginald felt excitement quicken in his chest, even as he took the trouble to hide the gleam of greed in his eyes. He lifted a disinterested shoulder, feigning impatience. "Then if it's not smuggling, what is it, Everett? You waste my time with these foolish games of supposition."

In the shadows, Phillip smiled again. All he had to do now was reel in his catch, slowly, slowly . . .

Reginald's words had been disparaging, but his body leaned forward in the chair, tensed, eager. "I want Letters of Passage," Phillip announced, "to allow my ship to trade freely in the French and Dutch West Indies. You have the power and the contacts to provide me with such papers."

The voice from the darkness was hard and business-like, stripped of the foolish drawl, the simpering accent, the fatuous giggle. There was a sharp, acute mind behind the prancing facade of Phillip Everett, a mind as shrewd and a character as unscrupulous as Reginald's own—almost.

Reginald's reply was smug and arrogant. "Of course it is within my power to arrange such letters . . . were I so inclined. But why should I? Stay with your smuggling, Everett. A clever chap like you should make a go of it in no time."

Phillip was not moved. Reginald could feel rather than see his companion's irritatingly confident smile reaching out across the silent room. "And I put it to you," Phillip replied. "Why should I? So much easier—and healthier—to sail beneath an honored flag. I have made it a policy to stay within the law whenever it doesn't inconvenience me too much. Sleep so much better at night, you know."

Reginald frowned. This matter was beginning to grow tiresome, and Everett had not yet gotten to the interesting part—Reginald's own share of the profits. For his trouble, Reginald determined, it would be a great deal. "My dear young fellow," he said indul-gently, settling back into his chair, "I find this entire

126

business most preposterous. Why should a respected man such as myself risk the besmirching of an honored name—no less discovery and treasonable charges—for such as you? Why, I could walk out of here this night and turn you over to the customs authorities. *My* reputation would hardly suffer from your arrest. Indeed, it would be your family who would bear the shame of your folly, and, I might add, the responsibility for that young baggage of a sister of mine. I've no stake in this whatsoever." Reginald sat back in his chair, pleased with his maneuver. Who did this young jackanapes think he was to threaten the Earl of Chatley?

Phillip's voice was low, calm, and as deadly as the blade of a rapier. "Your protestations are worthless, Chatley. Your aid is already guaranteed, you see. It was done so on a certain night not six months ago in an inn near Covent Garden."

Reginald blanched perceptibly. "Hold your tongue, Everett," he hissed. "You speak of things—"

"Unspeakable," agreed Phillip mildly, "but true nonetheless. I speak of a whore so badly beaten she did not live through the night. I speak of a certain member of the House of Lords who was seen leaving her quarters. I speak—"

"Lies, all lies, sir!" Reginald tottered to his feet and stood swaying in the candlelight, peering into the darkness and trying to focus on his tormentor. He could only see Phillip's form in the shadows; he could not read the expression on his face.

"Not lies, Chatley," Phillip answered easily. "Do you think I would be so stupid as to marry your sister without knowing something about the family with which I was about to align myself? It simply isn't done, sir. Not at all. After all, I have a name to uphold."

Phillip brought the glass to his lips and sipped again

127

leisurely. Reginald watched with something that felt like a cold hand squeezing at his insides, and the seconds of silence that passed seemed an eternity. "So"—Phillip shrugged—"I set about making investigations. If one has the right contacts, there is nothing that cannot be learned. My agents talked to the woman's family, her fellow whores, the innkeeper. You thought that bribes would buy their silence."

Reginald sank back into his chair. His face was pale and sagging, and he suddenly appeared ten years older. His leg throbbed abominably. He said nothing.

Phillip chuckled as he reeled in his catch. "It worked for awhile . . . until I paid more. Just a simple matter of economics, Chatley—buying and selling on the open market."

Reginald stared at him in dull defeat for a long, silent moment. There were no protests, no defenses. For perhaps the first time in his life, Reginald Winters had been bested, and by Phillip Everett. Reginald's hand trembled only slightly as he reached for the decanter of brandy at his elbow. His voice was somewhat hoarse. "How soon do you need the letters?"

"First, pour me a dram of brandy." Phillip's voice was pleasant as he extended his empty glass from the shadows. "And then I will tell you how very rich we are both going to be."

Well into the morning a figure entered Arabella's bedchamber and moved easily across the floor to stand at the foot of the bed gazing down at her. Arabella slept like a child, on her back with one arm flung out beside her and the other resting on her leg. Her white gown, now rumpled and twisted beneath her, exposed one slim white calf and thigh and gleamed in the moonlight that spread across the bed.

128

Tendrils of hair curled damply about her face, making her look even younger and more vulnerable. Occasionally she moaned, whimpering softly as though even in sleep she could not escape the cares that plagued her. Her breath was shallow and rapid as though she might be dreaming, and her moist lips parted in a sigh.

Silently, the figure knelt beside the bed, his eyes drinking in Arabella's lush young body. Slowly, the man lowered his head and let his lips touch the soft, delicate skin of her thigh. Lightly he ran his tongue along the smooth flesh, tasting the sweet-saltiness of her skin. Feather-light fingers pushed the gown farther up her leg, exposing more of the petal-soft flesh to his hungry eyes. Again his lips sought the silkiness of her body, dropping tiny kisses as soft as raindrops along the softly curving shape of her leg.

Arabella trembled in her sleep and stirred, this time moving so that one of her breasts, which had been hidden by the low neck of the gown, now spilled forth. The invader felt a primitive stirring within him, an ache as old as time, as he saw her lying beneath him, so innocent on the surface yet so maddeningly provocative.

He knew he should leave her while she still slept, before she chanced to awaken and rouse the house with her cries of alarm. There was danger in coming to her like this, but she had become a compulsion to him, invading both his mind and his senses, and perhaps the danger was part of her appeal. Never had he been so consumed by a woman as he was by this one, and her temptation was too great for him to resist.

Yielding to that compulsion, he leaned forward and touched the tip of her bared breast with his tongue. Her nipple rose pink and soft against the magnolia white contour of her breast, and as he teased it lightly with his tongue it hardened into a perfect bud. He knew how to pleasure a woman, and the thought of pleasuring her, even though she might take it as no more than a dream, heightened his own need to intensely sharp proportions. He felt his skin heat and desire thicken in his loins, and even though it had not been his intention to go this far, he could not turn away from her. Not yet.

Arabella moaned softly and moved beneath him, lost in a wonderful and incomprehensible dream, unaware that her dream was a reality. As his tongue lightly circled her breast in a moist, erotic path, Arabella, with eyes still closed, gave a soft cry and raised her arms to enfold the phantom lover who gave her such pleasure. When she found flesh and blood, muscle and sinew, beneath her hands her eyes opened wide.

The face that looked down at her wore a mask.

"You . . ." she said, and there was no fear in her half-dazed voice but only wonder. "You," she repeated.

"Yes, it is I, Lady Arabella, come to visit you in your dreams."

As the fragments of sleep slowly dissolved into a clear understanding of the waking truth, Arabella struggled to a half-sitting position and grasped at the open edges of her nightgown. Alarm surfaced as she felt the ache in her breasts, the moisture that still lingered there from the touch of his mouth—alarm, and the heat of embarrassment at such unimagined intimacy and the shameless pleasure she had taken in it. But most of all there was puzzlement as she demanded, "How . . . how did you get in here?" Her voice was a hoarse and strained whisper and her eyes searched his intently in the dark. "Where—"

He laid a finger lightly across her lips and she saw the gently mocking curve of his lips. "Ah, but haven't you guessed by now, my lovely? I am everywhere, watching you, waiting for you . . . and no door will keep me away from what I want."

Her heart was beating rapidly and her breath was a warm and shallow whisper against his fingers as he turned them to caress her lips. It surely could not be. It must be yet an extension of her dream that she should awaken and find him, Le Renard, sitting upon the edge of her bed, drawing her into caresses she had never before known were possible between a man and a woman. She whispered, hardly believing her own ability to speak, so intense was the pounding of her heart. "And . . . what is it that you want?"

The gleam of his eyes in the darkness was rapier sharp. "You haven't yet guessed?" His voice, as low and husky as she remembered, the accent distinctly American, went through her like a thrill. His fingers caressed the line of her jaw, then downward, to her throat. The motion of his fingers was mesmerizing, and his eyes moved lower as his hand did, focusing all her attention on the slow, insinuating path he was tracing. "Does it frighten you," he murmured, "to find me here?"

Arabella, as though compelled, found herself whispering back, "How can there be fear . . . when there is so much pleasure?"

His eyes gleamed at her briefly with a mixture of triumph and desire, and he gathered her into his arms. "Then let us not forsake the pleasure."

His hands moved over the smooth contours of her breast, touching the nipple with his fingers where moments before his mouth had found sweet succor. Something warm and sensual and strong blazed within Arabella and instinctively she shut her eyes and raised her face toward him, lips slightly open, moist, inviting.

Le Renard's laugh was low in his throat as he pulled her to him. "Oh, you want to be kissed now, Lady

131

Arabella. So different from the first night by the river when you fought me. Then you were all fire and fury, and tonight I find you honey and wine. Which are you, I wonder?" His mouth paused a breath away from hers and with narrowed eyes he studied the face that yearned toward him. There was pliancy and hunger in the warm, soft body he held, and irresistibly he was drawn toward her. "Some of both, I imagine," he murmured.

His lips touched her cheek and then slid downward to her chin and to the soft column of her neck. His tongue traced a hot path along the line of her shoulder, tasting the fresh dewiness of her skin. He wanted to taste all of her, to touch her, to rain kisses along the length of the slim, warm body that pressed eagerly into him. And it would be easy, so easy. She was ready for him, willing, yearning, stirred as much as he by the hot kisses in the night.

Her hair was tousled wildly about her face, her nightdress pulled low to expose the ripeness of her breasts, and her face ... her face was alive with a passion that matched his own. She was all fire and flame in his arms, feverish with desire, and he wanted her desperately, foolishly ...

His lips moved in hungry kisses back along the line of her shoulder, upward along her soft, sweet neck until his mouth claimed hers and he kissed her, a hot, greedy kiss that demanded as much as it gave. Arabella was no longer a novice and this time she responded instinctively. When his lips parted hers she was ready for the invasion of his tongue, she was as eager to taste him, tantalize him, explore him, as he was her. And she felt herself drowning within the heady rush of sensations their shared passion brought, the blending of their bodies in heat and taste and texture. Yet even as waves

132

of mindless pleasure washed over her, she was greedy for more.

He groaned and tore his mouth from hers.

Her senses inflamed and her pulses rushing wildly, Arabella looked at him in confusion and hurt. "Have I displeased you?" she whispered, wanting him against her again, his mouth upon hers and his touch upon her breast.

His laugh was low and bitter. "You have not displeased me, my lady. I swear that." His breathing sounded unsure, and there was a grimness in the set of his mouth. His eyes swept hers with a barely restrained greed that made her heart lurch and then resume its furious, ecstatic pounding within her chest. "There is nothing more I want than your sweet body beneath mine," he said hoarsely, "your arms around me, your honeyed taste enveloping me . . . but that will be another time, another place."

She caught her breath, barely comprehending the meaning of his explicit words, knowing only that she did not want him to leave her, that the wonder he had brought to her could not so abruptly end. But already he was rising to go and she reached out her hand to detain him. "No . . . wait . . ."

He took her hand in his and firmly removed it from his arm as he got to his feet. "No, my lady," he said quietly, determinedly. "I will not make love to you in your husband's house."

"But"—Arabella sat up and there was urgency in her voice as he moved away from her—"when will I see you again? We must talk. You—"

He smiled at her, lifting a hand as though to stay an impatient child. "Another time," he promised her and, with a billowing of his long black cape, he turned toward the window.

By the time Arabella could fling aside the covers and rush after him, he was gone. Though she spent a long time gazing into the shadows below while her pulses still raced and her cheeks tingled with the excitement of the adventure that had just befallen her, she saw nothing stir, for just as stealthily as he had come, Le Renard had disappeared into the night.

Chapter VIII

The waterfront tavern was dark and noisy; it stank of fish and sweat and old ale. The table at which Reginald sat was sticky with grease, and, as he watched, a fly circled lazily and settled on the rim of his mug. He brushed it away impatiently and said to the man sitting across from him, "Do you understand what you're to do?"

There was no need to lower his voice. Crimes were plotted and committed in this part of the city at the rate of a dozen or more a day—many far more despicable than the one he planned—and there was hardly any need for subterfuge. But still Reginald did not feel it necessary to draw attention to himself, and he kept his tone low and his face half covered by the handkerchief he pressed to his nose, ostensibly to guard against the smell. All he wanted was to dispense with this messy business and be away from here.

The man who huddled over a mug of dark ale across the table looked the type who would slit the throat of a finely dressed gentleman like Reginald for a handful of shillings and the boots on his feet. He was small, grizzled, and filthy, with narrow darting eyes and two missing front teeth. "Aye, guv," he replied, draining his mug and shifting restlessly in the low chair. "And you couldn'ta picked a better man for the job." He wiped his mouth with the back of his hand and showed Reginald his gap-toothed grin. "Now hand it over, and I'll be on my way."

Reginald had been in Norfolk less than a week before he finally made up his mind what he had to do; it had taken another week to finalize the details. Phillip Everett thought he was very shrewd, but he had underestimated the faculties of his business partner. Reginald, Lord Chatley, was not about to enter into any association as risky as this without protecting his own interests.

Reginald slid a small leather pouch across the table, withdrawing his hand distastefully as a greedy fist closed about it. The other man had only three fingers on his left hand and Reginald found the deformity quite sickening. "One hundred pounds sterling," he said. "There'll be another fifty every time you report to me. You have the address in New York. I don't care how you do it; just make sure that ship doesn't make a move without your knowing about it. And you report to *no one but me*." Reginald's eyes were dark and fierce. "Is that quite understood?"

The three-fingered man caressed the bag of silver lovingly. He would have killed a dozen men for half as much. "Put yer mind at ease, guv. Just leave it to me. Easiest money I've ever made, and that's a fact."

Reginald nodded curtly, satisfied. The man was shrewd enough to know his business but not bright enough to turn it to his advantage. And his loyalty could be bought. He was exactly the man for the job. "Then get on with it," Reginald growled, closing his hand about the mug with one last furtive glance around the room. "Get out of here."

Reginald sat there for a moment longer, feeling relief

settle upon him as he watched the little man, one hundred pounds richer, swagger through the crowd toward the door. He lifted his mug for a congratulatory drink, took a look at the filthy contents, and thought better of it. All in all, he had handled the matter rather well. So, Phillip Everett thought he could threaten Lord Chatley, did he? A frown came over his features at the very thought. Simpering jackass! He would just see who could threaten whom . . .

Everett would have his precious Letters of Passage as soon as the post could be dispatched from London. Let him continue his little enterprise beneath the full auspices of the British government, and if he was true to his word, then both of them would profit. But the moment he took it into his head to cheat the Earl of Chatley . . .

Reginald tossed a coin onto the table and got to his feet with a sigh of satisfaction and a self-congratulatory smile etching its way onto his dry features. New York. It was not an unpleasant destination, though he would have much preferred to have been on his way to England. But he had friends in the northern city, and he knew it would have been foolish to leave the Colonies before becoming entirely certain about what Everett was up to.

Yes, New York, he mused. He had made the right decision. At least, he thought as he lumbered out into the sticky heat of the filthy dockside street, it was bound to be cooler there.

The moments before dawn were dark and still. The moon had set; the sun had not yet risen. The band of men on horseback moved silently down the shadowy alleyways of Norfolk. A torch flared to life and sailed across the night toward a solitary guardhouse. Briefly the blackened faces of the silent band were illuminated by the orange glow of the conflagration, but at a terse order from their leader, they turned and made their way toward the high garrison wall. Under the cover of shouts and confusion generated by the fire, they began with swift efficiency to scale the wall and drop soundlessly onto the ground below.

Not until the last man had climbed back over the wall to safety did the cry of discovery rise up, but it was too late. The band of renegades mounted and rode swiftly into the dark from which they had come. Where once there had been six, now there were seven.

The man leading the pack rode hard and fast. He was Le Renard, and he had struck again.

It sometimes seemed as if Lady Arabella Winters, the bane of London and the rage of Devon gossip, had never existed. Arabella Everett, mistress of Shadowood, arose at dawn, dressed sedately, and had unlocked the storeroom, supervised the lighting of the fires, prepared the daily menus, assigned tasks to the household staff, and seen that breakfast was laid long before her husband thought of stirring. The life of the mistress of one of the great James River plantations was indeed a full one.

It had been Sam, not Phillip, who had taken Arabella on her first tour of Shadowood. They had gone riding early in the morning before the summer sun could burn its hottest and before her slothful husband had even arisen from bed. On that first ride around the plantation Arabella had been besieged by the sounds and smells and new sights that were a part of this strange world in which she found herself.

Behind the house and hidden from view by a well-placed stand of boxwoods were the outbuildings—the

138

kitchen, smokehouses, ice house, and cabins of the house servants. Sam, as the master's valet, had his own quarters inside the house near Phillip's bedchamber, where he might be no more than a step away from the master's imperious call, and Arabella, feeling a streak of amusement as he told her this, wondered if he might not have preferred the less privileged but doubtlessly more comfortable status of a mere houseman.

Attached to the kitchen was the laundry, where female slaves in bare feet and bright cotton had stood around huge steaming vats of lye. Each had held a long wooden stick that was used to stir the mixture. Some of the Negro women had called out to Sam, and others had nodded and dipped their heads to Arabella. Arabella had not been certain at that moment whether their deference was due to her newly acquired status or Sam's long-standing one, for it was obvious he commanded much respect among the other slaves.

"They're making soap," Sam had explained to her. "We try to make most everything we use on Shadowood."

Arabella had been intrigued by his comments, for they were made with a distinct touch of pride and proprietary interest. His use of the word "we" was hardly customary for a slave speaking about the place that owned him.

Sam had taken Arabella around the house, scattering the flock of chickens before them, pointing out the kennels where Master Phillip kept his prize collection of barking hounds, stopping before the large barns that housed the plantation horses and cattle. Livery boys had been busily scrubbing leather and polishing carriage brass under the strict command of a grizzled old groom; activity had been everywhere.

As they had passed through the grove of trees that set the slave quarters apart from the main house, little children had run alongside them, calling out Sam's name. He had seemed to be a great favorite among them all, including the tiny girl who had shyly brought Arabella a bunch of wildflowers she had gathered. "For Missy," she had whispered before running back to hide behind the cabin.

"Master Phillip don't hold with separating families," Sam had pointed out with an unmistakable nod of approval, "not like a lot of masters. The more children, he says, the better for Shadowood."

It had somehow seemed typical to Arabella that Phillip, if he thought of nothing else, would consider his own best ends. But the sight of all those scampering children had touched her in some way, as had all of Shadowood, so beautiful, busy, and teeming with life. She had not been able to fault Phillip for being a bad master or a slovenly landholder, no matter how much she might have wished to do so. She had been forced to give him credit for having chosen a clever overseer, at least, for there had been no doubt in her mind that William Hampton was primarily responsible for what she was seeing here. She had not been able to find fault with the life Phillip—oaf that he was—had made for himself and for the people of the plantation. In fact, she had realized she could learn to love this place, had even imagined life here very pleasant, if only . . . But Arabella had dared not let her thoughts stray, in the light of day, to thoughts of Le Renard.

Sam had been a thorough and competent guide, intent upon showing her every aspect of the huge plantation. Crossing a long stretch of pasture land, they had ridden to a sawmill where timber was being cut and planked to be used in the constant building that was the lot of a growing plantation. The artisan's huts were nearby, those of the tanner, the cobbler, the weavers. It had all seemed a complete village in itself, this Shadowood, and Arabella had been amazed—and unwillingly impressed.

"It's like a small kingdom," Arabella had mused, still looking about her in wonder as they had paused to water their horses at one of the estate's many tumbling streams. "And Phillip is the king." A mad king, echoed the unspoken words—a completely frivolous, unworthy, and incompetent king, who could not possibly rule this orderly estate by himself.

She had looked at Sam steadily. "But you, Sam," she had said softly, "you and William are the real power behind the throne, I suspect."

He had met her gaze evenly. There would have been no point to denying the obvious. She had heard the way he had spoken to the slaves as they had passed, noted the uncommon attention he had given to the smallest detail of the workings of the plantation, the way the field hands and house servants alike had responded to him with respect and obedience. He gave the orders; they complied without hesitation. She had not been able to imagine the ineffectual Phillip ever managing such a feat.

"Master Phillip is a good master," he had replied and there had been no defense in his tone but merely a statement of fact.

"But you run the plantation."

"He has other things to occupy him," Sam had equivocated. His expression had been quite unreadable.

Arabella had known very well what other things occupied Phillip—the fit of his clothes, the fall of his lace, the length of his wig. How unworthy he was of all of this.

She had looked at Sam. "You are not like the others," she had observed, revealing only what she must have known from the first moment she had met

141

him. "You are not a slave, are you, Sam?"

Sam had turned his horse and they had begun to ride slowly along the stream. He had sat easily in the saddle for such a big man, as though accustomed to being in charge. "Master Phillip won me in a card game in Williamsburg," he explained after a time, "not long after he arrived in the Colonies. I guess the ways hereabouts were strange to an Englishman, so he set me free. I have my papers."

Arabella had drawn up her horse slightly, positioning herself to look at him. She had not been able to keep the puzzlement out of her tone or the amazement out of her eyes. "But why do you stay?" she had insisted. "Why . . . ?"

He had leaned forward over the pommel, gazing upward at the way the mid-morning sun slanted through the leaves of the trees. "I've got my reasons, Missus," he had replied, somewhat enigmatically. And then he had looked at her. "There's freedoms, and there's freedoms. The most important one, to my way of thinking, is freedom to choose. And I choose to stay here at Shadowood." He had turned his horse, gesturing to a nearby path. "We'll be at the tobacco fields soon, Missus. Mind your step up this hill."

Arabella had followed in silence, knowing that Sam had said all he was going to say on the matter of his position at Shadowood and on the subject of Phillip Everett.

Arabella had seen the vegetable garden near the slave quarters and had understood that it supplied food not only for the main house and its occupants but for the slaves as well. When she saw stretching before her endless fields of green tobacco, she had been amazed at the sheer vastness of it. Along each of the long, curving rows had walked slaves, their eyes intent upon the stalks, a sack in their hands, bending and straightening

142

with careful attention to each plant.

"This is gold to Shadowood," Sam had said, that note of unmistakable pride again in his voice. "Tobacco. It's used for barter, shipping collateral . . . better than gold," he had decided with a grin. "It's a lot harder for a robber to make off with a bale of tobacco than a bag of gold. Now the field hands are picking off the worms and suckers," he had explained, gesturing. "Later on this summer we'll pick the tobacco and cure it in those sheds you see yonder before it's packed in the warehouses for shipping."

Arabella's eyes had followed the row of huge warehouses that lined the river and she had thought that, if tobacco were as good as gold, Shadowood was indeed possessed of its share of wealth.

Her eyes had moved back over the rows, to the men and women and children working the fields, and her heart had gone out to them. "It must be difficult to be a slave," she had said softly.

An ivory smile broke across Sam's ebony face. "It's better to be free, Miss Arabella," he agreed. And then a sobering expression had darkened his eyes slightly as he had looked out over the distant fields. "And it's not only black folk who are finding that out."

Since that first ride with Sam, Arabella had made her rounds many times. She prepared potions for ailing slaves, she bound wounds from field injuries, she supervised the dispensation of supplies and all activities relating to the maintenance of a household consisting of over three hundred people.

She had begun keeping the plantation account books and inventory after Phillip had complained with an airy wave of his kerchief, "I've never had much of a head for figures, m'dear, and I'm afraid the ledgers are in quite a tangle. Do see what you can do to set them right, will you?" There never seemed a lack of occupation, and Arabella embraced each new task with enthusiasm and gratitude. Shadowood was her home and she would make the best of it. The household, an orderly one before her arrival, now practically gleamed with the pride of its new mistress. The slaves came to her with their problems and left beaming from her ability to conciliate.

Even Phillip had had a word of praise for her when he had seen how she had rearranged his bookkeeping system. "Capital, m'dear, just capital. Can't make heads nor tails of it m'self, so it must be right." The slaves adored her, Phillip was pleased with her, and if the neighbors went away from duty calls still skeptical about the new mistress of Shadowood, they could not deny she was taking her position seriously. For a space of pages even her journal gave way from ruminations upon the Fox to her absorption with her new position.

> *Sometimes I marvel over It, how I came to the Responsibility of this Place . . . It is quite as well suppli'd as Chatley Hall, with all the Accoutrements of a wealthy Virginia Plantation—the fine Crystal and China from England, the well-wrought Silver Pieces, the fine Linens from Ireland . . . The kitchen Storerooms are replete with Bins of Flour and Cornmeal of such Quantities I should wonder They would not spoil before All are Used; great Shanks of Ham and Sausage hang in the Smokehouse, and the Root Cellar is fill'd with Potatoes and Turnips. But I find It a Curiosity that other Items, which are not common to the Virginia Home, are found in such Quantity Here . . . Kegs of Molasses and Rum from the Indies, Dutch Tea, and the little Gifts*

which Phillip brings Me from his Travels (think-
ing, as He does, that It is only proper husbandely
Behavior and He is always so Concern'd with
doing All that is proper!)—Chocolates and
French Silk and Brussels Lace . . . I know from
my reading that these Items are All but inaccessi-
ble to the Colonists because of odd Political
Reasons, and I cannot but think Phillip must
have come upon Them by no honest Means, for
He is not clever enough to do otherwise . . .
Whenever I have brought the Matter up with
Sam, who seems quyte sensible and accessible, He
has only laugh'd and assur'd Me of my Hus-
bande's Skill at the Gaming Tables, as though It
were Something to take Pryde in . . . !

As for Myself I find this Moral Turpitude quyte
distasteful and would much prefer an honest
Criminal to a Man who hoardes to Himself ill-
gotten Gains while his neighbours suffer without
for the Sake of what They believe to be right . . .

At such a point, her thoughts would inevitably turn
to Le Renard, and, as night follows day, so her pen
would follow her reverie.

The clink and scrape of foils rang out sharply
through the stillness of the forest glade, and an
observer would have been hard put to take the display
for anything other than a fight to the death. The two
men wielded their weapons earnestly and with zeal, and
it was readily apparent that they desperately strove for
skill, not idle exercise.

They were a peculiarly matched pair. The one, tall
and lithe, was obviously the more well trained, casting
the fencing poses and moving with a grace that only

could have been learned after many hours of drilling in the art. The shorter, heftier man had superior strength but lacked the skill and was already breathing hard from the exertion he was applying to the contest.

For a moment the mock battle was too close to call, but then, in a movement as swift and unexpected as it was vicious, the tall man thrust forward and the foil went flying from the other's hand, catching the glint of the sun as it turned a perfect circle in the air before landing with a slicing sound in a tangle of undergrowth and brambles.

The victor made a classic bow while his defeated partner swore ungraciously and trod off in search of his foil. "Damn my soul, you near broke my hand!" he exclaimed, cradling the injured limb in his other hand as he paused to glare over his shoulder. "There's no need to go for blood!"

"If I had been a member of the King's militia, I would have run you through," replied the other without mercy, but he crossed the ground to assist his friend in retrieving the foil.

After many a muttered curse, the item was pulled from its thorny bed and deposited unceremoniously beneath a tree. Sinking with a sigh beneath the shade of the oak, the shorter man looked up at his companion in disgruntlement. "And don't think I don't know the reason for your hellish temper, either. It's plain to any man with eyes to see."

"Oh?" Le Renard bent smoothly to lift the foil, examining its tip for damage. "And what might that be?"

The other shrugged. "It has to me the look of an unrequited lust of some sort. You're as nervous as a stallion with the scent of a mare—and about as obvious."

"An astute observation, my friend, but I can't say I

think much of your choice of analogies."

"For a learned man you can be as big a fool as I've ever known," he replied curtly. "It hasn't yet occurred to you, has it—the danger?"

Le Renard laughed softly. His eyes glinted with that restless, urgent energy his men had learned to associate with the excitement of the chase. To see it now, under these circumstances, was altogether unsettling to his companion. "But danger is the very spice of life, isn't it said? And never truer than in a case such as mine."

There were no secrets between the two men, though they did not always find themselves in agreement. The lieutenant was the wary one, often too pedantic and cautious for Le Renard's liking, yet he valued him for those very reasons. Le Renard knew that his friend disapproved of his recent exploits—undeniably for very good reasons—but they both also knew Le Renard was not in the market for, nor was he likely to accept, advice upon the matter.

The other man said now as he looked up at the lean, well-formed face of his commander and leader, "Do you know, sir, sometimes I think you are truly mad. Who else but a madman would take such chances as you have with the winsome Lady Arabella—and in the very halls of Shadowood?" His voice was sober as he insisted, "Have you no idea how easily you could have been betrayed had anyone seen you? All we have worked for this past year would have been for naught—not to mention your own fate, which hardly bears detailing."

Again Le Renard laughed. "I have outdistanced the gallows for all these years, my friend. I've no intention of making its close acquaintance at this late date. Lay your foolish anxieties to rest, sir, for they are of no account."

The other man scowled. "I can't help but be anxious

when the man I rely upon to keep a cool head has his wits centered beneath his breeches. If you're not careful, we could *all* go to the gallows for the sake of your consolation."

"More than mere consolation, sir!" replied Le Renard, feigning injury. "You may well be speaking of my salvation!"

The other snorted. "Your damnation, more likely."

"You are implying, sir," said Le Renard mildly, running his fingers suggestively over the smooth edge of the foil, "that the lady might betray me?"

"All women are treacherous at heart," replied the other reasonably. "It is in their nature. They're not to be blamed for it; they just can't help it."

"And you, a happily married man."

"Happily married," he pointed out triumphantly, "because I know when to keep my own counsel. I do not bring my private politics into the bedroom, which is as it should be."

"Hmm." Le Renard was thoughtful. "But as matters stand now, it seems I am helpless to do otherwise. Unless," he suggested, eyes glinting mischief, "you would have me unmask myself for the lady?"

"Lord no!" There was horror in the exclamation. "For God's sake, use your brain. She is a daughter of Britain, a confidante of the Lord Governor's—"

"And the wife of Phillip Everett," pointed out Le Renard smoothly.

"Precisely!" he agreed with a satisfied nod. "Which tells better than aught else where her loyalties lie! For what other reason would she have married if not to further her own ends? She is a frivolous, self-aspiring wench who cannot be trusted out of sight."

"I am not sure I like the way you describe the lady," murmured Le Renard with a sly look, and his friend had the grace to look abashed. "However," he continued more energetically, "you are right . . . to a point. She is also clever, ambitious—perhaps too much so, I'll grant—and quite . . . um . . . amenable. It would be expedient, don't you think, to attempt to tame her?"

"Make a friend of the enemy?" The other man smiled, perceptively. "A clever enough scheme, and quite your style, but I think perhaps it has gone beyond that in this case."

An absent look crossed Le Renard's face and for a moment he did not speak. When he did, it was very softly, almost to himself. "Perhaps," he admitted. "I never expected her to be so appealing . . . or so easily aroused to passion. Sometimes I think . . ." A shadow passed his eyes, hovered momentarily, and then was gone. He flashed a smile at his friend, wearing this time a mask of a different sort. "It is of no consequence, sir. I know what I am about."

And then in two quick strides he retrieved his own foil and tossed the other to his startled partner, declaring, "And now, you weakling, on your feet before you grow as soft and worthless as Everett himself! *En guarde!*"

Tales of the exploits of Le Renard were everywhere, and what once had seemed no more than a secret romantic dream to Arabella became increasingly, and excitingly, real. Even Caroline, on her frequent visits to the main house, brought news of the Fox in the form of the *Virginia Gazette*. On a particularly hot August afternoon the two women sat in the shade of the arbor at Shadowood with cool glasses of lemonade. Caroline sewed industriously while Arabella eagerly scanned the

149

latest issue of the *Gazette*.

VIRGINIA GAZETTE   15 August 1773

LE RENARD RAVAGES COUNTRYSIDE!

On the tenth of July a consignment of woolens
bound for the haberdashery of Simon and Son,
Williamsburg, was overtaken on the Norfolk
road by a band of unidentified ruffians who left
the rider bound and gagged and made away with
the wagon, horses, and goods. George Milkins,
driver of the purloined wagon, could not say how
many bandits attacked him in the dark of night,
but he recalled quite clearly their leader. "A
masked devil, he was!" decried Mr. Milkins.
"Swift as a fox and just as clever. He was upon me
before I knew what he was about." The distraught
Mr. Milkins went on to describe the bandit as
having eyes "as red as a demon's" and brandishing
a saber "as long as his horse." Mr. Milkins
survived his encounter with the attackers un-
harmed.

"My goodness!" exclaimed Arabella with a light
laugh that disguised the sudden excited speeding of her
heart. "Woolens, is it? Now what do you imagine he
wanted with those?"

"To swathe his wife and children against the coming
winter?" teased Caroline, enjoying the sparkle of
pleasure in her friend's eyes. Then, allowing her
imagination free run, she suggested, "Perhaps he
means to sell them on the black market . . . or perhaps
it was a raid designed only to annoy the tradesmen. I
vouchsafe most of these attacks are more for the spirit
of adventure than for any real purpose. It does appear

your Fox enjoys seeing his name in print."

Arabella looked quickly at her friend, hiding with a nervous laugh the flush of embarrassed uneasiness that unexpectedly tinged her cheeks. "*My* Fox?" she protested, fanning herself with the single sheet of newsprint against the still August afternoon and the new, even more unwelcome heat in her cheeks. "My dear Caroline, you credit me with too much!"

"Well . . ."—Caroline ventured a single sly glance from the neat, precise, hemstitch she was working on a square of cloth—"you *are* exceedingly fascinated by the antics of the renegade, you must admit."

Arabella felt the heat suffuse her entire body, though she knew her friend could not possibly know of her late-night liaisons with the selfsame renegade. Yet even thinking of them made her stomach feel shivery, her throat tight. To hide her confusion, she turned quickly back to the *Gazette*.

This is the fourth such incident in the past month, and though witnesses disagree on many details, all attribute the misdeeds to a tall masked man who stalks his quarry stealthily, makes his raid silently, and disappears without a trace. Despite the fact that no bodily harm has yet been inflicted upon any of the victims, Virginians are outraged. Under the very noses of guards, prisoners are stolen from their cells, and the harbors of Norfolk, the streets of Williamsburg, and even the governor's storehouse itself are no longer safe havens for decent folk to conduct their affairs. Is this an example of the protection afforded by the King's militia? How is it possible that a single criminal can outwit an entire army and menace the countryside at will? This writer proposes that the inability to deal with this so-

called Le Renard is yet another example of the
inefficiency of the rule of King George and calls
for an immediate stop to this horror. Let us join
our voices together and rid Virginia forever of the
curse of Le Renard!

Below the story in a squared-off advertisement,
Arabella read:

REWARD

One hundred guineas sterling offered by His
Majesty King George III for the capture of Le
Renard, the Fox, or any other answering his
description, for aiding in the escape of One
George Rafferty, merchant, a prisoner of the
Crown in the Norfolk Garrison, and for sundry
other crimes against the crown and the people of
Virginia.

Arabella smiled and folded the sheet. All over a
wagon of woolens? she mused, imagining that Le
Renard himself would laugh when he read this.

Caroline was right, of course. Perhaps it was
becoming obvious that she was fascinated by the
legendary pirate of the highways and the countryside,
yet, in truth, she could find nothing for which to
condemn him. His daring and his skill elicited only
admiration from her, and his flair for drama could not
help but appeal. He had done no murders, and he took
only from those who could afford to lose. How could
he help but stand apart from those other highwaymen
who pillaged and raped, or left their victims bleeding or
dead on the side of the road and all for no more than

the change in their pockets? Oh yes, Le Renard had been the subject of much tittering female gossip in Virginia drawing rooms this summer, for it seemed Arabella was not the only one whose imagination he had captured. But she was the one who had captured his heart . . . or so she wished to believe.

Arabella returned the paper to Caroline with a somewhat wistful smile. *Her* Fox indeed! she reflected. If only it could be truly so . . .

"Oh, no," insisted Caroline, barely glancing up from her needlework. "It is yours to keep. When a merchant passed by with it yesterday, I knew immediately how you would enjoy it. It must be very hard for you to adjust to provincial life after all the entertaining news of London."

Pleased, Arabella settled back with the paper, glancing over it again. Though she had never thought it would be true, the lack of news was among the many things she missed about London, and reading and rereading this broadsheet about the Fox would help her pass many a long night and fill her lonely hours.

The afternoons of Caroline's visits, which took place once a week or less, were among the few times Arabella could be found sitting in the middle of the day. It was a mixed blessing. She enjoyed nothing as much as the company of this mild-spoken little woman, her easy companionship, her gentle harmless gossip. But sometimes Caroline only served to remind Arabella of all she herself would never have.

Arabella looked at the small, delicate garment Caroline was sewing and she felt a brief, uncontrollable twinge of raw envy. The other woman's full skirt disguised her condition, but Arabella had known for some time now that a baby was expected in late fall. Caroline was radiant, and after seeing the way William fawned over and catered to his young wife, one would think he had fathered the next heir to the throne. Of course, Arabella was happy for them, but she did not like to be reminded of what might never be hers. And she did not like the looks of speculative sympathy William cast her or Caroline's tendency to end every discussion of the subject with, "But you will know for yourself soon enough . . ."

In fact, Arabella did not at all like to discuss the subject that was so greatly in Caroline's mind these days, and to prevent just such an eventuality she inquired now, carelessly, "Will you be accompanying us to Williamsburg next month?"

"I'm afraid not." Caroline's grimace was a bit dry. "William will not hear of my traveling, and, of course, with Phillip away so much . . ."

Arabella smiled in sympathy for William, but in her own heart she felt no sadness over her husband's frequent absences at horse races and gaming parties. In fact, it was a relief to be free of his silly prattling, but that she could never confide to Caroline, though how much the other woman suspected she could not know.

They talked for a while longer, with Caroline busily advising Arabella about whom she must expect to call upon while in Williamsburg and which merchants were the most reliable, but the sun began to sink low and soon Caroline began to gather up her things to depart. Arabella bade her good day with regret, for she did enjoy these carefree hours of female companionship and the excuse to retreat from the August heat for a few hours of rest.

There was much that awaited her doing, but Arabella sat for a few minutes longer, taking the opportunity to read one more time the account of Le Renard's latest exploits.

A soft step behind her startled Arabella. "Afternoon, m'dear," drawled Phillip, his voice weak and wilted.

"Hideous heat, isn't it? Wonder that you haven't taken to your bed with it, being as unused to the climate as you are . . . Well, what have we here?" Nimble fingers plucked the broadsheet out of Arabella's hand just as she was about to rise, greet her husband, and make some excuse to retreat into the house. "Is this how you have entertained yourself this afternoon? How amusing!"

He scanned the writing for a moment, then waved it away with a sniff. "Le Renard, Le Renard, Le Renard!" he whined, twisting his features into an expression of pained boredom. "That is all I ever hear these days. What drivel! This is what comes of teaching women to read—they fill their little heads with fluff and feathers and give us not a moment's peace."

He carelessly tossed the printed sheet onto the wicker settee where Arabella sat, and with a great effort Arabella gathered herself together to converse with her husband. Her voice was even and well modulated as she commented casually, "This Fox does seem to be making quite a name for himself."

"Fox, pox!" scoffed Phillip; then, pleased with the cleverness of the rhyme, repeated again, "A pox upon the Fox!" He giggled and declared, "I shall write *that* to the *Gazette!* Where is a quill? Where is Sam?" He raised his voice and shouted, "Sam!" then grumbled, "Blast the man; he's never around when you need him. I shall soon forget what it was I wished to write. Sam!"

Arabella seethed. She knew Phillip could hardly be blamed for being such an idiot, but she invariably felt control of her temper slipping whenever he was around. "Indeed, sir," she interrupted coldly, "I wonder that you bother yourself at all about such"— she enunciated the word distinctly—"*drivel*. Isn't it you who has accused me of making much ado about nothing?"

Phillip turned back to her, distracted from his quest for a quill, and straightened his lace carelessly. "And indeed it is nothing," he pronounced. "A common criminal making print in the *Gazette*—what is this country coming to? Time was when the broadsheets were devoted to matters of more import, like the placement of buttons and the *proper*"—he fixed this word on her meaningfully as his hand trailed to the simply tied neckcloth he wore—"decoration for the neck. I do say, Lady Arabella, I must take exception to—"

But Arabella had no intention of allowing him to launch into another discourse on the tying of his jabot. "It would appear," she interrupted mildly, "that someone thinks the exploits of the Fox are worth notice. The King has offered a reward."

Phillip lifted an eyebrow. "Has he indeed? Waste of good sterling, if you ask me. Why, I doubt very seriously that the fellow even exists—Le Renard, not the King—and if he does, he is hardly, in my opinion, the cleverest fellow who has ever lived—Le Renard again, not the King. Why, he hardly makes it worth his time to raid, from all reports! Passing by a good cask of Madeira for a worthless barrel of saltpeter! Setting fire to a wagon load of tea without bothering to empty it first! And this matter of woolens—how absurd! Far better to have robbed the driver and left the wagon be. Of what value can such merchandise possibly be to a filthy, diseased ruffian who has doubtless never felt anything other than animal hides against his skin in his entire miserable life? He will probably use the stuff to clean his boots with! Damned shame, if you ask me, begging your pardon, m'dear." He bowed lazily and, apparently quite satisfied with his speech, took out his snuffbox again.

"I beg to disagree, sir," replied Arabella smoothly,

"but it is common talk that Le Renard's motives go beyond profit, and for that he is considered quite clever. He has, in fact, become something of a hero among the patriots, has he not?"

Phillip gave an ungracious sniff. "Patriots! Rabble, I say. And I'm sure I don't know what that band of ruffians may or may not think about Le Renard."

"Indeed, sir, do any of us?" replied Arabella airily, waving the broadsheet to cool herself. "But I find the entire matter great fun to speculate upon, don't you?"

"I'm afraid I find nothing 'fun,' or even tasteful, in a discussion of this Fox personage," replied a bored Phillip, "and I should very much like a change of conversation."

Arabella was only too happy to oblige. Somehow even mentioning the name of the dashing hero of her fantasies in the presence of one such as Phillip seemed a travesty. She said, searching for a neutral topic, "Did you have a pleasant journey to Richmond, sir?"

Phillip extended his arm to her politely and they began a slow and stately promenade through the rose garden, presenting, as always, a perfect if not true picture of the contented couple to the world at large. She laid her fingers lightly upon his arm and looked up into a face that did not reveal even by a flicker or a blink anything other than lazy indifference. Phillip had been away from home more often than not since their marriage, sometimes for days or even weeks at a time, and it was a fact she had cause to bless. She had found she could not be in the same room with him for more than a few moments at a time without forgetting everything she had ever known about civilized behavior, and matters always went much more smoothly when Phillip was away.

"Tedious, m'dear," he droned in reply, "most tedious. My digestion suffers so terribly from strange

157

kitchens, and I found on Tuesday morning that I could scarce get my boot on. I think I may be contracting a touch of the gout."

"Then," ventured Arabella, trying to conceal her disappointment, "you will be at home for a time?"

"Alas, no. I must go early to Williamsburg." He paused with a slight grimace of distaste to pluck a withered blossom from an overblown rose bush. "My tailor and wig maker, the lazy fellows, can never seem to get my order ready for the season unless I keep after the louts."

"And what of me, sir? Shall I remain here alone?" She tried to keep her voice noncommittal, for the last thing she wished to do was to encourage her husband to stay and keep her company, but oh, how she would have loved a trip to town—even a town as provincial as Williamsburg.

Phillip assured her, "You will pack up the household and join me later, of course. And do not distress yourself, m'dear. You will find quite enough to occupy you in my absence." And then, as if stricken by a sudden thought, he turned to her, eyes widening dramatically. "Why, surely you are not distressed by all the talk of this Fox beast? You can't think he will come upon Shadowood and—"

"I assure you, I have no such fears, Phillip," Arabella protested quickly, but already her cheeks were warming with remembrance of the times Le Renard *had* come upon Shadowood.

Caught up in his own theatrical imaginings, Phillip declared, "What have we to fear, I ask you, from a dastardly coward who will not even show his face in the light of day and who hides his countenance behind a mask even in the dark of night? Why, should he ever dare to set foot on Shadowood I would slay him with a single slash of my sword!" He pulled out an imaginary sword and made a few dancing slices at the air with his arm. "Aha, you villain! Die!" He thrust the imaginary sword into the ground and swept Arabella a courtly bow. "There you are, my dear. All taken care of. Fret no longer."

Phillip, who was apparently accustomed to nothing but applause for his antics, met her lack of response with a quizzical look. His brow immediately cleared into smooth solicitation, however, and he patted her hand absently. "Never mind, m'dear. I'm sure it's quite dull for you here now that your beloved brother has sailed for home, but all will be put to rights when we go to Williamsburg next month." He clasped his hands behind his back and began his mincing promenade again. "The governor has invited us to dine with him, which I am sure will please you immensely. Only do me one service, dear wife, and pray refrain yourself from infatuated raptures over this Fox creature. It is quite a sore subject for his lordship, you know, and I can't help but think how the last time we dined together our meal was almost ruined by the selfsame villain—Le Renard, that is."

Arabella, who had been accompanying him at a restrained, sedate pace, now stopped, her temper roused almost to the bursting point. His patronizing, his nonsensical chatter, even his mindless lectures, she could endure to a point, but that he would accuse her of "infatuated raptures . . . !" She gathered up her skirts and turned to go.

A look of bored impatience crossed his face at the expression of flaring indignation on hers. "Come, come, Arabella, I ask so little. It is only that I hear so much of this fellow that I could be quite jealous, you know"—he cast her a self-satisfied smirk—"were I not so certain that the heart of my lovely bride belongs to no one but me."

His words almost stopped Arabella. If only he knew! she reflected with some bitterness. On the verge of whirling to face him with the truth written in the contempt gleaming in her eyes, caution halted her. Phillip might be a fool and a coward she realized, but there would be no point to making life more difficult for herself by goading him.

She squared her shoulders, swallowed her temper, and, without turning at all, replied, "Good day, sir," then retreated at a stately pace into the house.

25 August, 1773

How unkinde is Phillip to me, mocking our marriage in that Odious way of his. As once I Looked Forward to a Season at Williamsburg now I dreade it, For there I will be too much in my Husbande's Company and will have no chance of seeing my Fox again ... Caroline is Right, though she could not have Knowne. ... He is myne.

Le Renard ... What a figure of Romance and Mysterie he is! And only a Lande such as this could produce this man—Wilde, Untamed, Living his Life to Suit Himself ... He is the stuff of which Novels are Made, yet to think that I know him ... That he has invaded the very room in which I sleep ...

All the Governor's men are upon Him, yet he Manages to Elude them all, and though he Sounds quyte Dastardly, Sam, who seems Most Knowledgeable about such Things, says Le Renard is the Most Revered Among the Patriots, for whose Cause he Fights ... I know little of Causes and Patriots. I know only of the Man who

160

held me in his Arms . . . I Have seen his Strength and felt his Gentleness, and I long to see him once More . . . But he has not Again come to Me, and I despair at tymes of our ever meeting Again. For How Should I Finde Him when others have Failed? And How foolish he would be, to Come to Me again while I sleep under the Roof of his Sworn Enemy . . . Yet how I pray he is Foolish! I say true, I do not know how long I can bear this life tied to an Insufferable Man such as Phillip without the small breath of hope Le Renard brings into my life . . .

Perhaps, when Phillip has once again left me for the Lures of Frivolous Pleasures, Le Renard will deem it safe to Visit me Again and I will have sustenance for yet another space of Tyme . . .

Chapter IX

During the following two weeks, the Fox and his gallant raiders grew ever bolder, possibly in reaction to the news of further royal sanctions against the Colonies that drifted down from the north, or possibly, as one *Gazette* article speculated, in preparation for the reassembling of the House of Burgesses in September. The House had been dissolved by an angry governor in March, when disagreement over royal policy had become so heated as to make the convention entirely unmanageable, and perhaps this latest twist in the rebel raids was meant to warn the governor that, should he consider such rash action again, he would have more to answer to than a few disgruntled legislators. This explanation seemed most likely to Arabella, especially since the Fox had turned his attention away from the crowded cities and busy harbors of Virginia and toward the wealthy planters along the James River.

The most recent episode had occurred at a plantation not half a day's ride from Shadowood. An empty warehouse had been set afire while the contents of another was confiscated. No real damage was done and no one was injured, but had the fire not been spotted by the overseer, who was late returning from a neighboring farm after an evening of cards and drinking, the flames undoubtedly would have spread to the warehouses filled with dried tobacco and an entire year's work—and the fortune of the plantation—would have gone up in a matter of minutes. And was it coincidence that the owner of the plantation was quite vocal in his despite for the patriots and his support of the king?

There had been other incidents. A barge loaded with indigo and bound for the harbor had been sunk in the middle of the night and within shouting distance of the hills of Shadowood. A gathering of gentleman planters, stopping for a polite game of cards at a neighboring plantation after a successful horse-buying trip to Richmond, had been disrupted by a torch thrown through the window and rushed outside just in time to see several hundred pounds worth of prime horseflesh being driven off into the night. Coaches had been stopped, robbed, and overturned on the Williamsburg road. They had been nuisance raids, all of them, but nonetheless disturbing.

The other men of the county were already talking of organizing a posse to track down and exterminate the Fox; Phillip scoffed at their concern and entertained himself with bad jokes about the activities of the renegade.

Arabella did not understand the differences between the colonists and the King, and she did not care. She was not interested in the sentiments of the patriots, nor was she particularly absorbed by the rhetoric that was tossed back and forth among Virginians regarding their purpose. It was Le Renard who had captured her imagination and had stirred her romantic fantasies, for he seemed a dashing hero from times of old, cleverly outmaneuvering those who sought to oppress him, striking a blow for the justness of his beliefs. He was, quite simply, a symbol of all Arabella would like to be: free, unfettered, laughing in the face of convention and striking down all that would bind her.

Phillip had departed that morning for Williamsburg, leaving Arabella with numerous preparations to complete before she could close the house at Shadowood and join him in town. Her days were filled and eventide brought the slumber of exhaustion, and there was little time left even for daydreams. Of uttermost necessity was a complete inventory of the household. In Williamsburg she would place orders for imported supplies that needed replenishing, and the inventory she made now would serve as a guide until the process was repeated next summer. She listed the contents and the value of each item methodically, taking one room at a time, counting each cone of sugar, each cask of wine, each napkin and pillowslip, wick and candle. In the huge warehouses by the river, William was doing the same with bales of tobacco and sheaves not yet dried, so that by the end of the count the value of Shadowood and all its accoutrements would be known to the last farthing.

The library was the last room that Arabella tackled. It was a fine library, she admitted, certainly as fine as that of Chatley Hall, for it was a mark of a man's breeding that he owned many books, though no one dared ask how many of them he had read. Arabella doubted with utmost sincerity that Phillip had ever perused a single volume.

The shelves were lined with leather-bound works of the great thinkers of the world: Suetonius's *Lives of the Caesars* along with Virgil, Cicero, Herodotus, Socrates, and Plato. In addition there were more modern volumes: *The Prince* by the Italian Machiavelli, the works of William Shakespeare and his peer, Sir Francis Bacon. There were novels, too, by Smollett and Fielding.

On another shelf were kept the books that Sam often borrowed, the works of Locke, Voltaire, Rousseau, and other philosophers. It was among these volumes that Arabella noticed several blank spaces between red leather covers. She gave a cursory look around the room, although she could hardly believe that Phillip would be interested in any sort of philosophy that did not involve self-indulgence or hedonism. It was obvious that the missing volumes were in Sam's quarters, and she knew that before she could complete the inventory they would have to be returned to the shelf.

She made her way to Sam's quarters at the upper rear of the house. Sam was helping William at the warehouses and she entered his small room without hesitation. There on a makeshift shelf behind a table were the missing books. She picked them up, reminding herself to give Sam a lecture about returning books to their proper places, and from the pages of one a white piece of paper drifted down on the hot air, fluttering in the sunlight that streamed in the windows to land softly on the wide plank floor. She bent to pick it up, meaning to return the note to its place, when one word, written in an unfamiliar hand, caught her eye. *Fox.*

Arabella wasted no time wrestling with her conscience. Her heart had leapt into an incredulous rhythm, and with hasty, uncoordinated hands, she snapped out the creases in the paper and read the note, once quickly and then more carefully, committing the line to memory. *Tell the Fox the hunt is on for Friday Next.* Arabella's breath lodged in her throat and her heart ceased its beating for the space of a split second then resumed again, louder and more volatile than before. The Fox! Hurriedly, with the automatic movements of habit, not thought, she returned the books to Sam's shelf. The note she tucked in her sleeve, and with all the nonchalance she could muster, she quickly covered the distance from Sam's chamber to her own.

Once there, she sank to an embroidered sewing chair. Her breath came with difficulty in the early September heat of the upper floor. She pulled out the note and read it again, though its words were etched indelibly in her mind. Sam had in his possession a note obviously meant for Le Renard; he was only waiting for an opportunity to pass it on. All the while she had been wondering how she might see the Fox again, the link had been there—in her own house. The hand of Fate, which had guided her steps to this new land and into the arms of one so filled with the spirit of adventure as the Fox, had once again, in its infinite wisdom, reached out to touch her.

In retrospect, she saw how blind she had been not to have guessed before. Sam, so well spoken and educated, with all his talk of freedom and politics, and his defense of the rebels ... Had it been her own prejudice that had refused to allow her to attach importance to the behavior of a servant? She had never once guessed that he could be a part of Le Renard's band of raiders.

Arabella's pulses were racing and energy flowed through her like flood waters racing through narrow banks. She had her connection; dare she summon the courage to use it? This was her chance, perhaps her only chance, to close her hand about what she wanted, to experience the grandest adventure of all, the seeking of her own destiny.

Arabella carefully folded the note into her sleeve

again and, with her eyes fixed upon distant horizons, began to think.

Arabella had taken to riding early in the morning to avoid the stifling heat of the sun. But on this occasion, too excited by the boldness of her plans and too restless with urgency to stay inside the house, she had taken her horse into the cool of the forest trail at midday.

There was a different aura to the stillness of the earth at this time of day, a shadowed eeriness, an uneasy expectancy that seemed to hide adventure behind every tree and bush. *He may have traversed these very woods,* she thought to herself, and the realization tingled through her to produce a mixture of anticipation and fear. *He may have brushed this very branch aside, here, as I am doing, and he may have passed upon this very spot to look down at the lay of the land below . . . He may at this very moment be lying in wait, behind that tangle of vines or around that boulder there, watching me . . .*

A branch cracked loudly and Arabella started, then reined in her horse and looked about frantically. The horse gave an annoyed whinny, yet his ears pricked up in sympathy with his mistress's alarm as a squirrel, chattering furiously, rattled the leaves of the tree overhead. Arabella gave an abashed grimace and nudged her horse onward, toward the inviting stream below.

Because of the long, hot days and the absence of rainfall, the wells at Shadowood were running low. It happened annually, Sam had explained, and by October, when the rains began to fall again, any threat of drought would be alleviated. Until that time, water was to be conserved, and it was with regret that Arabella had been forced to give up her daily bath.

When she had come upon the small, spring-fed pond in the woods on one of her daily rides, she could not resist the temptation to bathe there, and since that first day she had returned each morning.

She knew that Phillip would be shocked at her private ablutions and Caroline scandalized, but Arabella had few reservations. As a child when she had roamed the gentle hills of Devon, she had longed to plunge into the slow-moving streams, but all her nanny had ever allowed was a modest wetting of the toes. When she had grown older, she had slipped away and had bared her legs to the knees in the stream that ran into the mill pond, but in Devon she had never had the privacy that she had here in Virginia. Now at Shadowood and mistress of the great plantation, she could do as she pleased.

She tied her horse to a low-hanging branch and extracted a linen towel and bar of soap from her saddle bag. Then she quickly undressed, slipping off her riding habit and tossing it across the fork of a branch. She pulled off her boots and tossed them upon a bed of ferns, and then she hesitated, her hands on the buttons of her chemise. Once more Arabella glanced around the woods. The trees overhead formed a cathedral of green, through which could be seen only shadowy patches of afternoon sky. All was quiet and still except for the whistling of a mockingbird upon the limb of an elm. With a little shrug, Arabella removed her chemise and pantalettes and stepped into the water.

Hidden in a thick patch of wild ivy, the man on the hill above her drew in his breath sharply as he watched Arabella's gliding descent into the water. She had not seen him, even though her eyes had studied her surroundings carefully before she had stepped into the pool. He had thought that she was only stopping to water her mount, but she had stunned him into immobility when she had begun to disrobe. Still as a statue, he had sat upon his horse and watched.

She was beautifully formed, this Mistress Everett. Her legs were long and slender, flowing into strong hips that seemed to have been made for bearing children and for giving pleasure to a man. Her waist was small enough to span with his two large hands. And her breasts . . . As he watched the woman slipping into the stream below, he could feel the heat rising within him, quite a separate warmth from the sun that filtered through the trees and burned upon his shoulders. This was an inner fire, one that flamed but did not consume as his eyes surveyed Arabella's slender form. Her breasts were creamy orbs, high and firm, their pink tips hard and taut as her body registered the coolness of the water. He could not help but imagine their pebbly peaks rising beneath the brush of his fingers, his tongue . . .

He knew he should not be in this place. He had concerns elsewhere that demanded his presence and there would be danger if he were to be discovered on Shadowood land. His business here was finished for a time and his wisest course would be to return to his ship, to organize matters for the next phase of his operation. And indeed, that had been where he had been bound, when he had happened to spy Lady Arabella. And now the urgencies of grander objectives were all but subdued by this new, more demanding need.

Arabella slid into the water, not at all dismayed by its chill. The cold was a relief from the discomfort of the summer day and the fever into which she had worked herself since her discovery of Sam's note. This was a needed respite, she mused, a time to reflect carefully and not impulsively, and the temperature of the water provided just the environment in which to do so.

Adjusting to the coolness with just a slight shiver, she went about her bath matter-of-factly, almost absently, her mind upon more weighty concerns than ridding her body of the day's stickiness. By tonight she could be in his arms, she thought dreamily—tonight, with the lingering scent of soap and sunshine on her skin . . .

He watched her rub the soap up and down one creamy arm before moving the bar to wash the valley between her breasts. As she lightly stroked each breast with actions as unconscious and as innocent as those of a child of nature, the man hidden in the trees moistened his dry lips with the tip of his tongue. It had been a long time since he had had a woman—too damn long. Why else would he find himself so consumed by the very wench who could be his undoing? Everything about her suggested danger and everything within him pulsed with need.

He tried to still his restless imagination, but his hands upon the reins were damp with sweat and his heart drummed powerfully in his chest. His clothing felt too tight at every point it touched his skin and the temperature of the day seemed at the same time suffocating and invigorating. *What fools,* he thought. *What fools they make of us all* . . . And yet, helpless and aching, he watched the movements of the woman in the water.

Arabella glided to the edge of the pool and, balancing one leg upon the rock, began to soap her calf and her thigh. He followed the motions of her hands with fascination, imagining his hands there on the smooth, satiny flesh, sliding up the wet, slick thigh to curl in the thatch of hair between her legs, perhaps to probe, delicately, oh so delicately, the heated secrets within . . . Would she be shocked, the very well-brought-up Lady Arabella Winters, to be touched in that way? Had her adventures in the game of love yet taught her about the fulfillment of a woman's pleasure? He found satisfaction in imagining that, though he might not be the first to have her, he should be the first to teach her . . .

These were dangerous, treacherous thoughts. He was much too wise to ever succumb to them. He was certain of it.

Her bath complete, Arabella dipped once, twice, and then again into the water to rinse the soapy residue from her skin. Reaching for the root of a tree, she pulled herself out of the pond, exposing to him the smooth line that flowed from creamy breast to waist and hips. She was just below him now, not more than twenty-five yards away, so close he could see the shiny little beads of water that trickled down from her shoulders between her breasts. One drop hung upon a glistening areola like dew, and again he wet his lips with his tongue. The engorged heat between his legs was insistent, powerful, painful.

Arabella reached for her towel and began to dry, not hurrying her task at all but appearing to luxuriate in the freshness of the air and the warmth of the sun that radiated in dappled patterns across her skin—the skin of a woman who responded to touch, who knew the sensations of pleasure and who welcomed them, eagerly.

How had it begun, he wondered, this insane wanting? Had it been an accidental meeting, a trifling mischief, a private joke upon the bride of Phillip Everett? And how had it come to this, spying upon her in the woods like a common thief, his body in torture and his mind aflame? There were other women in the colony, lusty, bawdy women who were eager to accommodate and demanded nothing in return. None of them could threaten him as did Lady Arabella, none of them could wound him . . . and none of them could stir him as much as did Lady Arabella. Winters, Mistress Everett.

Perspiration gathered beneath the thickness of his queue and rolled down beneath his shoulder blades. The urgency of his desire was hard and throbbing against the tight cut of his breeches. He could have her now; he knew it. He could swoop down and overpower her on the floor of the forest, using the soft green ferns for a bed here in the stillness of the day. She would resist at first, shocked, and would perhaps even fight him, but she would yield at last to their mutual pleasure . . .

A less controlled man, or one with less to lose, would surely have followed that instinct then. But he was well schooled in the ways of reason and accustomed to mastery—even of himself, when the occasion called for it. He sat still and watched as the lady, now dressed and groomed, untied her horse and headed back toward the plantation. As soon as the sound of her hoofbeats covered his, he turned and rode away, in the opposite direction.

Chapter X

Arabella waited until that evening to call Sam to her. She sat in the library behind Phillip's huge mahogany desk, a delicate figure caught in the light of two great candelabra. Her inventory lists lay beside her hands, which were folded tightly to keep them from trembling with excitement. Sam stood before her, seemingly at ease, but Arabella was certain she noticed a difference in his stance. He appeared more guarded than usual and very alert as he balanced on the balls of his feet, his white shirt and trousers gleaming in the candlelight.

She had chosen the library because it seemed the seat of power in the house, the one place in which she might intimidate Sam, and to gain the truth from him she knew she would have to use every advantage she could muster. As Sam stood quietly before her, Arabella chatted idly about the inventory and then casually, offhandedly, gestured to the empty spaces on the library shelves.

"Two books seem to be missing, Sam. I wonder if you might know where they are?"

"Yes, Missus. In my room. Master Phillip—"

"Yes, I know. Master Phillip allows you to use the library." She smiled up at him innocently. "And does

175

he also allow you to use his books for concealment of secret and treasonous messages?"

Sam did not blanch, nor did his eyes flicker. "I don't know what you're talking about, Mistress. The books are on my shelf. I'll go fetch them now."

"No, Sam. No, you will not." Arabella leaned forward across the desk, her palms braced on its spotless surface, her face tense with determination. "I have the note, Sam, and the game is over. You might as well tell me now how long you have been a member of Le Renard's band."

She sat back, pleased at the way she had thrown down the gauntlet with no preamble or warning. It would take a very clever man to elude her now.

And Sam was very clever. "You must be mistaken, Missus. I know nothing of a note. And all I know of Le Renard is what I hear."

His face had taken on a blank, stubborn look that Arabella found intensely frustrating. But she did not let her impatience register in her voice as she replied coolly, "We could bandy words about for hours, Sam—I accusing and you protesting. But why don't we look at the evidence, the note I found." With a flourish Arabella pulled the paper from her sleeve and flung it onto the desk. "You may deliver it to the Fox with my compliments . . . and a condition."

Sam looked at her blankly.

"I would meet with Le Renard," announced Arabella smoothly, "and you will arrange the matter for me."

Sam said, "I'm afraid I can't help you, Missus. But even if I could, I'm sure Master Phillip—"

"You will say nothing of this to Master Phillip!" she hissed, for the first time on the edge of losing her hard-won control. Curses upon the man! she raged inwardly. He was going to be a trying opponent, and her impatience, excitement, and wonder over her own daring were rapidly consuming her, making it difficult for her to remain reasonable. She had come so close. Must he waste her time with these senseless evasions?

She sat back, took a calming breath, and played her final card. "Or perhaps my husband *would* be interested in how a message meant for a notorious enemy of the crown came to be in the hands of his most trusted servant. Perhaps even the governor would be interested. I am on quite good terms with his lordship, you know. I'm sure that if I were to send a message to him, he would be here before daybreak."

And now she thought she finally saw a flicker of recognition—or alarm—in those dark, inscrutable eyes. She pressed her advantage. "All I ask is that you take me to the Fox, much in the same manner as you would have taken this note to him. That is not so difficult, is it?"

Again Sam's face hardened. "It is impossible, Missus. I do not know the Fox."

Arabella restrained the urge to swear aloud. Her nerves were stretched as tight as piano wire, but she bit back her impetuosity and said in a voice as deadly calm as she could make it, "But *I* know him, Sam. I know the identity of the Fox."

Her words hung heavily in the air, but Sam showed no sign of relenting.

Arabella's threat was nothing more than bluff and bravado, and she feared that Sam recognized this only too well. Still, she was determined to press her advantage. "A word in the governor's ear, Sam, is all that it would take, just a hint that I have the key to the puzzle of the Fox, a whisper that Le Renard uses a servant at Shadowood to pass his messages. Such information might very well bring the governor's troops to Master Everett's plantation. That could be

177

embarrassing for all of us and quite ruinous for your master . . ." Arabella spoke calmly and evenly. "It all depends on you, Sam. Will you take my message to the Fox?"

Sam's shoulders sagged slightly, and Arabella knew she had hit the mark in threatening his beloved Phillip.

"I can try, Missus."

"You will do better than that. Tell Le Renard I want to see him within twenty-four hours—here, at Shadowood." He knows the way, she added silently.

"That may not be possible, Mistress Arabella."

Arabella nodded. "Twenty-four hours, Sam. No more."

The large black man sighed deeply. "And if I see this Fox, what shall I tell him you want from him?"

"Just what I have told you. I want to see him. He will understand."

Sam spared her one intensely puzzled look, then bowed deeply and left the room.

When the heavy door closed behind him, Arabella felt some of the tension slide from her shoulders. Her hands trembled in the aftermath of the confrontation from the extent of her own daring. She was now within hours of seeing the Fox—mere hours. Perhaps it would even be tonight.

She was still keyed up and somewhat disturbed over the interview. Sam had been her friend, and she had threatened him, forced him to choose between Phillip and the Fox. He would think her the lowest kind of traitor now, for not only had she turned against him, but she had also made it clear that she would not hesitate to bring down ruin upon her own husband's head. Her conscience tormented her momentarily, then became still. In reality she would not have done anything to harm either Phillip or Sam, but it had been important for her to make Sam believe she would have.

178

It had been the only way for her to see the Fox—the only way.

The scene was an innocent one—two men out for an early morning ride, stopping among a stand of longleaf pines. Above them the bright flash of a bluejay cut the still air. One of the waiting men was tall and fair; the other heavier and more rough hewn. They waited in companionable silence, soothing their restless horses, ostensibly relaxed and enjoying the peaceful morning. But their eyes gave them away, for they were wary and searching, alert to the smallest sign of anything unusual.

A third man appeared on horseback, racing up the hill toward them. When he reached them he reined in sharply, his black face shining with sweat. "We've got trouble," he announced without ceremony. "Lady Arabella has found a message to the Fox."

The stocky man swore sharply under his breath.

Le Renard, his face implacable, extended his hand for the note. He glanced at it briefly, then pocketed it. "She returned it to you. No matter."

Sam's face was grim. "The message comes with a condition. She demands a meeting with you."

The Fox laughed at this, throwing back his head and shaking his hair in the bright sunlight. "The lady is hardly in a position to demand anything, I think. Why so grim, old friend?"

"There is more." Sam took a breath. "She threatens to go to the governor with what she knows."

Suddenly the slight twinge of a muscle marred the smooth, handsome face of Le Renard. He looked at the other man steadily. "And what, exactly, does she know?"

Sam met his gaze unwaveringly, although what it

179

cost him to do so no one would ever know. "She says she knows the Fox, knows his identity. But that I can't believe." Still looking his leader straight in the eye, he went on. "She does know enough to bring the governor's troops down upon me and Shadowood. Apparently she considers her husband—and myself—an expedient sacrifice for her cause."

"Damnit!" swore the shorter horseman, and in his agitation his mount veered and snorted nervously. "I told you, didn't I? Now the viperous wench has us where she wants us! Nothing but trouble. I knew it from the beginning, treacherous to the skin—"

"Enough!" snapped Le Renard, and the silence was immediate. He spoke in a moment, more calmly, to Sam. "And what does she expect to come of this meeting? Did she tell you that?"

"She said," replied Sam simply, "that you would understand."

A small, completely mirthless smile touched the lips of Le Renard. Oh, yes. He understood. But did she?

Unbidden came the memory of her body, smooth and lithe and glistening in the sun as she stepped onto the riverbank . . . Immediately he squelched the vision and the impulses it had stirred. This was no time for *jeu d'amour*. Whatever her intent, Lady Arabella had made it clear that she could present a clear and imminent danger. She would have to be dealt with.

Sam said courageously, "I take responsibility for the mishap. The note was delivered to me only yesterday, in a niche in the gatepost. All I had to do was keep it safe for a few hours." He swallowed. "I've forgotten, these past months, my first impression of Lady Arabella. She is indeed too clever for her own good, and I was a fool to grow lax around her. I can't excuse my carelessness."

"Nor can I," replied Le Renard coldly. "However,

the deed is done now, and we must take steps to ensure that the situation grows no worse." And then, thoughtfully, he added, "I do believe Lady Arabella's somewhat . . . uncertain temperament . . . would benefit from a cruise on the James. Bring her to me tonight. Arrange it, Sam."

"Are you mad?" cried his lieutenant. "After what she's—"

Le Renard's voice cut through his protests sharply. "See to it, Sam."

With a gesture that could have been a salute or a sign of resignation, Sam turned his horse and retreated down the hill, riding cautiously out of the pines and across a field to Shadowood.

"Come," said Le Renard, jerking his own mount around. He suddenly seemed to be in much improved humor. "We have preparations to make for the arrival of a female guest."

His friend, still seething, burst out harshly, "You are mad! After she's proved her treachery, you'd bring her into our very camp? Have you any idea of the risk you're taking?"

"Enough," cautioned the Fox again, though more mildly now. "We are in the business of taking risks. And if we do not deal with her now, she will only become more persistent, if I know the lady at all."

They rode a time in silence, and at last the other man spoke again. "What do you intend to do with her?"

Le Renard's lips curved into a slow smile, but his voice was cold and quite matter-of-fact. "Whatever I have to," he informed the other, "to keep her silent."

His companion felt a sudden chill as he studied the resolute profile of the man who rode beside him. Friends, confidants, companions in battle, they had ridden together on many nights, facing dangers and even risking their lives for each other. They had shared the closest secrets and the deepest pains, and he thought he came as close as any man ever would to knowing this enigmatic personage who called himself Le Renard. But there were times, times like these, when this man for whom he would have laid down his life without question was a stranger to him—when, in fact, he even frightened him.

"Sometimes," he said slowly, quietly, "I think I don't really know who you are at all."

Le Renard turned in the saddle to look at him, moving his large shoulders easily and gracefully as he tilted his head in a moment of consideration. His smile was absent; his eyes cold. "And sometimes," he replied as though to the distance, "I scarcely know myself."

Arabella's needle stabbed impatiently at the silk scarf, which for weeks she had been attempting to embroider. She found no comfort in the task, for she had never been of a temperament to enjoy the ladylike pursuits, and tonight her concentration was even more sorely tried than usual. The clumsy movements of her fingers did little to distract her mind or soothe her nerves as she waited for Sam.

"God's teeth!" Arabella dropped the scarf into her lap and sucked the tip of her finger, which she had pricked with the needle. A small red drop of blood marred the sheen of the imported material. "Blast it all," she swore again when she saw the stain, and her mouth curved downward with irritation. She rang impatiently for a servant.

The servants had been avoiding her all day, and with just cause. Her nerves had been in such a state that she had snapped at anyone who crossed her path. She had berated her poor maid for not being gentle enough when she brushed her hair, upbraided the cook for

182

overdone pork roast, and caused a scullery girl to drop a large bowl of applesauce when she had stormed into the warming kitchen to complain about a spot of tarnish on the candlesticks. And the tension had mounted as the day progressed.

Now, as swiftly and as silently as a mouse, a serving girl poked her head into the parlor and bobbed a nervous curtsy. Her eyes were white rimmed and wary. Arabella commanded curtly, "Bring me a cup of tea." Then, making an effort to gentle her voice, she added, "And a damp cloth, please. I seem to have pricked my finger."

With another quick curtsy, the girl scurried off, glad to have gotten away so easily.

The silence in the parlor was broken only by the ticking of the ornate clock above the mantel, and with each tick the sound grew louder and louder until Arabella could feel it reverberating within her head. The pounding in her temples, the deadly silence of the room, and the endless wait made her want to scream aloud. Instead, she deliberately took a deep, calming breath and tried to think of other matters.

She looked down at her needlework, then tossed it aside. This was not the way she had planned to spend this evening, sitting in her own parlor, sewing absurd designs on a swatch of silk with only an empty house as her companion. And it was no use. She could not think of other matters.

Soon she would be with him—with Le Renard. Sam would not fail her. He would not dare. It would be tonight.

What would it be like to be with him again? Would he be shocked at her brazenness? No, she thought not. He was not a man easily shocked. This time they would talk, but there would be more. Arabella thought of his kisses, remembered his caresses. That was what she

183

wanted—to be held in his arms once again. She felt feverish in her need for him, as though his arms were already about her, his breath already warming her . . .

Excitement for what she could hardly believe would come to pass swept through her and made her dizzy. This was an adventure more wonderful than any she had ever read, a drama more daring than even she could imagine. Yet it was real. And she, Lady Arabella Winters, had the courage to carry it out.

Arabella glanced at the clock. It was almost nine o'clock and there had been no sign of Sam. Yet it did not occur to her that he would disappoint her. She would not let go of her victory so easily, not when she was so close.

"Your tea, Miss Arabella."

He entered the room quietly for so large a man, causing her to start. "Sam!" The pink color of alarm and quickening anticipation stained her cheeks and brightened her eyes. It had begun. At last, the waiting was over.

He set the tray on the table and passed her cup to her with a bow. "I passed the girl in the hall and took this from her. I thought you wouldn't want anyone to overhear the news I've brought."

"Of course." Arabella tried to maintain a semblance of calm as she sipped the tea. "Have you arranged—" She broke off the question with a lift of her brow.

Sam nodded. "Plans have been made, but first we need to talk. There are certain precautions," he said vaguely.

Arabella nodded. The tea was lukewarm, but she drank it anyway. "I understand, Sam. This must be undertaken in absolute secrecy, and I am ready. Now"—she took a final sip of the tea and set the cup aside—"I am weary of this delay." She tried to inject authority into her tone, but the words did not come out

184

as she had planned. Her mouth seemed dry and she had difficulty forming the next sentence. She swallowed hard, then wet her lips with the tip of her tongue. "If you will be so kind . . . as to . . . get on with it . . ."

"As you wish, Missus. The gentleman in question has requested a slight alteration in your plans . . ." Sam's voice seemed far away and there was a ringing in Arabella's ears as she struggled to rise. She reached out a hand to Sam for assistance, but his image seemed to dance playfully before her, first moving away, then coming closer.

Shakily, Arabella reached out a hand behind her, grabbing for the back of the divan. Then the room tilted crazily around her and she felt herself slipping into unconsciousness.

Chapter XI

Arabella's eyes opened slowly and painfully. Misty darkness surrounded her, pierced by a fuzzy glow of light in the corner that tilted with a throb of pain as she attempted to move her head. Her arms and her legs were paralyzed and there was a powerful aching in her shoulders; her mouth was dry, her tongue immobile, and gradually she became aware that the cutting tautness across her cheeks was the handkerchief that held the gag in place. She tried to swallow and could not; tried to move her arms and discovered that her wrists were bound behind her with rough ropes. Her ankles were lashed together in like manner, and she lay at an awkward angle on her side upon a narrow cot. The cot seemed to be moving, rocking ever so gently up and down, swaying as that diffuse glow of light at the edge of her vision swayed, producing nausea in the pit of her stomach. She moaned softly and closed her eyes, seeking balance, willing the nightmare to go away. She heard a movement.

"So, Lady Arabella." The voice was hoarse and airy, terrifying by its sound yet causing her heart to lurch with a thread of recognition. "You are among us again. Welcome aboard."

Arabella opened her eyes and a mixture of shock and relief jolted her into complete consciousness. It was he—the Fox. She had been taken to him. Whatever disorientation she had experienced upon first awakening dissolved like morning fog. She searched the dark, making out the shape of a small, unfamiliar room lit only by the low flame of a single candle in the background; it was low-ceilinged, sparsely furnished. She twisted her head to look directly before her, and there, lounging in a chair drawn up beside her cot, was the figure of a man. He was masked, his face shapeless and diffuse in the dark. He wore a white shirt, no neck cloth, dark breeches, and riding boots. He sat back negligently in the chair, one ankle crossed upon his knee. The candlelight gleamed purposefully upon the blade of a short, wicked-looking dagger that he held in casual readiness in his hand.

Arabella's eyes went from the weapon to the figure before her, and her heart began to pound an uncertain pattern of alarm. This was not how she had imagined greeting him again—bound and gagged, staring into the cruel edge of a blade. Something was wrong. There was a misunderstanding. She tried to sit up and failed; tried to speak and remembered too late the impediment in her mouth; the sound came out as little more than a dry croak.

"Ah, so you would speak." There was satisfaction in his tone, and in an instant his shadow blotted out the light. Rough fingers fumbled with the knot of material at the back of her head; several strands of hair were pulled away along with her handkerchief and tears stung her eyes. Impersonally, he plucked the inner wad of material from her mouth and tossed it onto the floor. He stood slightly above her, and there was cruelty in his voice as he demanded shortly, "Speak then. I have little enough time to waste upon you this night."

188

Arabella could not have spoken had she wished to do so. Her mouth was dry, her vocal chords numb and swollen, her head swimming with confusion. She stared at the expanse of chest covered in white muslin, the flow of a full sleeve, the beginning of a strong throat, and before she could so much as attempt to moisten her cracked lips, he made a sudden movement and she felt the tip of his blade rest beneath her chin.

"Think not that I fear to use this." His voice was the hiss of a snake, the waiting growl of an animal stalking its prey; it chilled her blood to ice. His eyes were coal-like slits gleaming from the depths of the mask, his face a demonic blur above her. A slight increase of pressure upon the blade forced her to tilt her head back and she could only stare at him in mute terror, eyes widening, heart lunging to her throat. "Speak, woman!" he commanded, and his hand tightened upon the hilt of the blade. "What business do you have with me?"

"I . . . don't . . . I can't . . ." Her lips were numb and she slurred the words; fright choked her voice and made the sounds almost unintelligible. Her throat was still dry and aching, and the last syllable dissolved into a weak cough. "Please . . ."

He leaned back somewhat and, in doing so, eased the pressure upon the weapon at her throat. She could feel his quizzical gaze on her, and the time during which they were so poised—he above and holding her life upon the tip of his blade, she below, wretched and helpless—seemed interminable. And then he said thoughtfully, unexpectedly, "You have been bound some time." The dagger came away from her throat. "No doubt you could not speak if you meant to. I will free your hands and your feet so that you may sit up and drink, and then we will have a nice long talk, you and I."

In a swift, efficient movement he slashed through the

189

ropes that bound her ankles, and then her wrists. The blade came so close to her skin that she could not prevent a strangulated cry, but her hands fell free, throbbing and tingling, when he stepped back.

Stiffly she sat up, wincing as she braced her hands against the cot to do so. He was a huge, looming shadow above her and her heart was pounding. This was not what she had meant to come to pass at all. This was not the way she had intended it to be—held captive in this strange, dark place with a man who meant to kill her. Terror and confusion chased themselves around and around in her mind and she understood nothing except that she would have to get away.

She sat on the edge of the cot, every muscle in her body trembling as she rubbed her bruised and aching wrists and willed life back into her numb feet. Her panic-stricken eyes took in what they could of the place in which she was imprisoned. They registered a chair, a table, the low-burning candle. On the wall was some kind of drawing—a map, perhaps. She noted a trunk, several hooks for clothes, and, directly opposite, a door.

In a moment, he turned away and strode toward the table. She did not follow him with her eyes but heard the clink of a water pitcher against a cup. And then, without thinking or giving herself a moment to lose her courage, she bolted for the door.

She stumbled and almost fell on feet that shot arrows of pain upward the moment they hit the floor; she lurched forward and her hand touched the latch. She struggled, she tugged, but it would not budge. A choked sound of helplessness and terror escaped her and she tore at the latch, banged her open hands upon the door, and then his voice reached her, quite calm and somewhat amused.

"A valiant effort, my dear, and quite predictable, but

as you see, there is no escape. The door is locked from the outside and I do not have the key, so I'm afraid you are bound to stay here until I call my man to release you."

With her hands splayed helplessly against the door, Arabella turned to look at him, knowing from the tone of his voice and his casual, unconcerned stance that he spoke the truth. Slowly, the horror of her situation began to form and mount; it seeped into her pores and built upon itself with each long and painfully drawn breath. What had she done to herself? What incredible, foolish thing had she done? It had been a jest—no more—an adventure; a daydream born of desperation and loneliness that reality had turned into the starkest of nightmares. This man was no gentle lover of her rose-colored fantasies, no dashing hero of embellished legend. This was the man who, for years, had made ruthless raids upon innocent citizens, who had outwitted the governor and all his troops, who struck the unguarded in the dark of the night and made no effort to repent for it. He was an arsonist, a thief, a ruthless criminal who knew no remorse. He had had her drugged and bound and gagged; he had held a knife to her throat. He was clever enough to elude capture by the best of the king's men; he would not be careless enough to let her escape. He was the Fox, and she was at his mercy.

He gestured politely with the cup. "Will you sit?"

On knees that would barely support her, Arabella backed across the room, never once removing her eyes from his shadowy form. She sank down onto the cot again.

He placed the cup in her hands. The dagger was still unsheathed and held with unconcerned competence in his hand. She could not seem to keep from staring at it, even as with trembling hands she brought the cup to

191

her parched lips, nor as he moved again to resume his seat in the chair opposite her.

He sat there, leaning back comfortably, the flat blade of the knife resting upon his knee, and he simply watched her. He was always careful to keep the light behind him, and Arabella still could see nothing of his face and little of his figure. She sipped the tepid water, casting about frantically in her mind for something to do, something to say, that would eventually lead her out of this hideous situation. She tried to compose herself, to think calmly, but the cup shook in her hands, splashing water onto her fingers and the bodice of her dress, and rational thought seemed to be beyond her, for there seemed to be no escape. At last, when the silence could be borne no longer, she blurted hoarsely, despairingly, "What . . . do you mean to do with me? What is it that you want of me?"

His reply was lazy, his fingers upon the blade of the dagger caressing. "But it is I who should ask that of you. You, after all, requested to be brought here, and we have complied." Now his tone grew sharp. "What is it that *you* want of *me*, Lady Arabella?"

In a swirling vision wild with hysteria, it came back to her. There she had stood, taunting Sam with the purloined note, demanding to be taken to the Fox, dreaming insane, schoolgirl dreams of a romantic reunion with the dashing hero of her imagination . . . It had been a game, that was all, a silly game in which all the characters had lived solely in her mind, where she could manipulate them at will. But *this* was no game. This was real and dangerous, and nothing, nothing she could do or say could help her now. She had threatened the identity of the Fox and his band, and she had been foolish beyond belief.

"Sam . . ." she began to babble, "Sam knows where I am, and should anything happen to me . . . he will not

192

let you harm me . . ."

A sound, short and derisive, escaped him, and his words were harsh. "Sam," he told her mercilessly, "is only one of a dozen men who have sworn to live and die at my command. It is he who brought you here, and he let you live only because I wished it. As for myself . . . ,"—another small movement of his shoulder—"there is a price upon my head already, and I have nothing to lose. So you will speak now, because shortly it will be too late. My patience is not infinite."

She followed the movement of his fingers, which were long and slim and strong, as they glided down the edge of the blade, and she knew the truth of it. The power this man wielded was a tangible thing, and there was no doubt that it extended to command Sam's loyalty as well as that of the others who nightly risked their lives for him. How else could they have eluded capture so long? And now—a shiver went through her that defied the hot, close confines of the room—now she had threatened them, all of them, with her foolish charade. Now he truly believed, for she had taken great pains to convince Sam, that she would go to the governor with what scanty information she had. He truly had nothing to lose, and she would be of far more worth to him dead than alive.

"Believe me"—somehow she made her voice work and panic and hopelessness injected sincerity into it— "I mean you no harm." Clasping her hands tightly around the cup, she leaned forward slightly, pleading now for there was no other course open to her. "I came upon the note by accident and I never intended . . . I would not reveal its contents to anyone, even if I could. What would it avail me? I've nothing to tell!"

"Haven't you?" His words were easy, but there was a sharpening of his manner, a narrowing of his eyes. "You claim to hold the key to the identity of the Fox."

Arabella opened her mouth to blurt the truth—that she did not know him, that she could tell nothing, that it all had been a game. But the words were lost in a sharp intake of breath and she closed her mouth just in time. This was a reality more desperate than she had ever imagined and perhaps her only chance of survival lay in continuing the ruse, in bargaining for power by whatever means was available to her.

With all the courage she possessed, Arabella lifted her chin perceptibly. Her voice was almost calm. "And if I do?"

He was silent, frighteningly, thoughtfully silent, for a long moment. *Fox,* she thought somewhat incoherently. How very appropriate the appellation was. There was an animal power about him, a wildness shrewdness and an instinctive cunning that rendered human prey helpless against his wiles. He sat there, utterly motionless, releasing not even the sound of his breath to alert his victim, assessing, planning. Then, as swiftly as the wind, with no warning whatsoever, he said abruptly, "I do not believe that you do."

Arabella's frail hold on power was snatched away, leaving her swaying once again on the precipice of despair. He stood, moved silently to stand before her, and removed the cup from her numb fingers.

"However," he continued mildly, turning to replace the cup on the table, "you have somehow managed to discover the identity of one of my men, which is not good. You have also gone to a great deal of trouble to arrange this meeting, which does not bode well for your motives. I would know why," he said, turning easily, with the dagger still poised carelessly before him, "before I decide your fate."

And there, once again, was the question Arabella would not answer. She remained silent, her heart beating a slow, heavy rhythm within her chest. The Fox was cornered and he was a man who did not like to be placed in such a position. But worse, his lair had been exposed and invaded, his lieutenant identified. She had done this all inadvertently, unintentionally, giving no thought to the significance of her actions nor to the danger of the situation into which she was stumbling. For years this renegade had roamed and ravaged the countryside at will, living on nothing but wits and daring, and in one fell swoop—or so he now believed— she could spring the trap that would end his reign forever. With swift and unexpected insight, Arabella knew that he resented the manipulation more than he feared the threat.

"And now"—his voice was harsh as he loomed above her, feet planted firmly apart, his stance creating a formidable shadow that blocked all light and almost succeeded in blocking all hope within Arabella—"I will have my answer. What is it that is so important to you that you would risk your life to unearth the Fox? What do you want of me?"

Arabella took a breath. Dimly she remembered outrageous fantasies of adventure and romanticism, even that this man called Le Renard might care for her. She had believed—oh, greater fool she!—that he would welcome her into his arms. She had not taken into account the effect of her threats that she could expose and ruin him. Would he believe the truth now if she told it?

Her voice was so low and soft that he was not sure of her words. "I wanted to see you."

He leaned forward. "What is that? You wanted to see me?"

She felt her face grow hot with shame, but she answered truthfully. "To see you, to . . . talk with you. I had no way of contacting you. I thought, since the . . ." She drew up her courage. "I was foolish enough to believe that you might wish to see me, too . . . after the night you came to me."

Le Renard leaned back, a slow smile curling his lips. So that was it. It had nothing to do with the governor or Sam or the Fox. The little wench wanted him just as he did her. Lady Arabella Winter's reputation had not been exaggerated in London. She was a woman, obviously, with hungers as deep as any man's. The deprivation she had suffered since her marriage to Phillip Everett had no doubt worn sorely on her, leading her straight into the waiting arms of the first virile man who crossed her path. And with this he almost chuckled. He had played his cards right, and the timing could not have been more perfect.

He remembered the woodland scene the previous day—her lithe young body unclothed before him—and the recalled vision made his loins tighten with the heat of too-long-repressed desire. Oh, yes. Lady Arabella would in no way be disappointed this night, but for a while longer he would play the game.

He remarked dispassionately, "And your husband, Lady Arabella. Does he approve of your liaisons? I understand such things are quite the fashion on the Continent, but few husbands here in the Colonies would be so tolerant."

Arabella swallowed hard, steeped in misery. Would he mock her as well as humiliate her? She said, with great difficulty, keeping her head high, "He neither approves nor disapproves, nor does he notice my comings and goings at all. My husband cares more for his hounds and horses than he does for me, and he scarcely knows I am about most of the time." A slight bitterness crept into her voice as she added, "I have no idea why he even married me. We have no marriage— no marriage at all. But you know that." She looked at him hesitantly. "That night you found me by the river . . . was that the behavior of a woman happily married?"

"Then Everett is a bigger fool than I had imagined," he murmured, "to let such a prize as you slip from him."

Her eyes met his in a look that seemed to sear the air of the small cabin. It was clear now what was between them; something deep and unspoken that had begun the night he had taken her in his arms by the river. He wanted her, and she needed him. Her foolishness had brought her here; his passion would hold her.

He moved to the cot beside her. Silence hung heavily in the room as his face moved slowly, slowly, toward hers.

It was a rough kiss, though it was not meant to be punishing. There was an unexpected flare of passion—brought on perhaps by the past hour's tension and the surge of victory he knew when he finally held her in his power—that caused him to crush her to him, to devour her mouth with a greedy hunger that burned into his brain and threatened to shake his control to its very core. The taste and the feel of her were imprinted upon him, filling his mind with images and needs that built upon themselves, doubling and redoubling and honing into a sharp and undeniable demand. She was soft in his arms, warm and pliable, and her mouth was hot against his. How he wanted her!

But, slowly, with an effort, he withdrew from her. The seduction of this woman, like all other undertakings in his life, would be accomplished with control, discipline, and deliberation. He would not move rashly. And he would make it very clear who was the master here.

His breath fanned her cheek as strong fingers fastened around her chin, lifting her eyes to his. "And so, my dear," he said softly, "you have come to fill your

197

empty bed with yet another man. I will not argue your motives, but I am compelled to remark upon your wisdom in your choice of companions. I think consorting with known criminals cannot be acceptable even among your wild set. You could be hung for what you are about to do here tonight."

The first part of his statement was lost in the dizzying rush of blood that pounded into Arabella's head in the aftermath of his kiss. She had the strength to focus on only one thing, and to whisper an objection. "You . . . are not a criminal. I do not fear you."

He laughed, low, harshly, and his fingers tightened for an instant upon her chin before releasing it. "What an innocent—and all the more beguiling for it. I am almost moved to pity."

His eyes were upon her, steady and intense, and she felt the flush that heated her skin deepen beneath his gaze. What a master he was. He held his prey helpless in the dark, surrounded by water and the absence of sound, not allowing even the courage that could be derived from a link with the familiar to develop within his private prison. They were completely isolated, the hunter and the hunted; they might well have been in another world. Even his voice was not human. And when Arabella yearned to search his face, to derive some hint of his emotions or his thoughts from his eyes or his countenance, he denied her even that small advantage. He had calculated every last detail to leave her frustrated, helpless, and dependent upon him. She knew in that moment he was right; she should fear him. But she could not.

The sound of her gradually steadying breath and the lapping of the water against the hull were the only sounds. He leaned away from her with his weight upon his palm, studying her, his gaze a thick and palpable thing in the dimness. She said, mostly because she did not think she could bear the oppressive silence another moment without screaming, "Why do you wear the mask? Are you so ashamed of what you do?"

His hand lifted, and lightly he reached out to touch her hair. He did not miss her flinch as he did so, and he dropped his hand again with barely a caress. Never once did he remove his eyes from hers and his voice was smooth and husky as he replied, "Ah, but we all wear masks of one kind or another, Lady Arabella, do we not? Even you."

Arabella could no longer continue to look into that depthless shadow of a face, and his words, his tone, made her throat suddenly dry. Her own mask of brave nonchalance seemed at that moment very frail indeed. She moved her eyes over his shoulder, searching out the flickering light of the candle. A sticky film of perspiration was beginning to swathe her neck and her chest, and her hair felt very heavy. His closeness blocked whatever air might have been stirring in the tiny room.

Le Renard seemed very relaxed, almost amused, which in contrast to the violence he had affected only a moment ago was as puzzling to Arabella as it was unsettling. "You are a very foolish woman," he commented as though stating the obvious. "You seem to have a penchant for rushing headlong into danger without the least bit of thought or preparation. Did it never occur to you that your foolish boasts and absurd threats might mean your death? Were you not aware that you were dealing with a desperate criminal?"

The challenges were thrown out lightly, and beneath the words Arabella again thought she could sense a thread of amusement, a hint of gentle self-mockery. Arabella was so intrigued, she forgot to be frightened. "You moved to save my life once," she reminded him, her voice softening unconsciously with the memory of their night by the river. Intently, she tried to peer into the dark and the mask for a hint of the man beneath. "I had no reason to think you would take it now."

She sensed a tensing within him, and a quieting, as though he, too, were recalling the episode. The silence was brief in duration, but heavy. And then he drawled with deceptive mildness, "Ah yes, when you swore to fling yourself to your death before committing yourself to the marriage bed. A minor miscalculation on both our parts, Mistress, and you do make a great deal over nothing."

Arabella's heart began to thud, slowly, loudly. She could not see him, but she could feel him, and somehow the development of that insight brought on by the dark and the silence and her fear seemed to be telling her so much more than her eyes or her ears. It was a trick that the Fox had no doubt long since learned, and which he was now inadvertently sharing with her. There was no sense of danger about him now, no threat, and little cunning. But there was intense awareness, low-level alertness, and the gaze that she could not see felt like a physical thing upon her skin. She could feel his eyes upon her face, examining, assessing, and then lower, across her throat and her bare shoulders and her upper chest, until finally they rested upon her breast.

Arabella knew he was going to touch her before he made the movement, and her heart leapt to her throat, cutting off her breath. Abruptly she understood what he expected from her now; indeed, what all her actions to this point had led him to expect, and what she had been too frightened, too preoccupied and reckless to consider before.

She had not come here to offer her feminine favors to him, to deliberately betray her marriage vows and take this man as her lover. She had come because the loneliness had been overwhelming; because the cryptic attentions of Le Renard had been the only relief from a dreary and tedious existence with a man who did not love her; because when the Fox's attentions had suddenly ceased, she had despaired over the emptiness that stretched before her. She had come for adventure and had not thought past that. Le Renard assumed she had come to be his mistress, and nothing she could do or say now would convince him otherwise.

Nevertheless she formed an instinctive protest as his hand reached out, but it was lost in a gasp as his fingers caught the first of the tiny buttons that fastened her bodice. Breath and will left her at once as swiftly, effortlessly, first one button and then the other opened to his seeking hand. Part of her knew it was futile to resist his touch; another part, caught up in the trip-hammer tempo of her heart, awaited it with an anticipation that had nothing to do with fear of harm. His forefinger lightly traced a curving pattern upon the outer portion of her breast and her skin prickled with a heated reaction she had not expected.

She heard the rustling of the cot as he moved and felt the strong substance of his presence as he shifted his weight to bring himself closer. The rough but strangely gentle texture of his fingers grazed her flesh as he pushed the cloth aside, baring the thin, lace-edged chemise to the gleaming fire deep within his eyes. And she could not move, or breathe, or even think at all as for the longest time he simply looked at her.

Le Renard was accustomed to danger; he thrived upon it and had learned to call it friend. Dimly he was aware that the danger represented by this woman was unlike any he had faced before, and that, in the end, she was the one person in the world who could cause his destruction. He was a man of reason, not emotion. To become embroiled in the emotions of his own needs and desires could leave him vulnerable, defenseless.

He knew the danger. This was a woman who had no compunction about betraying her own husband for the comforts of another man's bed, who boldly and brazenly sought the affections of a branded criminal. Who was to say that she might not leave his embrace for that of one of the king's guarde, or that she would not betray him with as little conscience—but with far more deadly intent—as she had her husband? It was truly said that treachery was in the nature of a woman, and he was stepping willingly and consciously into her trap. He knew all of this, and he knew that the wisest course would be to turn back now, to remove her from his presence and his ship, for the game they were playing could all too easily find him the victim and not the victor. But he could not help thinking how easy it would be to shift the material of her chemise only a fraction lower, to expose the creamy fullness beneath, to cup its heaviness in his hand and cover it with his mouth.

Arabella felt a stab of alarm as his fingers moved downward, pushing aside the material. A gasp and an involuntary shrinking away followed as warm fingers drifted over the exposed flesh and feather-light touches traced the puckering nipple and the darker pink that surrounded it. And then she felt the warmth of his breath upon her flesh and moist heat as his mouth came to her breast, and though her instinct was to fight, to push him away, to cry out, the sensation was so strange, so joltingly, unexpectedly weakening, that she could do nothing for a moment but let it happen.

Arabella had arranged herself in a corner of the cot against the bulkhead, her legs curled beneath her in an instinctive gesture of self-protection. She could not have gotten further away from him if she had wanted to. At that moment, she did not want to. The sensation of his mouth upon her breast was like a sudden injection of hot fluid that penetrated every part of her body—melting, debilitating, overwhelming her. His tongue flickered over her small, taut nipple and made her moan aloud with the sudden charge of electricity that teased unexpected parts of her—her fingertips, her toes, deep within her abdomen and lower, to a pulsing, undefined tingling between her legs. The suckling motions he made seemed to draw the very life from her and her head spun. And then, so easily and so gradually she hardly noticed, he slipped the material of her bodice and her chemise off her shoulders, down her arms, exposing all of her to him. Only when she felt the heavy warmth of his hands close over both her breasts did her reason return to her with a jolt. Panicked desperation and confused alarm strengthened her to cry out a muffled protest and brace her hands against his arms in an attempt to push him away.

He did not release her. His lips made soothing, insinuating forays across her chest and her throat and upward to her face. His hands were caressing, adoring, and somehow protective upon her breasts. He whispered, "No, my lovely, do not fear . . . I mean you no harm . . ." And then his lips captured hers.

There was an urgency in the kiss now, a fierce mastery that had grown from something strong and primitive inside him, and he felt her respond to it, softening beneath him, melting against him. Le Renard knew how dangerously close he was now to the point of no return, but it hardly seemed to matter. He had been too long without a woman—without this woman. And he should have known, from the moment of that first kiss beside the river, that it would one day come to this between them. She was his by right, and with each passing moment he was more and more consumed by the urge to claim her as his. Too long he had been a martyr to his cause. For this one night he could afford

203

to be a little unwise.

Arabella felt herself sinking into the sensation, helplessly, remorselessly, a victim of all her fantasies come true. The passion he had stirred in her on that night so long ago resurged as though it had never been forgotten, and Arabella wondered dimly if this were not what she had been waiting for, since the moment she had awakened and found him standing over her, since the night by the river at Shadowood . . . no, longer; perhaps all of her life . . .

His arms slipped around her, pressing her slowly but strongly against him. Her naked breasts were against the coarse texture of his muslin shirt and she felt the heat of him beneath, the pounding of his heart, his strong hands upon her bare back, stroking, caressing, molding her closer. Her hands, of their own volition, ceased pushing against him and began to curl around his taut upper arms, feeling the strength of him, drawing him closer.

Yet it was wrong, her mind cried. It was dangerous and it was wicked and it was frightening. She had been a fool before, led too often by her desires and not her head, giving no thought to consequences.

"No!" It was a gasp that was torn from her as she twisted away, her hands tightening against him in resistance again, her chest heaving and her head ringing. His arms loosened about her, but he did not release her, even when she found the strength to struggle. He allowed no more than an inch between them, and he looked at her intently. She could feel his uneven breath on her cheek; she almost thought she could hear the pounding of his heart in counterrhythm to her own. And she knew at that moment that she was struggling as much against herself as she was against him.

She choked out, "Phillip," and she felt him stiffen.

Her hand closed into a fist against his chest, but she made no move to draw away. She could not look at him, for the words she spoke next were not those she wanted to say. "I . . . I am a married woman. I cannot . . ."

Her voice trailed off as she felt him relax. With one hand he covered her own against his chest; with the other he stroked her face, very lightly, and she could not be certain that the small curve of his lips was not mocking. "And so now you give thought to the poor wretch of a husband of yours . . . but a bit late, I perceive. However"—his chuckle was low and airy and brief—"to soothe your battered conscience, consider this: I think your husband will not mind if I take some of what he so seldom uses . . ." And then his lips captured hers.

Chapter XII

The tip of his tongue lightly caressed her lips, tracing their shape and creating a warm, tingling, hypnotic sensation that made her gasp with the pleasure of it. He lifted her hands and placed them upon his waist. "Touch me, Arabella," he whispered against her mouth. "Feel me . . ."

His tongue slipped past the fragile barrier of her slightly parted lips, invading her mouth, filling her, even as his arms wrapped around her and pulled her close. She was not aware of the moment her own arms came around him but only of the feel of taut, straining flesh beneath her fingers, the rippling muscles of his back, the heat of his neck, the silken queue of his hair falling over her questing fingers.

And such unimagined things were happening to her body—the complete, overwhelming invasion of her senses. She was lost beneath the strange intimacy of the kiss, the salty, brandy-laced taste of him, his tongue, slippery textured and strong, heated and demanding; a part of him inside of her, filling her, blending with her, drawing from her . . . Then there was his hand, seeking her breast again, cupping and kneading gently, the tantalizing pressure of his thumb against her tender, swollen nipple and the sudden heat that flamed to her loins and made her moan into his mouth. It was an ache, almost a pain, that tightened low in her abdomen and seemed to radiate tingling need between her legs; a yearning she did not know how to satisfy but which his every movement seemed to intensify.

There was no more hope for reason, no more chance for resistance, no more thought of danger. Arabella was too inexperienced and too much in need to know how to separate instinct from logic.

He lifted his face and his eyes were but a blur in the shadowed candlelight, yet the heat from him engulfed her and joined them even in the brief separation. He was breathing heavily, and there was an unaccustomed roughness to his voice as he commanded, searching her face, "It is too late, Lady Arabella, if you have doubts . . . for now I cannot turn back."

But she hardly heard him, for already her lips were seeking his again, her fingers creeping beneath the neck of his shirt to explore the masculine flesh beneath. And he was pushing her back, down upon the cot, his weight shielding her as his mouth fastened upon hers with a greedy hunger that sent her senses to soaring, blinding heights.

Her bodice was pushed away, and in a few deft movements her skirts and underclothes followed. Only when he lifted himself a little to gaze at her did Arabella realize that for the first time in her life she lay naked before a man.

She felt his sharp intake of breath, heard a slurred and murmured exclamation. With a sudden flush of shyness and trepidation, she made to draw her legs up, to hide from him, for the candlelight fell full upon her and left little shadowed to his gaze. But his hand descended then upon her knee, and his fingers, like whispers of fire, stroked gently upward, turning her muscles limp and immobile. He bent to kiss her breasts as his hand curved around her hip. All of her was suspended in rapt concentration upon him, his touch, his breath, each new and baffling sensation that assailed her and made her helpless, yet her mind seemed incapable of functioning. There was dampness between her legs and the twisting knot of longing deep within her only tightened with each moment. She thought her chest would surely break with the hammering of her heart.

Her skin seemed to be an entity of its own, contracting and straining with each kiss he placed upon her chest, her breasts, her abdomen. And all the while his hand was stroking her leg, her hip, moving upward and around until at last, to her shock, his fingers touched that most private part of her and instinctively her legs clamped tightly together and her muscles went rigid.

His words were soothing murmurs that held no reason; he kissed her, he adored her with his touch and his voice, and his hand grew bolder until at last her legs loosened and began to part. She felt his touch upon her, gliding like warm silk in caresses that shot bolts of fire through her veins and quivers through her limbs. Nothing existed in the world except this man they called Le Renard, his breathing, his fingers and the mindless pleasure they evoked, and that awful burning, twisting ache deep within her that made her writhe and moan with a mixture of discomfort and pleasure.

And then, too soon, his hand moved upward, his kiss seemed to hold a note of finality, and she could have sobbed out loud for the absence of him as he stood. She lay there, aching and confused, as he crossed the room and snuffed out the candle, abruptly plunging the cabin into inky blackness. She heard his steady, sure footsteps returning and the rustle of movement, and when he lay beside her again his nakedness was against her own.

Cautiously, encouraged by the feel of his own hands upon her fevered flesh, she began to explore the wonders of male chest and back, the strength of uncovered arms, the spareness of waist. She heard his little moan of pleasure with her touch and a rush of delight filled her that he could welcome her nearness as much as she welcomed his. His flesh was damp, like her own, and just as heated, its texture slippery and smooth beneath her fingers. But when she reached his face and discovered the barrier of the mask still in place, he caught her hand.

Puzzlement and hurt was in her eyes, and though he could not see it, he knew it. "Trust cannot be given lightly," he said softly. "It must be earned."

"But surely I have earned your trust," she protested. "I have told no one of your visits to me; I have kept the secret of the Fox locked in my heart."

She felt his sigh upon her face and he gentled her with the touch of his lips. "To keep my identity secret is the kindest thing I can do for you. To know the Fox is dangerous; to know his identity is certain death . . . for both of us."

With his words came a sudden rush of awareness of what she was doing, the long forgotten reason of hidden danger. The man who lay naked beside her, the man who caressed her body as no one had ever done before and who allowed her the freedom of his own, was Le Renard, a wanted criminal, a renegade, a traitor.

The knowledge should have frightened her, but it did not. The recklessness of her actions should have alarmed her, but rather she felt strengthened, powerful, eager to draw him to her again, for it seemed only natural, decreed by fate and ripened by time. She met the passion of his kiss with demands of her own rather than submission. She felt the strength of his chest against the softness of her breasts, the urgency and the strength that crushed her against him and ravaged her mouth; she felt the alien masculine hardness of him pressed against her stomach and a gasp caught within her throat.

Then he lifted himself slightly and one strong thigh wedged itself between her own, urging them apart. His face was a haze of heat and flaming need above her, featureless but strong; his breathing was harsh and his hands unsteady as they stroked her hair away from her face. She looked up at him in wonder and confusion, lifting her arms to draw him down to her again, and he whispered raspingly, "Forgive me, my dear. I can wait no longer. Another time we will go slower . . ."

His hands slipped down beneath her hips, lifting her, parting her legs on either side of him. Arabella's heart began a new and increased tempo of alarm and confusion at the strangeness of this and something within her rebelled even as her need rose another degree into twisting anticipation. She felt the strange, hard strength of him probing her tenderness and she tried to flinch away, but his hands tightened upon her hips, holding her steady, and Arabella cried out with the searing pain that thrust itself inside her, so unexpected and so enormous that she felt as though she were being split in two.

Le Renard's head was spinning. Too late he registered the resistance of unaccustomed flesh, the female cry of pain, the sharp bite of her nails on his shoulder. Instinctively she struggled and just as instinctively he pushed harder, for he could not stop himself. She sobbed again, and he was deep inside her, his heart thundering, his breath coming in panting gasps, his muscles straining to the breaking point. She was quivering beneath him, frightened and in pain, and the warm moisture that spread against him was the trickle of virgin blood. His mind could not accept it; he was far past the point of functioning rationally, and all he could do was bring his hands upward to stroke her damp and frightened face as he breathed, "Oh . . . Arabella. My dear love . . ."

He dropped his face to hers, kissing away the lines of distress, his hands maintaining their soothing stroking rhythm upon her face until the whimpering gasps of uncertainty and discomfort that issued from her throat gradually grew less frequent and the stinging cut of her nails upon his shoulder eased somewhat. He held himself still within her, whispering, "Relax, be easy . . . soon the pain will fade and there will be only pleasure . . ."

Slowly the tension began to recede from her muscles and her breath became less frantic. She turned her face to his gentle rain of kisses rather than avoiding it. One hand left her face and slid down her body, over her hip, beneath her knee, lifting and bending it; cautiously he settled himself more deeply within her. Arabella gasped with the sensation, but already the sting of torn flesh was beginning to ease. She felt little but the strange fullness inside her the renewed awareness of tightness at the core of her that he seemed to touch but not ease. Then the rigid control that Le Renard had never expected to exercise this night began to melt into the heat and the softness of her, and he began to move within her.

At first the sensation was not pleasant, and Arabella resisted it, expecting more pain. But gradually her tight flesh began to loosen and to mold itself around him, to concentrate on the rhythmic stroking pulse of his body joining hers. Something built within her that she could not define, an expanding emotion laced with wonder

212

over this act of coupling that brought him closer to her than it seemed possible for any human being ever to be, and yet she felt the need to draw him closer and ever closer still, to wrap her arms and her legs around him and to feel him pressed against her at every part so that they would never be separate again.

But even stranger to Arabella was the physical desperation that was building within her, the hard knot of yearning she did not know how to satisfy and which made her want to sob out loud from the frustration of it, the sense of reaching for a goal that was just beyond her reach . . .

He brought his mouth down upon hers and she opened to him, greedily accepting the thrust of his tongue as she arched to meet the thrust of his pelvis against hers. His thrusts became stronger, harder, faster; the desperation within her sharpened and expanded until she thought she would burst from it and she cried out with undefined need. Her breath came in short, harsh pants that mirrored his own. She clutched at him; she lifted herself into him; she sobbed with unfulfilled yearning that was deeper than any physical pain could ever be.

And suddenly there came a burst of blindness, of mindlessness, of shuddering relief that rippled through her in involuntary convulsions of unimagined intensity. She thought, *I am dying,* but there was overwhelming joy in the thought that she would die in his arms and that wherever she went he would follow, that eternity could not separate them. And from the dim edge of gilt-colored consciousness she felt his last mighty thrust, his gasp of breath, and the trembling rigidity of his muscles as he held himself deep inside her. Sated, he collapsed against her.

For a time, an endless time, he cradled her, his body full against hers, his whispers of adoration inter-

213

mingled with his broken breath in her ear, his lips caressing, his arms shielding, his hands adoring. Arabella hardly felt his weight or heard the words, for a strange lethargy had overcome her, a suspended wonder that allowed no thought, a heaviness of mind and body and a satiation that knew no bounds.

Then he moved from her, turning on his back, slipping his arm beneath her shoulders to draw her close. Their bodies were slippery with mingled perspiration and the untamed scent of shared passion permeated the room. Vaguely Arabella perceived his labored breathing, the jerky rhythm of his heart beneath her hand, but for the most part she knew nothing. She simply existed in the splendor of the moment that would change her life forever.

She knew not how much time passed. As though from the edge of slumber she was brought back to awareness as he moved away from her, getting to his feet and crossing the room. She listened to the sounds he made but did not try to decipher them. She had no strength for questions and her muscles were only a tangle of remembered usefulness, and, in any case, he was sitting beside her again in only a moment.

He touched her thigh, urging its parting, and when she hesitated he said gently, "A damp cloth. It won't hurt."

The coolness was soothing against her, his ministrations tender. He did not lie again beside her but simply sat there, looking at her, for such a long time that she began to think something was wrong. And then he said, "You should have told me, Lady Arabella. There are much gentler ways to lose your virginity."

It was difficult to determine the emotions that backed the tonelessness of his husky whisper, and she looked at him anxiously, fearing he was displeased. She did not know how to respond.

Finally she managed a stammering, uncertain, "My . . . my husband . . ."

He made an impatient gesture with his hand that startled her, and this time there was no mistaking the derision in his tone. "I know of your husband; it is not to him that I refer. Before your marriage you were rumored to have been . . . experienced in these matters. I had no cause to think you were not."

A sudden stab of hurt and disillusionment ached tightly in her throat, though her words were delivered without emotion. "I see there is nothing Sam does not tell you." She had to force herself to remember that they had met as enemies; he had not forgotten it even if she had. She took a breath and lifted her chin slightly. "At any rate, it hardly matters, for now I am what you thought me to be. I'm sorry if you were disappointed."

She heard his long, deep intake of breath and felt it released against her skin as he drew her slowly into his arms. "No," he murmured into her hair. "Not disappointed. Never that." His voice was heavy with regret. "Only that I cannot help but think that such matters belong in the comfort of the bridal bed with a loving and gentle husband rather than in the squalor of an unknown ship at the hands of a brutal stranger."

"Not brutal," she whispered, for already the hurt and the anger had dissolved within the comforting security of his arms. "And not a stranger . . ." She reached up to caress his masked face, lifting her eyes to his. "Not anymore."

He captured her fingers with his lips. "Sadly," he whispered, "'tis so. I am, and must always be, a stranger to you." He drew her down with him, entwining his body with hers on the cot, his arms around her and one strong, furred leg protecting hers, her head against the hard heat of his shoulder. "The hours left to us are few, and come morning I must be no

215

more than a memory to you."

Everything within Arabella rebelled at his declaration and she wanted to cry out, No, I will not leave you! I will stay with you forever . . . But even before the words were formed, she knew it could not be so. Would she stay with him—a criminal and a traitor—even if it were possible? Her soul cried out yes, but her mind was plunged into turmoil. She could not imagine returning to Shadowood, to Phillip, after this night that had changed her forever. All of it seemed to belong to another lifetime. Lady Arabella Winters, Mistress Phillip Everett, had departed Shadowood this night, but another woman would return to its confines on the morrow.

She heard her own voice, low and helpless, speak the words before she could think. "I love you. I would not part from you."

She felt his stiffening, the involuntary tightening of his hand upon her waist, and she knew she had said the wrong thing. Once again, she had led with her heart and not her mind, for of course it was impossible . . .

He said harshly, "You give your love cheaply, Lady Arabella, to the first man who crossed your path."

Le Renard knew it was cruel to discourage her fantasy so brutally, but already he was regretting the rashness of the act, wishing that somehow he could have controlled his foolish rush to passion. His mind was in turmoil and his will was weak. He had meant to use her, enjoy her, discard her, and he could not afford the tenderness that swept him as he held this small, fragile creature in his arms. His own vulnerability made him angry, yet the effort it required to hurt her made him angrier.

He felt her little shudder of pain at his words, felt the hotness of tears against his shoulder. He swore silently with a new wave of remorse, and his next words were

216

more gentle. "You will think you love me," he assured her, "for awhile, but it will pass. And you will realize that it is for the best. I endanger no one for my sake; those who risk their lives with me do so because their purpose is as strong as my own and their will is free. I hold no man—or woman—to me with promises I cannot keep."

Such a great sense of wonder and adoration filled her that she had to close her eyes to contain it. How could she leave him? How could she put this night behind her as though it had never happened? How could she forget him? What magnificent fate had brought a man such as he into her life, and how could she turn her back on it? *I would fight by your side,* she thought intensely. *I would learn to embrace your cause. I would risk my life with yours daily as long as we could be together . . .*

He bent his head to place a brief, tender kiss against her hair. "Now still your silly tears and rest a time. Dawn will come soon enough, and I must return you to the safety of your home while all is still quiet. Sleep."

Arabella had no intention of wasting precious moments with him in sleep; she could not imagine how she could do so, for so many confused thoughts pommeled her mind and heart. But, like an obedient child, she closed her eyes at his command, and her shocked and weary body betrayed her. She was asleep within the space of half a dozen breaths.

When Arabella awoke a pale gray twilight was filtering through the room. There was no disorientation, for she had slept lightly and the hardness of his muscles and the sticky warmth of his nakedness was never far from her consciousness. At first she felt a moment of shock and wretched embarrassment at finding herself unclothed in the arms of a man, for

217

never had she appeared nude before anyone except her maid, and then only in the bath. Then the rush of memories of the shared intimacy of the night before came flooding over her and the flush of shame and, yes, titillating excitement spread throughout her whole body.

He was asleep next to her. His breathing was deep and his arms relaxed, and the moment of tenderness and sorrow that overwhelmed Arabella made her want to tighten her arms around him, to hold him, to try to recapture the warmth they had shared only hours before so that it might be imprinted upon her memory forever. Was it possible that she must part from him now? Would he send her away so cruelly? Or perhaps, when he awoke, everything would be different, and he would look upon her with contempt in the light of day . . .

She could not pursue that painful, confusing train of thought, yet the experience of waking naked in a man's arms was so strange to her that she did not know what to do. She could not make herself look at his masked face, afraid that any moment those dark eyes would open and survey her and the signs of her embarrassment with mockery or with cool dispassion that would break her heart. Instead, she directed her eyes lower, to the strong masculine leg that was thrown over hers, to the sheet that was twisted between their bodies and its telltale pink stains that only increased the uncomfortable rush of memory.

But as she looked at him, becoming slowly aware of the unfamiliar soreness in her own body that testified to the intimacy they had already shared, new sensations overcame and pushed aside the embarrassment. Her heart began its slow, rhythmic pounding as, in the cool gray twilight, she looked for the first time upon the body of the man who had formed her anew. She noted his ankles, strong and firm, the length of his calf covered with its brush of light-colored hair, and his strong, muscular thighs. His waist was spare and lean; his chest and shoulders broad. The hair of Le Renard was tousled upon the pillow, having come loose from the narrow thong that bound it, and its color was light with highlights of gold, rather than dark as she had first imagined it. The sheen of his hair brought back memories of those long-ago days in Devon when Phillip was her dashing knight and the adventure that had lain in store for her in the future had not yet even been imagined . . .

His hand, so innocently cupping her shoulder in sleep, was long boned and slender, its nails well manicured, its shape graceful. A tightness began in her throat, a dim uncertainty that her exhaustion-fogged brain would not recognize, as she moved her eyes to his masked face. The shape of his chin was so familiar, as was the line of his lower lip with its small, almost invisible, scar near the corner.

A sense of certainty gripped her stomach and made her heart skip a beat. As a child in Devon, Phillip had fallen against a rock and had acquired such a scar. It could easily be hidden beneath his rouge and powder. But it could not be true. It was not true . . .

Her breathing was rapid and very shallow as very carefully she lifted her hand, drawn by a force she could not resist to the places where woolen ties secured his mask to his head. A single movement, quick and certain, and he would be uncovered before her . . .

His hand shot out like a snake to grab her wrist.

Instantly Le Renard was awake, furious with himself for having slept and allowing the dawn to creep up on him, for having lowered his guard even for a second, and cursing himself for his foolishness of the night before and its almost disastrous result this morning.

219

All of this took place in an instant as he looked down at her with eyes as cold as ice and as gray as the twilight around them. "So, my fine Lady Arabella," he hissed, "already you have stooped to treachery!"

But Arabella hardly heard the words. Her heart had stopped the moment she felt his crushing grip upon her wrist, and she screamed, *"No!"* She kicked out and tried to wrest her arm from his grasp, and his eyes widened with surprise as he automatically tried to subdue her. Eyes that were as gray as the Devon coast, hair that was tawny and tousled, lips that were . . .

"Bastard!" she screamed. "You vile, low . . . cur . . . *cochon*—" She was fighting wildly now, striking out with her fists and her nails, kicking him, twisting and bucking as he tried to subdue her with his weight, for outrage had consumed her, and with it the fury of a betrayal that was too great for comprehension, shock, and sheer, unadulterated hatred. Her head was roaring with it. A red haze blurred her vision and threatened to devour her, and though her mind shouted disbelief and horror, she fought against what she knew to be true. "You . . . unspeakable . . ." She struck out with her fists and when he caught her hands with cruel strength she began to use her feet, sobbing, screaming. "I hope they put you to the rack! I hope they draw and quarter you and cast the pieces to the birds! They will hang you from the highest tree and I will be there to dance upon your grave! I—"

"God's teeth, but you are a little wildcat this morning!" He gasped with exertion, but there was amusement in his eyes. "Even more so than you were last night," he amended, and he brought her hands behind her back, wrenching her shoulders painfully, holding her body still with the cruel weight of one knee upon her abdomen as he secured her hands together tightly with a strip of sheeting.

She bucked against his restraint, but it was not fear that drove her now. Blinding rage flamed through her, giving her strength, and she screamed again, almost incoherent by now—"Bastard! *Bastard!*"—until her voice was abruptly cut off as he shoved a wadded cloth deep into her mouth.

"And that," he pronounced grimly, "will be enough of that." He looked down at her, and when she lay still for a moment, desperate for breath against the impediment of the cloth and the choking weight of his knee against her diaphragm, she thought she saw a flicker of bitter regret in his eyes. "I warned you, did I not, Lady Arabella, that whatever small affection you imagined you felt for me last night would soon pass? Only," he murmured, and now the glint that came into his eyes was definitely self-mocking, "I did not expect it to be so soon."

He left her and the rushing return of air into her lungs was painful. But almost immediately she began to buck and twist again, trying to roll her weight to the edge of the cot, not knowing why, but only aware of the need to fight. Her screams of fury were muffled in her throat as little moans, and she was awash in a swirling nightmare of truth and disbelief and betrayal.

He came back to her, dressed in breeches and boots, and he held a small vial in his hand. His stance was powerful, his movements brisk, his lips grim, but his words were unexpected. "I regret that it must be this way—you have had enough distress for any one night, I think—but you leave me no choice."

He sat beside her and took a firm grip on the back of her skull, holding her head steady. "This is a sleeping draught—very powerful, but it won't kill you. We have lost too much time already and it will soon be impossible to return you in safety. I will remove the cloth from your mouth and you will drink. When you

221

are still I will clothe you and Sam will return you to Shadowood, where you will no doubt sleep until afternoon." His hand came down to pluck the suffocating cloth from her mouth.

At first she wanted to laugh hysterically, to scream at him and decry the foolishness of their night together, and then all she wanted to do was strike out at him, to rake her nails across his smooth skin and draw his blood as he had drawn hers, to tear the mask away and spit in his face.

But the instant the cloth was removed it was replaced by the vial, which was shoved roughly against the back of her throat as his hand grasped a handful of hair and jerked her head backward. She gagged and she coughed as the liquid trickled into her throat. She tried to twist away and spit it out, but the tightening of his hand upon her hair brought tears to her eyes and the bottle was shoved more roughly against her throat. "Drink," he commanded sternly. "For I promise you there are less gentle ways to render you unconscious."

At last she had no choice but to swallow, and when he took the vial away she collapsed, sobbing and coughing, face down against the cot. Already the laudanum was beginning to work, and in combination with shock and exhaustion, nothing remained within her mind except confusion, hurt, and the swirling of a nightmare that could not be true, all of which were pushing her toward oblivion at an alarming rate.

The last thing Arabella remembered was strong arms lifting her and her face being cradled against a bare chest. Then there was nothing but grayness.

It is now four Hours since I awaken'd from my drugg'd Sleep. I wisht that my Nytemare had been but a Dream, but I fear It is All too true. My Body still aches from my Venture into the Mysterie of Love and there are Bruises upon my Arms where he has graspt me.

Why, I have askt Myselfe over and over, why is my Husbande masquerading as the Fox? And the Answer that comes to Me is so despicable, so degrading, that I hardly can bear to contemplate It. The Phillip of Olde, that Phillip whom I Lov'd in Devon, though careless and reckless, would not have play'd such a cruel Trick as to come to Me in the Guise of another Man.

But This Phillip of Virginia, this Man I hardly know—Nothing seems past his devious Minde. Would He shame Me so that He could tell his Friends in Gaming Rooms and at Card Partys that He made Love to his owne Wife, pretending to be the Fox? Is He e'en now laughing at Me, at my Foolishness and Naivete? I thinke upon his Words of Trust, his Talk of the Danger that surrounds him, and I know that He was only making vile Sport of Me.

If only I had not flung Myselfe so impetuously upon him in his Cabin. Why did I not byde my Tyme and confront him then? But there is still Williamsburg, and Tyme there to finde Proof which will show the devious Nature of his Madness. Oh, myne owne Husbande has used and tricked Me, that I cannot deny, but He shall not prevail, for now I have the Advantage, knowing of his Secret Charade, a Secret which I shall fling into his Face when the Tyme is right . . .

Chapter XIII

In the early days the tavern had been known as Wetherburns, but with a new owner came a change of name and today the sign over the rambling clapboard building read "Southalls." Still, to the old-timers, it was Wetherburns, and little had changed. The new innkeeper stood behind the bar as Wetherburn had done and served up his tankards of ale and drams of rum while his wife passed the punch in the communal wine bowl from table to table, expertly dodging the pinches of the guests. Negro servants carried in platters of beef and fowl, bowls of peanut soup, and plates of spoon bread. The Bull's Head Room was crowded as usual, and fumes of tobacco from clay pipes mingled with the smoke from the fireplace. The succulent aroma of roasted skins of pork, fermenting apples, and spilled ale competed with the sharp underbite of tallow candles, and many jostling bodies crowded together on this hot September afternoon.

Phillip delicately brought a handkerchief to his nostrils and passed the dining room by. The hall was empty and, after a quick look around, he bent his head and ducked beneath the stairs where a door led into a private back room simply furnished with a table and chairs. Two men waited at the table, lounging comfortably before tankards of ale, engaged in desultory, sporadic conversation. One was short, stocky, and filled the room with smoke from his clay pipe. The other was large, plainly dressed, and dark skinned.

As Phillip entered, a young serving boy followed quickly behind with another tankard of ale and Phillip complained loudly, wrinkling his nose, "By all that's holy, William, must you pollute the air with that odious weed of yours? Of all the nasty peculiarities of you backwoods colonists, that has got to be the most distasteful. Why can you not learn to take your tobacco like a gentleman?"

As he spoke he arranged himself carefully in a straight-backed chair at the table and flipped out his enameled snuffbox. William replied mildly, "I wouldn't object too loudly, sir, about the consequences of the very stuff from which you've made your fortune."

The serving boy carefully wiped the table before Phillip and set down the overflowing tankard. He cast only one surreptitious glance at Sam before departing as quickly and as silently as he had come. Phillip Everett was well known for his eccentricities and if he wished to sit down at the table with a slave, it was, as his own employer constantly reminded him, the good man's own business. Besides, Everett was an Englishman and could hardly be held accountable for his actions.

When they were alone, Sam lifted his tankard and commented, "I thought you'd never get here."

Phillip returned his snuffbox without partaking and leaned back in his chair. "It was difficult to leave the house undetected," he answered vaguely.

William smothered a grin by bringing the pipe quickly to his lips, and Sam stared intently into his ale, murmuring, "Mistress Arabella does seem to be everywhere doesn't she?"

Phillip nodded. Since her arrival in Williamsburg, she'd attacked the house on Nicholson Street like a diminutive tornado, stirring up clouds of dust that had been accumulating over the summer while the residence had been closed, rearranging everything that could be moved and replacing everything that could not. "The good lady does seem to be taking her housewifely duties seriously."

"Miss Arabella is a hard worker," agreed Sam carefully, "and she's a cool one, too." He held Phillip's gaze. "She's never said a word to me about her little adventure."

Phillip felt his throat tighten, the way it always did when he paused to think on that night. He replied shortly, lifting his tankard, "She won't."

Watching Phillip with the same wariness that was in Sam's eyes, William said, "Maybe she forgot. That dose I put in your flask was pretty strong."

Phillip's lips curved downward tightly. "Not likely. It would take more than a dram of laudanum to affect that lady's memory—or anything else about her."

Sam scowled uncomfortably. "It doesn't make sense. She's said *nothing*—not to you, not to me. The woman was abducted, and she knows I'm the one who did it, yet she acts as though nothing happened at all. I don't like it," he confessed uneasily. "Not a bit."

And William exploded softly, "Damn it, man, I knew no good would come of this! I warned you not to bring her there! She's up to something; she's just biding her time—"

"She knows nothing," returned Phillip harshly, and his eyes darkened with a warning both of the men knew to heed.

He stared intently at the wall opposite, lost in his

227

own brooding thoughts. He knew perfectly well what was prompting his wife's strange silence, and had, in fact, counted upon it. The woman had committed adultery. Was she going to confess the same to her husband? No, it was not her silence that bothered him; he had predicted that. But the fact that she did, indeed, act as though nothing had happened—that annoyed him. What an actress she was. And how close he had come to underestimating her.

"She could have recognized you," William mumbled at last, unable to keep silent. He tapped out his pipe on the rung of his chair. "It was a damn fool thing to do."

With that last statement Phillip most heartily agreed, but he laughed. "Of one thing I can assure you, my friend—she did *not* recognize me." There was a trace of bitterness in his voice, which he quickly tried to swallow with his ale.

When he looked back at William, his face was smooth, his voice mild. He inquired, "Is everything in order for our lord governor's surprise *fete?*"

William hesitated only a moment before nodding. "Just as we planned. If you still think it's wise . . ."

Phillip gave an impatient turn of his lace-drenched wrist. "Will you stop prattling about that twit of a wife of mine? She will in no way interfere with our work, and the less said of her the better."

Sam offered slowly, "She does have a way of . . . blundering into things."

"A habit that could be more dangerous than I like," added William.

Phillip shrugged. "Then Williamsburg is a good place for her. She can stay occupied and busy—and out of our way."

After a single shared glance of doubt with William, Sam rose and straightened the front of his doublet. "Right now Miss Arabella's keeping me busy. She sent

228

me out of the house with a list of errands as long as my arm."

"Then do them, by all means," Phillip said with a laugh, relaxing. "We wouldn't want to rouse the lady's temper."

He sat with William for a time longer, finishing his ale, talking of inconsequentials, but soon he found himself too restless to stay still. William wisely did not bring up the subject of Arabella again, yet that was the only subject on Phillip's mind.

He had brought her to the ship to stem her threats, to frighten her a bit . . . and to have her alone. He could no longer deny that that had been part of it, and he knew that whatever more noble motives had prompted the action, at the base of it had been desire, pure and simple.

It had been foolish, no doubt of it—a foolish, selfish act that had endangered himself and his men more than he even wanted to consider. But he had wanted her since the first moment he had seen her, had determined to have her in that brief encounter on the stairway when she had looked at him with fire in her eyes and disdain on her features. And so he had taken her . . . and had been rewarded with the torment.

His broad shoulders hunched beneath the brocade of his peach-colored jacket, Phillip sat staring with unseeing eyes at the empty tankard, oblivious to William's sporadic attempts at conversation. A virgin. The foolish child had been a virgin. He wanted to laugh with a sudden surge of bitterness over his grand assumptions about the lady. How little he knew his wife. He wondered what other masks she was capable of assuming.

After a time he rose, tossed some coins on the table, and bid William an absent good day. After the governor's ball, William would have to return to

Shadowood for a time—until the Fox had need of him again—and see to the affairs of Phillip Everett. They had much to discuss, but William tacitly understood it would not be today. They were a difficult role they all played, to protect the Fox.

Phillip exited the way he had come in, nodding at Wythe and Randolph as they entered. Another time he would have stopped to pass the time of day with his fellow Burgesses, but today he had no use for small talk and little energy to play the foolish, prattling Phillip— a role that grew more tiresome each day, yet more and more necessary.

He walked along Duke of Gloucester Street, careless of the mud and straw that stained his impeccably polished boots. The streets had been dampened by an early morning rain, much to the delight of the free-roaming hogs who had found a particularly muddy spot in which to turn and wallow. Although the gardens of all Williamsburg houses were neatly fenced, citizens allowed their livestock to graze free, which added a unique quality to the odors along the main thoroughfares.

He smiled and bowed at acquaintances he passed, but again he did not stop. His spirits were dark, his mind greatly occupied. He could not erase the damnable wench from his thoughts. She was a witch, he mused, a veritable witch. She denied her husband his natural rights but gave herself eagerly to a stranger . . . and then showed not a shred of remorse or a trace of shame.

Familiar resentment mixed with puzzlement and an even more familiar frustration as he thought of her, for the worst of it was that the single night with her had not appeased his appetite but only teased it. He wanted her as much as ever, perhaps even more, for now he was driven by a need not only to possess her, but to *know*

230

her. He longed to understand what made that incredibly devious little mind work, to know the thoughts that spun in her head and the strength that enabled her to lie so coolly, to break down the cursed reserve she had cultivated so carefully around him, and to make her cry out with passion as she had before in his arms.

But that, he realized grimly, was the least of all things that was possible. He had taken far too many risks for her sake already. He had become careless in her arms; her warmth had lulled his caution and dulled his senses. He had almost forgotten who he was and what was at stake. She made him vulnerable, and vulnerability was one thing he could not afford.

The irony of it all brought a grimace of a smile to his face. She was his wife, but to bed her as a husband would be to reveal his identity and bring destruction upon them all. He was her lover, but to come again to her as the Fox would be to endanger her as well as himself. What a fine, taut web he had woven for himself. And there was no way out of it. None at all.

With a sigh, he turned his steps from Duke of Gloucester and crossed Market Square, toward his home and his waiting wife. When, he wondered wearily, had it all gotten so complicated, so out of his control?

The answer to that was quite simple, he reflected. It had been the moment Arabella had walked into his life.

Arabella spoke sharply to the Negro servant. "Just put the boxes on Master Phillip's bed and then get back to the parlor. See to it that the andirons in the grate are polished. I noticed a trace of soot this morning."

She held her imperious pose until the door shut and she was alone. Then she quickly looked around the room, indecisive for a moment about where to begin. This day was the first that she had been alone in the Williamsburg townhouse without Phillip or Sam. It had taken every ounce of Arabella's control to keep her cool veneer in place, and unless she learned the truth— the real truth—soon, that veneer would surely crack and leave her raving like a lunatic. She had to have evidence of Phillip's damnable trick, and when she held it in her hand, when she saw the mask and the cape, only then would she confront Phillip with his madness.

His room was on the first floor of the brick home, toward the rear, far away from her own room on the second floor that overlooked Nicholson Street. She had never been inside his chambers before, either here or at Shadowood, and she found the decor somewhat more masculine than she would have supposed. The plain but stately furnishings were accented in blue and white, and the elegantly patterned fabric had been fashioned in France, she realized, then wondered— could not help wondering—whether this was yet more evidence of his illegal shipping activities. And the ship . . . the ship he passed off as Le Renard's . . .

She stepped toward Phillip's clothespress and opened the drawers, her heart pounding hard. She had looked in every other room of the house during her housekeeping frenzy, but Phillip's own chambers were kept strictly private. Now she did not know whether the dryness in her throat was from dread or anticipation of what she might find.

Stealthily her hands moved through his clothing— the lawn shirts with their wide sleeves, the neatly rolled cotton stockings, the folded satin and brocade trousers. From the garden and the stables noises drifted in on the afternoon breeze—the sound of slaves' laughter, the clink of a pail against the stone well, the rattle of a harness. Her hands grew clumsy with the desperation of her search. It *must* be here, she told herself. She had to have some evidence, anything, to tie Phillip to the night on the boat, when he had so cruelly pretended to be Le Renard, mocking and humiliating her to his heart's delight.

Of course, as long as they both remained silent, no one would know of her degradation, but if it somehow slipped out that the flighty and silly Lady Arabella had been ravished by her own effete husband, believing him to be the dashing Le Renard, what a fool she would look. She would become the laughing stock of two continents. And there was no point in believing that a man twisted enough to concoct such a charade would have any scruples about making it known. This was more bizarre than any novel written by her English friends and more humiliating than any humiliation ever devised.

The anger that Arabella felt toward Phillip, tamped down over the past few days into simmering control, returned now in a great, roaring flame. She had hated him at first because of his foolish, simpering way, but she had at least thought him harmless. Now she despised him as a cruel and arrogant *poseur,* a man totally bereft of morals. Smuggling was certainly not beyond him in light of his capacity for cruelty, his lying, and his questionable sanity.

Arabella moved to one of the closets that flanked the fireplace. In one were the hidden stairs that led above to Sam's room; in the other were Phillip's belongings. No other house in Williamsburg had closets, but when the house had been built Phillip had insisted upon a proper repository for his clothes and wigs—far too many for a single clothespress and chest of drawers. Hurriedly Arabella went through the items neatly arranged on the shelves. How could a man own so many pairs of shoes, she wondered; so many pairs of

233

brightly polished riding boots, so many jackets, vests, and hats?

It was no use. Arabella closed the closet door and sank to a small footstool in despair. There was nothing here except the proper belongings of Master Phillip Everett, and the more she searched, the more she realized she had been a fool to expect anything. This room and every article in it cried out Phillip's presence, but it was the Phillip she knew, the prancing, mincing buck of fashion who had not a thought in his head beyond how to best present himself. The very notion that he could have the wits to impersonate Le Renard grew more absurd by the moment. Perhaps it was she who was insane, she thought on a rising tide of helplessness, and not Phillip. Perhaps her suspicions were only imagined ones, and perhaps she had imagined them because she had *wanted* it to be so, because she had wanted to believe in her Phillip of old, that the dashing lover of her dreams and the man she had married were one and the same . . .

She started guiltily to her feet as the door opened and Phillip entered. Any look of surprise on his face was quickly covered by a fatuous smile as he bowed low. "Lady Arabella, such an honor. What brings you to my sleeping chambers? Surely after your ministrations of the past days there cannot be a speck of dust left anywhere in the house."

Did she notice a flicker of apprehension in his gray eyes over her unexpected presence? She hoped so. Surely he could not fail to observe the bright spots of color in her cheeks or the dangerous gleam of fire in her eyes. Boldly she looked back, and though emotions were churning inside, she managed to keep her voice firm. "Indeed not, sir. I'm quite satisfied with the condition of your chambers. I was here only to supervise the unpacking of your costume for the governor's ball, which was delivered scarcely an hour ago." She gestured innocently toward the bed.

Phillip gave her a long, measuring look, which Arabella met without flinching. And then, with a smirk, he turned toward the large box. "My costume! What a lark. You will adore it, my dear. I vouchsafe that. Just wait until you see."

With a flourish, Phillip lifted the box's cover and tossed it aside. "Here," he cried. "Just what do you think of this?

In his hands, Phillip held a giant *papier-mâché* head of a fox.

They were an unlikely pair, the slim young lieutenant wearing the red coat of His Majesty's Royal Guard and the shabbily dressed seaman who had only three fingers on his left hand. They strolled along Duke of Gloucester Street past Chowning's Tavern to the edge of Market Square, ambling through the narrow passages created by wagons and stalls that were crowding the square's green lawn.

Today was Market Day and the farmers had brought their goods to Williamsburg. Girls with cheeks as red as their wares sold apples from the backs of wagons; farmers hawked fresh produce and offered their animals for sale—hogs and cows, sheep and goats. Chickens squawked from their wooden cages and geese added their nasal call to the general hubbub. Fresh-caught lobsters from the bay swam in huge wooden tubs, while less fortunate game, gutted and stripped, hung from hooks before the stalls, attracting flies and hagglers. To anyone observing the scene, the lieutenant and his companion were no more noticeable than any other interested shoppers come to market, and it was easy for them to become lost in the crowds.

"I've some information the governor would pay highly for," commented the three-fingered man at last, when the lieutenant seemed to slow his pace and relax his guard.

Lieutenant Warner Hastings looked with disdain at the man beside him. He hated contact with these scruffy, smelly types, but in order to satisfactorily perform his duties as aide to Lord Dunmore, he had found that such situations were often unavoidable. "The governor does not part with his coin so easily," Hastings warned mildly.

"But he's already offered five hundred guineas."

The lieutenant's gaze sharpened, but outwardly he gave no sign of interest. "What are you talking about?" he asked negligently.

His companion was wily enough to know when he had struck a spark of interest. He glanced up at the young lieutenant's face, which wore a look of studied indifference. The man decided not to dissemble any longer. "I've stumbled upon the whereabouts of th' bleedin' Fox."

There was a long pause. Hastings walked on with a measured stride, stopping to look at a string of rabbits whose lifeless legs were bound together with a leather thong. Blood ran from the gashes in their throats and trickled to the ground in a scarlet puddle, and Hastings carefully stepped around the mess, mindful of the polish on his boots.

"And *you* will lead us to him?" he said lightly to the other man, his lips curling in disbelief.

The lieutenant's remark brought forth laughter from the three-fingered man. "This is a catch that's worth more than five hundred, eh guv?"

Hastings was thoughtful. The man could be of value . . . "What's it worth? That is, of course, if you're telling the truth."

236

"Put a thousand in my pocket and I'll not only tell you where to find him, but I'll unmask the blighter meself right before yer eyes."

Was he bluffing? Hastings wondered. He stopped and rolled back on the heels of his high military boots, his blue eyes cold and questioning. "Many have sought the Fox; no one has found him. Why should I believe you? I want proof."

The spy shifted from foot to foot under the ice blue gaze, but he held onto his bravado. "Come with me on the next new moon and I'll show you where the contraband goods are hidden—goods bound for the Fox."

"Meet me tomorrow and we'll talk," Hastings ordered.

The spy waited for more words, but none were forthcoming. Making an obsequious bow, he scurried away into the crowd.

Lieutenant Hastings headed back down Duke of Gloucester Street toward his favorite tobacco shop, thinking all the while about the strange little man who had approached him. He knew the governor would give a great deal to snare the Fox, and he could hardly afford to pass by an opportunity like this. Who knew? Perhaps the lowlife did know something of Le Renard. At the very least it was worth investigating.

The palace grounds were awash with gaiety and activity as one finely drawn carriage after another pulled up to deliver its cargo of bizarrely garbed revelers. Despite the renewed tension between the burgesses and the governor, this was one event that was not to be missed. The most outstanding citizens of Tidewater, Virginia were present, and the atmosphere was light.

Arabella, devoid of jewels, was plainly clad in a long black traveling cloak. Her hair was simply dressed and almost mannish in a short queue that was drawn up to double back upon itself and was tied with a black thong at the nape of her neck. The arrangement was topped with a small cocked riding hat. Upon arriving, she gracefully accepted the hand of the footman in order to descend from the carriage. When her husband presented his arm, she took it with a regal smile that never reached her lips, and they glided silently through a wrought iron gate displaying the symbols of England— the lion and the unicorn.

If Phillip wondered at the absence of billowing skirts or a bejeweled mask, or if he gave any thought at all to what costume Arabella might be affecting beneath the cloak, he did not mention it to her. He seemed much too impressed with himself and the stunning sight he made in his lavender coat and breeches and the brightly embroidered waistcoat and profusion of lace with which he had chosen to set off the outrageously designed fox head. Arabella had to clench her teeth to prevent herself from snatching the mask away, flinging it against the wall, and screaming imprecations every time she glanced at him. Even now he would mock her—he would mock them all! How much more did she expect her to take?

She would take, Arabella resolved grimly, as much as she had to. He would find her a worthy match in his game, for she was far from conceding victory to him.

They paused in the dome-ceilinged entrance hall, awaiting presentation to the governor. As she glanced around, Arabella felt a little tremor of unease, not only for herself but for her foolish husband. Phillip might mock her, but dare he mock the authority of England?

All around them on the black walnut-paneled walls were arranged displays of muskets, swords, and

238

handguns—hundreds of them—harrowing portraits of power. The barrels of muskets were equipped with evil-looking bayonets, sharp enough to pierce the heart of a man. The swords were gleaming scimitars capable of decapitating effortlessly, their high polish reflecting the light of the myriad candles that flickered along the sideboard. Above it all flew the Union Jack, the flag of England, dominating all within its sphere, and the obvious display of arrogance and power seemed not at all an appropriate welcome for guests, but rather a deadly and frightening warning.

Raucous laughter and cries of delight reached them above the music as they were escorted down the elegant hallway toward the ballroom, and Phillip was practically rubbing his hands in childlike glee as he anticipated the reaction of the governor and his guests to his costume. Arabella felt a surge of despite for him so strong it tasted bitter in her mouth. What arrogance, what incredible naivete, she fumed silently. To play his nasty little tricks upon his gullible, unhappy wife was one thing, but if he thought for one moment that the lord governor would be amused to share his private joke, he was being foolish in the extreme.

The swords and guns that surrounded them brazenly shouted that England would not be mocked. Yet perhaps this was what Arabella hated most about Phillip—that he was confident enough in his position in the colony, and in the governor's friendship, to walk into this ballroom dressed as the Fox and expect to be received with nothing but laughter and admiration.

Arabella had refused to relinquish her cloak at the door, but now as they paused before open double doors of the ballroom, she reached up to undo the clasp, letting the garment fall into the hands of a waiting servant. Phillip stood before the doors, his companion completely forgotten in the delight of making his grand entrance, when Arabella took his arm again. "Shall we proceed, my husband?" she invited pleasantly.

He turned to look at her and the simpering smile died on his face. His visage, beneath the absurd snout of the over-dressed fox's head, tightened only the minutest fraction as his eyes swept over her, taking in the plain white shirt and genteelly tied stock, the coat in its distinctive red color, the tight-fitting dark breeches and high-topped boots, and, in her hand, the riding crop that she had kept concealed under her cloak. His eyes lingered for quite a long moment on the shape of her thighs, and she thought she saw the very faintest tint of color creep above his heavily laced collar. But absolutely nothing was in his face as he turned abruptly to the bug-eyed servant. "My wife's cloak," he requested smoothly. "I find we cannot stay."

Arabella widened her eyes for an innocent protest, but just then there was a stir in the commotion of the crowd behind them and a booming voice demanded, "And who is this who dares shadow my door?"

Phillip turned with a perfect court bow to meet the royal governor.

Lord Dunmore, dressed in the black mask and garb of a hangman, drew himself up short, eyes glowering at the travesty of justice the fox head represented. But as Phillip straightened and revealed the face beneath, his expression grew less formidable, more uncertain, until finally it erupted into a laugh. "Everett, by God! I should have known it was you! Who else would dare bring that filthy animal face into my presence but a man who hasn't the sense to come out of a storm!"

"I trust I haven't offended, my lord?" inquired Phillip anxiously, and that only precipitated another guffaw from the governor, accompanied by a mighty slap on the back.

"Papier-mâché and feathers, eh Everett? That's all

240

the substance to Le Renard! Capitol jest; simply capitol!" But his words trailed off as his eyes strayed to the smoothly smiling Arabella, and there was no mistaking the avaricious light that sprung to his eyes as they took in every detail from her thrusting breasts to her shapely legs to her curving hips. "Quite . . . unconventional, my lady," he murmured, and he bowed to her. His eyes fastened for a long and insinuating moment on the soft shape of her abdomen between waist and thighs, and then he forced himself to straighten, meeting her unperturbed eyes again. "And who," he inquired politely, his eyes flashing an unmistakable greedy message, "might you be?"

Arabella bestowed upon him a radiant smile and took the arm of her husband with both hands in an affectionate, wifely manner. "Why, my Lord Dunmore," she replied brightly, "I am the Master of the Hunt, of course!"

She felt Phillip's muscles stiffen beneath her hands with the governor's roar of laughter, and she reveled in the small humiliation she was causing him, though it was only a token repayment for the much greater and unredeemable humiliation he had brought upon her. It was, after all, a beginning.

"Oho, Everett," declared the governor slyly, "bested by your lovely bride once again! The Fox and the Master of the Hunt!" He burst into laughter again. "Deuced clever! Unsurpassed! Come, come, the both of you"—he gestured them into the ballroom, still chuckling with enormous pleasure—"welcome to my table! This will be one ball these wretched colonials will never forget, eh? The Master of the Hunt!"

Arabella held her head high, delighting in the turned heads, the outraged whispers, the quickly raised fans and averted eyes. A lady, to appear in public in breeches! And who else but Lady Arabella? It was

241

scandalous; it was unconscionable . . . and at the governor's ball! Of course the governor fawned over her—what else could be expected from an immoral Englishman? And with every gasp of shock, every murmured scrap of gossip, every distasteful glance, Arabella could feel Phillip's embarrassment grow until she thought he would surely wither with it. Not only had she made him the victim of public scandal once again and demeaned him before the governor, but she had done the utterly unforgivable—she had upstaged him. His grand jest of the elaborately designed fox mask went almost completely unnoticed in the stir of Lady Arabella's scandalous attire, and Phillip Everett, the great entertainer, faded quite ignominiously into the background.

Yet, predictably, he did not remain there for long. He greeted his acquaintances and accepted the boisterous jokes from his peers about the nature of the one who wore the breeches in the Everett family with a giggling delight, and soon he was taking credit for the idea himself. He did not disappear into the card rooms but remained diligently by her side, to all appearances enjoying the attention enormously. Only when the governor asked her to dance did Arabella have her suspicions of his true feelings confirmed. His face was smooth, his voice languorous, but she could feel the slight tensing of his arm beneath her hand as he replied before she could, "My wife will not be dancing this evening, your lordship. I'm sure you understand."

Lord Dunmore looked disappointed, but clearly he did understand, as just as clearly he reassessed the wisdom of dancing in public with a woman so attired. His smile was polite as he bowed away, but he could not prevent his glance from straying to her legs one more time.

"Why Phillip," inquired Arabella sweetly when they

were momentarily alone, "has my costume distressed you? I thought it would please you. Your own mask was so magnificent that I felt quite dowdy in the Joan-of-Arc I had ordered. I thought you would be amused."

His face was implacable; his eyes opaque. He deliberately did not glance below her waist. "I find your taste . . . questionable," he drawled at last. And then a small, self-satisfied smile caressed the corner of his lips as he decided, "However, you do seem to be drawing a great deal of attention, which happens to suit me quite well." And he smiled at her, fatuously. "Yes," he declared with some enthusiasm, "I think the evening will go even better this way. A cup of punch, my dear?"

Arabella kept the vapid smile upon her features until only the tips of his fox ears were visible among the garishly costumed crowd, and then they disappeared as abruptly as though a gust of wind had snuffed them out. Nothing remained upon her face but grim determination, and her eyes were as cold as ice.

Throughout the day she had tried to resign herself to it, but some things were simply too horrible for comprehension by the human mind, and every attempt she made to understand caused her senses to revolt. Only one thing was certain: Phillip Everett had, cruelly and deliberately, abducted his own wife, had engaged in an awful charade to mock and humiliate her, had cunningly seduced her and then had returned her abandoned. Once she had turned him from her bed. His revenge had been to take with guile and force what she had refused to give, and in a way that was far more brutal than any plain demands for conjugal rights could have been.

How he had managed the charade so effectively she did not bother to wonder. He lived to seek attention in the most outrageous ways possible, and therefore his jaded sensibilities would find the ultimate amusement in playing upon the fantasies and fears of the wife he despised. He would be laughing over this for years; he had completed the most spectacular jest of all time, and nothing could have been more rewarding to him. For that she hated him.

She did not know what he expected of her now. She did not know how he could look into her eyes and show no sign of smugness, of mockery, or of memory—how he could suddenly and completely be no more than the simple-minded Phillip Everett, bland and unctuous, wiped completely devoid of the character he once had played. She would have expected him to taunt her, to continue the mockery, to play up his cleverness for all it was worth, but she was only now beginning to learn how little she knew of her husband. Apparently he found more pleasure in imagining her private torture— or her private longing.

It would be his intention to play the game further, to wait for her to make a slip and then to pounce upon it in gleeful delight, lording his deception over her. Perhaps he expected her conscience to overcome her and force her to make a confession of adultery to him. He would take great pleasure in that before presenting her with the truth. Or perhaps he yet planned to return to her bed, to remind her as Phillip of the delights she had shared with Le Renard.

Her hands shook with hotly banked emotion even as she stood so coolly in the midst of the governor's gala reception. Her eyes narrowed with the intensity borne only of a woman most deeply abused, and the music and the laughter and the gay assemblage blurred before a more precious vision—that of Phillip Everett brought to his knees and begging mercy for his crimes. She did not know yet how she would accomplish her revenge, what method it would take, or even what it would avail her, but one thing she did know for certain:

revenge would be hers. Phillip Everett, always the fool, had overestimated himself in thinking he could make a fool of her. He would have his games, and she would bide her time, for he had not a chance. This time the *insouciant* cardsman had gone too far. Now he was playing against the master.

Charlotte Parkington arrived at the ball fully believing she had timed her arrival perfectly. Her sense of the dramatic told her it would not be wise to be the first to arrive in the crush of the crowd, nor the last, when the excitement had peaked and the governor's heady wine punch was overtaking the guests' sensibilities. No, there was an auspicious moment, one that was just right for her entrance upon the stage, and grandly she swept down the hall toward the ballroom, alone, for she wanted no escort to attract attention from herself.

She had chosen to come as a queen, for nothing less would suit her style. Inspired by Phillip's chance remark the last time she had visited his house, she had made herself up as Cleopatra.

Her gown was diaphanous and floating, the color of molten gold. Beneath it she wore no petticoats or corset, and the sheer material hugged her curves in a most delightfully scandalous way, caressing her breasts and draping over her full, voluptuous hips. On one of her milky white, well-shaped arms she wore a gold bracelet in the shape of a serpent writhing upward, and from her shoulders hung a cape of royal purple silk. She had gone to a great deal of trouble to make certain hers would be the costume to draw all eyes tonight, and if it drew a few shocked gasps and scandalized whispers as well, so much the better.

Her glossy dark hair was piled high on her head and

entwined with ropes of pearls. Her eyes were heavily shaded and outlined with charcoal, her face dabbed with rice powder and colored with rose petals, her lips brightly rouged. From her ears dangled intricately worked chain-and-jewel ornaments that she had had fashioned especially for the occasion, and a series of gold ropes were draped provocatively over her breasts. Her feet were bare except for delicate sandals woven of gold embroidery, and when she moved, the material of her gown clung to her calves and revealed more than a goodly portion of her exceptionally fine ankles. There was not a doubt in her mind that all eyes would be turned toward her entrance, and she anticipated with delight the months of gossip that would be fueled by the daring and originality of Lady Charlotte Parkington.

The entrance should have been astounding, drawing every eye and stopping all conversation in mid-syllable. Charlotte paused dramatically at the entrance of the ballroom, waiting for the attention that was her due, and she was utterly crushed to receive nothing more than a few jealous glances from the women and an occasional smile of pleasure from the men. All eyes were turned toward the dance floor.

In a mounting furor of resentment and anger, Charlotte followed the gazes toward the usurper who had spoiled her entrance. The man, tall and well formed, was wearing the long, dark cape and mask of a highwayman, but it was the woman who had stilled all tongues and bugged all eyes.

Her costume was the most outrageous device Charlotte had ever seen outside a stage play. She was dressed as a *man*. Not even Charlotte would have gone so far. With her red hair gleaming in the light of a thousand candles, the woman nimbly followed the steps of the dance, the tight cut of her breeches and

246

short jacket outlining every movement of muscle and flesh in a shockingly provocative way. And even as Charlotte watched, repulsed and insulted, she could not help but recognize a small stab of jealousy—mixed, perhaps, even with admiration—for the fact that *she* had not thought of it.

In truth, the Master of the Hunt's costume was much less revealing than the low-cut gown of Charlotte's Cleopatra, which exposed fully half of her ripe breasts and clung to her curves in a much more alluring way than was decent, but that was not the point. It was the very nerve of the woman that outraged Charlotte and every other female guest present. It was obscene, and Charlotte was astounded that the woman had even been permitted entrance.

Disguising her fury behind polite smiles and gracious bows, Charlotte drifted through the crowd, catching snatches of whispered comments as she passed.

". . . strictly forbade her to dance . . ."

"She is quite shameless . . ."

"Hastings will be answering to the governor himself, I'll warrant. I think our Lord Dunmore covets the wench for himself. . . ."

At last Charlotte paused by the side of an old friend, a man who once had been her benefactor and lover. "Who is she?" she demanded shortly, snapping open her fan. "Who is this jezebel?"

The gentleman greeted her with a low bow, his eyes sweeping Charlotte's outlined figure from head to toe. Charlotte was annoyed.

"You don't know, Charlotte?" he replied upon straightening. The lift of his eyebrow was coolly amused. "She is Phillip Everett's new bride, if you can imagine such an unlikely match. What a spectacle she has made of herself and her poor husband, and in front

247

of half the assembled company of Williamsburg and the lord governor himself. It is just as well we can't see poor Everett's face beneath the mask—I imagine it is quite green." He chuckled softly.

"Phillip? Where is he?" Charlotte looked sharply around the room, over the heads of feathered birds and monks and fairies, through the crush of potted flowers and floating silks and glittering masks.

"Over there." Her friend waved a hand. "The one in the mask of the fox." Again he laughed. "You should have been here when they arrived, Charlotte. Only Everett would have the nerve to bring the Fox to the governor's ball, and if one should ask, I would say that bride of his is no less than he deserves—"

But Charlotte did not ask. Without a bow or a by your leave, she departed his side and made her way across the room to Phillip.

"My dear, dear boy." She laid her hand upon his arm and sighed with exaggerated sympathy, lifting her wide, darkly rimmed eyes to him. "I can well imagine your chagrin. I am so sorry, but I did tell you this marriage was ill-timed and ill-suited. Just look at her."

Arabella was moving through the lively steps of a reel, alive with the music, her face glowing. She was a beautiful young woman, and Charlotte's resentment was only increased. Beautiful or no, Phillip might as well have married a trollop. And poor, dear Phillip, with his recently acquired obsession for proper appearances, would be ready to sink with mortification. Charlotte did not know whether the raw emotion that stirred within her now was on her own behalf or that of her dear boy, Phillip, and his injured pride.

She could see Phillip's tightened jaw below the mask as his eyes followed the direction of hers. But his tone was mild, drawling, and careless. "Quite disgraceful, I must admit. I doubt I shall ever live it down."

"I should lock her up, if I were you," Charlotte advised quite seriously. "No one would think less of you for it. And there is a most reputable institution not far from here . . ."

Phillip glanced at her, and she thought she detected a twinkle of startled amusement deep in his eyes. "Do not think I haven't considered it, my dear," he replied lazily, but his arm beneath her touch was very tense.

"The young man dancing with her seems quite entranced," Charlotte remarked after a moment, watching them. "I do not believe I've seen him about before."

He was quite a delicious specimen, at that, Charlotte reflected, and he was made all the more appealing because of his association with the woman she had immediately decided to hate. She would have made it her mission in life to snatch him from Lady Arabella had he been pockmarked, one-armed, and crippled, but fortunately she did not have those disadvantages with which to contend.

He was tall, as tall as Phillip, and young. His shoulders were broad and his face wonderfully accented by the domino, square and strong. His queue of dark brown hair was lustrous and full, and the effect was complimented by the rakish angle of his hat. He had fine legs, horseman's legs, with trim calves and muscular thighs that led the way nicely to a strong pelvis and well-defined—*quite* well defined—masculine attributes. Yes, Charlotte mused, eyes narrowing with the thrill of conquest, he would do rather well. This one she intended to have, by hook or by crook.

"His name is Hastings, I believe," Phillip said coolly, "an attache to the governor. Until now, I had thought him a man of breeding and good sense. I am saddened to see I misjudged."

Charlotte smiled, confident in her ability to relieve

249

Phillip of at least one burden his troublesome bride had brought. There would be no competition for the attentions of Mistress Everett from Hastings's quarter once Charlotte made his acquaintance.

Absently, her eyes roamed the room. "Lord Dunmore doesn't seem too pleased either," she commented, her tone much milder than her emotions dictated.

Her most prominent admirer stood across the room with his eyes fixed upon the swaying hips of Mistress Everett, and there was a dark and jealous scowl on his face. *That* she would not tolerate. When Charlotte Parkington was in a room, it was understood that the lord governor should have eyes for no one else. With determination and a sweet smile on her lips, she patted Phillip's arm consolingly. "Do not fret yourself, my dear. I will not have Lord Dunmore put out with you on account of your poor taste in brides. I will speak with him immediately."

Phillip bowed low over her hand as she departed, but there was gentle mockery in the curl of his lips. "How kind, dear lady, to concern yourself on my behalf! And how reassured I am that our host will find himself in much better humor once you have worked your charms upon him."

Charlotte's smile faltered only slightly at the hint of bitterness in his tone, for she was ever confused by Phillip's easy descent into duplicity. Yet what could she expect? The poor dear had been dreadfully abused this night, and he had been jealous of Lord Dunmore ever since Charlotte had turned her devotion his way.

Somewhat cheered by the reassurance that she still had the power to bring men to odds over her affections, Charlotte made her way to Lord Dunmore's side.

Governor Dunmore bowed low over her hand and made the obligatory charming remarks about her costume, but Charlotte could not help noticing how his eyes strayed to the dance floor, to the couple cavorting there, and especially to Lady Arabella. Yet as Charlotte chattered on with him, exchanging pleasantries and catching him up on the latest gossip, she seethed within. First the young wench had stolen Phillip and had made him dreadfully unhappy, and now the red-haired slip of a girl seemed to have caught the governor's eye—not to mention the way she had captivated the handsome young Hastings, whom Charlotte had marked for her own.

It was entirely too much. Lord Dunmore was a valued and important ally. Until now Charlotte had been very special to him, but his attentions now seemed to be totally fixed upon the firm young buttocks of Phillip Everett's bride. A tiny frown started to wrinkle Charlotte's brow, but she willed it away. Damnation! She would not have this party ruined for her, not by some chit of a girl who somehow seemed to have captivated half the men at the ball.

At last the quadrille ended, and Hastings bowed low over Arabella's hand as a wonderful smile lit his mouth. Whatever words he spoke brought an answering smile to Arabella's face, and Charlotte suddenly felt a deep stab of possessive jealousy for this young man whom she had never even met. It wasn't fair, she thought furiously. She had lavished too much care on her costume for all eyes to be on a silly girl dressed as a man!

The governor caught Hastings's eyes and with an imperious wave of his hand brought the young lieutenant over, along with Arabella.

The governor bowed over Arabella's hand. Charlotte could not help noticing the tiny squeeze he gave her fingers and the way he held them a moment longer than was strictly polite. "My dear," he murmured, "you dance charmingly, but I thought your husband had forbidden it."

"Indeed he has." Arabella's eyes gleamed mischievously. "But then Phillip and I always seem to differ about my dancing. I shall be able to placate him later, I am certain."

"My only regret, dear child, is that it was not I but this brash young lieutenant who first received the honor of your hand in the dance." Through his smile there was an edge of real anger, and Arabella noticed it with curiosity.

"Oh, do not fault Lieutenant Hastings," she reassured him quickly. "It was I who asked him, is that not so?"

The young man shook his head. "From the moment you walked in, Lady Arabella, I knew I could not rest until I had met you." He bowed gallantly over her hand and kissed it, seemingly oblivious to the governor's displeasure and the cold fury of the unknown woman beside them.

When he raised his head, he looked into the flashing brown eyes of the woman and was instantly alert. There was danger there, and he did not know the source. And there was also passion and a touch of malice. She was a dangerous woman—Hastings could tell that instantly—much more so than his dancing companion, who, despite her provocative behavior, was no more than a young girl having fun at her husband's expense. But this dark-haired queen, Cleopatra of the Nile, looked as though she might well live up to the bloodthirsty reputation of her namesake. He told himself to be wary, yet her dark eyes held him and he only half listened. Women, like battles, were as inately dangerous as they were exciting, and Hastings took his greatest pleasures from the thrills of both.

"Forgive my manners, ladies," the governor said with another bow. "I fear I am quite befuddled by the loveliness that surrounds me and have forgotten to make introductions. Lady Arabella and Lieutenant Hastings, neither of you have met my good friend, Lady Charlotte Parkington. Her plantation, Parkland, is quite one of the finest on the James—in truth as lovely as your own Shadowood, Lady Arabella."

Hastings bent low over Charlotte's hand and once more received a jolt of something inexplicable from the depths of her dark eyes. Her smile was alluring and explicit, her perfume heady, and the invitation Hastings received was unmistakable; it made his heart race with anticipation. She was lush and willing, and he was more than ready to oblige her.

But then those dark eyes swung from their sultry focus upon him to Lady Arabella, and the message there changed abruptly and most disconcertingly. It was hate. Lady Parkington hated Lady Arabella, and Hastings could not fathom why.

The two women locked gazes, green eyes measuring dark, and neither wavered. "So," Charlotte said sweetly, "you are Phillip's little bride. How charming. And how dreadfully pained I am that I have been unable to call upon you, but"—she waved a careless and dismissing hand—"so much demands my attention."

Arabella knew when she was being snubbed by an expert. Her smile was most gracious but mistook no charity. "How very peculiar," she remarked in the same sweet tone, "that my husband has never seen fit to mention your name. You must be a neighbor, I believe?"

A brief flash of something vicious registered in Charlotte's eyes for the match she had found in the young vixen, but her tone was light and superior. "Oh, indeed, much more than that! Dear Phillip and I have known each other for ages!" Again she waved a

253

graceful hand. "After the death of my beloved husband, Phillip was such a comfort to me." Her eyes were all innocence, but the meaning was clear.

On Arabella's part there was little but astonishment, which she hid admirably. Phillip and this cool, sophisticated woman who exuded sensuality from every pore? Impossible. Unless . . . unless her suspicions about that night on the boat had been right. Unless Phillip's duplicity extended even beyond what she had guessed.

Her heart was beating so loudly with this speculation that she barely heard the next words. Charlotte, sensing that she had struck home and struck hard, pushed her advantage. "That was, of course," she added with a trace of condescension, "long before your husband took it into his head to find a bride. He has changed so much since then," she mused innocently, and Arabella stared hard at her. What was this woman trying to tell her?

Before she could even begin to form a response, Phillip appeared by Arabella's side. His jaw was tight, his eyes angry, but his manner was as controlled as ever.

"Charlotte my dear," he drawled, "I couldn't help remarking from across the room how beautiful you look. Quite the center of attention, as ever. And what a pleasure it is to see a lady adorn herself so imaginatively yet remain forever within the bounds of acceptable taste." The remark was pointed and Arabella tensed, not only for herself but for Lord Dunmore and Lieutenant Hastings, who were observing the proceedings between the two women with ever increasing curiosity.

Charlotte laughed lightly, tapping him affectionately on the arm. "And your fox head, dear boy! You are far too clever by half. Do you not agree, my lord?"

She bestowed her gracious smile on the governor, who hastened to agree.

Arabella made a little *moue* of distaste at the turn of the conversation. The woman had obviously set herself up as Arabella's rival, and Phillip was abetting her. And if anyone should speak of acceptable taste, it most certainly should not be her husband.

She smiled brightly at Phillip. "Why, I do believe the music has started again. Perhaps—"

"Perhaps you and I shall have some refreshments." Phillip's hand clamped firmly upon her arm.

Arabella's brilliant smile vanished like wind into a pout. "But if I cannot dance, why should I stay?" she demanded. "How can you be so unkind? I think I shall call for the carriage straightaway."

Lieutenant Hastings made a move as though to volunteer to escort her, Governor Dunmore opened his mouth to protest, and Phillip's fingers tightened on her arm. It was he who spoke first, smoothly and calmly. "Of course you shan't, my love. The fireworks have yet to begin, and we would not wish to miss the best part of the evening."

"Indeed not, Lady Arabella," Governor Dunmore hastened to add. "Our illuminations are quite dramatic. Tonight's display will be one you are not likely to forget."

Lieutenant Hastings's smile was charming yet secretly amused. "Of that I can assure you, my lady," he said with a bow. "Please do not deprive us all of your most delightful presence. Stay for our spectacle, and allow us to entertain you."

Arabella pretended to consider, then turned her dimpling smile first on the governor and then on his lieutenant. "How could I refuse two such charming gentlemen? I admit I am quite intrigued. We will stay," she announced regally.

Phillip lost no more time. "Then come, dear, let us sample some of our host's most excellent refreshments. I am sure your dancing has quite tired you out." With a low, sweeping bow, Phillip made his farewells and moved toward the supper room with Arabella in tow.

Governor Dunmore's eyes followed Arabella's departure far too fondly for Charlotte's liking. And when he turned back to her, it was only to mention the wench's name again. "And what do you think of Everett's bride, my lady? Quite an addition to our colonial revels, eh?"

"Quite an addition," murmured Charlotte politely, but her eyes were glittering and Lieutenant Hastings was struck again by the malice within them. "I look forward to knowing her better." The lie came out smoothly and placated the governor, whose eyes were wandering elsewhere about the room among his brightly costumed guests. But Hastings heard it and again he wondered.

"Ah, excuse me, my dear," Lord Dunmore said, casting a vague smile in Charlotte's direction as he returned a nod to someone across the room. "I see Colonel Jameson bowing. Doubtless he intends to introduce me to another one of his tiresome daughters." With a short bow to Charlotte, and another to Hastings, he mumbled, "Your servant," and departed.

Charlotte could not help being somewhat miffed. Never could she recall the lord governor being quite so anxious to depart from her company and she knew it was because he was confident he had fairer game waiting as soon as Lady Arabella could be torn from her husband's side. Only Lieutenant Hastings's smooth words soothed her temper.

"And so Lady Parkington, the governor does me a great favor, leaving me alone with the most beautiful lady in the room." His smile was charming, his lips full and sensuous, and his teeth a brilliant white. He bowed and extended his arm. "Might I have the honor of escorting you to the supper room?"

Charlotte bestowed upon him an elaborate curtsy— one designed to give him the best possible view of her overfull bosom—and inclined her head in consent, resting her fingers on his forearm. He was quite tall, and, from what she could see beneath the mask, fully as handsome as she had first imagined. His eyes were a sultry blue-gray, his forehead wide, his cheekbones broad and well defined. She wondered with more than idle curiosity if he and Lady Arabella had already made the consummate leap together. Had the little wench cuckolded Phillip so soon?

"Have you known Mistress Everett long?" she inquired silkily as they made their way toward the double doors that opened into the supper room.

He shook his head. "Our acquaintance began only this evening, when we were introduced. She seemed so unhappy when her husband refused to dance with her that I offered myself as a partner."

Charlotte slanted him a glance that only a fool or an underage boy could misread. "You are a very accom- modating young man," she purred.

Hastings laughed softly, and his eyes sparked with promise. "I can be, my lady, I assure you," he murmured. And then he added, "Where Mistress Everett is concerned, however, I'm afraid I was only in for the sport. That husband of hers is—" He broke off. "My apologies," he offered. "I realize that you and he are friends."

Charlotte's smile was cool and inviting. "I am dreadfully fond of Phillip, of course, but sometimes his behavior mystifies even me. What were you about to say? Have no fear," she assured him as she ran her fingers lightly up the inside of his arm and lowered her

257

voice enticingly. "I am the very soul of discretion."

Hastings's eyes brightened instinctively and his thoughts were far from Lady Arabella and Phillip Everett. "I was only going to remark," he murmured, "what a very peculiar match it is. They seem so ill suited. I thought perhaps it could not hurt the fine Mr. Everett to see the futility of trying to hold such a bird as Lady Arabella on a string. Especially"—his smile glinted mischievously—"as I had no fear of finding myself across a dueling from the good gentleman come morning."

"Hmmm." Charlotte recalled that there had been a time when Phillip had been quite the swordsman—in bed and out. Apparently, however, for reasons known only to himself, that time had passed.

She favored Hastings with the full brilliance of her magnificent eyes. "So you felt quite safe in your little flirtation?"

Hastings stopped and looked down at her, into the beautiful camellia-pale face, into the deep, dark, glittering eyes, and he gave the only answer that a healthy young man could give. "Oh yes," he said softly. "I felt quite safe . . . until I met you, Lady Parkington."

Charlotte smiled the smile of the satisfied cat and tucked her fingers more securely into the crook of his arm as they proceeded into the supper room.

Chapter XIV

The illuminations, always the highlight of every social function at the governor's palace, began before eleven with bright streaks of color that cut through the dark sky and brightened up the night. The governor and his guests, raucous with wine punch and conviviality, pushed from the ballroom toward the terraces that overlooked the gardens. On the palace mall, the townspeople of Williamsburg, eager to see the display, passed jugs of rum from hand to hand and shouted out their approval as vivid fingers of red and blue and green blossomed into fantastical flowers and animals above them. Their cheers carried across the noise of the fireworks to the ears of the aristocracy when the image of a peacock, more elaborate than any strutting across the governor's lawn, was emblazoned for an instant in the sky, only to dissipate into a long gray plume of smoke before another burst of color replaced it.

Guided by Phillip's unrelenting fingertips at her elbow, Arabella moved with the other guests toward the ballroom gardens. He had insisted that she slip on her cloak, claiming the night air to be chilly. Arabella meekly complied, hiding a smug satisfaction in having already made her point.

The press of the crowd was close with guests jostling to reach the terrace and view the pyrotechnics, which the governor had promised would be even more spectacular than his last display. Once Arabella was pushed from behind and she lost her step. When she looked for Phillip's steadying hand, she found that he had slipped away from her. Glancing up, she saw at her side not the ruddy mask of the fox but the stern countenance of a dominie in gray. And beyond, across the masked heads of Roman generals, queens of England, birds of prey, and Egyptian pharaohs, she saw a fox's head moving slowly away from the flow of the crowd.

There was something so unexpected in Phillip's sudden desertion of her and such furtiveness in the way he moved away from the illuminations instead of toward them that Arabella's suspicions were immediately aroused. He had been beside her all evening, hovering about like a mother hen over its only chick, until she had been hard put to bite back a scream at his suffocating attentions and the constant touch of his hand upon her arm. And now he was leaving—no, creeping away—like a man on his way to a liaison.

Arabella did not hesitate. She turned and began to worm her way through the throng, keeping the red ears of the fox mask in view. Phillip was drifting slowly toward the large boxwoods that lined the ballroom gardens, and she was determined to follow him.

He was up to something, Arabella was sure, and, whatever it was, she wanted to know more. She had once thought that she knew everything about her foppish husband; she was now beginning to realize she knew nothing at all. She had thought him an effeminate weakling; he had proved to be a lover of consummate skill. She had judged him a fool and a ninny; she had learned he was cleverer than the

260

devil himself.

Arabella wrapped her dark cloak more closely around herself and stepped onto the path that Phillip had taken. The shrubs grew high on either side of the garden and she tried to melt into the shadows of a boxwood, kneeling down behind the bush and holding her breath, her eyes adjusting to the darkness as she watched Phillip.

His movements were no longer furtive, but quick and sure. Within seconds he had stripped off his lavender coat and mask and was pushing them into the hands of another who had appeared as if by magic from the darkness. The man hesitated for a moment and his words were voiced in a low, stunned rasp. "You? By God, I never—"

"There is no time for discussion," came Phillip's sharp response. "Just do as your instructions bid."

Quickly the second figure slipped on the fox head and the jacket while Phillip wrapped himself in the long black cloak of the highwayman, the high collar of which obscured the back of his head and the lower part of his face. In seconds the man in Phillip's mask and lavender coat came back down the path toward her, and Arabella, willing herself to be a part of the shrub, crouched lower into its shadow as Hastings hurried past.

Arabella caught sight of Phillip as a bright streak of fireworks flashed above them, illuminating the ebony sky. He was moving swiftly now, his black cloak billowing behind him. She drew her own cloak more tightly around her body as Phillip crossed the fruit gardens, using the dark forms of the trees to hide himself as he darted from shadow to shadow.

Pausing at the edge of the garden, Arabella hesitated momentarily. It was more than obvious that Phillip had a purpose, one that drove him to steal away from

261

the party like a thief in the night. For the first time she was struck by a premonition that something dreadful was in the offing, and the night air practically sang with the scent of danger. Phillip was not out for an evening stroll. His departure from the party had been well planned and deliberately acted out. And there had been another man involved, someone willing to impersonate Phillip. It was a conspiracy! But why? she wondered. Why this elaborate charade?

It had to be another one of Phillip's silly games, but who was to be his victim this time? There was only one way to find out, Arabella realized as she moved across the fruit garden, using the shadows as she had seen Phillip do.

The holly maze was ahead and Arabella's heart sank. Once in the maze, she would never find him. But Phillip ignored the intricate, concealed paths and suddenly turned right, climbing a small hill covered with clumps of trees.

He moved rapidly, his long strides covering ground effortlessly while Arabella struggled to keep up. Her breath was rasping in her throat now and her heart labored as she attempted to match his pace. Trying to move more quickly, she became careless, and a twig broke loudly beneath her foot. She stood immobilized, not daring to breathe, clinging to the trunk of a tree and wishing she could disappear into it.

Phillip turned, his eyes raking the line of trees where she stood. Arabella was sure that he had seen her, heard her choking, grabbing for breath, sensed her presence in the darkness. For a long moment he looked, then he turned and hurried on as another burst of fireworks lit the sky.

They were behind the fireworks now, the governor's palace effectively screened by the rows of trees, and at last Phillip seemed to have reached his destination. He stood, as though waiting, before a small brick building that looked military in design.

Arabella had no idea what mission might have brought him here. With rare good judgment, she had paused, hovering at the edge of the copse while he had weaved his way from shadow to shadow toward the building. And now, as he stood, other figures merged with Phillip's; men materialized from nowhere and began following Phillip's low, curt orders with military precision. This was not a band of friends gathered together for some haphazard reason, Arabella realized with growing puzzlement and fascination. These men had an objective, a cause, and, inexplicably, Phillip seemed to be at the center of it.

The sky above was lit periodically by the fireworks display, and great streamers of red and mauve and yellow cast an eerie glow over the men who worked so determinedly at their tasks. Arabella was too far away to see their faces; Phillip's was the only form she recognized as he worked in the midst of the men who carried casks into the building and then emerged empty-handed. Quick orders were given for the band to move away, and Phillip was again left alone near the building.

Arabella's mind raced with a thousand unanswered questions. What kinds of supplies would Phillip take into a building on the goveror's grounds in the middle of the night? Why this subterfuge, this surreptitious meeting in the dark? And then, in dawning horror, she had her answer.

Phillip removed a leather pouch from beneath his cloak and disappeared into the building. When he emerged, he was spreading a powder on the ground behind him, leaving a shining trail that snaked across the ground into the building.

Gunpowder! He was laying a line of gunpowder

from thè heavily fortified building. Mesmerized, seeing but not believing, Arabella watched as Phillip stooped and struck the flint. A spark caught the powder and raced toward the building. All of this flashed before her eyes, but none of it seemed real: Phillip swathed in black, bending to light the flame, the flame catching and burning, and, in the distance, the shouting of the crowd at the governor's palace as yet another illumination caught the fancy of the observers.

The tiny flame raced down the line of gunpowder toward the building, and Phillip straightened and began to run from the scene. In the darkness a voice shrill with excitement called out, "Only Le Renard would dare this on the night of the governor's ball!"

Only Le Renard. Le Renard . . . The words reverberated in Arabella's head.

With a sputter, the spark reached its goal and an ear-shattering explosion tore the building apart with the fury of an unleashed volcano. Arabella sank to her knees, peering at the burning building through trembling fingers as pieces of debris flew into the air like torches thrown by an angry giant. A great ball of fire, brighter than ten thousand suns, lit up the night with its angry glow and turned the sky red-orange with its licking tongues of flame. For an instant Phillip was silhouetted against the hellish inferno and, as he turned away from the fire, Arabella saw his face. On it he wore a black mask—the mask of the Fox.

Arabella gave a little moan and clasped her arms across her stomach, as if in pain. It was no game, no trick, no jest. Phillip—her Phillip—was the Fox, and on the night of the governor's ball, within clear sight of the palace, he had blown up the private munitions storehouse before the governor's very eyes.

*   *   *

If anyone had asked Charlotte Parkington to attest to Phillip's presence in the ballroom during the explosions at the munitions building, she would have done so without hesitation. Phillip she had seen and spoken to, but Hastings and Arabella had been nowhere in sight. About that she was very sure.

Always alert and intent for any kind of gossip that might be amusing enough to pass on to Lord Dunmore, or any information that might raise her in his esteem, Charlotte had found it extraordinarily interesting that both Arabella and the handsome young lieutenant had been conspicuously absent when the fireworks display had begun. Charlotte had seen Arabella and Phillip—how could one miss those fox ears bobbing above the crowd—making their way toward the gardens, and then they had seemed to disappear as if swallowed up by the darkness.

Hastings had been by Charlotte's side then, where he had spent the better part of the evening. He had been most attentive and Charlotte had been certain she had captured his fascination in every way she had intended. But then, suddenly—just as suddenly as Arabella and Phillip—he was gone. The three of them, she mused. Yet for all the devious twistings of her mind, Charlotte could not imagine why that trio should sneak away together, skulking into the night.

And then she realized that she was wrong. Phillip had not left at all, for there he was among the guests, his ruddy mask plainly evident. It was only Hastings and Arabella who were missing, and the reason for that was abundantly clear. What else but a lover's tryst?

Charlotte felt a sharp pang of distress. Despite Hastings's words to the contrary and his attentions all evening, he was evidently still taken with the red-haired vixen. He wasted no chance to be with her, even leaving Charlotte standing in order to take the wench right

265

beneath her husband's nose.

Her own fury and shame at being abandoned warred with her sympathy for Phillip. Poor boy. Poor, silly, cuckolded boy. Her eyes narrowed upon the fox figure across the way and her first instinct was to go to him immediately and inform him of the dastardly treachery being perpetrated on him this night. Fie on the handsome Lieutenant Hastings and his smug confidence, for he would feel the point of Phillip's sword before morning if Charlotte revealed the truth.

But then she hesitated. She had no wish to hurt her Phillip, for it was well known that the bearers of ill tidings often received the worst of it themselves. And perhaps, in Phillip's case, ignorance was bliss. Did he not have enough trouble with his bride without having her infidelity flaunted in his face?

Or perhaps he did know, it occurred to Charlotte, and did not care. Then the wiser man he. For if he were aware of his wife's unfaithfulness, he might be ripe to fall into the comforting arms of an old friend . . .

Charlotte was accustomed to playing her cues by ear, and she was not apt to miss any opportunity that could conceivably be turned to her advantage. As the fireworks began, she pushed her way through the crowd toward Phillip. She still was unsure of her course of action, but of one thing she was certain. Her knowledge of Arabella's and Hastings's tryst was far too valuable to be kept secret.

She would not tell him, she decided, not in so many words. She would only hint, and if Phillip cared, then he could do as he wished. Charlotte would be wise enough to protect herself against his wrath, and if all came to rights, he could be eternally grateful to the friend who had warned him of his wife's perfidy. By the time she reached his side, she had convinced herself that she was acting only as a friend, nothing more.

266

Alone, Phillip hovered uneasily near the door, watching the fiery trails of the illuminations streak across the night sky.

"Magnificent, aren't they, darling?" Charlotte laid her hand lightly upon his satin-clad arm.

The fox head nodded up and down.

"It's too bad your wife isn't here to see them." Charlotte looked at him expectantly. "Where can she have gotten to, do you imagine?"

There was no response.

"Perhaps she is startled by loud noises," Charlotte suggested.

Phillip was silent.

Charlotte pursued her point with no great amount of tact. "And Hastings, too. Why, I don't see him anywhere." Dramatically she looked about as if she expected to find Hastings hiding behind one of the potted palms.

As she spoke, she could feel the muscles of Phillip's arm tighten beneath her hand, and for a moment Charlotte felt a twinge of pity for him. Poor Phillip, married to such a conniving woman. He had done nothing to deserve such distress.

Charlotte decided that obviously she had been wrong to mention the vile woman's name to Phillip. Rather she should have kept the information to herself, for obviously there was no advantage in upsetting Phillip. Surely if she thought long and hard enough, there would be some way to use this evening's events to her gain. Nothing would bring her greater satisfaction than to bring low the high-flying Lady Arabella . . . unless, she mused, it would be to rekindle the interest of Hastings, which for a brief time had flowered so brightly. Perhaps, with luck, she could use her new knowledge of the two adulterers to do both.

Charlotte was just about to turn to Phillip and tell

267

him that perhaps she had been mistaken, when an enormous explosion set the air afire. It was huge, terrifying, brilliant, and certainly no part of the planned illuminations. Ladies screamed, gentlemen shouted and started for the gun room; the crowd surged forward. Roars of terror rose up from the streets outside. Somehow in the chaos Phillip slipped away from her, but Charlotte, her eyes wide with excitement and her hand pressed to her breast, hardly noticed. All thoughts of Phillip, Lady Arabella, and Hastings—as well as anything else—were pushed from Charlotte's mind.

Another explosion rent the air, and Arabella, kneeling on the ground, placed her arms over her head, shrinking as much from the noise and the danger as from the new and devastating truth she had just learned. Daring to look again, she saw no sign of Phillip, but she remained transfixed and on her knees, watching the fire that burned more fiercely than the flames of hell and shivering as the seering mass fed upon itself and grew brighter and brighter.

In the distance she could hear other voices, crying out in alarm or calling for help, and from far away came the ringing of the bells of the fire brigade. Soldiers began to appear at last, looking disoriented and confused, standing paralyzed for the most part as they stared at the conflagration that raged like a demon through the night. It lit the faces of those who watched, etching on them looks of fear and wonder at the blazing fury before them.

Then the figures moved to begin their futile efforts to put out the blaze, and Arabella rose to her feet, staggering a little at first, holding on to a tree until the spinning in her head cleared. Then she began to run,

268

faster and faster through the night, until at last she reached the safety of the governor's palace.

She pushed through the throng of bodies pressing to get out, their excited chatter sounding like the buzzing of insects in her ears. Her lungs were bursting and her head was swimming, and she clutched a marble support pillar for balance, desperately struggling for breath. And then a familiar nasal voice droned behind her, "Why, my dear girl, you are quite beside yourself! Such excitement, eh? I don't believe I've ever . . ."

She turned slowly to look into the painted, exuberantly chattering face of her husband. Phillip, complete with fox mask and lavender jacket, stood before her like a memory of a bad dream. She lifted a hand to reach for him, then she fainted dead away.

Arabella was not the only lady to swoon that evening, but her fainting spell was, no doubt, the only one that was genuine. She drifted back to the unpleasant aroma of burnt feathers being wafted under her nose, the irritating motions of languid fingers rubbing her wrists, and the hubbub of a dozen voices speaking at once. She made weak motions to push away the offensive scent of feathers, and her eyes focused reluctantly.

She was lying on a small and uncomfortable divan in a curtained anteroom off the supper room. A solicitous black face bent over her with the feathers, and it was Phillip's voice that kept murmuring an absent, "There, there." Beyond the curtain she could see the crowd of skirts and satin breeches, and hear the excited voices: "Le Renard! They say it was Le Renard!"

"Damn the creature anyway!"

"No, didn't you hear? It was the illuminations. A spark must have set off the munitions . . ."

"Stuff and nonsense! I had it from the governor's own guard. It was gunpowder . . ."

"Always said those blasted things were dangerous! Chinese, you know . . ."

"Deliberate treason! He set off the munitions dump hoping the illuminations would cover . . ."

"Le Renard? Did you hear? Le Renard . . ."

"Here on the very palace grounds!"

"Even now, skulking about . . ."

"Le Renard . . ."

Arabella murmured weakly, "No . . . ," and struggled to sit up, her thoughts awhirl and unfocused as her vision.

"There!" pronounced Phillip with satisfaction, dismissing the servant with a snap of his wrist. "I told you she was coming around. Such dreadful goings on! Gracious, m'dear, you're as white as muslin, not that I can wonder. Here, do lie back; there's a good girl."

The servant bowed away and Phillip pressed a cool, dry hand against her forehead, pushing her back. Arabella could do nothing but stare.

Someone poked a head in the curtain. "All right, Everett? Yes, looking right as rain. The ladies are dropping like flies; they are—"

Another broke in, "Did you hear? Oh, pardon, Mistress. Are you quite all right?" He added excitedly, "They're saying it's that Fox again, right here under our noses—"

Phillip waved them away, saying in a greatly pained voice, "My dear sirs, have pity please! Can't you see my poor wife is distressed enough as it is? Such distasteful talk before the ladies—"

"Yes, yes, of course . . . Mistress, your health . . ." Bowing and murmuring, the two men departed, but excitement was snapping in their eyes and on the other side of the curtain they resumed their declarations again. "You've got to credit the renegade! A stunt like this . . ."

"Blast and tarnation! I can't recall such a stir since . . ."

And Arabella simply stared at Phillip. There was no mistake. It was he, in lavender coat and fox mask, just as he had been standing so calmly before her after her frantic race back to safety . . . just as, to all appearances, he had been all during the Fox's escapades. If any of the guests were questioned, there was no doubt in Arabella's mind that each of them would testify to Phillip Everett's presence in the palace throughout the illuminations. Yet why should they be asked? He had done it—pulled off an unbelievable act of treason with a hundred witnesses to prove he was innocent. A sort of dazed admiration filled her and she thought, *Dear God, he is my husband*. He was astounding, the most devious man she had ever met, and also the bravest and most brilliant. He *was* the Fox; nothing was beyond him.

But now he was playing the role of Phillip, and he was playing it to its fullest. "Sweet Arabella, how distressed you've made me! Dreadful business, isn't it? Enough to make anyone faint. In fact I feel quite that way m'self, don't you know."

Arabella shook her head, then nodded dizzily. Nothing Phillip said made sense; in fact nothing in the world made sense this night. Solicitously he patted her hand and got to his feet with a great show of resolve. "I know just the thing," he declared. "Stay here and I shall fetch you a potion. Might take one for myself, come to think of it. The state of my nerves . . ." And he wandered through the curtain, shaking his head and murmuring to himself.

Arabella struggled to a sitting position, watching him depart, her heart thudding erratically in her chest.

271

Of course she should have known. She should have realized Phillip was not pretending. It was all there—in the way he carried himself, the breadth of his chest, the set of his shoulders, the tilt of his head. It had been there all along and she had been too blind—or too foolish—to see. But Phillip . . . Phillip . . .

It was too much to take in; too much for one night. She needed time to think, to absorb all of this, to think what to do, what it might mean. And over and over her heart seemed to pound with the music of only one incredible, joyful word: *Phillip!*

There was a new commotion outside, and Arabella got shakily to her feet to see what it might be. She reached the entranceway of her little alcove just as Lord Dunmore strode through the garden doorway, and the excited voices stilled expectantly.

Lord Dunmore, governor of Virginia, was livid. His face was the hue of freshly cut liver and his eyes bulged menacingly as he stalked into the ballroom. There was nothing he could do, nothing at all but put a good face on the whole affair, and that he did to the best of his noble ability.

"Good ladies and gentlemen," he began, raising his hand for attention. "The fire is under control."

Shouting and applause greeted his remark.

The governor held up his hand for silence. "These rebels—these abominations against God and country who dare to defile His Majesty's property—have not succeeded. We have munitions stored in other places, so there is no cause for alarm that the subjects of the Crown are without protection."

Dunmore took a deep breath and waited for the scattered applause to end. "And may I say that even now, our troops—the best-trained soldiers in all the world—are combing the streets for these nefarious renegades, and we shall find them."

The governor paused and wiped his purplish brow with his handkerchief. The night had been a long one, and he still had hours to go.

"And now, before I meet with my staff"—the governor cast a glowering look at the covey of embarrassed young officers huddled in the doorway— "I have one more announcement. We have reason to believe that we know the criminal who perpetrated this vile deed, and I therefore announce tonight that the bounty upon the hide of that villain known as Le Renard shall be doubled to one thousand guineas."

On the other side of the room, Arabella saw Phillip, smirking his own brand of restrained enthusiasm, lift his hands politely to join the applause. But Arabella, sinking back against the door frame, was gripped by an uncontrollable shiver as she listened to the crowd cheer for the death of her husband.

Chapter XV

Lord Dunmore arose late the next morning after a sleepless night that had left him bloated, suffering from a headache, and more irritable than usual. The fact that he was already too late to attend services at Bruton Parish only exacerbated his condition. The only thing worse than facing a church full of smirking citizens after the humiliation delivered to the throne by the Fox last night was to imagine them glancing at the royal governor's chair and speculating that he had not had the nerve to face them.

Damn. He brought his fist down upon the small fireside table with a force that rattled his untouched breakfast tray. Until last night he had held out some hope that things might be beginning to calm down. This session of the Burgesses had started out restrained, if not completely amicable, and he had even had some hope of resolving the differences between himself and the colonists that had made his life so miserable this past year. And to add to his own personal delight, there had been the knowledge that the winsome Lady Arabella would be in residence for some weeks, which provided the more than delightful prospect of furthering his acquaintanceship with her.

He had not anticipated the coming of Publick Times with greater pleasure since his arrival in Virginia two years ago. His idea for the masked ball had seemed just the thing to keep everyone's spirits on the right track, and everything had been going perfectly—most especially the unexpected appearance of Lady Arabella in a costume that it even now made his blood flame to recall—and then enter Le Renard, once again dashing his hopes, spoiling his plans, making him look the fool, and plunging his well-ordered world into chaos.

"Damnation," he muttered aloud, and his fist clenched against the linen table cover as his eyes narrowed at the congealed mess of ham, soft eggs, and cold tea in a china cup. He should have been celebrating this morning, but instead he was once more facing the prospect of writing a report to England regarding his latest failure, and even his breakfast was ruined. "Damnation," he growled again, and, at a soft tap on his chamber door, he snapped, "Come in!"

Lieutenant Hastings presented himself before the royal governor, looking reluctant, uncertain, and somewhat crestfallen, as well he should.

"And so," declared his lordship, welcoming the chance to vent his frustration upon someone besides himself, "you come skulking in here like the cowardly dog you are!" He pushed himself up from the table, a formidable figure in silk dressing gown and wig, his dark eyes narrowed and his color rising. "What happened to the hearty detail that was supposed to be guarding the storehouse last night? Have you managed to discover that? I would have an answer, man!" he bellowed.

Lieutenant Hastings had the grace to look abashed, but his gaze did not waver. "Our guards were found bound and gagged in a spring house some distance from the munitions dump, your lordship. Apparently the Fox was too clever for even our most stalwart militiamen. There was nothing that could be done to prevent it, for one never knows when or where he will strike."

That very obvious truth was the last thing Lord Dunmore needed to hear this morning, and he turned abruptly away, fuming impotently. "That dastardly renegade will be the ruin of us all," he muttered, fists clenching. "Do you have any idea how much we lost last night? Our militia will be virtually helpless for weeks, and Heaven forbid we should be called upon for a major defense . . ." He muffled another oath, bringing one fist forcefully into the other. "By God, if I could get my hands on the villain—"

"Then perhaps," ventured Hastings, taking a small step forward, "on that tact I might have some news that will cheer your lordship."

Lord Dunmore turned sharply.

"I have been in contact with a man," explained Hastings carefully, "who claims to be able to lead us to the Fox. Already he has taken me to a place where contraband goods are stored, and he assures me they are delivered into the hands of none other than Le Renard."

The formidable gleam of worried displeasure in the governor's eyes sharpened into avarice. "And you are convinced?" he demanded.

"I believe," reported Hastings firmly, "that we are closer than we have ever been." And then he hesitated. "My . . . informant . . . demands a thousand guineas before he will take us further."

But the naming of the sum hardly gave his lordship pause. "I would take it from my own purse!" he declared, his dark eyes suddenly alive with the taste of blood. He began to pace excitedly around the room, his head racing with the possibilities afforded him by

277

Lieutenant Hastings's revelation. He could almost feel his hand closing about the scrawny neck of the Fox; he could imagine the parade through the streets of Williamsburg—himself at the fore and the caged Fox dragged behind—the cheering crowds on either side. . . . They might be only days away from victory, and the next missive sent to England could record his triumph. He might even receive a commendation and a special place at court. He might be able, once and for all, to put this abominable colony behind him and return in honor and exultation to England.

The day was suddenly brighter, his head ceased aching, and his appetite was restored. "What are you waiting for?" he demanded when he whirled to find Hastings still standing there. With a grand gesture of his billowing sleeve, he dismissed him. "See my treasurer, withdraw the funds, and be off with you! We haven't a moment to delay!"

Hastings bowed out, and Lord Dunmore rang impatiently for another breakfast. He settled down before the fire with a great sigh of satisfaction to await it, his head filled with grand plans for his triumphant return to England.

Master and Mistress Everett were among the last arrivals at Bruton Parish that morning—Phillip preferred, whenever possible, to make an entrance—but they were surprised to find most of the parishioners still gathered outside the sanctuary, upon the stone steps or in the street below. The ripple of agitation that seemed to be gathering momentum within the crowd of sedately dressed men and women appeared to have its focus upon the man who stood at the top of the steps, reading aloud from the broadsheet he held in his hand.

Arabella's heart began to speed, but she kept her face

composed and her hands firmly attached to her husband's arm as he made his way to the forefront of the crowd, disguising his irritation over the fact that such excitement had begun without him with small bows and politely murmured greetings. "Can you imagine?" someone answered his inquiry, intrigue mingling with distaste in the tone. "It was found tacked to the door this morning, bold as brass . . ."

"After what happened last night I'm surprised it wasn't a fox tail tacked to the door!" came another subdued murmur and someone else hissed impatiently, "Listen!"

". . . the conflagration of last evening was but a sample of the delights to come," read the orator from the top step, "should His Majesty persist in ignoring our pleas. The anger of injustice burns hot in the veins of patriotic Virginians and we grow tired of complacency. Too long one man has carried our standard, but beware, Lord Dunmore, of casting the credit too quickly at the easiest target. The man called Le Renard would gladly claim the victory for yet another blow against inequity, but this time triumph does not belong to him. I suggest, Lord Governor, that you cease concentrating your efforts upon one man and realize that the Fox has an ally in battle and a rival for your attention . . . It is a force that burns hard and long and will not be subdued as long as a single man, woman, or child lives to draw royal breath in Virginia, and its name is the flame of liberty."

Arabella watched through shaded lids as Phillip snatched the paper from the reader and scanned it himself. Only she could see the tightening of his rouged lips, the slight tinge of color that began to creep through his heavily powdered face, and the force with which his long, delicate fingers held the broadsheet, which was in danger of being crumpled in his hand.

From around her rose cries of "Will this insanity never end?" and "Wasn't it bad enough we have a fox to plague our shores, and now what is this to add to our trouble—a flame? A flame of liberty? Soon a man will not be safe walking in his own garden, so bold are these criminals that breed and multiply like rats!"

"Nonsense! It is nothing! Another Fox trick to divert attention, that's all it is!"

And another voice, stronger, more thoughtful. "I wouldn't be so sure. Perhaps it *is* time the governor realized there is more than one man against him. How long are we going to let the Fox fight our battles for us?" he demanded and was met by a cautiously growing murmur of agreement, a nodding of heads, a shifting of the crowd into an unconscious alignment.

Arabella could feel the mounting electricity of emotion that was like a physical thing, a uniting of citizens behind a cause, an unexpected challenge to the true loyalties of each and every one of them. The pounding of her heart registered amazement over the stirring of emotions that could be wrought with a few deft strokes of a pen, a little awe at the discovery of how intense those emotions ran, and beyond it all, a small but unmistakable twinge of power. And then Phillip, thrusting the broadsheet back to its original caretaker, complained nasally, "What tripe and foolishness! Not even the Lord's House is sacrosanct to this abominable Fox! I am appalled!"

Arabella, grasping the moment when attention was momentarily diverted to them, once again slipped her hands protectively through Phillip's arm. "My husband is so right," she said, her voice cool and sweet and carrying just the right amount of maidenly alarm. "This is blasphemy in this holy place. Let us go in to worship, as we have come to do."

She deliberately ignored her husband's guarded

glance of surprise as they glided into the sanctuary, a somewhat chastened crowd following slowly behind them.

But not even the inner sanctum was safe from the Fox's influence. Emboldened, perhaps, by the governor's conspicuous absence from his customary throne-like chair in the position of honor across from the pulpit, the rector extolled the virtues of dedication and courage demonstrated by those brave, anonymous few who fought for the liberty of them all. And through it all Phillip Everett, the Fox, sat with an expression of studied indifference upon his face, occasionally making a discreet check of the burnish of his buttons or the state of his lace—innocent, oblivious and stalwartly anonymous.

23 September, 1773

Ev'n though his cruel Masquerade has caus'd Me much Pain, I can now begin to understand my Husbande . . . When I first came Here, He could not trust Me; I was a Stranger and foolishly I saw only the Mask and not the Man beneath . . . Phillip, my Phillip, my Love of olde, is the Fox of my Dreams . . . Oh, Phillip, I knowe You now, and I believe in You . . . I would be your Wife, your Helpmate, and I would fight alongside You if need be, for having just found You, I cannot lose You again . . .

Yet I can never speak these, my Heart's Deepest Longings, aloud. What would it avail Me to go to my Husbande and assert that I have penetrat'd his Masquerade? Would He not merely deny my foolish Claims and grow even further away from Me . . . for, in truth, I have done Nothing to earn

281

his Trust, and he made It abundantly clear, that Night aboard his Ship, that his Trust is not given lightly, if at All . . .

No, I will not confront him. It is for Phillip to confess to Me, to willingly and gladly come to Me, confyde in Me, ask Me to join him . . . Trust, like Love, cannot be coerced or demand'd, and it is up to Me to earn them Both.

I will be a Wife to him, in every Way and by every Method known. Day by Day I will grow to become Everything He has ever want'd, and I will prove to him that I am worthy of his Confidence. And soon, as Man and Wife, We will once again know the Joy we shar'd so briefly and so poignantly . . . for the one Place that allows no Room for Secrets is the Marital Bed, and I Knowe that when Phillip comes to Me again all Masks will be cast away . . .

The look of shock on Mistress Jane Woolcot's face was barely masked by a smile of politeness as Arabella came toward her. The older woman was in her garden at the back of her house on Nicholson Street, scarcely a block from the Everett home, and this morning, as on many others, she was sitting under the shade of the grape arbor. Even in early fall the sun was still hot in Virginia, and Mistress Woolcot, like Arabella, wore a broad-rimmed straw hat to protect her fine skin from its rays.

"Lady Arabella?" The words were more a question than a greeting.

Arabella found herself dropping a low curtsy, feeling suddenly somewhat nervous before this *doyenne* of Williamsburg society. Wife of a wealthy lawyer who sat in the House of Burgesses, friend not only of Lord

282

Dunmore but of his predecessor, the popular Lord Botetourt, Mistress Jane set the standard for the rest of the gentry. The look that she gave Arabella now was as frosty as the one she had given her the night of the ball when she had cut her dead, and Arabella knew that winning over Mistress Jane was going to take all of her skill and charm—and an inordinate amount of subterfuge. But Arabella was determined to ingratiate herself with the icy woman who sat before her, not only to make a friend of her, but to become her *protégée*. For what better protection for her husband than for Mistress Everett to be on close terms with the leader of Williamsburg society? Painting a smile on her face that bordered on being a simper, Arabella spoke.

"Mistress Woolcot, I am so grateful to you for receiving me. After that terrible debacle at the governor's ball on Saturday last . . ." Arabella cast her eyes downward and attempted to look contrite, but Mistress Jane had mistaken her meaning.

"The dreadful explosion, yes. We were fortunate that someone wasn't killed." Her voice was high and precise, perfectly modulated in rounded syllables. Her nose was hooked, her eyes large and protruding and a very pale blue. Her small mouth was bow shaped and her high forehead gave her the distinct look of a bird of prey.

This will not be easy, Arabella thought before she spoke. Still, it was entirely necessary. "That, of course," she demurred. "But I was thinking more of my personal humiliation—that hideous costume. Oh, Mistress Woolcot, I had no idea that the ways were so different here. I am so in need of guidance. That is why I have come to you."

"Indeed," the good lady responded after a long moment. "If not I, then who indeed could guide you?" She looked Arabella up and down, registering again

283

the appropriateness of her attire. This young lady was indeed quite removed from the hoydenish spectacle she had presented at the governor's ball.

"Why did you do it, child?" she inquired, her voice softening now. "Whatever could have possessed you to choose such an outrageous costume."

"Why . . ." replied Arabella, widening her eyes innocently, "for a jest, Mistress. That and nothing more. On the continent such things are quite acceptable." Well, almost, Arabella added to herself, but Mistress Jane could not possibly know that.

Mistress Jane picked up her fan and spread it wide. "Then you must travel in far different circles than we are accustomed to here in the Colonies." She moved the air briskly with each flick of her wrist. Then, more politely, she added, "But you are young, and there is nothing that cannot be repaired in this life."

"I do so hope you are right," Arabella said with a sigh. "For I want nothing more than to be an acceptable wife for my Phillip and to make him proud of me."

Mistress Jane could not help but be touched by the genuine emotion in the younger woman's voice. Phillip Everett had surprised them all with this marriage, and there were some who said that the vixen of a wife he had acquired was no more than he deserved. Still, it was the wife who was seeking counsel, not the husband, and far be it from Mistress Jane to turn her back upon the opportunity to redeem a member of the gentry and prepare her to take her rightful place in society.

"Was your husband much distressed over your costume at the ball?"

Arabella nodded. "I am certain he was, but Phillip is too much the gentleman to ever criticize me openly. No, it is I who must be distressed . . . over my lack of judgment and disregard of the customs of my new homeland. For this," she said staunchly, "will be my home and that of my children."

Mistress Jane's eyebrows rose. "You are . . . " Delicacy forbade her to go farther.

"Oh, dear me, no." Arabella colored prettily, and then cast a shy glance in the other woman's direction. "But one always hopes."

Mistress Jane closed her fan and tapped it against her skirt as she looked out across her garden toward the Woolcot house. It was a view she liked—the well-manicured gardens blooming with flowers in season, ripe with vegetables and fruit. The gardens represented the order and respectability of life in Williamsburg, an order that must be kept intact.

She had come to this colony as a bride herself, married to a man whom she scarcely knew, and together they had made a life in Williamsburg. They had seen four children born and two of them die, and they had carved a niche for themselves here in the bosom of this new land. It could be the same for Arabella; she too could belong and find the contentment that others had. All she needed was a guiding hand, someone to show her the way. Mistress Jane had decided she would be the one to turn the scandalous Lady Arabella into a quite respectable matron of the colony. She delved into the small basket that held her sewing and her skeins of thread and pulled out a small volume. "Have you ever had occasion to see this?" she asked.

Arabella reached for it and read the title out loud. *The Lady's Calling*. No, I have never seen such a book." It had certainly not been on her father's bookshelves, nor had it been a topic of conversation at Mrs. Montagu's salons.

"Then you must have one of your own. They are offered for sale at the Post Office, I believe, but you may use my copy until you have acquired your own. My dear Arabella"—Mistress Jane put her hand on Arabella's—"this will answer many of your questions and solve many of your problems."

Puzzled, Arabella looked down at the book in her hands.

"I sense in you," Mistress Jane went on, "a rebellious nature, one not easily tamed. Am I correct? Only such a nature could have impelled you to wear that most incorrect costume at the ball."

Arabella nodded. She could hardly deny the obvious.

"If at times you feel too much the pull of that rebelliousness, that need to act upon your impulses, then I beg you—no, beseech you—to read in this little book. Here, let me show you." She took the book from Arabella and turned to a much-used page. "'It is a wife's duty to her husband's person and reputation not to bring upon him any cause for embarrassment or distress. Rather, it is the wife's duty to set forward her husband's good qualities in the brightest of all lights.'" She put down the book and looked at Arabella. "If you had read that—if you had only thought upon it—surely you would not have behaved so outrageously."

Arabella nodded. "I have caused my husband pain and embarrassment, and I want to atone for it any way that I can."

"It will take work," Mistress Jane warned sternly.

"I am ready," Arabella declared, wondering what this work would entail. "I shall endeavor never to embarrass my husband again."

Mistress Jane nodded. "How you deport yourself in public is but a start. There is more. A man's home is his castle in which he commands patriarchal sovereignty. Your husband must be king there, my dear, high priest."

At Arabella's sudden quietness, Mistress Jane went on. "I know that to some younger women this must seem old-fashioned, but it is the only way, Lady Arabella. You must bend to your husband's will in everything. He must be your master. It is the only way to achieve true accord with the nature of the universe."

Arabella held her tongue. Indeed her husband was already her master. Phillip Everett did exactly as he pleased, when he pleased. The only freedom she had was that which he had given her, and now, in retrospect, she saw that it was merely to keep her busy and out of his way. She had yet to best him, and whenever she thought that she had, he turned the tables on her.

But certainly she was not here to argue with Mistress Jane over *The Lady's Calling* and its efficacy in dealing with Phillip Everett. She was here to present to the world a picture of a dedicated and dutiful wife, who was devoted to her husband.

"But what of love?" she said suddenly. "Does your book speak of love?"

Mistress Jane looked closely at Arabella to see if she were making sport, but the look on her lovely face was one of yearning. "Of course my book speaks of love—the grandest of all callings." Mistress Jane closed her eyes and repeated the passage from memory. "'Without love, marriage is nothing but a bargain.'" She looked at her young companion. "But I am sure such is not the case with you and Master Everett, for indeed if you care so much to please him, you must love him deeply."

For just a moment a shadow seemed to flicker in Arabella's eyes, and Mistress Jane saw reflected there pain mixed with tenderness. "I do, Mistress," Arabella said softly. "I do."

Mistress Jane was thoughtful. She had seen much in

her life—satisfied wives and unhappy wives, husbands who strayed and those who were faithful. She knew that all marriages had periods of difficulty; certainly hers had. She could sense something about Lady Arabella, something more than her asking for forgiveness for her scandalous behavior, more even than her seeking advice on wifeliness. There was almost a desperation about her to put her marriage right. Arabella needed her help, and she had found in Mistress Jane a staunch supporter.

"I shall be having a small dinner party later in the season and would be pleased if you and your husband could attend. There you will have a chance to meet some ladies and their husbands who might be most helpful to you in society."

Arabella smiled her thanks. "We should be most pleased—" Then she caught herself and corrected, "I shall ask my husband, and if it pleases him, then we shall be delighted to attend."

"Ah, Lady Arabella," replied Mistress Jane with a smile, "you will have no problems with your husband or with this new society. You are quick to learn, and besides your lively mind you have been blessed with great beauty. I hope you use it well."

Arabella lifted her graceful shoulders. "But is it not said that beauty is only skin-deep." Arabella had found her own fine looks to be of little help to her during her lifetime; in fact, often it seemed a detriment to her.

Mistress Jane was quick to disagree. "Oh, no. Why *The Lady's Calling* says that if love is the key, then external appearance is the gateway to the heart. And you are very beautiful, child."

"But perhaps I do not display it well," Arabella objected modestly. "My London gowns do not seem quite in fashion here." She looked down at her dress, which seemed so out of place in the brilliant morning sun.

"That is no problem. Our dressmakers are quite talented, especially the one I use. I shall write you an introduction at once."

"You are too kind, Mistress Woolcot," Arabella said.

The other woman sighed happily. What could be more heartening than guiding someone along the correct path to lifelong contentment?

As Arabella was departing, Mistress Jane tried to press *The Lady's Calling* into her hands, but she demurred. "I shall purchase my own copy at once, for I'm sure that you would not wish to be long parted from your own. In fact, I shall call my carriage and go to Duke of Gloucester Street straightaway."

Arabella left for the crowded thoroughfares of Williamsburg quite satisfied with her morning's work. Soon, she knew, word of the chastened, most-anxious-to-please Lady Arabella would spread throughout the matron's circle, and to be taken under Mistress Woolcot's wing assured only the best for her reputation—and that of her husband. On one score, at least, that silly book had been right: the deportment of the wife did reflect directly on the husband, perhaps more strongly than any other influence in his life. And she was determined to see that hers was above reproach.

It was a fine day, and she left her carriage before the Raleigh Tavern to stroll down Duke of Gloucester Street. She had few purchases to make, but she was tempted by a handful of ribbons at the milliner's, and she stopped by to make herself known at the shop of the dressmaker Mistress Jane had recommended. She found that the craftsmanship displayed at the silversmith's was more than impressive, and there she placed an order for a sterling christening cup—a birthing present for Caroline and William.

Her last stop was the Post Office, where she planned, true to her word, to buy a copy of *The Lady's Calling*.

She had no intention of reading it, but it would do no harm to leave it lying about the parlor, proclaiming to all the world her devotion to wifely duty. Her visit to the Post Office took more time than any of her other stops. In addition to *The Lady's Calling,* there were copies of other books, some that had been bound and printed in Williamsburg. There were copies of the *Gazette* for sale, along with stationery and writing supplies, of which Arabella purchased a great quantity.

Beyond the Post Office were the printing presses for the *Gazette,* and Arabella was drawn there even though it was an unlikely place for a lady to go. An idea had been forming in her mind, a vague, amorphous notion without substance, and it required investigating. She stood outside in the small courtyard and watched the printer at work as her idea grew and took shape.

It seemed a simple enough task, Arabella mused, intrigued. And so very efficient. What once was written by hand could be reproduced in moments to prepare a dozen—a hundred—identical copies. And with those copies a few scrawled ideas could be spread more miles, instead of blocks, could be read by dozens, instead of one . . .

The printer picked his type from a drawer and set it by hand in a wooden frame. Then he applied his ink, laid out his paper, and applied a blotter against the paper. The task seemed to require no great skill or strength, although the machine, she had to admit, was quite unwieldy.

For a long time she stood and watched. Only when the printer looked up to ask if he could be of service did she turn and walk away.

Chapter XVI

After only the briefest of taps, the door to Phillip's bedroom was flung open and Arabella sailed in, servants in her wake laden with boxes and baskets. Phillip, who now had cause to regret that the nature of his work occupied him mostly at night, roused himself from the settee on which he had been napping. He rose up on his elbow, a mixture of disbelief and irritation clouding his eyes as he observed the entourage that had invaded his chambers.

"Lady Arabella—"

"So you *are* awake," she declared with a coquettish nod of her head. "I thought so, even though Sam said you were sleeping." Phillip, still somewhat dazed, struggled to a sitting position and watched as his wife swept to the window and flung back the heavy draperies. "How unbearably hot it is in here, Phillip! We must let in some air."

The bolt of sunlight shot through his head like a rapier, capturing the astonishing vision that was his wife in its golden fingers. Phillip closed his eyes against the glare and leaned back on the pillow, too weary at the moment to spare much energy for deciphering his wife's strange behavior. "My dear Lady Arabella, you must forgive my lack of hospitality at this most unexpected visit, but I find myself quite indisposed. Most devilish headache, you know." He pressed a languid hand to his brow. "Perhaps another time I will be more prepared to receive guests."

Arabella's look was of ultimate concern. "Fa! Guest? I am your wife, Phillip, and therefore distressed that you are unwell. It is no wonder, though, lying in this steam bath of a room."

Arabella beckoned imperiously to the servants, who had been standing near the door uncomfortably. They had learned early on that Master Phillip's privacy was never to be intruded upon, yet their new mistress seemed determined to break that rule along with so many others. "Put the boxes over there"—she pointed to the bed—"and on Master Phillip's shaving stand, and on the chest there, and then you may leave." Phillip's eyes opened slowly, narrowing with suspicion and dislike as she chanted this string of orders, and Arabella turned back to him with a most enchanting smile. "Master Phillip needs his rest, so be quick about it."

"Thank you, my dear," was his dry response. As he realized his domain had been successfully—and irrevocably invaded, Phillip stirred to prop himself up on the pillow. "You are too kind."

Arabella smiled ingenuously. "What I am going to show you will cheer you immensely and drive away that dreadful pain in your head, I promise. You will be so pleased."

Phillip, resigned, rearranged himself with as fine a show of grace as he could muster. He had slipped off his boots and jacket before lying down, and he now faced his wife in a state of *dishabille* most improper— his waistcoat undone, his stock and wig discarded, his hair tousled, and in his bare stockinged feet. The correct thing for the very correct Phillip Everett to have done would have been to don his jacket and boots and tie his stock, or to at least fasten his waistcoat, but it was too damnably hot and he felt too sluggish to do either.

But he was intrigued by Arabella's appearance in his private chambers and by her great show of ebullience. His wife was definitely up to something, and it would be great misjudgment to send her away without discovering her plot. "Then pray tell, m'dear," he invited with lazy magnanimity, "do let me see your prizes."

If Arabella noticed any reluctance in Phillip's manner, she ignored it and delved into one of her boxes. "Look Phillip, is this not wonderful?" She held up a cloak of deep purple velvet trimmed around the front with a rich band of beaver. "I was at the dressmaker's having a fitting for my new gowns—"

Phillip's eyebrows quirked upward.

Arabella's look was innocent. "I know you want me to look stylish for the season. I visited Mistress Jane the other day, who was most helpful in—"

"You are always lovely, my dear," drawled Phillip with customary gallantry. "You need no frills and furbelows to enhance what is already yours."

Arabella colored prettily and beamed at him. "But I want to be lovely especially for you. You are the most excellent authority on fashion, and it is only my duty to live up to your very fine taste."

A muscle in Phillip's jaw tightened. So now she wanted to be lovely for him, did she? Now, after she had given her most precious jewel to another, she would play the devoted spouse for her husband. There was something laughable about the entire situation, but Phillip found it difficult to be amused.

Arabella pulled the cloak around her shoulders and

pirouetted before the bed. Her hand smoothed the soft velvet across her breasts and waist and ruffled the deep pile of the fur. "Oh, Phillip," she breathed. "You should feel this. How luxurious it is beneath my hands."

She moved close, but Phillip shook his head, instinctively retreating. The sensation, he imagined, would be very much like that of her hair drifting through his fingers . . . "Much too warm, m'dear. Do put it away before you suffocate."

"The seamstress had this made up for someone whose husband could not pay, and when I saw it . . ." The cloak slid from her shoulders and fell like a cloud of violets to the floor. Arabella retrieved it and tossed it across a chair. "I told her that *my* husband was Master Phillip Everett and she was most pleased to part with it. She will send a messenger with the bill," Arabella added airly, digging into another box.

"Oh, I'm quite sure she will."

Arabella pulled out a hat of turquoise-blue topped with a fan of pheasant feathers. "I am not really sure of this one . . ." Her voice was hesitant as she stood before the pier glass, adjusting it. "When I visited the milliner's, both she and her assistant insisted this was just right for me." She turned and looked at Phillip, her lips forming a doubtful *moue*. "What do you think, Phillip? Do you like it? Tell me true."

Arabella's cheeks were flushed with the heat and the skin of her chest and neck bore a trace of rosy color. Phillip found it difficult to keep his eyes upon the hat.

Her dress was of a shiny golden material, and its tight corset accentuated her tiny waist and pushed her breasts together, exposing half the creamy orbs above the lace bodice. It had not been suitable for an early-morning shopping trip, and Arabella had known this, but now Phillip might be thinking how beautiful his wife was, how desirable, and, as she stood before him asking his opinion as though it were the most important thing in the world, how vulnerable she was as well.

Arabella's behavior was, as usual, very disquieting, and despite his languid appearance, all his senses were alert. What a chameleon this woman was. Scarcely a fortnight ago she had attempted to humiliate him at the governor's palace. Today she begged for his advice upon her foolish hat. Now roused from his languor, he was curious enough to play along. There was a reason for this abrupt change of heart, if only he had the patience to discover it.

Phillip placed his arms behind his head and crossed his long legs before he answered, drawing out the reply in his most affected tones. "The color is divine on you, of course. And those feathers! *Tres chic.* Very continental."

Arabella clapped her hands with delight. "You are right! Exactly." She checked her appearance once more in the glass before she removed the hat. "I knew I could count upon your most excellent judgment." She smiled winsomely and blew him a kiss. "Now I have one more."

She held up a fluff of mauve feathers and bows. "This is quite lovely too, but . . ." She tossed it aside. "I must get to my best surprise. Look! Look at this, Phillip. Is it not spectacular?"

Arabella displayed for him a silvery white wig, puffed high with rolls and pads, curls and twists. "From Mr. Charlton's, your very own wig maker."

Phillip kept his voice mild. "A wig? But my dear, I was under the impression you eschewed such attire."

"Anyone can change, Phillip." She balanced the wig in her hands, looking at it intently. "Hmmm, it's heavier than I thought. Oh well, I suppose one adjusts.

Mr. Charlton told me that it was of the finest hair, from Flanders. It seems the cider and the beer they imbibe make the hair especially shiny and strong. But then, of course, you know all about that." She glanced at the three that stood in line on Phillip's wig stand.

"Charlton is a superior wig maker," Phillip agreed. "But you have not assuaged my husbandly curiosity. Why this sudden interest in fashion, my dear? You've never displayed such before."

Arabella carefully replaced the wig and lifted out another. "He insisted that I take this one, but again I am unsure." She displayed a hairpiece of palest pink. "He said this color was all the rage on the continent—"

"But it is not for you," Phillip interrupted impatiently. "Have your girl return it, and now that that is settled, I would like an answer to my question. Why the wigs? Why the frills and baubles?"

Arabella looked at him anxiously. "Have I displeased you? In truth, I meant just the opposite."

She held out her hand to him, and in a gesture that was purely reflexive Phillip reached for it. Her hand was smooth and soft and slightly damp with the heat, and the touch of her flesh against his in that intimate and spontaneous gesture sent messages of remembrance coursing through him.

"The answer, Phillip," she said softly, "is that I want to please you. I realize that we shall be married for many years—forever—and our disagreements produce nothing but unhappiness for us both. Therefore I thought to begin by dressing as you would have me, for no detail is too small to be ignored if it will bring you pride in me." She lifted a graceful shoulder. "If I must wear wigs to please you, then I shall."

Phillip let go of her hand and rubbed his temple with his index finger, all the while watching her covertly. It was an excellent performance, so much so that it was difficult to remember it was nothing more than a performance. It had just the right amount of pathos and sincerity. Her full bottom lip trembled slightly and her dark lashes brushed modestly against her rosy cheeks. Was it guilt over her adultery, he wondered, or guile that motivated this remarkable change, this sudden domestic docility?

As Arabella continued talking, she moved to sit on the narrow settee beside him. Phillip listened with only half an ear. Her actions were a little overblown, he judged, for a woman who had engaged in but one night's infidelity. Was there something more going on in her devious little mind? What did she expect him to do to assuage her conscience?

As beautiful as she was, he could not trust her; nor could he allow himself to become beguiled by her. He could feel the heat from her hip pressed against his thigh and with all his will he tried not to focus on that light pressure, to prevent the almost unpreventable reaction. She was leaning forward slightly so that her breasts almost spilled from the low neckline of her gown. He could see the slight sheen of perspiration on her creamy flesh, and he could imagine the taste of it against his tongue, salty sweet, heated, silky . . .

Arabella saw his eyes change, darken slightly, and she heard the quickening of his breath as his gaze traveled up the column of her neck, to her chin, and then to her lips. He was so casually attired, this Phillip, lounging and at ease, so unlike the Phillip of his public image and so like Le Renard, whom she had known so intimately. His hair, slightly disarrayed from its queue, was a pure tawny color, and it shaded his temple as it was pressed forth against the pillow. There was a flush against the coarsely textured flesh of his throat, and the very faintest stain of masculine perspiration lining the stitchery of his collarless shirt. The heavy brocade of his waistcoat fell open over his chest. Absently she mused that only the barrier of thin lawn material would be left between his flesh and her hand . . . if she should be so bold as to touch him. She could feel the heat that would rise from his chest if she did so, could remember the firm-muscled flesh, and the mere memory did odd things to the pace of her breathing, to the inner regions of her abdomen.

She did not touch him, of course, but she watched him intently, and when his eyes met hers they locked and held. A long, slow moment passed. In the motes of afternoon light that streaked in through the window a fly buzzed lazily. Outside a carriage passed, its wheels creaking noisily on the street, but inside there was only the slow intake of breath, the pounding of hearts.

She is yours, Phillip thought. *She has come to you willingly* . . . Whether it was to learn the differences of her husband's bed after having known those of another or to ease her aching conscience for her imagined betrayal of her marriage vows made little difference at this point, for she was here, and unprotesting, and his . . .

His heart was a heavy, powerful muscle thudding out the rhythm of his desire. How simple it would be, as she pressed so close, to let his hand drift down and discover the small turn of her ankle as revealed beneath her slightly disarranged skirts; to run his hand up the stockinged length of her leg that was lost in the dark heat beneath her heavy skirts; to trace the fine weave of material that shaped her curved calf until it gave way at last to bare flesh at her thigh. And there the heat of her skin would sear his fingers; and there he would push her skirts upward and drag her down beneath him . . .

The tight cut of his breeches concealed no secrets. The growing tumescence of his loins was heated and painfully evident as her hip pressed so innocently against him, and like a boy he was moved to hide it from her, to shift away with an embarrassed cough or to move his hand casually to his lap . . . But of course Arabella would not notice, or understand, he reflected silently. No lady would notice such a thing, and he tried to put his great discomfort out of his mind, to better deal with it.

Arabella noticed. She noticed and felt a surge of triumph, of power, of memory. He *did* want her. She had not been wrong . . .

She leaned forward, only fractionally, her lips moist and parted, her breath suspended with hope, with anticipation . . .

Phillip was unable to move, or look away, or do anything at all but let the sensations of promise and desire wind their treacherous tentacles about him. *She is yours. Take her . . .*

His hand moved slightly, the fingers curling into the material of her skirt that spread along the settee. It would be madness. She was no fool. She had been with only one man; she would not fail to remark the sameness. She would know the minute he came to her . . .

Arabella's face drifted closer, and with all the intensity in her soul, she thought, *Phillip . . .*

"God's blood, Arabella. This headache strikes me like a bolt of lightning." He turned his head sharply on the pillow. "I am dreadfully in need of sleep."

Arabella's dulcet tones masked any frustration that might have crept into her voice. "Poor Phillip, and here I am prattling on about fashion while you are in pain." She reached out a soft hand and placed it on his forehead. "You seem feverish from the heat, but I can remedy that."

"It is not necessary. Sam—"

"Sam? Certainly not." Arabella slid from the settee

and moved to the nightstand. Phillip, taking advantage of her momentary absence, shifted his position, attempting to make the prominent bulge in his breeches a bit less obvious. He prayed that she would simply go away, for this test of his control seemed too cruel a one to pass.

She poured cool water from a Staffordshire pitcher into a matching bowl, her voice cheerful and determined. "This is a wifely duty, and I intend to perform all wifely duties for my husband from now on."

Phillip stifled a groan.

Arabella wet a cloth in the water and wrung out the excess moisture. "This cloth will cool you."

Phillip's protest was weak. "You take too much trouble for me, dear."

"It is no trouble. I had no idea that September would be so warm. I am quite parched myself, and you, poor darling, lying in this dreadful heat." With seeming absentmindedness, Arabella patted her neck and the tops of her breasts with the damp cloth. Phillip's eyes were riveted to the movements, and a thin line of perspiration broke out across his forehead. She was a witch, this woman.

She is yours . . .

"Umm, how cool this feels," she murmured, her eyes half-closed in innocent sensual enjoyment. "You have no idea what women suffer for fashion. These stays, for example, seem to trap the heat."

Arabella loosened the fastenings at her bodice and pushed away the edging of the silk chemise that had given her breasts some semblance of cover. Now they were almost completely exposed, revealing the deep cleft between and a hint of the rosy areola that surrounded each nipple.

Again she pressed the cloth against her breasts and the moisture darkened the gold cloth of her gown,

300

delineating the tight buds of her nipples and putting Phillip in mind of how the moisture from his mouth would leave a similar stain if he were to press his lips there. Phillip took a breath and tried to look away, but his eyes were drawn back to a speck of glistening water that clung to Arabella's neck and then, like a drop of dew on a flower petal, slid down along her chest and into the valley between her breasts. His finger longed to follow that path, to gather that moisture. He remembered the morning when he had seen her bathing in the pool, and the darkness of the night when he had felt the softness of her breasts beneath his hands. It could be so again, so easily . . .

Arabella saw the look in Phillip's eyes and she forcefully refrained a smile of triumph. There was pleasure in seeing him yearn, as once she had yearned; in making him aching and confused as once he had made her. But there was also frustration, for it would be so simple, if only he would believe in her . . .

She walked slowly to the settee and laid the cloth across Phillip's brow. "Is this not soothing?" She fitted herself beside him again.

"I believe you are right, Arabella." Phillip's voice revealed only a slight strain as he tried to ignore the warm press of her thigh against him.

"That is most pleasing to me, dear husband," she replied softly.

Phillip's brow formed a frown beneath the cloth. *She is treacherous* . . . Her voice was too sweet, her tones too honeyed, to be sincere. She was a woman who promised her undying love to a renegade and then made deliberate attempts to seduce her husband. He must not forget that. Arabella as a virago was a nuisance, to be sure, but as a charming seductress she was both dangerous and unpredictable. He had risked too much at her hands already.

301

"I have another idea," she whispered. "A massage to help you relax."

Phillip's throat convulsed. "I do not think—"

But Arabella's fingertips had already peeled away the cloth and were gently massaging his temples. "Why Phillip, your muscles are like iron here." Her fingers moved in small circles, sliding over his damp skin. Her hands moved down his cheeks to the muscles of his jaw. "So tight. Poor Phillip," she murmured, "so many worries, and I am sure that a scandalous wife only compounds your cares. Well, that is all in the past. Mistress Jane says a wife must never reflect poorly on her husband and that she must . . ."

Her voice droned on but Phillip lost the context of her words. Arabella shifted her weight, leaning forward to stroke Phillip's brow, running her hand across his forehead. Her breasts loosened from their confinement and swayed enticingly before his face. When she stretched her arm to smooth back a lock of damp hair from his forehead, one breast lifted from its scant cover, exposing the rosy tip of a nipple. And she seemed so innocently unaware of the provocative pose she struck, her hair curling softly around her face, her lips pursed in concentration, her ripe, full breasts so temptingly close to his face.

All he had to do was raise his head—inches, only inches—and capture the taut nipple in his mouth. And would she be startled, would she protest . . . or would she melt into the pleasure he could give her, as she had done before? How easy it would be to slip his arms around her, to pull her on top of him and lose himself in the mindless pleasure of her flesh. He longed to take her fiercely, savagely, an exploding release to the pent-up fire that boiled in his blood . . . and then to take her lingeringly, adoringly, until she wept with the pleasure of it . . . to make her his—completely his.

Phillip's need was sharp and painful, and close to blotting out reason. This physical longing was compelling but easily understood, a purely visceral reaction to Arabella's mysterious blend of sensuality and innocence. But it was his other need that surprised him—the aching urge to hold her, to claim her, to be within her mind as completely as he could be inside her body. It was this emotional longing that made him want to reach out and cup her face, caress her cheek, and tell her how much he wanted her before his lips drank the sweetness from hers. He recognized the sheer pleasure of her presence that made him want to laugh aloud from the ever-increasing wonder of her, and he felt a deep, abiding longing that demanded he wrap himself around her and keep her beside him always. He yearned to expose all of his secrets to her, and to take all of hers into himself.

And that, of course, was the danger. She made him weak. She was the key upon which all their destinies were hinged. Should she guess his identity—which she surely would if he made love to her—she would have knowledge that could endanger not only his life and that of his men, but hers as well. And the future of a cause that she could not begin to understand would be in her hands. He would not place that burden upon her, no matter what her devotion, what her charms. Too much was at stake.

Phillip sat bolt upright, dislodging a startled Arabella's hands from his temples. "What a miracle worker you are, m'dear. Why, my headache has quite vanished." Phillip swung his stockinged feet to the floor. "In fact I feel quite well enough to attend Colonel Durham's card party this afternoon, after all."

Now on his feet, he bowed low to Arabella. "With deepest gratitude, my dear, I must beg your pardon and prepare my *toilette*. I know you are exhausted by this

303

ordeal of nursing me and beg that you rest yourself."

"No, I—"

"I shall brook no arguments, my dear." Phillip clasped her arm tightly and guided her through the boxes strewn about the room toward the door. "You have done too much, and I shall monopolize you no longer with my silly ills."

Arabella sighed and allowed herself to be ushered from the room. Once again she had been bested by the wily Fox.

The townhouse was still with the heaviness of the hot autumn night, the thick, humid air broken only by an occasional flutter of a warm breeze through Arabella's open window. The servants had gone to bed, the lamps had been turned low, and Phillip had not yet returned from his card game. Arabella was, for all intents, alone in the house.

She sat at the elegant *escritoire* in her bedchamber, clad only in her dressing gown, a quill in her hand. Her brow furrowed thoughtfully as she paused in her writing, and she tried not to dwell with too much concern on her husband's whereabouts. A game, he had said. And Phillip did love his games. But did the one he was playing tonight involve the relatively harmless accoutrements of cards and pegs, or was it something a bit more exciting, like masks and swords . . . ?

Oh, Phillip, she thought, and a mixture of anger and despair clenched at her chest, *can't you see that the trap is closing in upon you, and that now, of all times, is not the time to advertise your presence?* It was one thing to create havoc among the widely scattered plantations of the James and along the well-traveled roads of the tidewater, but here, in Williamsburg, right under an irate governor's nose . . .

Arabella told herself she wanted only one thing: that she and Phillip should live to enjoy each other. And it was indeed true that this concern played an important role in moving her toward the action she had decided to take.

When she had stood in the midst of the ballroom listening to the governor furiously double the bounty on her husband, she had known something must be done, and she had set about helping in the quickest, and the safest, way she could think of. But she had not imagined it would work so well, if at all, and now, in the stillness of the night, she could not deny she felt a small thrill of power to know that she held Phillip's safety, in however small a way, in her hands.

Phillip would not give his trust; he would not accept her help or her allegiance, even when she had lain in his arms after the deepest intimacy a man and a woman could share and had offered it willingly, and had meant it. But she could fight his battles with him, even if he did not know of it. She could help him, though it be in secret. She could play some small part in giving the Fox the freedom to continue his fight, and for now that would have to be enough.

Arabella was not certain she understood the nature of his fight, or the reason for it, but she did not have to. She only knew that he believed in it, that his courage was the thing she had first loved about him, and that such nobility of purpose must be cherished and protected. The rhetoric of colonial politics as quoted in the *Gazette* and as expounded by Sam was appealing and ear-catching, and though it had little meaning to her in a grander sense, the phrases she had chosen for her own seemed to exemplify precisely the feelings for her husband that consumed her. *Men who stand above the crowd and are unafraid to demand their right to do*

305

so ... Strength of heart and loyalty to one's own ...
Liberty ... Freedom from oppression ... A vision of
tomorrow. ... Those things she did understand, and
those things she envisioned when she thought of
Phillip.

Arabella would show him, through constant devotion, that she could be the perfect Tory wife for Phillip
Everett; she would reinforce his disguise rather than
undermine it. She would keep the governor so well
occupied, both personally and politically, that the last
place he would ever look for treachery would be within
the Everett household. And slowly, day by day, she
would chip away Phillip's restraint until at last they
would lie once again in each other's arms and there
would be no more games between them.

But for now, the most important thing was to keep
Phillip safe. And, at last emerging from her reverie,
Arabella dipped her quill once again into the inkwell
and signed the parchment before her with a flourish.

This love letter to her husband would be posted
tonight on the door of Bruton Parish Church, and it
was signed, "The Flame of Liberty."

Chapter XVII

"Think not that we are defeated before we have begun, my noble Virginians, for the mightiest armies are composed only of so many beating hearts, like our own . . . As Moses delivered the Israelites from the evils of captivity through the Might of Divine Guidance, so shall we, my Valiant Patriots, dethrone the Oppressors for the sake of Divine Right . . ."

In a small clearing in the depths of the forest perhaps a dozen men were gathered beneath the light of the moon. Near them the occasional soft whinny of a horse added its voice to that of the reader and, further beyond, the murmur and whisper of the James provided a soothing background. For the moment all attention was focused on the voice of the man who held the parchment, his hushed tones adding unexpected vehemence to the stirring words of inspiration and victory he read. Abruptly, one man, masked and cloaked, stepped forward and snatched the paper from him. "Enough," he said sharply.

Le Renard stared at the wrinkled parchment in his

hand, a mixture of anger, frustration, and an unequaled sense of confused admiration going through him. The injustice was that this Flame creature, whoever he might be, had captured too closely his own sentiments, had elucidated far too convincingly the motives and the concerns of himself and all like him. Had he not gone to great lengths to assure himself otherwise, Le Renard might even have thought it was one of his own men who had, for reasons unknown, embarked upon this new mission. But it was not one of his men, or anyone known to them, and therein lay the problem. Le Renard had had enough dealings with spies of late; he needed no new mystery to complicate his life.

"All right," he said, and his eyes swept slowly around the group of men who sat upon the ground, straddled logs, leaned against trees—farmers, fishermen, merchants, professionals—every one of them known to him, every one of them loyal. "I've had enough of games. This Flame of Liberty was amusing at first, but I begin to suspect it has gone too far. Already"—he gestured to William, who had been the reader of the pamphlet—"these circulars have reached every merchant and tradesman in Williamsburg, and I dare not think how soon it might be before they travel further. I think it's time we discovered this Flame's identity."

"We know every patriot in the county," declared a henchman from the side, "and three counties beyond. How can this man continue to elude us?"

"It stands to reason," returned the Fox impatiently, "that this man did not spring up from the ground full grown two fortnights ago. Publick Times brings people from as far away as the mountains into the town; we obviously do not know everyone. My patience wears thin with this nonsense. I will know his identity."

"He fights for our cause," murmured Sam, chewing

thoughtfully on a blade of grass. "Yet he keeps himself hidden from those who would be his friends. I wonder . . ."—he cast a sly glance at his leader—"what would cause a man to do something like that?"

Le Renard returned a mildly damning look. "Perhaps," he replied distinctly, "because he is not a friend."

William chuckled softly, his teasing eyes glinting at his friend. "It's beginning to sound as though Le Renard is jealous. This mysterious stranger has attracted more attention with his pen in a few weeks than we have in months of raids. It cannot sit any better with our noble leader than it does with ourselves."

The lips below the dark mask relaxed into a careless smile, and Le Renard admitted lightly, "Perhaps. Or perhaps, in one way, he has done us a service, for we could use a bit less attention now and more privacy in which to carry out our plans. But that is neither here nor there, for I will not deal with friend or foe unknown to me. This entire matter reeks of a Tory trap."

His statement had a sobering effect upon them all, and the Fox paused to let them digest it before continuing with more force, "We who sit here are among the cleverest and the most skillful in all Virginia; it is beyond me to imagine we could be outwitted by one cowardly scholar who wields a pen instead of a sword." He turned sharply upon a slight, bespectacled young man who hovered at the outskirts of the gathering. "And what of you?" he demanded harshly. "What have you been doing while the villain plants his treacherous scribblings beneath your very nose? Sleeping?"

The young man ventured, stammering, "It is difficult . . . that is to say, one never knows. . . . He comes so silently, and in the dark of the night, and is gone as swiftly as a—" He broke off, blushing to the roots of his wiry brown hair before uttering the word "fox."

Le Renard's scowl deepened, and the sight of it was enough to set the young man to quivering in his boots. He turned abruptly away, directing his attention to another man, and an equally important matter. "And what of our ever-vigilant spy?" he inquired in a tone that spoke loudly of forced mildness.

Lieutenant Hastings straightened with easy confidence to deliver at least one positive report. "In the palm of our hands. The governor has released a thousand guineas to him on the promise of your capture, and is, even now, planning a feast whose main course, I wouldn't doubt, features roast fox."

Someone muttered, "I still don't understand why you don't just throw the vermin overboard."

Le Renard returned an enigmatic smile as he moved toward his horse. "Too simple, old friend, and much too predictable. That would quite take the sport out of the game, I think. Much more preferable to let the cur swing from his own rope, and, with any luck, take the governor along with him."

He scowled again, briefly annoyed. The matter of the spy was not greatly inconvenient, but it was troubling to his temper. Unbeknownst to his erstwhile partner, the treachery he had enacted would serve Le Renard rather than threaten him, yet it had taken all of his self-restraint and a good deal of Sam's persuasive reason to deter him from tracking down the whereabouts of Lord Chatley and fastening his strong fingers around his flabby throat. A message, curtly phrased and discreetly delivered, would end their partnership and serve the purpose of revenge just as neatly as an impetuous action would do, for it was well known that nothing could hurt Lord Chatley except an attack upon his pocketbook.

Shrugging away uncomfortable thoughts of the

author of this treachery, Le Renard continued easily, "We'll bide our time, and at the most propitious moment make certain our worthy spy receives just enough information to hang himself with. In the meantime"—he swung lightly into the saddle and paused to look down at them all with an air of easy command—"we have more pressing matters to deal with." His eyes swung to the bespectacled young man, who met the challenge with great trepidation. "I suggest," he said, "that you increase your vigilance." His eyes swung around to include all of them. "All of you. For I *will* have this interloper, and before the week is out."

He spurred his horse and disappeared into the night. They stood there for a moment in the sound of retreating hoofbeats, looking at each other uneasily as they digested the enormity of the task that had been set before them. Then Sam straightened up slowly, tossed the blade of grass to the ground, and surveyed his companions with mild resignation. "That, gentlemen," he said, "unless I'm very much mistaken, was not a request. I suggest we set to it."

In the still, quiet hours just before dawn, a silent figure, heavily cloaked and masked, made its way with an almost ghostly grace through the heavily shadowed churchyard. Keeping close to the walls and shrubs, it appeared not to move but to flicker into presence and then disappear again so that anyone observing could almost count it as nothing more than a momentary lapse of imagination.

In the past month, revolutionary pamphlets authored by the Flame of Liberty had appeared at the rate of almost two a week, each one more incendiary than the last, and each one causing more excitement and speculation than the one before. Slowly but inexorably they moved attention away from the Fox and focused it instead upon this new troublemaker, The Flame of Liberty.

Arabella had never intended it to go this far. That hideous night after the ball, when she had paced the floor of her lonely bedchamber agonizing over a way to keep Phillip out of danger for only one more day, she had finally hit upon a solution, which, at the time had seemed like grasping at straws; she had doubted it would help; she had only hoped it would not hurt. She had wanted to have the governor's wrath focused on someone else for a moment, and the simplest way to do that had been to let someone else take credit for the Fox's infamy. And it had worked. Though the governor still sought the Fox with a vengeance, he now had new troubles to occupy him. Daily he was becoming more and more uneasy about what he presumed to be the growing tide of dissent in his colony. The Flame could hardly cease her writings now, just when they were beginning to have an effect.

But more inspiring was the reaction her writings were causing among the people of Williamsburg. The handwritten pamphlets were passed around, read from the steps of buildings and in Market Square; from the market they made their way into the countryside, where the cry of The Flame of Liberty was taken up by farmers and yeomen and soon perhaps would begin to spread to other colonies.

Arabella could not pass a day without hearing the name mentioned in whispers or in admiration, or find that a quote from her own pen was being passed around like a talisman, and the power she had unknowingly acquired was heady and overwhelming. She had an audience. People were listening to her, waiting for her, depending upon her. She was beginning to make a difference, and this was more than an adventure. It was an enterprise.

Arabella had learned her lesson, however painful it had been, about impetuosity and foolhardiness, and she planned her missions with a care and cunning that might have done Le Renard himself proud. Her movements were restricted to the early morning hours, before dawn yet well after the time even the most decadent citizen would be asleep. She wore the trousers and the shirt of her costume from the governor's ball, and covered it all in a long, dark traveling cloak. She blackened her face and her hands with coal to more easily fade into the shadows, and she fashioned a domino from a dark square of silk upon which she had once begun embroidery. Her hair was bundled beneath a dark woolen cap she had appropriated from a stable boy. Not even after the closest of scrutiny would anyone have recognized the dark, boyish figure in heavy cloak and cap as Lady Arabella Winters, Mistress Everett, for her disguise was perfect. She had, after all, learned of such matters from the master.

Neither did she make her movements easy to follow. She varied the time and place of her dispositions; once at midnight upon the door of the courthouse, again at cock's crow upon the steps of the Raleigh, sometimes tacked upon a tree in Market Square. The location of Phillip's townhouse on Nicholson Street gave her easy access to many places of prominence. She found she could steal silently down the back steps and through gardens, down alleyways and across shadowed thoroughfares to her destination, and be back in her own bed with her costume stored away beneath the clothespress, the coal washed from her skin, and her hair and her eyes closed in feigned sleep before the great clock downstairs struck the half hour.

When Phillip was home, however, she took even

313

fewer chances, knowing from experience of his diligence and his shrewdness. Yet stealing out of the house to perform an act of sedition beneath the very nose of the Fox was too great an adventure for Arabella to resist, and she could not let his presence curtail her activities entirely. On such nights, rather, she chose to go only as far as the church, which was well shadowed and less than a five-minute walk away. It was there her steps took her tonight.

Arabella was swift, efficient, and silent. She secured her latest writing to the door of the church and turned with a movement as smooth as the wind to depart. It was then she saw a form emerge from the shadows.

For a moment her heart lurched before she recognized the timid, bespectacled face of the assistant rector. Knowing he could not possibly know her, or even see her very well in the darkness, she nonetheless turned quickly to put her back to him and make her way into the churchyard, where he could not possibly follow. A whisper, urgent and almost desperate, made her pause. "Please . . . wait." And, in a rush, his words tumbling over themselves in his shyness and excitement, he said, "I have a message. A friend would meet with you."

Arabella's heart was racing, but it could not keep pace with her thoughts. *Run,* she thought. *A trap.* But if it was a trap, why did he not take her now? A friend . . . ? Who could it be who wanted to meet The Flame? If not an enemy, then it could only be . . .

She half turned, keeping her own face in shadow while affording herself the opportunity to observe the timid, excited face of the young rector in full. She thought it reflected no duplicity. "What friend?" she demanded.

Quickly he pressed a scrap of paper into her hand. He whispered, "Le Renard!" and then, as though

314

suddenly afraid she might spring on him, he scurried back into the shadows from whence he had come.

15 October, 1773

This could be my Chance, the One I have wait'd for. To unmask Myselfe before Phillip and allow him to do the Same. To free Ourselves from these Silly Games . . . When He comes to the Church-yard expecting to meet an Ally and fynds instead his Wife, can he fail to give Me his Love and Trust? If I can willingly cast aside my Mask, cannot He?

Arabella stopped and looked about her room. It was on the second floor of the house, far from Phillip's chamber, and she felt safe writing in her journal. Her room was bright and sunny during the day, cheerful with its chintz prints on the canopied bed and side chair. She sat at a walnut desk that had been made in Virginia but was as fine as the Chippendale chest of drawers against the other wall. It was a beautiful room, well proportioned and elegantly furnished. It did not seem a room in which one would conjure up thoughts of treachery or betrayal, but now such thoughts came to Arabella. Living with Phillip Everett had taught her well.

I am sure It is his Hand, for I have seen it many Tymes upon the Documents at Shadowood—but what if I am mystaken? What if This is a Trap? What if I should meet the King's Guards and not Le Renard? There is always the Possibility of Treachery and against that I must be wary. This is not a Lover's Tryst that I am keeping Tonyte, no matter how glad my Heart might be for the Chance to show Myself to Phillip. No, this is a Dangerous Mission, laced with Intrigue, and I cannot be too cautious. . . .

Late in the afternoon, as a small test, she casually mentioned to Phillip the possibility of gathering a small, impromptu supper party. "Tonight, m'dear?" he drawled, barely glancing up from his languorous inspection of the cards and invitations Sam had just brought. "Afraid I won't be able to attend. I won a devilish amount from some of the fellows last night and they demand a rematch. Probably go on all night, don't you know. But do go ahead—have some people in." He patted her cheek affectionately as he passed. "So pleased to find you're keeping yourself occupied, dear. By all means, give your little party; I doubt I shall be missed."

Arabella smiled sweetly and demurred that she would not think of entertaining without her husband's most welcome presence, and her heart gave a little surge of triumph. So indeed, Le Renard had plans for tonight. And so, had he but known it, had she . . .

Dressed in all his finery, Phillip left for supper and cards about ten. Arabella, her nerves wound to the breaking point, did not trust herself to bid him her customary affectionate good night, but she watched from the landing as he primped and postured before the pier glass in the hallway, fussing over the way his cloak hung and the turn of his hat, tossing out whining reprimands to Sam each time he tried to assist. Arabella could not help but be amazed at the depth of his performance. Could anyone have guessed that in two hours he would be, not in a smoky gaming house

316

drinking wine and dipping snuff, but waiting in a damp and foggy graveyard to meet with an enemy of the King? Indeed, his performance was so expert that sometimes Arabella herself began to doubt all that she knew to be true.

But tonight it was a risk she had to take. Tonight she had to believe that it would be her husband who waited for her and she would not—she could not—disappoint him.

At eleven o'clock the household was still. Sam had been instructed by Phillip not to wait up, which meant that either the servant had gone to bed or he had slipped out of the house to accompany his master to his rendezvous. Either way, there were no sounds from the attic room in which he slept, and Arabella felt confident she could leave the house unobserved.

Dressed in her breeches, boots, and shirt, she carefully blackened her skin and covered her hair once again, for the possibility remained now, as ever, that she would be spotted by some passerby who would wonder why Lady Arabella traversed the streets of Williamsburg alone at midnight. And then, ever aware of an even more ominous possibility, she took from the bottom of her traveling trunk the leather-embossed case that held her father's dueling pistols.

At the time she had packed for the trip to Williamsburg her mind had been greatly concerned with thoughts of brigands and robbers, and she had had no intention of leaving something of such great personal value behind in a house unguarded. She had never dreamed that she might have real and definite cause to be thankful for their presence.

She held one of the heavy weapons in her hand, and an instant rush of familiarity and confidence came back to her. She had learned to target shoot with her father's pistols, and she had no doubt of her ability to make the weapon perform now if the need should arise. She loaded it with a single shot and tucked it into her waistband, trying not to think how much use such a precaution would be should she find herself surrounded by the King's army, trying not to think that this time her target might be human.

Arabella's heart was in her throat as she crossed the familiar paths and hugged familiar shadows, her night-bright eyes seeking out signs of danger or treachery. The streets were not quite as silent as they were usually when she made such trips, for the early hour gave occasion for sporadic trails of music or laughter from a nearby tavern, the jingle of a carriage harness or the closing of a gate, and with every sound her nerves tightened, her breath lurched. She would arrive at the meeting place early, the better to be prepared should anything seem amiss, and perhaps in time to warn Phillip should there be signs of danger.

And suddenly Arabella realized exactly what she was doing, stealing through the streets of Williamsburg dressed as a man, with a weapon in her belt and treachery on her mind—treachery. She could be executed for what she had done as The Flame. If that note had not in truth come from the Fox . . . If the young man who had delivered it had first shown it to the captain of the guard . . .

The gate to the churchyard swung open easily and closed silently behind her. The light of the new moon was just enough to darken the elongated shadows of the stately monuments and the spreading oaks that stood, like ancient sentinels, to guard this holy place. All was still; so silent that Arabella could hear the sound of her own heart, the whisper of her own breath as she made her way with stealthy, searching steps deeper into the cemetery, seeking a vantage point from which she hoped she could spot danger before it spotted her.

Crouched at last behind the huge canopied monument that protected the final resting place of Governor Nott, Arabella willed her breath to slow and her eyes to see through the darkness. Any one of the stones might shadow the form of a man, a spy, an armed guard, a dozen armed guards, she realized. Her palms were damp, her pulse strong, her ears straining for a sound, the crack of a twig, the rustle of a footstep, and her hand unconsciously clenched the pistol, knowing that any sound she heard could herald the approach of an enemy, not a friend.

The sound she heard was not as loud as a step, not as subtle as a breath; perhaps it was not a sound at all. But with the aid of senses she had learned to use so long ago on a ship in the middle of the James, she knew a presence was behind her only a fraction of a second before a hand reached for the ties that bound her mask.

Arabella was on her feet, whirling to face him, the pistol clenched in both hands and leveled directly at his chest, and all this in the instant before either of them had taken a breath.

It was Le Renard.

He stared at the figure before him, momentarily nonplussed by the sight. Small and slim it was, garbed in a cape that enfolded the slight body and disguised in a ridiculous woolen cap and some sort of scarf that had been fashioned into a mask. The hands and face had been blackened with coal. Why, this was no more than a boy, he reflected in amazement, and for a moment Le Renard was certain there had been a mistake. Then he noticed the cocked pistol only a few inches from his chest, and realized that, whether in the hands of a man or a frightened boy, such a weapon could prove equally dangerous. Though his instinct was to laugh out loud, wisdom dictated that he take a small step backward.

The relief that Arabella might have felt upon discovering that her stalker was none other than her own husband was momentarily swallowed up in a surge of outrage. She had come here, risking life and limb for his sake, fully prepared to unmask before him and share her secrets with the one man who could be counted upon to protect them, only to find that it was *he,* not their mutual enemies, who had set a trap for her. He had claimed friendship, but all along he had planned treachery. How foolish she was to have forgotten his cunning, his wariness, his suspicious nature. And how naive of her to imagine he could offer friendship when he would not offer trust.

Willingly she would have revealed her identity to him, but she would not have it taken from her by force. And Le Renard had, with typical duplicity, broken the rules before the game had even started.

She lifted the pistol a fraction, her eyes narrowing, her hands steady. Her voice was cool and low and laced with the Virginia accent she had so painstakingly acquired from Caroline. "Think not that I fear to use this," she said, unconsciously—or perhaps consciously—mimicking his own words to her from that night on the boat. "I learned to shoot at my father's knee and I doubt I could miss much at this distance, at any rate. You'd best keep your hands at your sides."

It was damned uncomfortable, being held at gunpoint by a young whip barely out of the nursery, and a momentary flash of irritation went through Le Renard and almost forced him into rash action. But a nervous hand upon the trigger was worse than an experienced one, and more embarrassing than the present situation was the prospect of explaining to the surgeon how he had come to be wounded in a churchyard by a boy half his size and age. He decided a more rational approach was in order.

"Put the pistol away, son," he said gently. "There is no quarrel between us."

For a moment Arabella was startled to hear him call her "son," and then she realized that that was exactly what she must look like to him—a young, overdressed boy, wielding his father's pistol and wrapped in his mother's cloak. A surge of triumph went through her, and she thought grimly, *So much the better, for I shall treasure the expression on your face when you find it is only your wife who has tricked you.* After all she had suffered at Phillip's hand, this small embarrassment seemed no more than his due, and she could barely restrain a smile of anticipation as she thought of it.

She replied sternly, "I find a quarrel with any man who claims friendship and then tries to overtake me from behind, and in the dark. I had thought better of the great Fox," she sneered.

"And it is difficult," returned the Fox smoothly, "to know a friend by the name of the weapon he draws. As you can see"—grandly he spread the folds of his cloak to reveal the snug-fitting breeches and unadorned shirt beneath—"I am unarmed."

Arabella conceded generously, "You may keep the dagger that you have so cleverly concealed at your waist, and I will keep my pistol." She did not lower the pistol even as she smiled mirthlessly. "It is always best, I think, to keep the scales balanced."

Though Le Renard gave no indication, his mind registered surprise, and not a small amount of disturbance. A boy perhaps, but a deuced clever one, and not to be so lightly reckoned with as he had originally thought. He surveyed the figure before him with new interest, his mind working rapidly. Though at first glance the boy had barely seemed old enough to be out of smocks, it was apparent he was somewhat more competent than appearance would lead one to believe. A student at William and Mary most likely, whose intellect and small size had set him apart from his peers and whose proclivity for prose had led him to express his support for the patriots' cause in the best way known to him.

It was a pity, for under other circumstances such zeal could have been useful, and even seriously sought, by Le Renard. But he had no use for glory seekers and suicidal patriotism, nor was there room among his well-disciplined band for those who persisted in taking on the king and all his men single-handed, as this headstrong lad was apparently bent on doing. Besides, he was not yet fully convinced of the boy's motives. Why had he chosen this particular season to make an appearance? Why had he done so directly after the governor's ball? And why had he capitalized on the Fox's legend to make his own fame? Something about it did not sit quite right, and it still could be a Tory trick. The greatest dangers, as Le Renard had learned so well from his lovely young wife, often came disguised in the most innocent packages.

Arabella kept her hands firmly on the pistol, glorying now in the confusion she could sense beneath the implacable surface of her husband, delighting in the purely ignoble sensation of having him at her mercy, just as she once had been at the mercy of his dagger. It had been a game then, just as it was a game now. Only this time it was the prey who made the rules, and not the hunter.

She said gruffly, "What is it that you want of me? Why did you ask for this meeting?"

Le Renard surveyed the small figure through expressionless, hooded eyes. The scarf from which the mask was fashioned was silk, he noted, and had some sort of design sewn upon it, which, when slits were cut for the eyes, resembled a flame. Theatrics, or cunning? It was the uncertainty that he did not like. "Only," he replied, for prolonging the encounter seemed the only sure way to an answer, "to warn you of the dangerous game you are playing. Your writings are pretty, I'll grant you that, but I suggest you turn your talents to treatises upon Homer and Plato, for the matters you stir up now can have greater consequences than you guess. You are but a lad; you know nothing of the things of men. Leave the politics to those who are wise enough to deal with them."

And slowly Arabella realized that his purpose in this meeting had not been to draw an alliance at all, but instead to dispense with his competition. Le Renard brooked no interference with his work, and neither did he accept aid. She had come willing to bare herself before him; he had come willing to do nothing but brush her away as if she were nothing more than an annoying insect that had happened to disrupt his concentration. She had risked her *life* to meet with him tonight. She had tasted fear. She had known danger, bitter and sharp, coursing like liquid metal through her veins, tainting the very air she breathed. She had known what it was to face capture upon the charge of treason, to risk disgrace, betrayal, and even execution. She had known it all, just as well as he had, yet he dared this condescending manner. He dared to dismiss her with a wave and a sneer, a bothersome obstacle to be skirted or trod over.

The familiar outrage began to gather within her, and then she understood something more: No matter what the circumstances, if Phillip found out who she was now, her work would cease. As the Fox he scorned her, as Phillip . . . Would any man allow his wife to face the dangers she had faced tonight, to go up brazenly

323

against the king and the royal governor, knowing discovery would mean certain death? The cold truth of her dilemma crept through her as she became aware however unwittingly, that she had stumbled into folly. *I am the Flame,* she thought, and the surge of power and pride that went through her was imcomparable. But just as swiftly came the opposite knowledge. *And I am your wife . . .*

Must she make a choice?

She eased her grip on the pistol somewhat, knowing instinctively that the time of its effectiveness had passed. Yet her head tilted in confidence; her words were cool. "Wise, sir?" she questioned evenly. "I wonder which one of us now is less wise. You risk your life in daring raids and shows of bravery; I risk nothing but pen and ink. Yet each of us achieves his end, and only time will tell which way is most effective."

Only barely did Le Renard restrain the glint of admiration in his eyes. Damn, but the young cur was cool under pressure. He almost found himself wishing the lad were a few years older, a few pounds heavier. And he was almost swayed to believe him.

He said sharply, "What proof have I that you are not a spy? That all of this is not some elaborate Tory trick designed to weave a web around the Fox?"

Arabella now uttered words that must have been waiting for just this moment in her life to be spoken. "You cannot know. You must trust me."

Unbidden, his mind swept back to a night not so long ago, in a darkened ship's cabin, with the smell of tallow and river, and Arabella, so frightened, so brave . . . She had begged for his trust then, and he had not given it. "One other person asked my trust . . ." he said softly, "and I was wise to withhold it." His eyes sharpened and his voice took on strength. "Do you think I would offer it now to a stranger?"

This, the final rejection, was almost more than Arabella could stand. Her shoulders squared, the muscles of her neck tightened, and her eyes did not waver. She said, unable to disguise the harsh mockery in her voice, "Are you so confident, oh great Fox, that you have no need for allies? You have a friend in me, one who is willing to fight for you and advance your cause, yet you turn your back. Are such as I so easy to find? Perhaps it is *you* who doesn't realize the true danger in this game!"

Le Renard felt his patience snap in a single motion, perhaps because he recognized too great a truth in these words. "I need no lectures from a young pup like you," he flung back angrily. "Especially one who dares to take credit for my deeds and then holds a gun to my ribs! Is this your show of friendship? I can do very nicely without it, thank you!"

Arabella surveyed him coldly. "Does it matter, sir, who takes the credit, as long as the deed is done? We are, after all, fighting on the same side."

"Indeed," said the Fox at length, softly. His eyes were sharp and glittered cunningly in the dark. "But are we?"

Arabella had no answer for that. She had demonstrated her loyalty as best she could, and still he would not believe. A despair as keen as she had ever felt swept through her, but she could not buckle beneath it. Something strong and as yet undefinable within her would not let her abandon the disguise, not now, not after having come so far. She said quietly, returning the pistol to her belt, "So be it then. We could have made a strong alliance, you and I. But now we must wait to see which way the coats turn when the bullets begin to fly."

Again he experienced a moment of hesitation. Something deep within him knew the lad who called himself the Flame spoke the truth, yet another part,

325

just as strong, knew something still was not quite true. He was in no position to take chances. At best, he would be saddled with a headstrong youth who would bring nothing but trouble to them all; at worst he would be walking into a cleverly laid trap.

Le Renard said abruptly, "I want no part of you and your seditious writings. You are a half-wet whelp who brings nothing but problems upon an already troubled colony, and this you may take as a warning: Go home to your mother and leave this business alone, for if I hear of you or read of you again, there will be more to answer for than you care to know."

Arabella's temper flared. This was too much. She had been cast aside, rejected, mocked, and now threatened—all in the name of friendship, and for the sake of love. *I am the Flame,* she thought fiercely, unshakably. *Though I cannot be your wife, this one thing I am and will continue to be. There are those who recognize me, if you do not. You will not stop me. The governor will not stop me. The King himself will not stop me. For I am the Flame, and I will not cease to be!*

She lifted her head, and her eyes caught by the thin light of the moon for an instant, glittered dangerously. "I will go," she said coldly, angrily, "but to my pen. With or without your permission, Le Renard, the Flame of Liberty will continue to burn, and you have not heard the last of me."

She turned abruptly, and in only another instant the flutter of her cloak had blended into the shadows of the night.

Chapter XVIII

It was among Lieutenant Hastings's privileges as a high-ranking officer and personal aide to the governor to enjoy private quarters in the military barracks of Williamsburg. His duties were light, his evenings his own, and, within certain restricted limits and subject to the needs of the governor, he could come and go as he pleased. His position was enviable from any standpoint, and for Hastings's personal goals and ambitions, nothing could have suited him better.

He had first made the acquaintance of Le Renard two years ago and had never once regretted the association. He had been involved in some minor pilfering and selling of the governor's troop supplies—nothing grand, to be sure, but just enough to see him court-martialed and hanged, had he been discovered. And so he might have been, except for the timely intervention of a yeoman farmer named Hampton.

Hastings had never wasted a moment's concern on thoughts of treachery to the king or betrayal of his post during this episode. It might have been different had he been taking the food from the mouths of babes, but in his opinion the Crown's contingent was well oversupplied with munitions for use against colonists who

327

meant them no harm. A display of arms against a people on their own land seemed to Hastings the height of bad taste, and no one would suffer for it if he were to line his pockets a bit with the profit made by taking from the king and selling to the colonists what, after all, was rightfully theirs. He even thought of himself as evening the odds, should it ever come to an unlikely display of force between the royal troops and the colonial militia.

He kept his operation small, to better reduce the chances of being caught, and made certain that the weapons he sold left the colony immediately. But at one point he had gotten careless, and the governor was more than a little surprised to find several of his missing British-made rifles appearing in the hands of the Virginia militia. Hastings felt the noose tighten about his neck and knew he had but two options: to disappear into the wilderness, or to seek an honorable death on the blade of his own sword. Neither alternative appealed to him.

That was when William Hampton had come in, and, acting upon a scheme concocted by Le Renard, he had not only saved Hastings's neck but had advanced him in position and confidence so that his position of trust with the governor was more secure than ever. Hastings had been allowed to prove to Lord Dunmore that it was the Fox, not one of the governor's own men, who had been stealing the weapons, and the scheme had been so brilliant that no one, least of all Hastings, could have been blamed for the split-second turnaround that had allowed the wily creature to slip through their fingers.

From that moment on, Hastings's loyalty had been secured. It was his great admiration for Le Renard, as much as his own personal motivations, that allied him to the mysterious man. Hastings was young, passionate, and adventuresome. He was no stranger to the thrill of battle, but it was the power of intrigue that drew him into the behind-the-scenes war being fought in Virginia. No man alive was match in wits for Le Renard, and Hastings dearly enjoyed being on the winning side.

That was why discovering the identity of the brilliant general to whom he had pledged his life had been such a shock. Now he paused with the boot brush in midair and let it wash over him again. Everett. He still could not quite believe it.

Hastings was meticulous in his appearance, and the sheen of overpolished leather was a mirror that reflected a thoughtfully arrested face. He stared into it, barely noticing, as he would have on any other occasion, the handsome lines of his face, the shrewdly appealing eyes, the neatly brushed and healthily gleaming hair, about which he was especially vain. And as he stared, a faint scowl line appeared between his brows.

Everett. No, he must have been mistaken. He had only been told that, as the illuminations began, he was to trade costumes with the Fox. All evening he had been busily trying to guess which of the elaborately disguised guests might be the man with whom he had ridden so often and in whose hands he had entrusted his safety more times than could be counted with no real thought of ever learning his identity. Yet he was still enough of a military man to obey orders without question . . . until he stepped upon the path and found a fox awaiting him, not *the* Fox.

He had pondered it for days, thinking that surely he had misinterpreted. Phillip Everett had appeared at the ball wearing the costume of a fox, but that in no way indicated that he was, in fact, Le Renard. Yet there was no getting around the fact that Everett had been involved in the victory struck against military imperialism that night—involved, perhaps, in a very major way. And when he had removed the mask, when he had spoken to Hastings, he had not been Phillip Everett at all. The face had been hard, the eyes alert, the voice one that had issued dozens of commands to which Hastings had responded without hesitation.

He had turned it over and over in his mind and had tried to reject the obvious, but he had been forced to return at last to the only possible truth. The costume Phillip Everett had worn to the governor's ball had been no costume at all. The mincing, prancing fool who was the darling of Virginia society was also Le Renard. And he was far, far more clever than even Hastings had imagined.

This new knowledge sat uneasily with him; in fact, it even frightened him a little. It was well known that the identity of Le Renard was protected to the death; only a man with extraordinary courage would want to be burdened with the responsibility of knowledge upon which the lives of dozens of men hinged. Yet such responsibility had been thrust upon him. Why? Would he prove equal to the challenge? And if he failed, what price would be exacted?

Thus far he had had no opportunity to speak alone with his leader. He had studied him carefully upon the occasion of their last meeting in the forest and had seen nothing that had not been there before. The transformation had been so complete, in fact, that he once again was thrown into confusion, thinking he had been wrong. He had waited for a word from Le Renard, a challenge, a warning, some acknowledgment of the secret they now shared and its implications. When there had been none, he was more at a loss than ever.

One thing only he knew. He must be very, very careful from now on. With the privilege of being one of the few living men aware of Le Renard's secret also came a terrible liability. A single misstep could result in his being branded a traitor by the one man in the world whom he never, ever wished to cross.

A short rap on the door jerked him out of his reverie, and Hastings straightened quickly, his nerves jolted. Then he cursed himself for a weakling girl as the boot brush dropped from his startled fingers. Since the night of the ball he had been walking on eggs, and if he had learned one thing from Le Renard it was this: a cool head was a safe one, and nothing could lead to an early grave quicker than a hasty hand.

Taking time to straighten his coat and polish a brass button with his sleeve, he strolled over to the door. He greeted the small Negro boy there with an irritable scowl and a terse, "Yes? What is it?"

"Beggin' pardon suh; a message for you."

Hastings snatched the folded note from him and, turning to the table near the door, picked up a coin and tossed it in the boy's direction. He was still scowling as he closed the door with his foot and tore open the note.

The paper was of fine quality and scented, and it bore an aristocratic seal. The flowery writing read:

My dear Lieutenant Hastings:

I would be most honored to entertain you at a small supper at my home this evening at eight. I think it urgent that we discuss your involvement in certain matters that transpired on the night of the governor's Masked Ball.

Fondest regards,
Lady Charlotte Parkington

Hastings went cold. A fine sweat broke out on his

forehead and he felt ill. So this was it. So soon was he being called to the test.

His fingers crushed the paper and, with a low, muttered oath, he took two pacing steps across the room. He should have known. He should have known the troublesome woman would bring him to no good end.

He had failed, somehow, in his mission. Such a simple thing, to stay quiet and be seen in the costume of Phillip Everett for a matter of moments while Le Renard performed his deed. It would have been no great enterprise, with all eyes on the fireworks, had not that Parkington woman, with her shrewd smile and her sharp gaze, come over to strike up a conversation with her good friend Everett. All the while Hastings had been so intent upon avoiding Lady Arabella that he had given no thought to others who might penetrate his disguise.

But Charlotte Parkington had come, had laid her hand upon his arm, had attempted to engage him in conversation. He could still remember the fever of fear that had gripped him when she had approached. There had been no way to outstep her. He had been terrified she would notice something amiss—his chin, his eyes, his hand—something that would reveal he was not Everett. He had been afraid to speak to her, knowing she would recognize his voice. When the explosion had allowed him to turn from her and disappear into the crowd, his relief at the narrow escape had been enormous and, apparently, premature.

Charlotte Parkington knew. And how the devil was he supposed to shut her up?

He glanced at the crumpled note and for a moment considered sending his regrets, then rejected the notion immediately. That she knew something was evident; how much she knew was up to him to discover. And the

332

only way to do that was to play her game.

Should he try to contact Le Renard? The danger in that was clear, especially for the sake of the small amount of information Hastings had. And would he go crying to his leader like a frightened child at the first sign of trouble?

No, he decided grimly. This was his responsibility, his test. He would prove himself worthy. He would find out on his own exactly what Lady Parkington knew, or suspected, and he would discern how best to deal with it. Then, and only then, would he report to Le Renard.

After all—and he smiled faintly, engendering his confidence as he turned to the pier glass to straighten his stock—there had never been a woman born he could not handle.

Charlotte lay back in the porcelain tub, luxuriating in the creamy white liquid that surrounded her, her eyes closed, a faint smile gracing her lips. She was thinking about her intimate supper party this evening and the tall, handsome young bull who would be her guest. Never had she anticipated a *tête-à-tête* with such eagerness.

The solution in which she bathed was pure mare's milk. The odor was quite rank, so much so that the servant could not even come into the room without much gagging and moaning and waving of burnt feathers, but the mixture was sheer magic for the complexion. Charlotte had long since grown accustomed to the smell, and the behavior of the servants she met with nothing but scorn. In fact, she was appreciative of the privacy. She enjoyed her little moments of reflection.

So far the season had been quite disappointing. Phillip, poor dear, was carrying on bravely, quite the life of any party, but she knew his heart was breaking inside. She knew it by the way he made the most imaginative excuses to avoid her little soirees and teas. He simply could not bear to be reminded of what he had left behind in Charlotte for the sake of the red-haired viper he had taken to wife.

Moreover, the governor seemed to be chasing after the vixen as well, and that knowledge put Charlotte quite out of temper. Not that she hadn't already grown bored with the old lecher, but it irked her to see her place usurped by a younger woman—and one who plotted against her darling Phillip as well.

So distressed had she been by the upsetting events of the season that she had quite fallen off in her quest for excitement. There had been no new lovers to distract her, no new amorous adventures to offer challenge, and despondency had loomed ever nearer—until she remembered Hastings.

Now there was a challenge, if ever there had been one. Military men were of a nature so stuffy and self-contained, and she did adore peeling away the layers and exposing the passion that lay behind the thrust of the sword and the explosion of the musket. And the fact that he was so young, so handsome, *and* in the very close confidence of the governor was all the more delightful. There was nothing she would enjoy more than to turn from the governor to one of his young aides and hope he found out—that would give the old dictator something to crow about!

Smiling to herself, Charlotte arose from the mare's milk, blotted herself on a sheet of lambswool, and stepped into a warm tub of rosewater to rinse. Arising, she wrapped herself again in lambswool and called imperiously for the servants, who lost no time in beginning to empty the offensive tub of milk.

Thoughtfully she perused the garments her maid had

spread over the bed for her inspection. It would be an intimate affair—her eyes glittered with the prospect—*very* intimate, and elaborate attire would be superfluous. A light supper would be drawn up before the fire in her private sitting room, the lamps would be dimmed, and they would enjoy a repast upon the settee.

She chose from the array of dressing gowns one of deep crimson trimmed in rabbit fur. The color did magnificent things for her skin, and its silky texture would drive any man to distraction. Already her hair had been perfumed, pomaded, and wound into gleaming coils atop her head. Letting the lambswool slide to the floor, she crossed over to her dressing table and applied the finishing touches—a dab of perfume behind her wrists, knees, and upon her throat, and a delicate coloring of rouge to the areolae of her nipples.

Charlotte was at her best when she could assign humanitarian motives to selfish pleasures, and the affair with Hastings fit her prescription precisely. She would be doing a great service to an old friend by warning Hastings away from Phillip's wife, and yet she would derive double satisfaction from striking a blow against the shameless Lady Arabella and claiming the spoils of the victory for herself. Yes, it would be one of the most delightful enterprises she had ever launched.

It troubled her briefly that Hastings, strong young stallion that he was, might not be so easily dissuaded from the charms of Lady Arabella. But almost as immediately as it had occurred, the notion was dismissed, and Charlotte smiled secretly to herself as she took from the lower drawer of a bureau a small amber vial. Where there was a will there was a way, for there had not yet been born the man Charlotte Parkington could not handle.

*　　*　　*

335

Upon the hour of eight precisely the resplendent young Lieutenant Hastings was ushered into the lady's private sitting room. He made a striking figure indeed in full dress regalia, with his scarlett coat, snug breeches, and gleaming black boots. He carried his hat beneath his arm in the military fashion, and when Charlotte arose from the chaise, he paused for only a moment, surprise registering in his eyes, before making her the proper deep bow.

During the afternoon Hastings's confidence had waned considerably, and he had kept the appointed rendezvous with the greatest of misgivings. This could be a serious business, and one he was not entirely certain he had the authority, or the skill, to engage in without the advice of Le Renard. Yet it had been his mistake that had aroused Lady Parkington's suspicions; it would be his duty to allay them. How else could he prove himself worthy of the trust Le Renard had placed in him?

His uneasiness only increased as his eyes swept the room, which had been intimately arranged for a cozy supper before the fire, and the lady who approached him. She was wearing a dressing gown of floating crimson, each fold and plane clinging to her figure in the most alluring fashion. A swath of white fur dipped into her breasts, a single jewel adorned her throat, and, as she lifted her hand to him, the full sleeve of her gown fell away to reveal smooth white elbow and a great portion of her upper arm. He had seen more subtlety in a brothel. What was her game?

"My dear Hastings," she crooned, placing her sweet-smelling palm in his. "I do hope you don't mind if we dine informally. I do so tire of the constant whirl of social engagements I am forced to attend. I find intimate suppers so much more conducive to"—she paused meaningfully, glancing at him through slanted lashes—"special friendships, don't you?"

"Indeed, my lady," he responded smoothly, "and I am most honored to be counted among your special friends."

She took his hat and led him to the settee, then went to pour a sherry. Hastings could not help but notice that there were no servants about. He had heard rumors of Lady Charlotte—indeed, who had not?—but he had never expected anything like this. The door was open onto her softly lit bedroom just a few steps away. He forcefully reminded himself to stay on his guard—at least until he discovered the meaning behind her enigmatic note.

Charlotte pressed the sherry into his hand and sank down beside him, very close. Her body was half turned toward him, pulling taut the material that barely covered her lush, creamy breasts, and she lifted her elbow to rest it against the back of the settee, almost brushing his shoulder. Her sweet scent enveloped him. She smiled and said, "Now, isn't this comfortable?"

He unhesitatingly agreed that it was.

She sipped her sherry, glancing up at him. "Do tell me about yourself, dear. Where are you from?"

He had to clear his throat. The room was very warm. "From London, actually."

"Is your family military?"

"My father was, yes." He was telling her something anyone who wished might know. "He, too, served with a detachment to the Colonies and always spoke of coming back to settle here. Unfortunately he died in service before he was able to."

"Ah, so the son followed his footsteps. How charming." Somehow her fingers had drifted behind him and now brushed a strand of hair that had curled from its queue against his neck. It required all the military training Hastings could command to restrain a shiver of awareness.

Her eyes were wide, interested, and unfathomably deep as she suggested, "But I'm sure you miss your . . . ah . . . family, do you not, so far away in London town?"

To the point, Hastings reminded himself sternly. *This is no lighthearted wench ripe for a dalliance. This woman possesses information that could endanger us all.*

He shifted away slightly and found it much easier to speak after another sip of sherry. "In fact, I do not," he confessed. "Coming from six brothers and sisters in a small pensioner's cottage, I am more than happy to be on my own."

Charlotte seemed not in the least disconcerted by his formal behavior, and she smiled as she reached for a platter on the table before them. "Do have one of these oysters, Lieutenant. They are most delicious and attributed to have, I am told, highly desired properties of health and fortitude."

Hastings watched as she took an oyster shell and tipped it upward to her lips, allowing the meat to slide smoothly down her throat. In a moment he did the same.

"So," she inquired, lifting another shell, "you admire our colonies, do you?"

"I have seen a great deal of them in the time of my service," he agreed, "from the wilderness forest to the charming towns, and I confess I understand why so many have chosen to make their fortunes here. It is a ripe land, ready for the taking, and I shall be sorry to leave it behind for the little that awaits me in England."

"I, too, find the open spaces appealing. So much more freedom to do and behave as one pleases . . . to take what one wants . . ." Her eyes had taken on a seductive gleam. "Perhaps," she suggested, "if you had a reason to stay, you would not be so quick to desert our fair land for Mother England." And then, slowly, purposefully, she brought the oyster shell not to her lips, but to his.

Automatically, Hastings parted his lips and let the rich meat slip inside. He swallowed without tasting, his eyes fixed upon hers, his head reeling, his senses pounding with warning and awareness. What kind of trap had the seductress laid for him? What was her talk of desertion and freedom and affection for the Colonies? Did every word she uttered have a double meaning, or was it only his desperate imagination? How close was she to knowing of Phillip Everett's double identity? And how much did she know of what Hastings knew? With a slow, sinking feeling, Hastings began to suspect he was in over his head.

To his great relief, a knock sounded just then, and Charlotte, without ever removing her eyes from his, called out to admit the servants bearing the supper courses. They arose to take seats opposite the small table, and under the attentive gaze of the ready butler, Hastings began to relax.

Lady Parkington's appetites in cuisine—as well in all else, Hastings suspected—were richly sensual, and the meal served them was exquisite. Following a creamy peanut broth, they were served slivers of fresh flounder in tarragon sauce, each separately delightful to the palate. She spoke very little during the meal, but her eyes spoke volumes as her tiny white teeth tore off a bit of pheasant thigh. Her lips were sheened with juices, and she chewed with sheer sensual enjoyment, each movement erotic and powerfully suggestive. She ran her fingertips over the leg of the bird as though caressing natural flesh, then slipped one finger inside her mouth. Arousal mixed with anxiety within him, and Hastings lost his own appetite in his fascination with watching her.

At last Hastings could stand it no longer. Whatever fate awaited him at the hands of this woman—whether a lover's tryst or a military intrigue—he would know it now. More of this suspense and he would surely go mad.

The servants began to clear away the dishes, leaving on the table before them a plate of Stilton cheese, fresh apples, and a decanter of port. Hastings cleared his throat. "Your company is delightful, Lady Charlotte, and your meal excellent, but I confess to some curiosity as to why you asked to see me. Your note"—he had to clear his throat again—"mentioned something about the evening of the governor's ball . . ."

Her smile was secret and she arose gracefully, reaching for the decanter of wine. "Do let us make ourselves comfortable, Lieutenant." She gestured to the settee, and Hastings, tensions rising with every moment, moved to it while she poured the wine. He did not see her tip a small vial of amber liquid into his glass just before she brought it to him.

He took the glass of port from her and she settled close, her thigh brushing his, her arm uplifted to the back of the settee near his shoulders, and her breasts, full and thrusting, positioned in the direct line of his vision. Her eyes were delighted, glowing, wicked.

He held her gaze with a very great exertion of will. But his collar was tight and it was difficult to speak. "You wanted to discuss something with me?" he prompted, pleased he was able to keep his tone even.

"Indeed." Her eyes dropped to her glass, studying the rich red liquid while her forefinger traced a languid, erotic pattern around the rim of the glass. She lifted her eyes to him again. They were dark and unfathomable, and her voice was husky. "You see, I have formed a special fondness for you and felt compelled to speak to you on a matter of some delicacy. One might even take it as a warning. Phillip Everett, as you know, is a very great friend of mine . . ."

Hastings's throat constricted. *She knows,* he thought. *She knows all.*

"And the governor is close to me, as well," she continued, watching him. "I wouldn't want to be caught in the middle of a distasteful little affair like this . . . no more, I'm sure, than would you."

Panic seized him, sheer and terrible. He took a hasty gulp of the port to calm his nerves. It was worse than he had thought. Not only did she have information that could destroy them all, but it was her intention to betray them to the governor. The safety of all depended upon him now, but he could think of no way out. He felt flushed and his hands were damp. He took another sip of the port for courage.

In the end he could see no approach but a direct one. If Everett were indeed her friend, perhaps she would not truly bring him harm. He said quickly, "Lady Charlotte, before you go to the governor, I implore you. This is a matter of the highest discretion . . ."

She arched an eyebrow, swaying a bit closer. Her breast brushed his arm and sent bolts of electric awareness through his nerve endings. She murmured, "But isn't that always the way with affairs of the heart?"

He paused, looking at her quizzically, wise enough at least to keep still. His pulses were pounding and his head felt fuzzy. He was overly warm and his clothing felt constrictive. The ache in his loins was a dull, almost painful thing that made it difficult to concentrate on the course of the conversation.

She explained, "Your liaison with Lady Arabella. For one who speaks so highly of discretion, Lieutenant, you seem sadly lacking in the same yourself. I can only advise . . ." Inching closer, she slipped a finger

341

beneath the tight binding of his collar. Her touch against his bare flesh caused nerves he had not even known he had to scream in awareness.

He could hear the roar of his own blood, heated and swift and rushing by volumes to his engorged loins. His skin tingled and burned unbearably at every point and he was terrified that he would soon be unable to resist the urge to tear off his jacket. Desperately he tried to concentrate. "You think"—his voice was hoarse— "that I left the ball for the purpose of a lover's tryst with Lady Arabella?"

Cool, deft fingers began to work the buttons of his coat, relieving the awful pressure against his skin. His head was roaring. *It is the wine,* he thought. *She has drugged the wine.* But there was not even room for fear. His body was on fire.

She whispered, her eyes dark and gleaming and taking up all the universe, "You would do better, lovely Lieutenant, to dispense your affections to one who can appreciate them . . . and in whose arms there is no danger."

Relief was so great that he almost shouted with it. His mind latched on to two words and sang them over and over again. *No danger, no danger* . . . She knew nothing of the events of the ball. She was merely jealous of Lady Arabella.

With a not-quite-steady hand, he set his wine glass on the table, and when he turned back she began to slip his coat off his shoulders. It was a sweet, sweet agony of sliding movement against bursting flesh, and he did not know how he would be able to speak. "There is," he managed, "no affection in me for Lady Arabella. How could there be"—a gasp as her nails brushed against the inside of his wrist and the coat fell free—"when I have eyes for only you?"

Her smile was infinitely satisfied as she leaned closer,

working the buttons of his shirt. A fine sheen of perspiration singed his skin, and she murmured, "You will not regret your choice, lovely boy."

It was me, he thought and wanted to laugh. *It was only me she wanted, and all the fear was for naught.* He had passed the test; he had kept the secret; he had been in no danger at all. He tried to think of Le Renard and pride in his duty, but he was on fire, burning to ashes, and all he could gasp was, "What did you put in the wine?"

Her laugh was low and throaty as she leaned over him, pressing his aching flesh into the cushions. Her breasts seared his bare chest, her fingertips ran alongside his inner thigh, and he bit back a groan. He was bursting. His clothes would no longer contain him. His hands ached for her, but he could hardly move them.

"An ancient potion," she murmured, her breath teasing his mouth, "but have no fear. You have not been poisoned"—again she laughed huskily—"though you may think so on the morn. For tonight, my little concoction has done nothing but push away some of the sternness that might have kept you from me and infused you with strength and endurance that will surprise even yourself."

"There was no need for such devices," he muttered, and then he could stand it no longer. He crushed her mouth to him.

Madness overtook him, devouring him, searing him. Her teeth bit his lips and tongue, her nails raked a burning path down the flesh of his chest, and when her fingers closed over the throbbing tumescence of his loins, he filled her mouth with a savage cry. She was a wildcat, fierce and brutal, but no more than he. Together their fingers tore at the material of his breeches and they tumbled to the floor. He felt her sharp teeth sink deep into his shoulder, her stiletto nails draw blood upon his back, and he thrust deep and hard, again and again, seeking only surcease from the agony of fire that consumed him. And no sooner was satisfaction reached than the burning began again, for there was no end to it, not to her desire or to his.

Hastings gave not another thought to Phillip Everett, the governor, or Le Renard. He had always prided himself on his experience along the paths of passion, but he had never known anything like this. And for the next twelve hours he thought of nothing and no one but Charlotte Parkington.

Chapter XIX

Drawn by four matched bays the great coach rumbled through the dusty streets of Williamsburg toward the party in progress at the Woolcot's elegant townhouse on Prince George Street. Inside the coach rode a magnificently attired lady and gentleman, epitomizing the splendor and pomp of the Virginia aristocracy. Over a vest and breeches of plum-colored satin, the man wore a coat of peacock blue velvet, its lapels richly embroidered with gold and silver threads. Buckles studded with semi-precious stones adorned his high-heeled slippers and his wig was in the latest fashion. The entire effect was crowned by a tricornered hat of deep burgundy that rode stylishly above his heavily powdered face.

His companion, in a dress of sea green silk intricately ruffled with yards and yards of imported French lace, was protected from the chill of the October air by a cloak of purple velvet. Her splendid wig, rising two feet above her head, was sprinkled with a lacing of pearls and diamonds, which rivaled the brilliance of the choker about her neck. The season in Williamsburg had begun, and Master and Mistress Phillip Everett were on their way to yet one more *fete*.

One of the wheels of the lumbering coach caught momentarily in a pothole in the uneven street, and the horses heaved mightily, struggling to free the wheel. In that moment of unsteadiness, Arabella was jostled against Phillip, and when the coach righted itself Arabella kept her position next to her husband, hip pressed against hip, thigh resting alongside thigh. Phillip could move but half an inch toward the door, and Arabella had no intention of moving the opposite way. Turning slightly, she studied Phillip's profile, her warm breath near enough his ear to stir the tendrils of his wig. "Did you enjoy the play, dear?"

Phillip pretended interest in the darkness outside the window. Since the governor's ball, Arabella had been unceasingly attentive to her husband's needs, unflaggingly interested in his opinion on every matter, relentlessly devoted to her duty as Mistress Everett and her responsibility as a member of aristocratic society. If her cloying sweetness was unnerving, her sudden dedication to all that was right and proper was nearly overwhelming, and Phillip had lost many a night to sleeplessness since her arrival in Williamsburg.

At last he turned to answer her question. "I found the bard a bit tedious tonight, m'dear," he drawled. "Three hours is overlong, I think, to keep one's eyes open. The mind keeps wanting to flit off, don't you know."

Arabella's concern was beautifully feigned. "But I thought surely the theater would be one of your greatest pleasures. You know, Phillip"—she favored him with a coy smile—"I've always thought you would make a fine actor yourself."

And you, my dear, Phillip thought, *are an actress* nonpareil. His expression of bored disinterest did not change as he replied, "Why how flattering of you, my dear. And in truth at one time I did consider treading the boards. Such a jolly life, don't you know? But that was in my younger days, and of course I soon came to realize that such a vocation was totally out of question for a gentleman of my social standing. However, you are right; I do enjoy an evening at the theater."

He glanced at her, observing nothing in her face but a look of artless interest. With a rueful smile he turned back to his nonexistent view from the window and drawled easily, "But then we are all actors of a sort, aren't we, dear wife? I would have thought you might have had an interest in the calling yourself."

Arabella's brow furrowed at the hidden import of the words. How slippery he was, she thought, and how clever to turn her remarks back on herself so that her own playacting of the perfect Tory wife was subtly brought into the conversation. Since the day she had come to his room—since that hot afternoon amidst parcels and packages and the fever of needs unfulfilled—he had made no comment on her change of behavior. Yet he had watched her; he had noticed, with puzzlement as much as amusement. What did he think, she wondered. Did he realize she was doing all this for him, and could he begin to guess why? Or did he resent her interference and suspect her motives, as he had always done?

She had had no way of knowing, for Phillip had made certain they were never again alone.

Arabella decided not to engage Phillip in a verbal battle about the complicated art of dissembling. In that, Phillip would always emerge the victor. Instead she steered the conversation into safer waters. "Hamlet is a magnificent role for any actor."

Phillip seemed bored by the topic now and yawned, raising a ring-bedecked hand to cover his mouth. "Actually," he said, "I've always found the story a bit bloody for my taste."

"Yes, I was quite trembling myself by the final act—

347

all those bodies piled up on the stage." She gave a forced, ladylike shiver of distaste. "But you, Phillip . . . I thought you would be moved to admiration for such fine examples of swordplay."

"Nonsense, my dear," he replied disinterestedly. "Fencing is a bore, and the sight of blood makes me quite ill. I've never understood society's fascination with so useless a sport."

What a skilled liar he is, she mused angrily, that he could sit in the carriage so close to her and speak nothing but lies, as easily as lines from a play.

"Hmmm," she murmured, as if giving serious consideration to his words. "Most men—and even some women—find a certain excitement in danger." Arabella was reliving in her mind the excitement of the midnight meeting in the graveyard with Le Renard and the danger implicit in their first coupling on his boat. And there was the growing intrigue of her own duplicity, deceiving her husband, the Fox, and all of Williamsburg with her identity as the Flame. Yes it was dangerous, sometimes even terrifying, but there was power in the game and allure in the power. Could not Phillip sense, even now, that they were two of a kind?

She could feel the tensing of his long, sinewy muscles at her touch, and the slight catch of his breath. Was he remembering their time together? Did he never yearn for her at all?

His jaw, in profile to her, was hard and contained. With all her heart, Arabella wanted to lift her fingertips and trace the shape of that jaw, to touch his lips, his throat . . . He must want her. He *had* wanted her that afternoon she had come to his room, yet he had pulled away as he was so very close to doing now. How was she ever to get through to him? The intent of her entire charade had been to win his confidence, to prove her loyalty, to draw him into closeness with her. But the

348

effect it was having was entirely the opposite, and Arabella did not know how much longer she could maintain her ruse.

What more could she do? As Le Renard, he had made no move to come to her again, and she felt a strong certainty that he would never do so. After the way she had behaved with him the morning she had awakened on his boat, he could hardly be blamed. And he had no way of knowing that now her attitude had changed, that now she knew the truth and understood it.

As Phillip, he was determined to keep himself away from his wife, for reasons Arabella was only just beginning to fathom. He was not yet ready to trust her, and never once had he let his facade slip. Yet surely there was something of him that she could reach.

She let her fingers drift a few inches along the musculature of his thigh, looking up at him with eyes that were large and brilliant. "Phillip," she insisted huskily, "can you mean to say that you yourself have never felt the enticement of danger, the allure of taking risks?"

Again she noted the tensing of his muscles, the hardening of his jaw. She sensed he might be wavering. But in an instant the mask was firmly in place again. "My dear, what a lovely ninny you are. The only danger I've ever faced is the risk of losing my shirt at the gaming tables."

He was still chortling over his own jest as the carriage shuddered to a halt. "Here we are, and not a moment too soon. I'm quite parched and eager for a glass of punch, I must say!"

But Arabella refused to give up so easily, not when she was so close. "Phillip, why don't we go home? We could have a hot toddy and sit before the fire—"

He looked astonished. "And disappoint the estima-

349

ble Mistress Woolcot when she has gone to so much bother on your behalf? My dear, I'm surprised that you would even consider such a thing. Why, should we fail to show without regrets, we would be ruined, simply ruined, and all your hard work to redeem yourself among your peers would have been for naught."

He raised his gold-topped walking stick and rapped imperiously on the roof of the coach, bringing a liveried footman to the door. "Out of the question, my dear, simply unthinkable. Besides, I have a new wig I'm dying to flaunt, and I wouldn't wish all your finery to go to waste."

He moved from her touch and clambered down from the coach before Arabella could even begin to form another protest. "Come now," he invited with a smirk. "Take my arm and let us show society that we are quite the most well-matched couple in the city."

Arabella, smothering a sigh of disappointment, had no choice but to do as he asked.

The narrow private room in the main barracks was dim and sparsely furnished, and it smelled of stale clothing and vomit. A narrow wedge of morning sun that filtered through the drawn blinds was the only light, but that thin sliver persistently found the eyes of the man who lay weak and moaning on the cot, no matter how often he tried to twist his head away from it.

Captain O'Donal looked down at his friend in sympathy and amusement. "I warned you, didn't I, Hastings, that one day your decadent ways would lead to your ruin?"

Lieutenant Hastings groaned a little, gripping his convulsing stomach as he opened his eyes a crack. "Those . . . damned oysters . . ." he gasped with dif-

350

ficulty. "If I ever get my hands on that cursed bitch that served me them . . ."

O'Donal brought another cool cloth for the lieutenant's head. "Nothing to do now but wait it out," he advised. "Don't worry about your duty—I'll cover for you. No sense having the colonel down on you over one mistake."

Hastings looked up at him weakly in gratitude, then grimaced again and groped for the slop bucket.

O'Donal winced in distaste and backed away. "No disrespect intended, old friend, but I'm devilishly glad it's you and not me." He turned toward the door. "I'll send a boy round to check on you later. Can you manage?"

Hastings, caught in another fit of retching, could not answer.

Captain O'Donal closed the door behind him and stepped out into the morning light and almost immediately came upon a sergeant who was escorting a rather unsavory-looking man directly toward the lieutenant's door. The sergeant snapped him a smart salute, and when it was returned, he addressed Captain O'Donal.

"This ruffian here," explained the sergeant, "claims he has business with Lieutenant Hastings."

O'Donal looked at the disreputable, scruffy-looking man with suspicion. The villain, he noticed, was poorly clad, unshaven, and had only three fingers on his left hand. "What kind of business?"

"The king's business," replied the man slyly. "And I would do it with Hastings, guv. Nobody else."

"The lieutenant," replied Captain O'Donal, "will see no one today. Whatever business you have you may discuss with me."

The ruffian looked at him doubtfully. "Well . . . I don't know. 'Tis Hastings that struck the bargain, and it's a matter close to the royal governor's heart, you know . . ."

O'Donal's attention pricked. He had been ready to dismiss the laggard as a fool, but he quickly decided that it might be worth his while to listen to what he had to say. He nodded curtly to the sergeant and ordered, "Dismissed." When the sergeant had removed himself he turned to the ill-dressed man and jerked his head toward the curving walkway that led away from the barracks. "Come. We'll talk in private."

"My thanks for the game of whist, my lord. How gracious of you to entertain the ladies of Williamsburg so pleasantly."

"The pleasure is mine, Lady Arabella." The lord governor bowed from the waist, and then, seeing her attempt to rise from the brocaded chair in the dining room, he raised a hand to stay her. "Pray do not desert me." He stood posed by the fireplace, his great bulldog snoozing at his feet, the very picture of a man confident in his authority.

"But the other ladies have long since departed," protested Arabella. "I fear I shall outstay my welcome."

The governor smiled. "An impossibility, my dear," he declared grandly. "An utter impossibility. In fact"— he lowered his voice reassuringly as he moved toward her—"I am not displeased that we are alone. I have ordered high tea so that we may have an opportunity to"—his eyes fastened intimately on a point just below her collarbone—"commune in private."

He sat down in a chair close to hers, then inched it closer so that their arms were almost touching. "I have scarcely seen you since the masked ball."

Arabella sighed and looked down at her hands

folded demurely in her lap. "What a ninny I was to behave so outrageously that night. I must apologize for my unladylike behavior and for any embarrassment I might have unknowingly caused." She smiled up at him winsomely.

The governor's eyes swept over the delightful vision only inches before him, taking in her beseeching eyes, her full, rouged lips, the perfect line of neck and shoulders, the proud bust pushed up high and firm by the tightness of her bodice. Yes, she was a ripe, magnificent creature, this Lady Arabella Winters, and all too well he remembered her appearance at the ball. His tongue licked his lips as he thought of her in those breeches, her delectable round bottom so clearly outlined that he had hardly been able to restrain himself from running his hands across her enchanting form—and with her spineless husband looking on!

He reached for Arabella's hand and planted a moist kiss upon her palm. "There is no need for apology, dear child. I ask only that in penance you stay and talk with me."

"How can I refuse, sir?" she asked, disengaging her hand from his grasp and returning it to her lap, knowing that for a time she was trapped. Having apologized to the governor and thereby firmly ensconcing herself in his good graces, she had no desire now to cause him any displeasure.

As soon as the heavily laden tea cart was rolled in, Lord Dunmore dismissed his servants. "Nothing is more delightful than watching tea being poured by a beautiful woman," he said gallantly. "Will you do the honors, Lady Arabella?"

"Of course, my lord. I shall be delighted."

Arabella poured the strong dark tea into thin china cups, keeping a gracious smile upon her face and trying not to let her eyes stray to the clock upon the mantel.

"Ah, now, is this not a treat?" asked Dunmore, cup in hand, leaning back in his chair. Upon close inspection Arabella could see that his face was ruddy, the pores of his skin large, and that upon his cheeks and upper lip there was a faint tracing of a dark beard that his morning shave had not removed.

"This is quite pleasant," Arabella agreed, adding cream to her tea and wondering how long she must remain before she could take her leave without offending this man whose protection and friendship were so important to her husband, and to herself. To that end, for awhile at least, she would bear with a smile his obvious but harmless flirtation.

The governor put down his cup and smiled. Arabella noticed then that his smile held no joy or pleasure, but rather it was cold and calculating, as would be the leer of a wolf before it made its kill. She had once thought Lord Dunmore resembled his bulldog, Glasgow, but now she saw him as an animal more dangerous, and more deadly.

The governor's blunt fingers were picking through the candied fruits upon a silver platter on the tea cart. They had been arrayed in a cone, the apricots at the bottom, then cherries, dates, candied lemon and lime rinds, and sugared strawberries on top. It had been a most attractive display but was now mangled by the governor's greedy gropings.

"My cooks have prepared some special delicacies for you my dear, treasures to match your sweetness," he said. "Here, for instance, a strawberry as ripe and red as your lips." He leaned toward her, holding the sticky fruit by its stem, touching Arabella's mouth with the strawberry and running its candied sweetness along the full line of her lower lip.

To turn her face away in refusal would be rudeness beyond possibility, and Arabella, surprised by the governor's action, could think of no quick retort to stay his hand. She could do nothing more than what Lord Dunmore expected; therefore she opened her mouth, took the fruit between her lips, and hastily chewed and swallowed. A bit of candied sugar became adhered to her lower lip and reflexively her tongue darted out to lick it away.

Watching under heavily lidded eyes, the governor saw the movement and experienced an even greater desire for Arabella, a yearning for her sweet, pink tongue to trace a hot path across his skin . . . Ah, what thoughts of unadulterated bliss filled him when he looked at Lady Arabella.

Embarrassed by the forced bit of playful intimacy with the governor and by his intense scrutiny, Arabella looked away, inadvertently revealing for his deliberate perusal the perfect line of her profile, the long column of her throat, the jutting thrust of her half-bared breasts. God's breath, he thought, his pulses quickening, it was immoral that this succulent morsel belonged to that effete twit, Everett. Why the man—if he could be called one—could not begin to satisfy the juices of passion that flowed in the wench. No, she needed a man, a real man, experienced in the ways of love, to unleash her passions. He thought again of her delicious little body packed into those tight breeches, clinging to her abdomen and hugging her buttocks.

And here she was, within his grasp. With a hand almost shaking with the thrill of conquest, Dunmore lifted the cover from a plate of pastries. "I had my chef prepare these especially for today. They are all the rage in Vienna, where they are called, I believe, Ladies Teats." He let his voice caress the words.

Arabella looked down at the plate the governor displayed so proudly. The soft white of the pastries' meringue was formed into a pointed mound, not unlike the breast of a richly endowed female, and in the center, slightly puckered and standing up with proud immodesty, was a bit of candied fig. Arabella looked down at the pastries, then back at the governor, whose hard black eyes were on hers.

"Not inaptly named, eh? And may I be so bold as to say that the snows of the Alps could be no more pure or white than the loveliness of your own sweet bosom." His eyes dropped deliberately to the neck of her gown, which showed the rounded curves of her breasts and the deep cleavage beneath. The governor licked his lips again, lasciviously this time. How he yearned to knead that soft flesh with his eager hands, to bury his face in the valley between those exquisite mountains . . .

Arabella gave a little shiver of apprehension, a sign which the governor deliberately misread and Arabella quickly tried to disguise. He reached for her hand and Arabella managed a light, careless laugh, tossing her head. "Fie, my lord, how you do go on!" Inwardly she decided that she had done enough for the sake of her husband's good reputation. There would be no more private meetings in the palace. This was fast slipping beyond a light flirtation and she had a dreadful suspicion that the governor's attempts at seduction were serious.

"Well, Lady Arabella, I want an answer." He deliberately kissed her fingertips.

Her eyes reflected the confusion that confounded her mind.

"About the pastries. Do you not find them exquisite?" he insisted.

"Quite unlike anything I have ever seen," she replied honestly, pulling her hand away.

The governor smiled at her reticence. The chase was always more interesting when the quarry prolonged the pursuit.

"Then let us try these new delights," he suggested, "together." His hand reached for a pastry, hovered over the white mounds, hesitated, then plucked the hard bud from the center of one. He held it in his fingers for a moment, gently rolling it between thumb and forefinger, and all the while his jaded eyes watched Arabella. She closed her eyes, and when they opened, he was smacking his lips in pleasure. "And now you, my dear. Will you not taste this delicacy?"

"Why . . . surely." She realized her voice sounded somewhat strangulated. The oppressiveness of the room was suffocating. The flames in the grate flickered hotly, but that was not the heat she felt; it was from her own shame and awkwardness. The governor's intentions were blatantly obvious, but as yet she had not discovered a way to retreat gracefully from his lechery. As her mind worked furiously, searching for a means of escape, she reached mechanically for one of the rounded white pastries. When it was almost to her lips, the dog suddenly sprang up from the hearth and rushed to the door, barking vociferously.

"Damnation!" shouted the governor. "Quiet, you beast, or out you go." But Glasgow continued to bark, more fiercely now, as the door opened and an officer wearing the uniform of His Majesty's Guard stepped in.

"Lord Dunmore," he began, obviously unaware as yet of Arabella's presence.

"O'Donal!" The governor was on his feet, his face red and bilious, whether with suppressed desire or rage Arabella could not tell, shouting at the officer. "Who gave you leave to enter here?"

"Pardon, my lord. Your servant said you were at tea. He did not say that a lady—" O'Donal bowed distractedly to Arabella while trying to assuage the governor's fury with meager excuses.

357

Arabella saw her opportunity and leapt upon it. "I have monopolized your lordship's time far too long," she said. "I am sure that the captain has important matters to discuss, business that has no place in the ears of a foolish female. With your permission, sir, I'll take my leave."

She began to make her curtsy, but the governor's quick hand stayed her. "Nonsense, Mistress, this will take but a moment. We shan't spoil our tea. I'm sure O'Donal will be quick about this . . . or delay his news until another time," he added pointedly.

O'Donal, knowing the governor's penchant for beautiful women, shifted from one foot to the other. Lord Dunmore would make him pay for this interruption, he knew without a doubt, but he could not walk out without delivering his message. "I do beg your pardon, madam, for the inconvenience, but I need the lord governor's ear . . ."

The meaning was clear. O'Donal wanted to be alone with him, but Dunmore, so close now to the prize he lusted after, refused to have it snatched away from him by this damnable intruding young man. He brushed aside O'Donal's suggestion of privacy with a wave of his hand. "If you have something to tell me, then out with it. Lady Arabella is a loyal subject of the king's and a close confidante of the royal governor's," he added with a barely restrained smirk. "We have no secrets from our citizens. Now what is so important, sir, that you must break in upon me and this gentle lady?" The governor delivered this with a threatening smile to the captain.

O'Donal swallowed so hard that his Adam's apple bounced up and down above his stiff collar. It was obvious he was caught now. He would have to retreat or spill out his information in front of the woman. He saw no choice. "It is the Fox, sir," he said guardedly.

"The Fox? Has the devil been captured?" The governor forgot his annoyance momentarily.

Arabella willed herself to sit quietly and betray none of the tumultuous emotions that hurtled through her. The Fox . . . Phillip . . .

"Not yet, sir," O'Donal answered.

The governor's snarl of disgust overrode Arabella's stifled sigh of relief.

"But I have had a strange meeting with a three-fingered fellow. He claims that Hastings gave him a thousand guineas for information about the Fox."

The governor became impatient again. This fool was bringing him no new information, and the lady's mood was fragile. If he delayed much longer, she might slip through his fingers. . . .

"Yes, I know that," he snapped. "I authorized the funds. Now what is it that this informant has for us?"

"He tells me that the Fox himself will be unloading contraband at Shelton's Cove tonight at midnight."

The governor pursed his lips thoughtfully. The Fox might at last be within his reach. He glanced out the windows of the room. Darkness was already falling on this late autumn afternoon. There was not much time to instruct his men before they would have to ride. Dunmore glanced at Lady Arabella, who sat as still as a statue, her eyes bright with interest. Alas, he must give up one chase for the sake of another. As beguiling as she was, the Fox was his nemesis and his true obsession, and catching the villain, watching him tortured, drawn and quartered, and his pieces fed to the birds . . . *that* would be equally as exciting as bedding Lady Arabella. Indeed, he might yet have both pleasures . . . in time.

"Tell the men I shall meet with them in half an hour with instructions."

With a bow and a click of his heels, O'Donal

disappeared, relieved that his message, once delivered, had been well received. Who knew? There might be a promotion in this for him. Too bad Hastings had become ill, but those were the chances of the game, and now the quarry—and its rewards—were his.

The governor turned back to Arabella and picked up his cup of tea. His smile was regretful, but there was an avarice in his eyes that went beyond the lust she had seen there such a short time ago. The passion of it made her shiver with far more dread than she had felt when she herself had been its victim.

"And now, my dear," he said, raising his cup to her, "before we must most regrettably part, let us drink one more toast—a final one—to the capture of the Fox."

Chapter XX

The small figure was hunched low in the shadows of the shrubs, every sense alert, her heart beating loudly in the deadly still silence of the night. The moonlight encountered dark reflection of itself in the small natural cove, so that it was impossible to tell land from water except by the soft lapping of wind-stirred waves against the short wooden pier. Her breath frosted in faint, jerky streams before her eyes, and she drew the woolen cloak more tightly around her to still the trembling of her muscles. But this did not help, for she was shaking, not with cold, but with fear.

Arabella had rushed to the house on Nicholson Street from the governor's palace, ready to abandon subterfuge, to risk Phillip's anger and her own need to have him come to her willingly, to risk anything for the sake of warning him of the trap the governor had laid for him this night. But the house had been deserted. Even Sam, who would have served as competent an emissary in this as he had in every other mission, was absent, and the only message left from her husband had been that he would not be at home for supper. She had been too late.

She had paced the house, frantic, trying to think of

something to do, racking her brain for clues as to the identity of others in Le Renard's band to whom she might go, and realizing at last, with a cold shudder of insight, that there was no one who might help her. If anyone was to save the Fox, it would have to be she. And she would have to do it alone.

She had dressed for ease of riding in the trousers and cloak she kept hidden in her room and at the last moment, had covered her face with the mask and her hair with the cap. She had had no intention of being caught—prayed she would not be caught—but if she were to be seen, she knew that the boyish disguise might buy her a few moments to escape and protect her identity from the governor's greedy eyes.

It seemed she had been here forever. Her fingers had grown numb around the small tinderbox she held, and her muscles were stiff from crouching. Her plan was crude and could break down at any one of a dozen points, but it was the only thing she could think to do. She could only hope that the ship was not late, that Phillip was not careless, that the master of his ship was as shrewd as the Fox himself was, and that the governor was not hasty.

She was so attuned to the sounds of the night and the colors of the dark that she sensed the approach of the ship before it was actually visible, while it was still just a shadow among other shadows along the wide expanse of the river, while the creaking of its boards and the whisper of its sails were no more than the sighing of the wind. Her breath stopped, her heart stopped, and her mind screamed at her to act. Clumsily, shakily, she tried to open the tinderbox and it fell to the ground. Her numb and stiffened fingers wasted precious moments fumbling among the dry leaves for flint and steel, and all the while the danger inched nearer, nearer . . .

Catching her underlip between her teeth, she grasped the flint firmly while rearranging a small pyramid of crackling leaves and branches on the ground. The ship was visible now, a dark swan gliding toward its river nest. She struck the flint against the steel. A wayward gust of wind caught the spark and extinguished it. She cast a frantic glance over her shoulder. Were they there, hiding in the woods, the troops who meant to kill her husband? Was Phillip even now guiding his horse down to the pier, unaware that the circle of death was closing in on him?

Please, please . . . , she prayed silently, striking the flint again, biting down hard on her lip. The small spark caught, and her breath rushed out slowly as a shred of the dry tinder began to glow, then died abruptly.

It was not going to work. She was too late. She would never be able to warn them, for by the time they saw the beacon they would be unable to turn the ship.

Was that a voice she heard on the night air? Could it have been the faint scuffle of footsteps on the deck, the soft relay of orders? Or had it been horsemen in the distance, the jingle of bridles, the murmured neigh of animals unaware . . . ?

Oh, dear God, please. . . .

She struck the flint again.

The band of horsemen moved slowly through the woods, and the sounds of creaking leather and breaking twigs beneath heavy hooves stirred the night silence. It was a routine mission and there was no need for stealth; still, out of habit, they exercised it. As they reached the top of the incline that swayed gently down into the cove below, the leader of the band pulled up, refusing to move out of the shadow of the woods. There he paused, his aristocratic head tilted backward slightly in an instinctive alertness of senses, like an animal scenting danger on the air. His eyes narrowed thoughtfully behind the mask, and he held up a hand to stay his men.

Sam edged his horse close to Le Renard's. "We'll wait here," the Fox answered his unspoken question, "until the ship is at dock."

Sam glanced at him, curious over the break in routine. "Something wrong?"

The Fox was silent for a time, his eyes carefully scanning the darkened landscape below. "Something makes me uneasy," he answered absently after a time. "I'm not yet sure what it is."

Sam had seen his own neck saved too many times by this man's intuition to question his judgment now, but still he felt compelled to protest, "We would have been warned if anything were afoot."

"Hmm." The murmur was neither assent nor disagreement, and he kept his eyes focused on the barely discernible shape of his ship, heavily laden with contraband and headed for the safety of this secret cove. "It strikes me strange, though, that our spy let this opportunity pass. I am not usually so wrong when it comes to predicting treachery."

"There was no word from Hastings," Sam asserted. "And he was prepared to look for trouble tonight." He chuckled softly. "Maybe the good spy drank up his profits and was in no condition to make the kill."

But Le Renard did not share his mirth. His eyes were still fixed, intensely, alertly, on the shoreline the little ship intrepidly approached. At last he shrugged, an easy, dismissing gesture that fell only slightly short of its intent. "Perhaps it is nothing but that I am missing our friend William. It's been a long time since I rode without you both at my side."

"Babies will come at inconvenient times," agreed Sam.

And with that, Le Renard's harsh features relaxed into a near smile. "A son, did you say?"

Sam nodded. "That was the word from Shadowood this afternoon."

Le Renard nodded decisively and lifted his reins. "A good omen. And now let us set about the business of making Virginia a freer land for this new generation."

He lifted his hand to signal his men to follow, and at that moment the movement of a shadow below caught his eye. It was followed almost immediately by a streak of color, a spark that grew into a smoldering flame.

Le Renard reined in sharply, his features etched into harsh disbelief as he saw the dry leaves in the clearing below begin to kindle and flame, fanned by the river breeze and licking toward the wooden pier. The yellow-gold aureole spread, dancing on the water, brightening the rough ground and casting in its aura the unmistakable silhouette of a figure, cloaked and masked, racing for the shelter of the woods.

"Damn the meddler!" he hissed and was off his mount in an instant, tossing his reins to the incredulous Sam. "Stay!" he shot over his shoulder harshly as the men, soothing their restless horses against the scent of smoke that bit through the air, gathered closer in confusion and disbelief. "I'll deal with this treacherous whelp myself—and this time for good!"

Fury coursed through his blood like a winter's storm, sharp and icy and heavy with the sting of death. It was as he had at first thought—the young cur was a glory-seeking troublemaker, a traitor to the Cause who hid behind the pen of the Flame of Liberty and at the first opportunity turned upon the very notions he espoused. To think that he had almost been tempted to

365

take the snake to his bosom! That night in the churchyard he had almost been fooled into giving his trust to the bastard, had even thought to admire his wits . . . Well, he had wits, all right. But if Le Renard had his way this night, he wouldn't live long enough to use them again.

The dry timber around the pier caught like kindling and in a matter of moments was a roaring bonfire. Little torches of dried leaves and crumbling wood drifted through the air, smoldering in the tops of trees, sifting downward and sizzling on the water. The once-empty landscape was alive with sound and color, a wash of sunrise gold and red that threw up a beacon for miles around and bathed the night in the glow of midday. The pier was a writhing tongue that lapped the water, snapping and groaning and falling by pieces with a great hissing sound to its death. From offshore came shouts of alarm and confusion, and the ship slowly began to heave to.

It was too late for the Fox to call back his ship, too late to save a hard night's work. But despite the rage that came near to blinding him, he moved with silent, catlike efficiency, taking no chances on frightening his quarry into a premature flight. The ship was gone, its cargo bound for Lord knew what trap yet awaiting it, but the author of this treachery was but a few steps away and the night would be well spent once the hands of the Fox closed around the scrawny neck of the Flame of Liberty . . .

Arabella gasped as she felt the strong fingers crush her upper arm, flinging her around with such force that she lost her balance and would have fallen backward had he not jerked her roughly to her feet.

For a moment the thundering of her heart choked off

366

her breath and whirled the sightless, dizzying red-black colors through the night, and her instinct was to scream, to kick, to claw her way to freedom, for she was certain the man who grabbed her so ruthlessly wore the red coat of the King's Guard. Before her paralyzed lungs could draw breath however, the face before her sprang into view, a devilish cutout in the dancing red flames that caught his hair and skin above the mask and shot twin sparks of danger from his eyes. *Phillip* . . .

She went weak with relief and almost cried the word out loud, but then his hands grasped her slim shoulders and he was shaking her, his rage a pure and viable thing as it coursed through fingers that threatened to snap her bones.

"You treacherous dog!" he growled. "You will pay for the infamy you've committed this night!" His hot breath seared the acrid, smoke-filled air and his words whirred through Arabella's head as her neck snapped back with helpless force. "But first," he demanded and pushed her hard against a tree, pinning her there with the weight of his hands and the hatred in his eyes, "you will talk. How did you know of our plans? Who—"

And then, abruptly, he was silent, every muscle in his body stiffening, those animal senses of his springing to instant alertness with visible intensity. It was a long time later that Arabella, through the hiss and rush of her own breath and the chest-crushing thud of her heart, became aware of the commotion that had first alerted him.

The thunder of hoofbeats echoed over the roar and crackle of the fire along with shouted curses and the whinnying of frightened horses. Red-coated officers reined in their dancing stallions, barking orders and imprecations. "Blast the devil! He's on to us! He's warned his ship away!"

"We can comb the woods for them, sir! They can't have gotten far!"

And O'Donal, rigid with anger at being cheated of his prize, shouted back, "And what if we find them, you fool? There's no law against a man taking a ride by the river! *Damn* the villain anyway!" O'Donal's face, illuminated by a sudden leap of flame, was white and grim. "I'll take an oath he's a sorcerer, that one, with all the demons of hell on his side!"

Half a squadron milled about the once placid cove, their horses chewing up turf with great, restless hooves, adding frightened whinnies and jangling bridles to the confusion of smoke and sparks and the crack of smoldering branches and bits of the pier as they hit the water with a hiss and a slap. The men, promised the biggest prize of their careers, were angry and disappointed, and they sharply reined in their mounts, muttering curses and waiting for orders to proceed.

Abruptly, O'Donal gave them. "Close ranks!" he barked curtly, swinging his horse around with a ruthlessness that evoked a startled, shrill cry from the animal. "There's nothing for us here. We're going home."

"What of the fire?" the second-in-command shouted after him.

"Let it burn!" tossed back O'Donal furiously over his shoulder. "Let the whole damn colony burn!" He spurred his mount onward. The sooner he delivered this latest news to the governor, the sooner the sorry affair would be done with.

Not until the last hoofbeat had died away did Le Renard release his fingers, which had been tightened in an unconsciously cruel grip, from about the thin-boned shoulders of the boy he had only moments ago intended to beat to within an inch of his life. And it was not until then, as he took a slow step backward and stared into the masked face of his adversary, that he was aware of releasing a breath that had been held for so long that his lungs actually hurt.

For the first few moments, standing there with the scent of autumn wood smoke in the air and the glow of dying flames warming his blood, all he knew was relief—relief that the captain had been unwise enough not to search the woods; relief that the noise of the fire and the troops' own clumsy entrance had hidden the whinnies of other horses waiting in the woods; relief that his ship had taken the signal for the warning that it was and had turned back; relief that he had not led his men blindly into a trap as he so easily might have done had he not paused those few extra moments atop the hill. And then there was anger—anger at the closeness of the call; anger that he had not foreseen it; anger that at this very moment he owed his life to a young pup with half his size and experience and whose aid he had so arrogantly refused less than a fortnight ago.

Yet despite these thoughts his voice was smooth, controlled, and with barely an edge to it as he drawled, "So, the Flame of Liberty has saved my ship."

Arabella, too, breathed for the first time, it seemed, since the thunder of the troops had broken into the fire-bathed cove. She had hardly even realized relief, or triumph, nor had she had a moment to understand the consequences of what she had done, or the wonder of it. All she knew was that Captain O'Donal had sat astride his horse less than ten yards from the stand of pines in which she hid, his eyes surveying the landscape that was illuminated like day from the burning pier, and that the snuffling of her own horse, tethered to a tree almost within touching distance, had sounded like thunder in her ears and that even the beating of her heart had seemed loud enough to summon an entire brigade. Yet he had not seen her. He had ridden away without seeing her, or Phillip, or Phillip's horse, or his men, who were no doubt hidden elsewhere in the trees. They were safe. It was over.

Her voice was hoarsened from smoke and fear as she spoke, and she forgot for an instant who they were and who they pretended to be. "It was a trap. You have a spy in the governor's pay."

His eyes narrowing speculatively upon the masked face, Le Renard murmured, "I know. I, too, have a spy. But it seems he has failed me tonight."

Some instinct—perhaps a sudden and fierce rush of pride for what she had done and a need just as fierce to receive some applause for her efforts—prompted Arabella to continue the masquerade a moment longer, to force from the arrogant Le Renard, who had used her so badly the night she had come to him seeking an alliance in the churchyard, some token acknowledgment, or even gratitude. Lifting her head slightly, she pointed out in her deliberately roughened colonial drawl, "Fortunately for you, sir, your friend the Flame of Liberty did not fail you."

The moment was suspended between them as Arabella waited for his response and he withheld it, pointedly, purposefully. And then the crack of a twig behind them made Le Renard turn his head.

Arabella suspected the shadow in the forest belonged to Sam, but he kept himself well hidden. How very wary and well trained were the men of Le Renard! she mused.

"All is well," said Phillip. "I have yet a few matters to settle with"—he cast a shaded glance in her direction—"yon Flame of Liberty. Disperse the men; there will be no work tonight."

They waited in silence for the footsteps to retreat, and the dying flames, as they crept toward the water, shed less and less of their yellow light, so that by now the two of them were almost in complete darkness again. Only the glow of his ice gray eyes as he looked at her indicated that the man who stood before her was real, not a phantom.

And when at last he spoke, his voice was as cool as the November night, as distant as the dying breeze. "I warned you once before, whelp. You have had a bit of luck tonight; next time the fates might not be so kindly disposed toward you. You will be wise to heed my advice because I will not give it again. Keep your games to the nursery, and leave the matters of men to those who can deal with them."

The breath left Arabella's lungs in one incredulous gasp. "I saved your hide tonight!" she hissed.

Those steely gray eyes narrowed sharply. "You committed dangerous folly that could have gotten us all killed."

"Ah, far better that I should have let the Fox hang from the tip of the lord governor's sword than to attempt the *folly* of warning him!"

"Your impetuosity will lead you to an early grave, pup," he said softly, and she could sense the tautness that strengthened his muscles just as certainly as she could feel the rage that stiffened hers. "I told you once I hold no truck with foolish schoolboys and their dreams of glory."

Where once she had been cold with fear, she was now burning. She had risked her *life* for him—for him and his foolish masquerade—and he dared berate her now. If only he knew who stood before him, masked and cloaked and daring to play his game; if only he knew to what lengths she had gone for his sake. But she would not give him the satisfaction. Not yet.

She said, keeping her voice just as cool and just as low as his, "Methinks the great Fox is jealous. He

371

doesn't wish to share his fame with anyone—not even with someone who fights on his side."

"What do you know of fights?" he scoffed with a short laugh. "Or of causes, for that matter? You see nothing but the adventure, the glory, and the high theatrics. You have proven this so tonight." And then his voice became harsh and he reached out to grab her arm roughly. "Well, I am here to tell you there is no glory in this business and we play no games! I did not ask for your allegiance and I do not accept it. You speak of causes you do not understand; you write of principles without having tasted the blood that formed them, and recklessness such as yours is the very thing that sends thoughtless men to their deaths. No one"— he gave her arm a rough shake—"*no one* risks his life for my sake, do you understand that?"

Arabella jerked her arm away imperiously, the harrowing remnants of terror mixing with her anger to embolden her beyond reason. "I understand," she shot back, her eyes glittering, "that Le Renard is too proud to admit he owes his life to another. How much greater an injury to that pride, I wonder, would he feel if he knew he had been bested by a woman?"

And with that, she tore off her cap and stood before him, her red-gold curls tumbling down about her shoulders, her chest heaving, her eyes shooting sparks.

He stood immobilized, his eyes dark, his face like marble. She saw, in the moment of his astonishment, the beginning of recognition and the horror of denial, and she felt a surge of power more precious even than the victory of this night's work. Oh, yes, she was the Flame of Liberty and, as such, a match for the Fox; perhaps, in this brief, charged moment, even the master of the Fox. But she was more. She was his wife, his helpmate, his lover. And it was time he knew it.

She took a step forward. He did not move; he

seemed, in fact, incapable of doing so. She raised her hand and very deliberately fastened her fingers upon his chin, holding his eyes with hers. Madness coursed through her, wild and brilliant, and a passion only the truest sense of power could bring, and she knew in this moment—and perhaps for this moment only—she held the man she loved in the palm of her hand.

"Someday," she said softly, huskily, "when you are old and gray, and you look back upon the days of your wild youth . . . remember that on this night you were kissed by the one whom legend has deemed to call the Flame of Liberty."

She stood on tiptoe and pressed her mouth to his, fiercely, possessively. She felt his sharply indrawn breath as he came abruptly back to reason and the swift, instinctive move he made to break away. But she was riding the crest of intoxicating power, a surge of triumph sweeter than anything she had ever known, and anger, hurt, and intense assertive pride inflamed her passion beyond the point of determined reckless-ness. She brought both her hands up to fasten on either side of his wool-covered face and kissed him then as he had taught her—her tongue flickering along the inside of his lips, her mouth opening to devour his. She felt him grow weak with the unexpected onslaught, and then, abruptly, strong again.

His hands fastened hard around her elbows and he pushed her away. He looked down at her, breathing hard in streams of smoky breath, his eyes like chips of polished coal in the night. And he said softly, "Damn you."

With a swift movement he reached up his hand and swept away her mask. His wife stood before him boldly, her face flushed and triumphant, her eyes as bright as stars, her breasts, now visible through the parted cloak, rounding out the material of the man's shirt with the strong rise and fall of her breathing. And everything inside Phillip was battered, reeling, enraged, twisted, and in turmoil. *Arabella*. Arabella who inflamed the city with her writings of political rebellion, taking credit for the Fox's work; Arabella who crept through a misty graveyard to meet with an enemy of the crown and then who held him at gunpoint and demanded an alliance; Arabella who risked her life this night so that he might live . . .

A great shudder shook him, though whether it sprung from rage, incredulity, or unsupposed terror for what might have happened here tonight, he could not be sure. A streak of wild hilarity struck him and felt, for the briefest moment, very much like pride; and, too, there was a note of rueful admiration—Arabella. It had been Arabella all along, and he should have *known* . . . Lord, what a woman she was.

And then the anger, and the fear, and the deadly seriousness of what she had done surged back in full force and his arms tightened again, painfully, on her upper arms as he growled, *"Damn you."*

He meant to fling her away, to storm at her, to give her the tongue-lashing she deserved, to shake her until she could not stand any more and then to fling her across his saddle and deliver her safely to her townhouse in Williamsburg from which, he vowed, she would never stir again.

But instead, and without knowing how it happened, he had crushed her to him, his mouth closing over hers with a brutal, possessive force. He wanted to punish, to claim the mastery, to hurt and to frighten. But beneath his, her lips parted willingly. He tasted their sweetness and their softness, and he paused. With that hesitation, with the gentle flow of her breath into his mouth, desire, pure and simple, rose in him and caught flame, burning brighter and hotter than the flickering fires

374

that still singed the woods around them.

Arabella slid her arms around his neck and pressed herself tightly against him. Through her clothing, even through his wool shirt, she could feel the quickening of his breath, hear the pounding of his heart. His lips pressed fiercely against her, his kisses rough with need. His tongue surged into the sweet confines of her mouth, examining the satin lining, thrusting against her tongue in a hungry, greedy exploration.

As Arabella clung to him, her mouth sealed to his, a warm, glowing radiance began in the lower regions of her body and moved upward, suffusing her in its heat. Her knees grew weak and she swayed against the Fox's strong body, breaking the kiss, resting her forehead against his chest.

Almost frantically his hands threaded through the soft tendrils of her hair, as if he needed proof that the Flame of Liberty, the woman he held in his arms, was really Arabella. He tilted back her face, his strong fingers hard against her cheekbones. "You were mad to come here . . . ," he murmured. "Mad."

"No more than you that first night when you brought me to your ship. I came to you that night knowing nothing of love. But now . . ." She raised her mouth to his and drank deeply. Their breaths mingled, their bodies meshed as if they had always been together. Beneath the confines of his trousers Arabella could feel the hardness of his manhood pressing against her, and its power was hers, hers alone.

As if with one thought, with one movement, they sank together to the ground. His cape was their bed, the heavens their canopy. He knew this was wrong; he should have sent her away from the very first moment as he had intended to do. But once his lips touched hers, he knew he was lost. For so long he had ached for her, this woman who was his wife, and now she was in

375

his arms, flesh and blood, and it was too late to turn back or to encourage regrets. The sharp-witted Lady Arabella Winters, his wife, had bested him. The Flame of Liberty, his enemy and his ally, had saved him. They were one and the same, and he was helpless in her arms. With a groan of mingled passion and inevitability, his lips sought hers again.

Arabella's hands wrapped themselves in his thick hair and held his lips to hers. She had not imagined this would happen. She had only thought to warn her husband, to save his life. Yet it was meant that it should come to this, she believed, after tonight, there would be no more masks.

Her fingers found the ties that held his mask. All she need do was loosen them. But she let her fingers fall away, seeking again the strong cords of his neck, the heavy fall of his hair. He would come to her willingly now and remove his mask of his own accord. She was certain of it.

His lips moved from hers and kissed the line of her chin, the softness of her neck, while his hands fumbled with the buttons of her shirt. She felt his warm fingers brush against her skin and then the coolness of the night air against her flesh. His fingers pushed aside the material of the loose shirt and the silkiness of the camisole beneath to find her breast. Arabella's nipple hardened, not with the chill of the autumn air but with the heat of his touch, with the pleasure of his fingers as they teased the pink rosebud and sent shivers of anticipation coursing through her. The heat of desire that had begun with his kisses was fast building into a raging fire.

The roughness of his mask grazed her satiny skin, rubbing erotically against the tender curve of her breast. Then his hot, moist mouth claimed her turgid nipple, enveloping, sucking. Arabella's body tensed as a whole series of sensations assailed her—the warmth of his mouth upon her breast, the cool night air upon her exposed skin, and the slightly abrasive touch of his mask and shirt grazing her flesh. She gave herself up to the feelings completely and threw back her head, closing her eyes and arching upward toward him, toward the man whose mere touch could give her so much pleasure.

There was a wildness building inside her, pulsating with an intensifying rhythm, straining to break free of the bonds of flesh that contained her. She could hear the harsh gasps of his breath as his lips moved to the valley between her breasts. Her own breath was short and tremulous, torn from her rather than surrendered willingly, and her heart pounded like the hoofbeats of a thousand horses.

She hardly felt his hands as they fumbled with the buttons of her breeches and pulled them away from her unresisting flesh. His hand trailed a band of white-hot fire across her belly to the bright flame of feathery curls between her legs, while his mouth still worked its magic upon her breasts. His fingers found warm and waiting flesh, moist, honeyed sweetness. She cried aloud then, little whimpers of joy and passion, as his hands and mouth inflamed her desire.

She was magic, this Arabella Winters Everett— impetuous, quick to anger, quick to passion. She was on the edge now, on the verge of breaking through the cocoon that kept her bound within the realm of mortal beings, and he was on the edge too. Her full breasts were satiny soft beneath his hands, her lips moist and demanding beneath his kisses. All the sweetness of her body was flowing toward him, welcoming him, inviting him to enter.

He struggled with the buttons of his own breeches, then she was helping him, her quick, eager hands brushing his arousal, sending a thousand daggers of desire into his aching groin. Briefly, almost shyly, she caressed the velvet-hard length of him, murmuring a little cry of wonder before quickly withdrawing her hand. He thought he would explode; there was innocence in her touch, a curiosity to explore, but he could wait no longer. With a groan of pure lust he moved so that he was above her, parting her legs with his knees and looking down at her face.

Her eyes were passion dark, her mouth swollen from his kisses, her hair a living flame spread out behind her on the black cape. When he entered her she gasped and pulled away for a moment—but only for a moment. Then she arched toward him, welcoming him inside.

"My love," she whispered. "Oh, my love . . ." And with that he was lost again. He tried to move slowly, to control his thrusts and to prolong the pleasure he knew would not come again soon, but there was no way to stem the raging tide within him. Nor did she seem to want that. Instinctively, she wrapped her legs around his hips and grasped him tightly with her arms, matching her rhythm to his.

With each powerful stroke, he drove her closer and closer to the edge, stoking the flame of her passion until she was filled with him. There was nothing in the world but the man in her arms and the pleasure that he gave her. The shirt he still wore created an erotic friction against her breasts and her tender, swollen nipples, a textured, abrasive counterforce to the smoothness of his manhood inside her. Together they moved, faster and faster, hearts pounding as if they would burst, lungs gasping for air. The wonder of release, the explosion that rocked them both, was so intense that they held tightly to each other, fearing that if they let go they would fall into an endless abyss from which there would be no return.

He buried his head in the hollow between her neck and shoulder, feeling drained, weakened, transformed. He reached for the edge of his cloak and pulled it tightly around them, holding her close against his chest, his thoughts too confused to put into words.

His silence, so intense and indecipherable, frightened her. Arabella's muscles were still quaking, her breath disjointed, her body tumultuous and glowing with the wonder he had wrought within her. Yet as tightly as he held her, he seemed to be no longer with her. And he still wore the mask.

She looked up at him hesitantly. "Your thoughts?"

He smiled very faintly, but it seemed an empty gesture without meaning. "If I did not know otherwise, I would say you are a witch, Lady Arabella, whose spell causes me to forget who I am."

Her fingers reached up, lightly caressing the smooth flesh of his face below the wool. "Then take away the mask," she whispered, "and I will tell you."

She felt him stiffen, felt him pull away from her slightly. His voice was harsh. "You would have me bring the troops down upon your head as well? If you have not already done so with this foolish charade you play as the Flame."

"If I am caught," Arabella replied boldly, "I shall be as well hung for two crimes as for one."

"You cannot confess what you do not know," he returned stubbornly, averting his face. "And you will not be caught, for, as of this night, the Flame of Liberty shall cease to be."

Arabella sat up, fighting back the tide of helplessness and despair that threatened to overtake her. "What must I do to make you trust me? I have embraced your cause, I have fought by your side. I have risked my life to be with you, and I have kept our secret. Tonight I *saved* your life, yet in return I receive nothing but

379

threats. Why will you not accept my loyalty?" She could feel the sting of tears in her eyes and a thickening in her throat, but she would not give in to feminine emotion; not now, not when Phillip was so close—and yet still so far.

He sat up, reaching for his trousers. The warm glow of their shared intimacy had abruptly disappeared, and he felt its absence acutely. He stood and began to dress.

She could sense the stiffening of his muscles, the fight against an emotion he held inside. Yet whether that emotion was anger, impatience, frustration, or helplessness, she could not tell. His voice was sharp as he responded, "You can do nothing but return to your home and husband. Forget this reckless masquerade . . . and me."

Arabella looked at him as if from within a deep well of despair. She wanted to scream at him, *I am your wife, Phillip Everett. How shall I forget about you? You are my husband. How can you think to conceal yourself from me?*

Yet concealing himself he was, for with each moment he grew further and further away from her, and nothing she could do would reach him. She whispered, "Why?"

He said, buttoning his trousers, "I have problems enough of my own, and I am not certain I can protect you from the consequences of your own actions. Leave it be, Arabella."

Arabella shivered and drew the heavy folds of his cloak more securely about her. Nothing remained of the fires except the taste of damp smoke on the air, and his words were as chilly as the night that surrounded them. She said softly, "I love you. All I ask is that you love me as well—if only a little."

He paused only briefly in his motions, and now there was no mistaking the pain that lined his mouth as he looked back at her. His voice was harsh. "I know nothing of love," he said, "just as you know nothing of the Cause of which you write so eloquently. I can only tell you that neither one is a game."

"Then make me know," she pleaded. "Tell me of this Cause for which you so blithely risk your life. Pray do not send me back . . ." Her voice softened to barely a whisper as she lifted her hand to him. "Not yet."

He looked at her and saw those wide, innocent eyes, the small hand reaching for him, the fragile figure alone on the ground and wrapped in his cloak, and though he cursed himself, he too knew he could not send her away so soon. How little time was left to them, and how greatly she had complicated matters with her masquerade. His mind was still reeling with the shock of a hundred decisions to be made in light of this new development, his emotions were in turmoil from sources unknown, and his wisdom dictated that he stride away from her this moment and never look back. But she reached for him, and he sank slowly to the ground beside her, enfolding her small figure in his arms.

A great rush of relief washed through her as she pressed herself against his warmth, felt his breath stirring her hair, his heartbeat steady against hers. Only to hold him, for however many moments they had left to them this night, was all she could ask now. She had no way of knowing how long this embrace might have to last her.

Finally he lay back, bringing her with him to lie cradled against his chest, his fingers stroking her hair. "All right, my dear," he said huskily, and there was tenderness in his voice and the faintest suggestion of a tremor. "We will lie here together for awhile, shall we, and count the stars, and hope that one of them will be lucky for us."

Arabella laid her hand against the warmth of his throat, lightly caressing, then curling her fingers to rest against the dip of his strong collarbone. She tilted her head so that she might look at him. "And will you tell me of your Cause?" she whispered. "Will you tell me how it is you came to be the Fox?"

She sensed again the stiffening, as though against pain, and the withdrawal. But his arm tightened in a brief embrace, and his tone was light as he replied, "A boring tale, dear lady, and not one I wish to inflict upon you. Surely we can talk of more pertinent things."

She looked up at him and her fingertips lightly stroked the shape of his chin beneath the mask. "Why do you do it?" she persisted.

He lifted one shoulder dismissingly. "Why, for the sport, of course."

Arabella said slowly, "I think not." It had suddenly become very important to her to understand him and what he believed in, even if he would not let her know him. "Such greatness is not achieved by whim."

He laughed softly and shook his head. "Greatness belongs to the speakers of words, my dear, the weavers of rhetoric and grand inspiration. The battle belongs to the generals, for soldiers like myself are unknown and soon forgotten. I prefer it that way."

"I do not understand," she whispered softly, and a desperation began to tighten within her at all she did not comprehend, for the thought of him being hunted like an animal for crimes that made no sense, tempting death for a purpose she did not know, was more than she could bear. She made her voice strong and intently she tried to find his face in the dark. "If I am to read of your death one morning over tea, I would like to think that your life had not been lost in vain. I would know what differences have set you against the king so that

382

you are now a wanted man. Can the talk of politicians and parliamentarians an ocean away," she demanded, tightening her fist against his chest, "really be worth risking your life for?"

He looked at her sharply. "And you, my dear? Have you yet realized that you are doing exactly that—risking your life for talk of which you understand little if anything at all?"

But no, it was not words for which Arabella risked danger; not meaningless platitudes and empty political ideals. Rather it was for a very real and concrete cause: the safety of the man she loved. He must surely know that, and yet, for him, it was not enough. And suddenly it was not enough for Arabella either. She reasoned, "How can you know that I would not believe as strongly as you unless you tell me what it is we fight for?"

Le Renard could have laughed her questions away or ignored them. He could have told her one of the many colorful tales he was so adept at spinning. He would never understand what prompted him to tell the truth then, and to this woman. He began carelessly, "There are many reasons, I suppose. The rhetoricians have their answer. Jefferson, Washington, Randolph—they speak so stirringly of noble ideas like freedom and fair dealing that it quite sets the blood to racing to hear them." He tok a barely perceptible breath, and the next words were peculiarly flat, heavy, and tinged with bitterness. "They are fools."

Arabella waited, very still, her heart aching for him in the dark as she felt him retreat into himself. Instinctively she knew that what he was revealing to her now had seldom been spoken before, and she strained to catch every nuance of it, to decipher and absorb and retain every memory of it.

383

"I was a spoiled child," he began slowly, almost absently, "a reckless youth eager to seek out excitement, never caring much for the rules . . . not a very admirable fellow all in all, I think. I first became aware of the patriots some years ago, in Boston, where I had friends. Patrick Henry was making quite a stir back then, with grand talk of treason and dissension, but in Virginia that was all it was—talk. In Boston it was somewhat different. The town was under military rule, and in the time I stayed with my friends there I began to understand some of the anger that was building. Peter, a young merchant with whom I had grown close, told of how his grandfather had settled the land and had built the home in which they all now lived—he and his mother and his sisters—how they had fought off Indians and famine and the bitter winters and had survived the generations to build Boston into what it is today. They had no need for the foreign soldiers who ruled their town and invaded their homes and confiscated their property. They were angry.

"Sometimes Peter would meet with his friends under cover of night in the cellar of some tavern and they would plan great acts of daring and revenge . . . such innocents." She thought she might have detected a bitter smile with these words. "Such fools."

There was a brief silence heavy with remembrance, and then he continued, "But it was a sport, and it eased the tedium. They seemed to want to follow me when I offered advice, and soon we were riding together, half a dozen young men and I, pulling pranks upon the soldiers in the dead of night, taunting them, outwitting them. It was great fun, though of no consequence, and whenever I was in Boston I knew there would be a diversion waiting.

"Peter was to be married one January and I came up

for the wedding. We were at the tailor's, fitting his bridal suit, when there arose a commotion in the street. A group of children had begun throwing snowballs at some of his Majesty's soldiers on patrol, and soon their elders joined in, throwing taunts and jeers and tossing snow at the clean red uniforms . . ." His voice became a monotone now, detached and emotionless, as though the vision of the scene that returned to him was too painful to be revisited in detail. "Peter and I came out to watch the sport—a crowd had gathered around, laughing and mocking and thoroughly enjoying the small power they had gained over oppression—and suddenly there was a musket shot, and another, as the soldiers opened fire, and there was screaming and falling and blood upon the snow, and then next I found I was holding my dying friend in my arms . . ."

Arabella could feel the tension in his body, the great stiffness that seemed to rise up from the core of him as he fought against emotions that threatened to devour him. Arabella wanted to hold him close, to cry out her understanding and give her comfort, but he was very far away from her now, lost in the world of men and the trials that made men great. She could only lie against him, aching for him, waiting for the easing of his pain and the end of the silence that seemed to last forever.

When next he spoke his voice was matter-of-fact. "I saw then that it was not a game, and I knew only one thing—this must not happen in Virginia. The men of greatness—the politicians and the philosophers—they speak of economics and trade and freedom to govern; they shake their angry fists in the face of the king and they ask for a war they do not believe will come. This is a land divided, and everyone, whether they wish it or not, must choose a side to defend. I have chosen Virginia."

A fierce, protective instinct rose up in her, and she whispered, "But there is no war. Men die in war. There is no reason—"

He interrupted tersely, "War will come, whether we are prepared for it or not, and this is what our great citizens cannot see. It is a war that will be fought upon the shores of Virginia, the tidewater, the hills, the forests, and the streams. It will be fought by men who are defending their own, just as they have defended for generations against starvation and nature's cruelty and savage Indians. I know the British, with their love of order and method and tradition, and I know the patriots, who know no rule except survival. The British invaders will be driven from our shores in short order, as long as we are prepared. And that is what I have set about doing—preparing."

And then he looked at her, and his expression was very grim. "And that is what you fail to understand, my dear, with your flair for the dramatic and your prettily couched incendiary phrases. Wars may begin with words, but they are rarely fought with them. Patrick Henry, Tom Jefferson, Peyton Randolph . . . and you . . . are voices crying out for the pleasure of their own echo, having no concept of what their pretty phrases will bring back to their doors. You sow ideas, but you will reap blood. And it is a notion to which you had best resign yourself now, for soon we all will be called upon to defend our pens with our swords."

"No," she whispered hoarsely. No. He was wrong. The way of words was the way of reason, and she could no more abandon her calling than she could abandon him or the terrors against which he fought, and which she only tonight had begun to understand. "Your words have only proven what my writings have said. We fight the same battle, you and I, and our only differences are in our choices of weapons. We will both have need of one to defend the other before this thing is through."

She knew, more surely than ever, that her pen would not be stayed—not when the life of this man, and so many like him, depended upon it.

"Perhaps." There might have been the faint curve of a smile in the darkness, for his tone had lightened somewhat. "It is always wise, I think, whenever disagreements occur, to arrange to be on the winning side." And then, more soberly, "The time of old kings is past, my lady; a new world awaits us on the horizon. We can move toward it or be drawn away. I choose to walk forward."

"And what of my choices?" she demanded.

"You have but one, my dear." His drawl was easy and smooth but unmistakably forceful. "To return to Williamsburg and to your husband and hope the poor cuckolded fool has enough sense to get you to Shadowood, where you will be out of danger . . . and unable to meddle in matters that don't concern you."

Anger rose up in Arabella, swift and hot. So that's it, she thought. That is the way it will be. He will bare his soul to me but not his face. *Phillip,* her heart cried out, *why can you not trust me?*

And she knew the answer. Despite all that she had done and had been through, in his eyes she was still only Lady Arabella Winters, Mistress Everett, to be sent safely to the country at the first sign of trouble, away from men and their grand missions. She could argue with him; she could shock him with the revelation that she knew his identity, or she could do as he asked. And in the end, would one course of action serve her better than the other? What she wanted from him he must give willingly; all else meant nothing. And

387

despite all they had shared, he was still unable to give her the one thing she desired.

Arabella got up slowly and began to dress. He was right; she had but one choice, and that was to wait until he was ready to allow her into his life, his secrets, and his heart.

Until then, the game would go on.

Chapter XXI

"But what if I refuse to go, Sam? Surely you will not truss me up like some common prisoner and drag me back to Shadowood." Arabella feigned a lightness in her tone she did not feel. In truth, she was tired to the point of exhaustion and in no mood to bandy words with anyone but her husband, who was conspicuously absent this morning.

Sam stood solidly in the door of the dining room of the townhouse, not the least concerned by her argument. He had expected as much from his mistress. "It's Master Phillip's order, Miss Arabella. He said for me to bring you back to Shadowood—"

"And you always do what he says. I know, I know," she ranted, no longer bothering to conceal the rising irritation in her voice. "Well, certainly I cannot fault you for your loyalty to Phillip, but the point is that I won't go back to Shadowood." She took one last sip of her morning chocolate and said with all the firmness she could muster, "Now, please have the carriage brought 'round. I have shopping to do on Duke of Gloucester Street today."

Sam shook his head. "I'm afraid you can't do that, ma'am. Master Phillip wants that carriage back at

Shadowood, and he wants you in it."

She had seen this side of Sam before, this implacable, uncompromising facade that could not be swayed by bribes or moved by threats. But there was a way—one that she had used in the past—for there was someone that Sam loved more than he cared for Phillip Everett.

"I can't go back to Shadowood," she said. "I'm waiting for the Fox." Arabella spoke with as much conviction as she could muster. "In fact, I have a message of the utmost urgency to deliver to him."

A slow grin broke across Sam's dark face. "Then you'd do well to go to Shadowood, Mistress Arabella. The Fox has left Williamsburg, and if he comes to you at all it will be at the plantation, not here."

She knew then that she had fallen neatly into Sam's trap, caught indeed by her own lies about the Fox. There was nothing she could do now but give in. "All right," she answered with a resigned shrug. "Gather the servants and tell them to begin packing. We'll leave for Shadowood tomorrow."

Hastings swallowed dryly as the cabin door clicked closed behind him, leaving him alone in the shadowed room with the man in whose hands his fate now rested. The ship swayed slightly beneath his feet, and the masked man in the corner made no sound or move. He simply watched, and waited.

"I had to see you," Hastings said hoarsely.

There was no reply.

Hastings clenched his fists, summoning courage. His heart was pounding. It was very quiet here in the middle of the James, very dark and very lonely. No one would ever know if . . .

"I have not betrayed you," he said forcefully.

Le Renard replied simply, "I know."

All the strength seemed to leave Hastings in a single breath of relief. Le Renard stood and crossed over to a central table, lifting a glass of wine. He added casually, "But it is good of you to come and tell me so."

He poured two glasses and lifted one to Hastings. Hastings came forward gratefully. But he had to ask, "If I had . . ."—his throat clenched briefly—"betrayed you, what would you do?"

Le Renard's glance flashed like a glint of steel in the candlelight. He gave the matter little thought. "I would kill you," he replied mildly, lifting his glass.

Hastings had no doubt of it. He never had. He drank deeply of his wine.

"It is good to know," continued Le Renard, "that you are ever being watched, and good not to know by whom. Those who pledge their loyalty to me also forsake all secrets." He sipped from his glass, his face in profile. "I am aware of your . . . indisposition . . . on the night in question, and"—Hastings thought he saw the quirk of Le Renard's lips beneath the mask—"can well imagine how it came to be. Pray tell me what it was Lady Parkington wanted from you . . . beside the obvious, of course."

Hastings felt himself relax even as a flush stained his neck and a good portion of his lower face. His relief was immeasurable at not being required to explain the embarrassing events that had led up to his being absent from Shelton's Cove at the time he was needed most, to say nothing of having allowed the disastrous information that had almost resulted in the Fox's capture to fall into the wrong hands.

He said, "I was not sure. On the night of the ball she came up to me while I was disguised as . . ." He cleared his throat. They had not yet spoken of Le Renard's true identity. "Well, as Everett, thinking I was he. I thought my behavior on that occasion," he confessed, "might have made her suspicious, though I couldn't be certain how. Then she sent me a note referring to the events of that evening, and I saw no choice but to obey her summons."

Le Renard nodded. "And what did she suspect?"

"Nothing," Hastings was relieved to announce. "Nothing except that I was somehow involved—romantically—with Lady Arabella."

The glint of Le Renard's glance was sharp and strong. "And are you?"

"No!" The breath left his lungs with a forceful expulsion, for it was impossible not to remember that the lady in question was also this man's wife.

Again Le Renard nodded, apparently satisfied with Hastings's sincerity. Hastings relaxed visibly. "I would not even have danced with her," he went on to explain, "had I known . . ."

Le Renard lifted his glass, watching the patterns made by the candlelight in its burgundy depth. "The female of the species is a devilish wonder," he mused. "How quickly they can bring us to ruin, and with so little effort. So." He drank from the glass and directed himself to Hastings again. "A cozy tête-à-tête with Lady Charlotte, a potion in your wine, perhaps"—Hastings flushed deeply—"and your head began to spin. Did you perchance say anything out of turn while under the . . . er"—his lips twisted mockingly—"influence of the lady's charms?"

"Nothing," Hastings asserted.

Le Renard chuckled. "Doubtlessly you had not the breath to, had you wished it."

He grew thoughtful, and Hastings's hand tightened about the glass. The thought that occurred to him was dreadful, but it was not new. "Do you think," he made himself say, "that Lady Charlotte plotted . . . to have me indisposed when the spy arrived with our information?"

Le Renard shook his head. "No," he murmured. "I know the lady well, and though she is bright, she rarely thinks beyond herself and lacks the wherewithal to concoct such a scheme."

"I am glad," Hastings said frankly, and there was amusement in the other man's glance.

"You have developed a fondness for the lady?"

Hastings grinned. "For certain parts of her."

The smile that curved Phillip's lips was measured and thoughtful. "You are well suited, I think. Be not surprised should the dalliance become something more."

Obsessed as he had been with the magnificence of the night spent in Charlotte's bed, Hastings had given that matter more than a little thought, but he would not admit as much to his leader.

"Though if you continue your liaison with the lady, be warned that men in our position cannot afford to give their trust lightly—if at all. It is a dangerous line we walk, my friend."

Hastings, with no small amount of uneasiness, asked the question that had been burning in his mind. "Why did you choose me? Why did you allow me to know your identity when no others are permitted?"

Phillip strolled casually over to the porthole and gazed out. "A matter of expedience, nothing more. And"—he glanced back at Hastings—"I was assured I took no chances with your loyalty. Your position, you must realize," he continued matter-of-factly, "is very vulnerable. That of a spy always is. Should you choose to betray me and should you escape the blade of my sword or those of my men, it would be no great matter to let certain information leak to the governor about your activities. The justice of the military in which you serve would do the job for me."

Hastings nodded, unoffended, undisturbed. The logic was impeccable, as that of Le Renard always was. For precisely that reason he inspired both fear and admiration in his followers, and there was security in the knowledge that they were being led by a master of cunning and force.

"Yet"—Le Renard lifted his shoulder gracefully— "I had no worry for that. I know you very well, Lieutenant, and knew you long before you were invited to join us."

"You cannot have been so certain of my loyalty then," Hastings felt compelled to point out. "I am a soldier in the British army, the latest in a long line of such. You cannot have guessed which way my coat would turn."

"You are," pointed out Le Renard smoothly, "a soldier's son, raised in crowded quarters with too many mouths to feed, who through cunning and determination managed to obtain a commission and use it to achieve your own ends. You are not afraid to break the rules if it serves yourself. You have no great political passions, either for Mother England or for the country that struggles to be born from her loins. You are not afraid of battle or capture, and the risks you take are for your own sake, none other. You are precisely the type of man who serves me well."

Hastings was silent for a moment, digesting all of this. He was amazed, not by his leader's insight, for that was well known, but by the choices he made in selecting his men. The very virtues Le Renard extolled were the ones years of military training had tried to teach him to deplore. Fortunately, it had not worked, for Hastings was as selfish, ambitious, determined, and independent as ever he had been. He was a new breed of man, well suited for this new land.

"My father," he said quietly after a moment, "was decorated a hero for service in the Colonies. He left his blood upon this ground, and a part of his heart, too, I think. I grew up on his tales of vast acres and freedom to roam, where any man might have land of his own if he would but claim it."

He looked at Phillip. "I determined then to have something for my own, and I do not mind fighting for it. I will not leave here when the battle is done."

Phillip looked at him soberly. "If it comes to war—and I think it must—you will have to make your loyalties known to all. You will be branded a traitor then."

Hastings only smiled and lifted his glass to him. "And so will you."

After a moment, Phillip returned the smile and the toast. "Then here," he said, "is to the work that must be done."

Hastings put down his glass and said soberly, "There is one of whom we have not spoken, the most wily and dangerous foe of all."

"I know," Phillip replied. "His Lordship, our royal governor. I am well aware of the man's capabilities and treacheries."

"He is single minded in his desire to capture the Fox, and I am convinced that he would use anything—or anyone—to attain that end."

Phillip nodded, his face reflecting the truth of Hastings's words. "That is what I have been warning you of, Lieutenant. Dunmore will use not only his troops and the power of his office but also anyone that he can manipulate—women as well as men. And so beware of those who are close to the governor, lest you yourself become tainted."

*   *   *

Arabella gazed out across the lawns of Shadowood. The moon was a pale, cold sliver in the sky, remote and heartless. She shivered slightly and let the curtain fall back across the window of her room. Wrapping her shawl more tightly around her, she made her way to the low fire that burned in the grate.

How many days, she mused, have I been here at Shadowood waiting for a sign, and there has been nothing. She had expected to see her husband the day of her arrival, but he had not appeared that day or on all the others she had waited.

To her many questions, Sam only replied, "He has business, Miss Arabella, but he'll be here soon, I guarantee." And as for William, when she asked him of Phillip's whereabouts he only shrugged and changed the subject to talk of Caroline and the baby.

The whole situation was highly unsatisfactory for Arabella. She had returned to Shadowood specifically to confront her husband—whether in the guise of the foppish Phillip or in the person of the Fox—and tell him what she knew, but the lord of the manor seemed loathe to cooperate and Arabella was left to pace and worry and wonder when she would hear his footsteps on the stair.

The air was growing cooler, and reluctantly Arabella went to her bed, slipping inside the heavy curtains that blanketed the canopied frame and kept its occupant safe from winter drafts and chill. Inside it was dark and warm, and only a glimmer of firelight penetrated through a small slit in the hangings. Arabella shut her eyes and like some small, hibernating animal burrowed beneath the covers.

Sleep did not come easily, for her mind was filled with many memories—the night by the river when she had first met the Fox; his visit to her bedchamber when he had kindled her passion; their time together on the

396

boat when he had awakened her to the fullness of her womanhood. Each meeting had been fraught with emotion and desire, with wanting and yearning, and each time she had sought a phantom, a stranger, when the man she really cared about, the one she loved, dwelt within the confines of her own home.

As Arabella lay waiting for the sleep that would not come, she made a vow: that no matter the price in emotional agony, she would not confront him. She would wait—wait until he was ready and until at last he trusted her enough to tell her the truth.

Shadowood slumbered in the cold light of the moon. In the kennels the hounds huddled together, seeking the warmth of one another. In the quarters, the slaves drew close to the fires that warmed their cabins and they wrapped themselves more tightly in homespun blankets. Far above the plantation, in the dark, chill sky, a night hawk cried out and was briefly silhouetted against the moon before he dived into the shadowy shapes of the pines after his unwary prey below.

Along the darkened halls of Shadowood, stealthy footsteps made their way toward Lady Arabella's room. Quietly the door opened and the footsteps moved across the carpeted room toward her bed. Hands reached out to pull aside the curtains; eyes gazed down at the figure who lay upon the sheets.

Her red hair was tousled upon the pillow and, in her sleep, in her tossing and turning, she had partially thrown off the quilt that had covered her. He had come only to look at her, to be sure that she was all right, but he could not stay the hand that reached out to rearrange the covers and then strayed to touch her cheek, so soft, so smooth beneath his fingers.

She moaned and stirred a bit, and his fingers slipped

across her lips to stem her little cry. As he traced the full, sensual lines of her lips, he knew what had brought him to her side. It was what always drew him, no matter how dangerous each rendezvous might be.

His hand touched her chin and then the line of her neck, across the slanted length of her collarbone to the round, sensuous curve of her breast. He knew that he should stop, that he should leave now, before she awoke. But he could not stop, not with her breast so sweet and warm in his hand, not with her nipple peaking involuntarily against his palm, not with all his senses reeling as if he had drunk an entire bottle of Shadowood's most potent brandy.

But Arabella was more intoxicating than any strong spirit, more addicting than any drug. He could not stay away from her; he could not. For one whose very existence was built upon control, he was in danger of losing it—and more—each time he came near her. All his determination was swept away by the sight of her, by the tightening in his loins with need and wanting, by the quickening of desire that knew its only satiation through her.

Without thinking, he slid into the dark, secret warmth of her bed and took her in his arms. He told himself he meant only to hold her, to draw comfort from her warmth and sweetness, but the need inside him was so powerful, so strong, that he could not stop his hands from touching her, his lips from seeking hers.

When Arabella awoke, it was not with a sense of alarm or fear; it was with a wonderful sensation of glowing warmth. Welcome hands touched and loved her, and her mouth parted under kisses familiar and druggingly potent.

"Oh, you have come to me," she whispered. "You have come to me at last."

"You knew I would, my lady."

The voice that answered her was not the one that she expected, not the tone of her husband but the low, rasping whisper of the Fox. And so it was not yet to be, not the complete and total sharing of the truth. Holding back a sigh of disappointment, Arabella moved her hand to touch his face and felt the mask, soft against her hand. And so it must be, she decided, until he is ready. For had she not resolved long ago that a part of him was better than none at all? As long as he would be with her, as long as she could lie in the circle of his arms and know that he loved her—on whatever level—she would be content.

Her hand caressed his cheek beneath the mask as she kissed the line of his full lower lip. "But what of my husband?" she asked, still playing the game. "Is it not dangerous for you to be here?"

"Your husband is far away tonight, and there is no danger of my discovery. And by dawn's light, I shall be gone."

"Then the night is ours," she murmured.

"And we must enjoy every moment." He kissed her fully then, deeply and hungrily, his tongue invading the silken recesses of her mouth, finding hers and drawing it into his own mouth, drinking all the sweet nectar of her.

Arabella's hands reached for him, drawing his shirt up over his chest so that she could touch his muscular chest and feel the hardening of his nipples. At her caress, he groaned slightly and tried to hold her more tightly, but Arabella pulled away from him.

"I want to undress you," she whispered, "to take your clothes from you and feel you next to me." Even as she spoke her hands reached for his shirt and pulled it over his head. In the darkness everything was more sensual, more potent. The sounds of their breathing, the rustle of the sheets, the whisper of his shirt against his skin seemed magnified, intensified.

Her hands slid down across his abdomen, across his hips to the buttons of his breeches. She realized that she was trembling and clumsy with excitement, but she brushed away his hand when he tried to help. "No, no. I must do this myself."

In the enveloping darkness her fingers worked the buttons and at last she was pulling his constricting breeches down across his strong, muscular thighs and calves and over his bare feet. Then her eager hands slid back up his legs, his thighs, until she held the hard, swollen evidence of his desire. Gently she caressed him, and as he trembled beside her she could feel her own desire begin to grow, and little blossoms of flames seemed to shiver throughout her veins and set her skin afire.

Soon his own hands, hurried and eager, reached for her and pulled her nightdress above her head, then tossed it aside. "This is the way it should be—always," he murmured in the low tones of the Fox. "Your body pressed tightly against mine." As he spoke he pulled her against him so that her breasts pushed against the hardness of his chest, her abdomen against the swelling of his need for her.

"Yes, yes," she cried. "Always." Her lips met his and teased and kissed and tantalized, her fingers pushing aside the edges of his mask so that her mouth might fully cover his.

He could feel his passion like a living fire within him, devouring, burning, flaming, as her mouth slid to his chin, his cheek, the line of his neck, the hollow of his ear. His words were muffled by a low moan of pleasure. "Though I am naked and vulnerable before you, you have not tried to remove my mask—not this time."

Her lips were only inches from his, but in the darkness he could make out only the silhouette of her face. Her words were clear and distinct. "You know everything about me," she said simply. "I have told you all my secrets—of my own free will. And in my love for you, I have learned that trust cannot be forced. Both love and trust must be given willingly. I love you enough to wait—to wait forever if I must—until you take off your mask without my requesting it."

At her words, he could feel something warm and tender rising inside him, something quite apart and separate from the sharp ache of desire that tortured him. Gently he reached up and cupped her face with his hands. "Oh, my dearest Arabella, you touch me so. God help me, but I do love you." And then his fingers moved to untie the strings of his mask.

The last barrier fell away and her hand reached up to touch his smooth, bare cheek. She whispered, "Oh, my love . . . my very precious love . . ."

Their bodies met in a kind of divine madness. They were lovers who had hungered forever for each other, whose arms now reached out and clung, whose lips sought and yearned. Each was a part of the other. When his mouth found her nipple, swollen with desire, tender and aching for his touch, she could feel a white heat surging through her veins and sinews. When his fingers discovered and explored the secret treasure between her legs, she answered with a wonderful flowing pleasure that beckoned him. As his hands and mouth played upon her yielding, pliant flesh, she arched toward him and begged with her body and with her voice for release from the burning spirals of desire that consumed her.

And soon he was deep within her, strong and pulsating, finding her welcoming moistness again and again, thrusting deep within. She wanted to be closer to him, part of him, as they moved ever faster in their mystical dance of love. Her fingers dug into his back;

she arched toward him, closer and closer, as the ecstasy built and spiraled until neither could contain it any longer. With a last powerful thrust, he exploded deep within her.

For Arabella, the moment was so magical and the pleasure so intense that she could not hold back and she cried out her love and her need. "Oh, Phillip. Oh, my Phillip, I love you so."

And then the magic ended.

With great effort he pulled himself away from her, his body miraculously regaining its control, stiffening and hardening against the pleasure that they had just shared. For a long time he sat upon the edge of the bed, and she could feel his gaze upon her, his face in shadow, his eyes as distant and as untouchable as the moonlight. And then he spoke, coldly, flatly.

"I am not, nor could I ever be," he said simply, "your Phillip."

With a quick motion, he retrieved his clothing and stepped outside the confines of their shadowy, curtained world.

Arabella reached out her hand to stop him and her fingers found nothing—nothing but the velvet hangings clutched in her fingers. Her heart was pounding with a slow and awful agony, and her breath was choked in her throat. "Phillip," she whispered, but her answer was only the sound of the closing door.

She knew that to pursue him would be fruitless; he would vanish into the night with the same stealth with which he had come. She fell back against the pillows, cursing herself for her foolishness, aching with his absence. Why had she not waited? Why had she not been able to still her tongue until he had spoken for himself and confessed willingly? Just when the truth was within her grasp she had pushed him away with her impetuosity, and he had given her no chance to explain her knowledge or how she had come by it. This time he might not forgive her.

All she had wanted was an end to the deception, to have them become husband and wife complete and fully sharing. But all she had succeeded in doing was setting up one more barrier between them—and it seemed a barrier that she might never be able to breech.

Chapter XXII

Warner Hastings stood in the dusty street in front of Lady Charlotte Parkington's townhouse without the slightest idea of how he had gotten there. He had intended, when he had left his barracks, to join a group of fellow officers at the Raleigh Tavern for a tankard of ale and perhaps a game of chess. Instead, his steps had taken him unerringly to Francis Street and Charlotte Parkington.

Despite the Fox's oblique warnings about a continued liaison with a woman whose ties to the governor were far too close, Hastings had not been able to clear thoughts of Charlotte from his mind. At the strangest and most inconvenient times—when he was barking out orders to his men or explaining a particularly complicated strategy of arms to his recruits—he would be suffused by memories of Charlotte, insistent memories of her hands upon his body, her eager mouth upon his, images that washed over him as fiercely and relentlessly as the tide upon the shore.

Hastings stared up at the house. She was inside waiting; in his heart he knew that. All he had to do was open the gate and climb the stairs.

*   *   *

Charlotte Parkington was bored and restless. None of the activities she had undertaken that day had held her interest for more than a few moments, not her early-morning visit to the governor or an opportune meeting with an old lover on Duke of Gloucester Street. Neither of those could take away the pervading sense of unease that cloaked her in its unwanted folds. She felt empty and lonely, with a longing for something she did not have. In point of fact, the longing was most certainly for some*one* she could not have.

Sighing, Charlotte picked apathetically at a bowl of candied fruit on the table beside her, wondering uncomfortably if she might be losing her appetite not only for food but for all the other good things of life. She had returned irritable and out of sorts from her morning outing, had uncharacteristically refused her midday meal, and had gone to her room where she had undressed and lain upon her brocaded chaise, giving all her thought to the lieutenant.

Why was it, she wondered, that this young man, above all the others she had known, appealed to her so much? Certainly he was comely, with a wonderful, strong body, and she could not deny that he had been a lover of extraordinary skill and stamina, but there was more.

Charlotte did not want to admit that part of her unease and dissatisfaction lay within herself. She was tiring of the game, of the flirtations and liaisons, the sudden meetings and the equally sudden partings. Could it be that she was ready at last to bestow all her affections on one man—one man only? She had not had a thought like that for years, and it frightened her as much as it amazed her.

Irritably she dropped a half-eaten candy back into the bowl, disappointed that not even its sweet familiarity was giving her pleasure. All of this was most unlike Charlotte—the loss of interest in things that usually appealed, the constant obsession with Hastings, this intense powerful longing for a man she scarcely knew.

Where was he, she asked herself for the hundredth time? She had expected him to dance attendance upon her, but he seemed to be blatantly ignoring her, and Charlotte despised nothing more than being ignored. Of course, there was an answer for her question, one that Charlotte had tried to push from her mind but one that kept returning again and again to torment her.

A most unwelcome vision came to her mind—that of Hastings dancing with Phillip Everett's chit of a wife the night of the governor's ball. Charlotte's own passionate night with the young lieutenant had, at least for awhile, wiped away all thoughts of Arabella as a rival for his affections, but now, with the young man so inattentive, she began to wonder. Hastings had never really explained why he and Arabella had been absent from the ball at the same time, but there was obviously only one conclusion to be reached, and it was one that Charlotte wished she could ignore.

The more she thought about the evening, the more confused she became. Phillip had acted very strangely that night also; there had been something different about him, something that she could not quite put her finger on. It was only a glimmer of memory that lodged irritatingly in the corner of her mind, just out of reach of conscious thought. But it was there, and if she could ever rid herself of her obsessive thoughts of Hastings and his remarkable prowess in bed, she was sure it would come to her.

When the house servant knocked at her bedroom door announcing that Lieutenant Hastings was waiting in the hall below, Charlotte felt an immediate improvement in her spirits. Her heart quickened and she felt a rush of color to her cheeks, like a schoolgirl who was entertaining her first beau. But Charlotte was no child, and she knew this meeting would have to be orchestrated perfectly. She could not appear too eager—not at first.

She plumped up the satin pillow behind her back and carefully arranged the folds of her green velvet dressing gown to show her full figure to its best advantage. When Hastings entered the room, hat beneath his arm, Charlotte extended a languid hand in greeting.

"My dear Lieutenant, how charming to see you."

"And you, my lady." He took her hand and kissed the petal-soft skin of her palm. Lord, she was beautiful, he thought to himself, like some kind of exotic tropical flower, lush and sensual. Her perfume was seductive and heady, and the heavy folds of her dressing gown only accented the female attributes of the wonderful body that he knew lay beneath the velvet. He could not hold back his feelings at seeing her again, the mixture of delight and a very potent desire.

The moment that he looked into her dark, liquid eyes, he knew that once again he was under her spell. The aura of sensuality that exuded from Charlotte Parkington was as powerful as any potion, and the memory of their night together came back as bright as the flame that burned in the hearth before Charlotte's chaise.

Nervously, he wet his lips with the tip of his tongue. "I was just passing; I did not mean to intrude . . ."

"But my dear, an intrusion such as yours is always welcome. Here, come and sit near me." She shifted on the chaise so there was room and drew him down beside her. Seated so close, he could feel the warmth of her thigh pressing against his hip, see the rise and fall of her breasts, smell the wonderful aroma of her scent, and all the while he was drowning, drowning in the dark, fathomless fascination of her eyes.

Carelessly her fingers stroked the sleeve of his jacket, and even through the material he could feel the warmth of her hand. His head began to pound and he could feel a familiar heat rising within him.

"And what have you been doing, dear boy, that has kept you away from me?"

In truth, now that Hastings was with her, Charlotte cared very little where he had been or what he had been doing. All that mattered was that he was here. She was on fire, merely at the sight of him, her desire catching flame from his first touch, the feel of his lips against her hand, his virile presence so incongruously perched on the chaise beside her. She could feel the heat of his body and smell his wonderfully manly scent. Oh, how she wanted him. Her conversation was merely the prologue to what she knew was only moments away—that time when she and Hastings would be joined in that most intimate of battles, the age-old act of love.

Somehow Hastings managed to tear his eyes away from hers and to enumerate his activities, the training of recruits, the maneuvers near the river, his riding.

"So you are a rider?" Charlotte interrupted. "I thought so." Her eyes drifted slowly, lazily, along his torso, drinking in fully his manly form. "You have such fine, strong legs and thighs—just right for a horseman." She leaned forward to run her hand along the woolen fabric of his breeches.

Hastings felt a film of perspiration dampen his hairline and there was an immediate tightening in the pit of his stomach.

"I do admire a man who rides well," Charlotte went on, managing to slip her hand inside of his thighs, resting it there with only the slightest bit of pressure.

He was having difficulty breathing now and his heart pounded frantically and erratically. He tried to look away, but her eyes held him as powerfully as the warmth of her hand against his leg.

"You have a fine steed, I warrant," Charlotte went on, her voice honey soft. "Something worthy of you," she murmured huskily. "A powerful mount . . ."

Hastings's need for her was immediate and painful. Never had he wanted a woman so much. Never. Somehow he managed to rasp out a few words. "A stallion . . ."

"One eager and strong, I'm sure." Charlotte's hand moved upward and unerringly found the burgeoning center of his desire.

"Charlotte, I . . ."

But even as he tried to force out his words, her greedy fingers were undoing the buttons on his breeches, her fingers like fire, caressing him, stroking him, bringing him to the peak of his passion. "Oh, a fine stallion indeed," she teased. "One eager to roam free."

Her eyes were bright with anticipation, and all traces of her former malaise dispelled by the excitement that flashed between them like summer lightning. Never had she felt so alive, or so eager. Her voice was heavy with desire as she lovingly held that most manly part of him in her hand. "I do not think we shall need a glass of port this afternoon, do you, my love?"

But Hastings had long since lost the power to speak. His only vocalization was a moan of pleasure, which was soon followed by a groan of complete surrender as Charlotte's eager mouth followed where her hand had been.

"Well, my dearest, I do believe my appetite has quite recovered itself." Charlotte raised her arms above her head, exposing fully half of her creamy breasts above the covers, and stretched with feline grace. "I feel extremely satisfied—at least for awhile." She smiled at Hastings then, her lips curving provocatively.

She was irresistible, he thought as he pulled her close, hardly mindful of the crumbs and bits of cake that littered their bed. He had never taken high tea in bed before, and when Charlotte had rung for her servants and they had appeared with trays laden with chocolate and tea, scones and clotted cream, assorted cakes and candies, he had tried to make himself as unobtrusive as possible, sinking low beneath the covers. But Charlotte's staff had served the repast without a flicker of an eyelid that might betray that this was an unusual circumstance, finding their mistress and her lover in bed. And perhaps, Hastings thought with a brief stab of jealousy, it was not.

Charlotte's curves fitted delectably against him, and once again he let his hands explore the hidden valleys of her body. "What a wonder you are," he murmured. "How lucky I was to meet you."

"And I. I never thought that I would find someone like you." There was not a hint of flirtation in her eyes or a trace of coquettish teasing in her voice. And that surprised Charlotte as much as it did Hastings. For the first time in her life, Charlotte was being totally honest with a man. She had thought that she might not see him again and, now that he was with her, she found him more precious than ever.

Hastings held her more tightly then, loving the feel of her full, heavy breasts against his chest, the curve of her abdomen against his hip. Softly he kissed the tendrils of ebony hair that curled about her face, luxuriating in the satin softness of her skin. "The question, I think, is what do you see in a lowly officer like me, when there are others—" His voice broke off with a trace of bitterness, and he felt again a surge of jealousy, white hot and acid.

"Come, dear boy, you are much more than that— and you know it." Charlotte's finger gently touched a scratch along the line of his shoulder, a mark that she herself had put there an hour earlier when she and this man had been locked in the combat of love. "You are strong and handsome—and a marvelous horseman." She punctuated her teasing remark with a kiss before she continued, "And I believe that you are quite clever . . . and perhaps have a touch of deviousness within you, which suits me very well. It is not usual, you know, to find such an abundance of intriguing characteristics within a body so young and skilled."

Hastings was thoughtful for a moment, half thinking she might be serious. Then he decided that her words were only playful talk that lovers share when their passion is temporarily sated. And so, in the same vein, he responded, "In truth, I am known as quite clever— but not clever enough to deceive you, dear Charlotte, about my need for you. I quite adore you." He followed his words with a kiss, licking the last trace of sticky- sweet cream from her lips. "Do you believe me?"

"Yes, I think I do," she answered softly, a bit shaken by the intensity of her own feelings. "I know that I want to, and while you are in Virginia, before the generals send you far away, I hope that we can be . . . close."

Hastings shifted so that he could cradle her head against his shoulder and feel her warmth along the length of his body. "I am not sure how long I will be in Virginia, Charlotte. I have dreams and ambitions . . ."

"Well, of course you do, my love, else I would not find you nearly so attractive. I am sure you have a fine career ahead of you."

"I am not interested in rising in the ranks, but rather in building my own fortune." He spoke without

412

thinking, and almost to himself, forgetting, as it was so easy to do in the arms of this woman, that danger could accompany a loose tongue. "There is so much of this land I have not yet seen, and I think that beyond the western mountains there lies land for the taking, miles and miles of it, and a chance for a man to become anything he wants, to rise to whatever heights he aspires."

Like a braggart boy, he was seized with the fierce desire to impress Charlotte with the grandeur of his vision. "The country is vast and rich with timber and furs and gold and silver," he added recklessly. "And it is there for those clever enough to claim it." And then he looked down at the beautiful, pampered woman in his arms and tried to hold on to his excitement, and his dreams. "Of course, it is not a life for a woman," he amended.

Charlotte raised her head and looked sharply at him. "Why? Because you think women are not strong, brave, or daring? I am ashamed that you would entertain such a thought! Did I not follow my late— and beloved—husband from the courts of England to this new land? And before that . . . well, I have seen some of the world." She gave an imperious toss of her head and her eyes were bright with challenge.

Hastings looked at her face, so alive, so filled with passion and excitement, and his heart leapt inside. A foolish daydream, yet . . . "If such an opportunity presented itself, to leave and travel west, would you not regret abandoning your townhouse and your plantation and all the luxuries to which you've grown accustomed?"

Charlotte gave his question due consideration. She did truly love the luxuries that surrounded her in Virginia; on the other hand, they were primitive compared to the life she had led in England. And there was something so enchanting about the young man who lay beside her, so daring and exciting, and the scope of his vision made her heart beat faster. To think, at her age, that she could have found such a man, could have the chance at such an adventure . . .

She answered honestly, "Of course I might miss all my pretty things, but then could I not expect someday to have more? That is, if this new land is as filled with possibilities as you expect. Ah, darling boy, do you not see what an adventurer I am?"

Hastings kissed her then, deeply and hungrily, and then he said, "I plan to be a very successful man, and if I were to hope that you might be beside me . . . well then, how could I fail?"

"Hmmm, how indeed?" Charlotte mused, smiling. "But, as delightful as your plans are, you have overlooked one minor impediment. You are a soldier in the king's army, and you belong to him."

"Things can change," Hastings said enigmatically.

"Whatever do you mean?" With her body pressed so close to her lover's, she could not help but notice the slightest change in his breathing, the alteration in the beating of his heart, the tensing of his muscles. The signs were slight, but they were there, and Charlotte was curious.

Hastings had no idea why he continued to talk about a subject he knew could be ultimately dangerous, but his usual good sense was overpowered by his need to share everything with the woman he loved; not just his kisses, or his body and his affection, but his hopes and his dreams. "I refer to the . . . disagreements between the patriots and the king. When two forces clash—and these ultimately will—there are prizes to be gained for the victorious."

"You speak in riddles," she chided, and added irritably to herself, *just like Phillip*. "You are a

414

representative of the king's and already on the side of the victor."

"Not necessarily," Hastings murmured heedlessly. "Of late, some of these dissidents have given imperial authority an impressive show of strength. As I say, matters could change—more easily, perhaps, than you realize."

"Ah, you mean the Fox," Charlotte said perceptively. She rose on one elbow so that she could look down on her lover's face. "The explosion on the night of the ball—and right in the governor's garden. I do see what you mean; they are a clever lot." Little pieces of memory came back to her like sunlight dappling the water, but still there was no clear picture. Her brow furrowed thoughtfully. "I have wondered how he managed to accomplish his ends so smoothly. Surely there must have been accomplices."

She could see quite clearly the expression that passed over Hastings's face, a look that he tried to conceal that seemed a mixture of fear and regret.

Abruptly he moved, half rolling on top of her, burying his head against her breasts. "Come, let us forget this foolish talk of patriots and fighting. I did not come here to talk. This is what I came for, my love." And with these words his mouth sought her taut, hard nipple and his hand slid across her abdomen toward the sweet treasure between her legs.

But Charlotte, for once in her life, was almost totally unresponsive. Something was nagging at her, some elusive bits of puzzle that involved this man with whom she was very much afraid she had fallen in love . . . and something that involved another, for whom she still cared deeply. The little memory in the corner of her mind was almost within grasp.

She pulled away from Hastings and captured his wandering hand in hers to distract him and to give herself time to think. "Such beautiful hands," she murmured. The memory was stronger now, her instincts surer. "Such strong, lovely hands. A woman never forget her lover's hands . . ."

Quickly he drew his hands away. "No more talk. I insist, my love, and since you care so much for my hands, let me show you what they can do . . . here." He rolled the tip of her nipple between two fingers. "Or here." He traced the softness of her thigh and grazed the silkiness that guarded her secret sweetness.

Charlotte allowed a brief shiver of pleasure to wash over her and, for a moment, she almost lost her train of thought. But with a deep breath and a supreme burst of resolve, she pulled away from her lover's arms and moved to the far side of the large canopied bed.

"We speak of a future, of a life together, yet you will now turn your clever powers of deception on me," she accused quietly. "I think you have only been toying with me with your pretty words and, in fact, I believe you have been lying all along about the night of the governor's ball."

"Lying?" Indignation sharpened his voice. "Don't be ridiculous. For what purpose?"

Charlotte narrowed her eyes and watched him carefully. How foolish men were to think that the women who loved them could not see through their petty deceptions. "Of that I am not certain. But something occurred that night that you do not want to talk about."

Hastings tried to control his racing heart, pounding now with alarm and not passion, but his words were easy. "Darling Charlotte, are you still jealous over the Everett woman? I am touched! But I assure you I have told you everything."

"Oh, I think not," Charlotte answered, and the glitter in her eyes warned him that she was not satisfied.

"All right, I confess. You have found me out." He gave a little laugh of mock defeat. "In truth she did ask me to meet her in the garden, but when we talked I made it clear that all my thoughts were of another . . ."

At last the pieces came together for Charlotte. She could see it so clearly now. Phillip leaving the ball, Phillip returning—Phillip, but not Phillip!

"No, my dear Hastings, you were not in the garden with Arabella." She looked at him with growing wonder and perception. "You were in the ballroom wearing Phillip's mask, talking to me. You could not conceal your hands—not from me." And as incredible as this sudden truth seemed, a yet more perplexing question remained. "But why? I cannot understand why you would want to pretend to be Phillip."

"What a foolish idea, Charlotte." His words were quick and terse, and his harsh tone was not mitigated by the easy smile that backed them. "Actually it sounds quite mad, and I think you are teasing me. Now come here. Come back to me." Though his persuasion was soft, there was a hint of something hard and steely in his eyes, a warning that Charlotte would have been wise to heed.

But she was reckless and filled with the heady victory of her clever wit over the mystery. "You were wearing Phillip's fox mask, leaving him free . . . but free for what? Surely he did not need a disguise for a tryst with his own wife . . ." Her voice trailed off. "Then it must have been involved with the explosion. Did Phillip try to stop it?"

She narrowed her eyes in concentration. The answer that had been eluding her was within her grasp. And then her eyes opened wide in shocked amazement. Phillip. The fox mask. The Fox. The explosion. "Oh, dear Lord in heaven! Phillip! My Phillip is the Fox!"

Hastings no longer made any attempt to conceal his

anger. His body was tense with it and his words exploded with a venomous hiss. "You are mad, mad and foolish, and should be locked away for spouting such drivel! Phillip Everett is no more the Fox than I am King George!"

By now Charlotte's initial shock at her discovery had turned into delighted glee, and she clapped her hands with childlike enthusiasm for her own cleverness. "Phillip! My dear, daring Phillip is the Fox! Oh clever, clever boy. I should have known he was far too much the young blade to continue to play the role of gentleman farmer. Oh, how could he deceive me so, the naughty rake? And how could I have been so blind! *Of course* it is he! I should have known it!"

With a strangled oath, Hastings threw back the covers and sprang from the bed. "You are insane! Your words are nothing but a woman's foolish fancies and imaginings." With controlled fury he pulled on the clothes that hours earlier he had so eagerly abandoned. His hands were shaking, more with fear than with anger. "If you are to repeat this demented gossip, I swear—"

"You have no need to swear," Charlotte shot back. "And it is not gossip. It is the truth, and you know it." Charlotte, wrapped in a sheet, slid off the edge of the bed, her head still reeling with the joy of discovery. "And you, my fine lieutenant," she declared triumphantly, "are obviously an accomplice! Oh, this is too, too fine to be believed!" And she broke into delighted laughter.

Hastings broke off his dressing and looked at her fiercely. "Dare not speak such a thing," he hissed. "In fact, don't even think it!"

Charlotte lifted an eyebrow in mild consternation. She did think his reaction was somewhat overplayed, when now they were not only dear friends and lovers but allies in crime as well. "My dear boy, aren't you a

418

bit impetuous to be rushing away before we've even had a chance to talk? I want to know when and how, every juicy detail . . ." She reached out a hand to stay him and was rewarded by his fingers biting viciously into her wrist.

"There is nothing to discuss, Charlotte. Nothing. As far as you know, the Fox does not exist. Do you understand?" His eyes were dark and his voice low and, as he spoke, his fingers tightened on her wrist painfully.

Suddenly she did understand. "Why . . . you are afraid!" she gasped and did not know whether to be amused or insulted. "Afraid that I will betray you and Phillip!"

"And what else am I to think? I know of your relationship with the governor. You are far too close to him to—"

"Be trusted? Is that what this is all about?" She wrenched her arm away from his grasp, searing indignation wiping out all traces of her former good temper. She was so angry she did not even notice the purplish bruises that were already beginning to form on her perfect skin. "So I am someone to sleep with and make promises to but not to trust! I think you are the liar, Hastings, and not I!" Her cheeks were flushed and her eyes sparked dangerously as she stared at the angry face of the man who so recently had held her in his arms.

"And you are nothing but a woman of disputed virtue," he tossed back bitterly, "who has done nothing to earn my trust."

He expected fireworks from Charlotte, but what he got was cold contempt. "And you are nothing but a lowborn lout who will live to rue those words. I am well rid of you, Lieutenant. Get out of my house."

"Not until you promise never to repeat your foolish accusations."

Hastings felt trapped, imprisoned by his own impetuous words and Charlotte's knowledge. It was all his fault—only his—yet he could not allow her to betray the Fox. He took a step toward her, to reach for her, to convince her somehow of her foolishness. But Charlotte raised her hand as if to slap him and, in a movement of self-protective instinct, Hastings's hand slipped around her throat. He stood very close to her, intent upon frightening from her what loyalty would not give.

"Your word, Charlotte," he persuaded softly. "Promise me that you will never talk of Phillip Everett in the same breath as the Fox."

Charlotte's eyes glittered and she did not flinch. "No," she said clearly, her voice icy with disdain. "You will not intimidate me. More clever men than you have tried."

His hands tightened imperceptibly on her smooth, white neck. "My fingers could snap your neck like a twig. You know that."

Defiantly she met his eyes. "Then kill me if you must, but you cannot frighten me, and I shall not promise."

He stood there, his hands around her throat, at war within himself, torn between loyalty to his leader and his tangled emotions for this beautiful woman who so proudly defied him. Slowly he dropped his hands.

"Get out of my house," she spat furiously, taking a step away from him. "I never want to see you again."

His eyes were cold and hard. "Say a prayer, my lady," he responded quietly, "that you do not. For next time I cannot promise our meeting will end so peacefully."

He turned sharply on his heel and strode away.

Chapter XXIII

23 November, 1773

I despair of ever knowing Myne Husbande, for just as I believ'd Mutual Trust had brought Us together, He is more a Stranger to Me than ever before. When He remov'd his Mask last Nyte, I was sure, so very sure, that We would be as One, but as soon as I call'd out his Name in my Joy and Passion, He turn'd on Me and left Me, and my Heart is rent . . .

Since that Tyme I have not seen Phillip, nor ev'n heard his Presence in the House. Has He departed again, this Tyme never to return? When I ask Sam of my Husbande's Whereabouts, He says only that He is away on Business on his Ship, and I despair. The Cruelty of Uncertainty, when my Heart is fill'd with such Longing, is too unjust . . .

Oh, why did I not wait until He was ready to speak to Me of his Double Life? Why was I in such Haste to tell him that I knew?

The Day is fresh and beautiful, the Sky above is bright and blue and All at Shadowood lies in a

glorious State, but inside my Heart is impover-
ished, for All I care for in the World is absent
from Me . . .

A wondrous leap of her pulses accompanied the
sound of the familiar footsteps upon the stairs, and
from long habit Arabella quickly put down her quill
and hid her journal. She was halfway to the door with
the welcome of relief upon her lips when it was abruptly
flung open and Phillip strode in.

He was dressed such as she had never seen him
before, and the mere sight of him, so strong and
handsome and without artifice or pretense, was enough
to take her breath away. The powdered wigs, the
foppish garb, the paint and powder were cast aside on
this day. The cloak and mask were absent. He wore
simple riding togs, a plain butternut waistcoat, and
rough-weave breeches of hunter green, with a muslin
shirt and casually tied stock. His silky hair was bound
away from his face with a leather thong, and his boots
bore the mud and scratches of a hard ride.

She could not tell why, in that one glorious moment
of seeing him again after being so long unsure she
would ever see him at all, she believed he would open
his arms to her and that she would run into them. In
fact, she stood poised to do so, her heart beating out a
wild rhythm of joy and anticipation. How beautiful a
man he was! How wonderful he looked to her. And
though he stood half the length of the room away from
her, she could feel his warmth, taste his skin, know the
mind-weakening surge of pleasure the strength of his
arms would bring to her. And then she saw his face.

He was tired. The lines about his eyes and mouth
bespoke his weariness; his carriage was that of a man
who had traveled long and ached for rest. Her instinct
was to give him that rest, to lay him down upon her bed

and to stroke his brow until those eyes that had seen so much, suffered so much, closed to the respite of her care. She wanted to hold him and soothe him and beg him to sleep in her arms. She wanted to lift some of his burden from him.

But immediately she knew that this would not be possible. He stood before her, tight-lipped and grim. There was caution in his eyes and anger in the hard lines of his face, and he was more remote from her than he had ever been before. If there were words to be spoken between them, Arabella knew they would not be of a personal nature.

She drew herself up before him bravely, steeling herself against the hurt. Once before she had tried to reach him with an expression of her love; she had succeeded only in driving him further away. She would not make the same mistake again.

She said quite calmly, "So. You are at home. You have dispatched your ship to safety?"

There was a flicker of something in his eyes— surprise, perhaps—as though he had not completely resigned himself to the fact that now there were no secrets from her. Or perhaps it was apprehension, as if he realized she had stolen his secrets from him and was not certain what she intended to do with them. And Arabella felt a swift, bitter surge of impatience. What more could she do to prove herself?

She turned away with a graceful twirl of her skirts. "A foolish question, I perceive. Of course that would be your first order of business."

"Indeed." His voice behind her was mild. "And now I find another item of business that presses me just as severely."

Arabella turned, the expression upon her face relating only the vaguest curiosity. Phillip came a little way into the room, his stance casual and relaxed as he perused with absent interest her belongings. Occasionally he would stop and pick up some small item—a silver-backed hairbrush, a tortoise-shell comb, her porcelain ink stand—and examine it briefly, turning it over in his long fingers before replacing it and moving on. His lean, taut body seemed to fill up her feminine *boudoir,* radiating danger of a most primitive kind. Arabella watched him with narrowed and alert eyes, and though her senses thrilled to a sharpened awareness of him, her pulses began to throb a slow, heavy rhythm of wariness.

Yet her voice was cool as she invited, "If you will tell me what you're looking for, perhaps I can help you find it."

He stopped and looked at her, his lips curving into a slow, easy smile that never quite reached his eyes. He held her freshly stained quill in his hand, fingertips stroking it with an unconscious sensuality, soothing the feather, caressing it. He said negligently, "I hardly think you realize yet what problems you have caused with your interference, my dear. And I think something must yet be done to convince you of the seriousness of your folly. Unfortunately, however"—very politely, very carefully, he replaced her quill in its stand—"I do not have time to deal with you now."

He took from his waistcoat pocket a key and looked at it for a moment before turning toward the door. "One thing is clear: You cannot be allowed to roam free. I think it best that I keep you where I will know where to find you for the next few days."

Arabella should have been outraged, but all she felt was a mild incredulity mingled with sadness. Still, after all they had endured together, he had no trust in his heart for her. What manner of man was this? Was there a word that went beyond stubborn?

She merely shook her head, her lips softening into a distant smile, and her voice was quiet with simple certainty as she said, "How little you know me yet, my husband, if you think a locked door will keep me from where I want to be."

He paused and turned to her, the key still held loosely in his hand. The look in his eyes caught her unawares, for there was a leap of subtle fire within them, of yearning, of uncertainty. And he inquired softly, without moving, without taking his eyes from hers, "And where is it that you want to be, my lady?"

She thought without hesitation, *In your arms . . .* , but she could not voice the words. The moment between them was charged and poignant, alive with half-formed thoughts and unspoken needs. These elusive threads reached out between them and ensnared them both, pulling them with a look, a breath, to where they belonged, until the yearning strengthened into action and Arabella, with the whisper of skirts and the gentle wafting of perfume, moved toward him.

She stood before him, her eyes wide and clear and filled with all her heart as she looked up at him. She would come this far, but no farther, and Phillip knew she had made the move to meet him halfway; if there were more, it would be up to him.

The sweetness of her scent filled his head; the warmth of her body caressed his senses. Her skirts just brushed his calves, so close was she standing, and the curve of her breasts was at a level with his arm. *How easily,* he thought distantly, *this fragile creature controls me; how effortlessly she takes my reason . . .*

And, hardly aware that he made the motion, he lifted his hand to grasp her chin lightly between his thumb and forefinger, and he looked into that sweet, inviting face intently.

Arabella's lips parted; she barely breathed. Only the smallest movement would close the distance between them, and once his lips touched hers, once they stepped into each other's arms . . .

She saw his eyes darken, felt his fingers tighten briefly, almost convulsively, against her flesh, and she knew it was not to be. He let his hand drop; he took a step back. And when he looked at her then his lips curved into a small, rueful smile. "I think," he informed her simply, "that you are right. Locks will avail me nothing against you."

He tossed the key negligently on her wash stand and turned toward the door. "Be about your business, my lady, but don't think to get too reckless. You will go nowhere unescorted, and I will know of your activities every minute of the day."

"Phillip," she called after him, somewhat desperately. "We cannot go on forever as though nothing has happened. We must talk. What is to become of us?"

He stopped, but he kept his back to her, his broad shoulders firm. "I cannot tell you," he replied soberly after a moment, "what I do not know."

He departed then, but he did not close the door.

Arabella's heels clicked sharply on the highly polished floor. She paused before a glass to adjust the veil on her small riding hat and breathed the first easy breath she had taken in almost two days. At least Phillip had spoken to her. True, nothing had been settled between them and his words had given her no reason to believe that that state would be changed soon, but at least he had acknowledged her presence. At least he was home.

She had heard him tell Sam less than an hour ago that he had estate business to attend to with William, and the moment he had departed Arabella began to make her own preparations for a ride. There was no point in testing Phillip's temper needlessly, but as long as he was out of the house she *did* long for fresh air and the company of an old friend.

It was good to be back at Shadowood, to be done with the ornate wigs, the powder, paint, and endless fetes, which had been so much a part of their life in Williamsburg. Here she could be herself, the Arabella who was only a shadow away from the Flame of Liberty.

Sam's ebony face gleamed beside hers in the looking glass. "Sam, I was just going to look for you," she greeted him. "Please tell Master Phillip when he returns that I've ridden over to the Hamptons to visit Miss Caroline and deliver her gifts. I shan't be gone long." A small leather case hung from her arm, holding the silver christening cup and a cluster of lace ribbons that she had spied in Williamsburg and had immediately thought would compliment Caroline's coloring magnificently.

"There's no need for a message," Sam responded. "I'll be riding along with you today, Miss Arabella."

Arabella turned to face him with resigned impatience transforming her features. So Phillip intended to be true to his word, she mused angrily. "Don't be absurd, Sam. I've ridden to the cottage dozens of times. I'd know the way in the dark with my eyes closed."

Sam's voice was soft, but she recognized the implacable look on his face that signified he would not be moved or deterred, no matter how vigorous her protests. "Master Phillip asked that I ride with you, Miss Arabella, and so I must."

A corner of Arabella's lips turned down wryly. "No doubt," she murmured, "he is concerned for my safety, with such dreadful rumors flying about Le Renard."

Sam did not blink an eye. "No doubt."

She turned for the door; Sam respectfully opened it for her. The November air was crisp and sharp, with an invigorating freshness that immediately buoyed her spirits. The trees on the wide lawn were barren now, their leaves of gold and orange and red blanketing the ground.

As she descended the steps, she called over her shoulder to Sam, "Tell the yard hands to get these leaves swept away this afternoon while I'm gone."

"Yes, Missus."

She crossed Phillip's rose garden, where spindly bushes stood forlornly in the sunlight, shorn of all their beauty and color. The seasons were changing at Shadowood from the lushness of summer into the abundance of autumn. The smokehouses were filled with sausages and hams from hogs butchered in the frosty early mornings. The granaries were bursting with fodder and winter feed for the livestock and the storehouses overflowed with the harvest of autumn—pumpkins, apples, chestnuts, squash, and onions. It was a season of fulfillment—at least for some.

As Arabella neared the stables, she looked back over her shoulder. Sam was there, striding a good ten paces behind her but still there. Her smile was half amused, half annoyed as she stopped to wait.

"If you must dog my footsteps, then make yourself useful." She handed him the satchel with the gifts, and if Sam was hurt by her sharp tone, his calm face showed no sign of it.

He quickly saddled their horses and they rode along the edges of the field toward the Hamptons. Once again Arabella was taken with the beauty of the land, and she realized how very much she loved this place. It had begun on that first ride with Sam, when all had seemed so strange and new, but even then this land had called to her like a lover. Even then she had felt as though she had come home.

Arabella looked over at Sam and smiled. How could she stay angry on a day like this? Besides, it was not Sam's fault that he was loyal to his master. Rather she should be grateful for Sam's devotion to the man they both loved.

"It's good to see you smile, Miss Arabella."

"I have a great deal to smile about, Sam. Being home again, with my husband . . ." Her voice drifted off. Determinedly optimistic, Arabella was certain that soon all would be righted between her and Phillip. All it would take was time . . .

The horses picked their way daintily along the path, blowing softly in the cool air. Their coats were full and glossy in readiness for the cold that would soon come. The sheep, shaggy in their winter wool, looked like white puffs of cotton as they grazed upon what sprigs of grass they could find in the pasture below. The slaves were warmly dressed too now in sturdy homespun, each with his own pair of shoes from Shadowood's cobbler.

Just as they turned to ride out toward the woods that separated the overseer's cottage from the rest of the plantation, Arabella and Sam stopped to greet a group of female slaves who were dipping spun wool into vats of dye. There was brown from walnut bark, blue from indigo, and cranberry from the berries of the same name.

"This color be pretty on the Missus," remarked a fat old woman, her face as wrinkled as a walnut itself, as she held up a strand she was dyeing a vivid yellow in a liquid made of apple bark.

"Or even better for a baby," another voice called out.

The woman laughed, hiding their smiles behind their hands until they saw that the young mistress was not offended. Then they laughed long and loud. No, Arabella wasn't offended at all. Once the thought of having Phillip's child had made her weak with revulsion, but now she was eager to bear his son or daughter. And she would—as soon as she discovered a way to bring him back to her bed.

As they rode on, Arabella was struck again by how

much like a little kingdom Shadowood was. It was as complete as Williamsburg, as self-sufficient as a small town. There was nothing about Williamsburg she missed, and nothing she could not find at Shadowood, except . . .

She remembered the day she had bought the gifts for Caroline that she now rode to deliver. It had been that long morning she had insinuated herself into the good graces of Mistress Woolcot, then traveled to the Post Office in search of that silly book. And later she had stood watching the printer.

She had thought of it then. How easy it looked, and how simple it would be for her to master. Why not? she thought. Why not a printing press at Shadowood? It would be much more difficult to deliver her pamphlets now that she was no longer in the city, but if she could prepare a hundred instead of only one . . . if her writings could make their way into the hands of many instead of a few . . . Farmers and laborers, small shopkeepers and yeomen who did not have the luxury of traveling to Williamsburg would be able to hear of the great injustices afflicting this land, and of the plans to overcome them.

"Sam," she said abruptly, "are there any vacant outbuildings near the main house?"

Sam answered cautiously, "Over past the blacksmith's shop there're several buildings we once used for storage. But they've been empty for a year or so, Miss Arabella. Probably full of lizards and rats. Not the place for you."

"Then we'll just evict the tenants." She gave a decisive nod and turned her horse. "Come on, Sam, let's have a look. I'll still have plenty of time to visit Caroline."

With a look of puzzlement on his face, Sam led the way toward the empty buildings.

430

Chapter XXIV

Reginald Winters, Earl of Chatley, was in a foul temper. He had returned to Williamsburg expressly to talk to Everett, but a servant sent to the house on Nicholson Street had told him that Arabella and her husband had left town for Shadowood. Reginald read again the letter he had received from his brother-in-law, the letter that stated their partnership was at an end, but Reginald was not satisfied with Everett's reason. There was more to this betrayal—he was sure of it—and Reginald was feeling very uneasy. Things had not gone well at all with their importing scheme, as Reginald preferred to call it—smuggling being much too unfortunate a term to apply to an arrangement between gentlemen. Everett, for all his silly prattling and posing, had had the upper hand all along, deciding when they would begin and when they would call a halt.

Reginald sighed and looked around his room on the second floor of the Raleigh Tavern. The simple wooden beds, the one sturdy chair, the white china chamber pot, the thin window curtains, were hardly the accoutrements expected by a peer of the realm in his lodgings, but then what could one ask in this barbaric country?

Reginald had come to Virginia to dispose of a troublesome sister, but greed had made him stay, and the promise of a quick and easy profit. He had managed to rid himself of the red-haired minx, but he had hardly found the fortune he had coveted. Nor had his spy provided the information he needed to control Phillip Everett. That repulsive three-fingered man— Reginald shuddered to think he had once shared a table with the vermin—had disappeared suddenly and without any warning, and Reginald had been left without an informant in Everett's camp.

And now Everett dared to shut him out of their agreement! Reginald's fingers curled around the paper, crumbling it into a ball, then he tossed it into the corner. By all rights the Earl of Chatley should be the one to control the situation, not that lily-livered fop of a Virginian. But control him Everett did; he held all the cards. And he knew about that cursed woman who had expired so unfortunately in London and what was more, if the fool were ever caught smuggling, Reginald's name could be traced to the Letters of Passage. It had not been wise to arrange for those documents—he knew that now—but at the time it had seemed a quick and easy way for a profit, and he had thought that with a spy aboard the ship he could easily manage his brother-in-law.

Reginald closed his eyes and wished he were back in London. He thought about the gaming tables at White's, the platters of rare roast beef at Claridge's, and an elegant little house he knew in Mayfair where a delightful woman supplied him with all the young girls he wished. Reginald's eyes opened and he gazed once more around the room. Here he was in this so-called capital city of this uncivilized colony in one devil of a tangle.

But there had to be a way out of it. There always was.

How easy it all would be if Everett disappeared, vanished from the face of the earth, went down with his ship on one of his smuggling *sorties,* but Reginald would have to have supreme good fortune for that to happen. And fortune did not appear to be coming his way. Far better if he could himself contrive to get Everett out of the picture. Arrested for smuggling . . . No, he reflected, that wouldn't do at all. Before the fool was dragged whimpering and screaming to the hangman's noose, he would surely implicate Reginald as deeply as he could.

There was a way, of course—one certain, infallible method of getting rid of Phillip Everett forever. If he should die . . . be killed perhaps in a duel . . . Reginald grimaced at the thought. He had never been worth much at paces, and the boy, ninny that he was, was half Reginald's age and in damned good shape. But at close range, of course, if he could arrange that, even he might be able to outshoot Everett. Or, better yet, if Everett were unarmed . . . If perhaps he were trying to escape the governor's troops . . .

Reginald replayed various scenarios in his head and, for the first time that evening, he smiled. Phillip's inopportune demise in a scuffle with his brother-in-law, who was only trying to convince him to give himself up to the authorities, would solve so many problems. No one could trace Reginald's involvement with Everett's nefarious activities, and, moreover, Arabella would be left a rich widow. Reginald was not sure just how he would carry out his plan, but he knew there would be personal gain to be made from his poor sister's tragedy.

When the girl knocked at the door, Reginald was almost in a jovial mood.

"Sir, they said in the taproom that you'd asked for a woman."

433

Still sunk into the room's one chair, he motioned the girl to approach. "Come," he said. "Let me see what I've bought."

Wordlessly she moved toward him, eyes downcast, the very stance of her body showing her servility. Reaching forward with fat, clumsy fingers, Reginald unlaced the top of her bodice. Impatiently he pulled the dress from her shoulders, exposing the whore's breasts, blue veined and small. As a draft of cool air blew through the cracks in the window, her nipples hardened into purplish peaks.

"God's breath, you are a scrawny one," Reginald growled as he plucked carelessly at one of her distended nipples. She stepped back slightly, raising pale blue eyes fearfully to meet Reginald's. He read the look easily and raised his hand to pat her face awkwardly. "But you'll have to do this night. Undress and get yourself on the bed."

She obeyed, her childish fingers shaking as she dropped her skirt on the floor and slipped off her patched stockings and slippers. Reginald watched stoically, remembering other women he had known, buxom women with pendulous breasts and broad hips, women whose flesh had been like warm dough beneath his hands. This one would be different, he thought, so small and fragile she looked as though she might break in his hands.

Reginald heaved himself to his feet and tottered across the room, favoring his gouty leg. He dropped his breeches to the floor but still wore his long shirt, which covered his generous belly and buttocks and concealed his mottled thighs.

The girl lay on the bed waiting, her smooth, almost hairless limbs trembling in the cold of the room.

He had demanded clean sheets from the landlord, but his request had not been granted. Instead, the linens had been turned to reveal coverings only a bit less gray than before. Lord only knew what kind of diseases ran rampant in this dismal place.

As Reginald sat beside the woman on the bed he tried to put aside his memories of silk sheets and pink-fleshed women. He could see the line of dirt around the girl's skinny neck and the grime encased beneath her short, bitten nails. A stale odor rose from her, the scent of fear and desperation and poverty.

His fat fingers played roughly with her large, tender nipple. "Do you have the pox, girl?" he demanded, pinching her flesh.

Her eyes closed in pain and she shook her head. "No sir, I don't. Believe me, sir, I'd tell you."

"You'd best be honest with me." He cupped her flat breast in his hand, digging his nails into the soft flesh until she whimpered with pain. When she closed her pale blue eyes and bit down on her bottom lip with small, crooked teeth, Reginald smiled and continued the pressure. The evening might turn out to be salvageable after all.

"I will sir. I promise."

Her eyes opened and Reginald took her cold hand in his and thrust it up beneath his shirttail. "Then begin to earn your money, girl."

When Reginald arrived at the palace the next day, he was escorted almost immediately into the governor's presence while a young captain of His Royal Majesty's Army sat morosely cooling his heels in the anteroom just off the great hall of the palace. He had been summoned earlier by Lord Dunmore's aide, who had given a hint of what awaited him—yet another dressing down about the incredibly inept handling of the raid upon the Fox. Lord Dunmore, a master at politics and the manipulation of human motivations, added insult to injury as he forced O'Donal to wait upon him, first while he completed his *toilette* and dressed, then as he drank his tea and breakfasted, and now as he entertained the Earl of Chatley.

The governor received Chatley at his desk, which occupied a discreet corner of the formal dining room. He pushed aside the documents he had been studying and waved Reginald into a chair at the same time sending a servant for morning tea. Reginald would have preferred a glass of port, a suitable refreshment for two men of the world no matter what the hour, but he was in no position to make demands on Lord Dunmore's hospitality.

Over a cup of tea, the two men talked of Reginald's stay in New York, mutual friends, and the vagaries and inconveniences of travel in the Colonies. Dunmore did not particularly care for Reginald Winters, but the Englishman's visit served a dual purpose. He wanted to let his officer know he was no better than a schoolboy awaiting his punishment. But more importantly, the governor wanted to know what information Reginald might impart concerning the Lady Arabella. His last visit with her had been abruptly curtailed—again because of the damnable Fox—but Lord Dunmore was not about to concede defeat.

When the second cup of tea had been poured and Dunmore had selected a hot cross bun from the platter of pastries, he brought up the topic that had been on his mind since the earl had been announced.

"And your charming sister, is she well? Her delightful wit and beauty have added much to our season this autumn."

This was just the opening for which Reginald had been waiting. "It is for my sister's sake that I am here." Reginald drew his thin lips into a semblance of distress.

"She is not ill?" The governor conjured up his last memory of Mistress Everett, here, in this very room. She looked well then, glowing with good health, wearing that low-cut gown that showed off to such advantage the lush curves of her body. He hated to think that all that ripe beauty might waste with illness.

"No, Arabella is fine as far as I know . . ." Reginald let his voice trail off. "Everett has taken her back to Shadowood."

"How irregular," protested Lord Dunmore. "The season has not yet ended." And Dunmore was deucedly disappointed. He had counted upon more intimate afternoons with Lady Arabella, and now to have her wrenched from him so inopportunely . . .

"I thought so myself." Reginald pretended thoughtfulness. "But that husband of hers is a strange bird."

Dunmore nodded glum agreement.

Reginald leaned forward as if to assure that they would not be overheard, although they were quite alone except for the guard at the doorway. His voice was low and conspiratorial. "I have reason to believe—strong reason—that Phillip Everett is involved in smuggling.

The governor threw back his head in spontaneous laughter that sounded very much like the bark of a dog and caused Glasgow, lying beneath the dining table, to lift his head. "Smuggling? Everett? My dear sir, surely you are joking." He managed with difficulty to control his mirth, for, after all, Everett was related, at least by marriage to Chatley.

But Reginald did not mind the laughter. "I know full well what the man is like. He seems foolish as a hare, but my information is not false."

The governor was far from convinced. "Preposterous. Everett doesn't need money. The man is damned rich."

"Sometimes wealth only breeds desire for more. Surely your lordship has observed as much . . . in his acquaintances."

Governor Dunmore scowled. He had a point.

"How did you receive this information?" he demanded. "Some disgruntled loser in a card game? For that is one area in which Everett does seem to excel."

"Indeed not. I engaged a man—a highly respectable seaman—to hire aboard Everett's ship. Since I was to be absent from Virginia, I felt it necessary to have someone be my eyes and ears, to keep watch on Everett and the welfare of my sister, you understand." As he talked of his spy, he tried to dismiss from his mind the image of the three-fingered man who had so discourteously disappeared.

"That you are concerned about the Lady Arabella is easy to understand," the governor murmured, but his eyes, as he spoke, lit up with an avarice that was difficult to mistake. "It would be difficult, I'm sure, to abandon such a lush beauty to the wilds of Virginia."

Reginald nodded, his mind working quickly. So that was the way the wind blew. The old goat was interested in Arabella. No . . . more than interested. He lusted after her, and Reginald was quick to turn that bit of information to his own use. It all seemed to be falling so easily into his hands."

"This fellow, this seaman that I hired, informed me that Everett, on a regular basis, smuggles goods into Virginia—all quite illegal, I'm afraid—and if he is allowed to continue, I fear the ramifications that could endanger the Winters name . . . and the person of my sister."

Both were thoughtfully quiet for a while, their minds busy with Machiavellian schemes, each attempting to work the situation to his own best advantage. "You have proof," the governor asked, "—irrefutable proof of this contraband?"

"There is but one way to be certain," asserted Reginald, bold now that he had captured the governor's interest. "Search the warehouses at Shadowood. I've no doubt that you'll find a quantity of goods that doesn't belong there. To be sure there isn't enough tobacco in all of Virginia to fill those damn warehouses." Reginald had no idea if the smuggled goods were at Shadowood, but he could not think where better they would be. Besides, it was a worthwhile gamble, and the perfect way to get the governor's troops, their guns, and Everett together at once.

"Smuggled goods . . ." Dunmore thought of the latest debacle, when his troops had lost the Fox and the contraband that might have been delivered into their hands. No doubt if Everett had had the wits to sneak anything at all past the customs examiners, it would be nothing more than a few kegs of rum or casks of Madeira; certainly nothing like what they had lost at the hands of the Fox. But, damn it all, he reflected angrily, it would be something, a chance to snatch some small victory from the ignominious jaws of defeat—and humiliation. Dunmore thought of the latest documents from Lord North containing his demand that Dunmore control the rampant smuggling that flourished along the coast. It was his duty.

But still . . . Everett. If those warehouses turned up empty, Dunmore would experience another embarrassment. Could it really be worth the risk?

Reginald saw the wavering in Dunmore's eyes. "Contraband," he insisted. "Right there at Shadowood, and to think my dear sister is in the hands of this smuggler, this traitor to the Crown and all that we believe in."

The governor was thoughtful. Even if the trip were a wild-goose chase, all would not be completely lost. He would see the Lady Arabella within the day and have a chance to sample the fine wine cellar at Shadowood. And if by some chance Reginald's story were true, and the man did seem sincere . . .

Reginald slipped in the final inducement. "As you said that first evening at Shadowood, these colonials must be kept in their places, running all over the countryside stirring up trouble, breaking the laws . . ."

The governor was not sure he had spoken those exact words, but the sentiments were his. He had one final warning for Reginald. "You know the penalty for smuggling is death by hanging."

Reginald sighed deeply. "A tragedy indeed, but if one is a loyal subject of the king's, one must see that the laws are enforced."

The governor nodded. "If indeed we find Everett to be guilty of this heinous act, your sister will be left a widow. Would you take her back to England then?"

Inwardly Reginald recoiled at the possibility of having Arabella once more on his hands, but his voice was smooth. "No, Arabella is far too fond of her new home and friends to ever leave. If something were to happen to my brother-in-law—and we can only pray that I am wrong—I would of course stay for a time to help her with the estate. The fortune is considerable, I imagine. But duty would eventually call me home, and on my leaving I would only hope that my Arabella might be in the care of someone responsible—a protector, if you will."

The message passed from one pair of eyes to the other and was understood. Lord Dunmore no longer had any questions about his motives for turning his brother-in-law in. The fortune of Shadowood was, indeed, considerable, and Arabella could not legally inherit. For the cooperation of the colonial governor, Reginald was bargaining his sister, and Lord Dunmore thought he could have done worse. He had no scruples about the situation whatsoever. If Everett was guilty, then guilty he would be found, and the winsome widow could make a far worse choice of protectors than Lord Dunmore himself. It all would work out quite nicely, he thought—if indeed there were a shred of truth in what Chatley was saying.

The two men, wigged and decked out, looked the epitome of English gentlemen. The governor was hard and muscled and Reginald portly and soft, but in their powdered headdresses and satin coats, united by the hard glitter in each pair of eyes, they were of a kind. Without a word or a handshake, the deal was consummated, and once again Reginald had sold his sister to the highest bidder.

"Don't be ridiculous, Charles. I refuse to be announced this morning. Governor Dunmore and I are never so formal with each other."

"I know, Your Ladyship," the agitated majordomo sought to explain, "but he has a guest already, and he has kept Captain O'Donal waiting for nearly an hour."

Charlotte took in the figure of the dejected officer and shrugged. "But then the captain is in the employ of the governor and must wait until his master calls, while I"—she smiled beguilingly—"I have only this special tin of tobacco, recently imported from the islands, to give to the governor. It is a special favorite of his, one that he is looking forward to. I shall just slip in for a moment—no more, I promise you—and deliver my gift. Why, he will scarcely know that I have been in the palace." Even as she spoke Charlotte was leaving the anteroom and moving down the hall.

As she drew near the dining room, she could hear the voices of two men, that of the governor and a stranger.

She paid no attention to their words at first, intent on making her entrance and claiming the attention of both men. Then she heard a name. Everett. Phillip Everett.

They were talking about Phillip and, as she moved closer, she could tell that the words were menacing and very much tinged with evil. As if a sixth sense were warning her, Charlotte paused before she reached the open door, then in an action that startled even her in its boldness, she stepped behind the folds of a heavy velvet curtain, not so near that she could be seen, but close enough to hear every word.

The governor barked out a loud order to his majordomo. "Send O'Donal to me and be quick about it." Then, in a muttered aside to Reginald, he added, "Perhaps the young ass can redeem his reputation as a soldier with a quarry as slow-witted as Everett."

When the officer appeared at the door, without so much as a word of greeting Lord Dunmore snapped out his orders. "I want a company of men ready to ride within the hour. We're going to Shadowood Plantation in search of smuggled goods."

O'Donal stood at attention, uniform freshly pressed, buttons gleaming gold, boots highly polished, and a face mirroring disbelief. "The Everett plantation? Sir, may I inquire on what evidence we ride to Shadowood?"

The governor pushed up from his desk, his voice sharp. "Upon the evidence of contraband concealed in the warehouses there."

The governor spoke angrily now, his face becoming mottled and the veins in his temple throbbing and prominent. "My well-trained British troops have bungled the capture of the Fox more times than I care to think about. But perhaps, if you act quickly and with any manner of military demeanor, we may be able to apprehend Everett—if, of course, the task does not trouble you too much."

The officer kept his face implacable and expressionless as he stood stiffly at attention and answered his commander. "My men will be ready to ride for Shadowood within the hour. Any other orders, sir?"

"Only to saddle my horse and one for Chatley. We shall be coming with you, and this time you can be assured that we will not return empty-handed."

Hastings frantically paced the length of his small room in the barracks. With each step his soul cried out at his foolish betrayal of his leader. He had been warned; he did not heed. And at this very moment, Lady Charlotte Parkington was no doubt pouring out every word of the secret of Phillip Everett's double identity to the governor. When he had seen her carriage pull into the stable yard, Hastings had almost panicked, thinking to go after her and stop her. But by then the lady was within the palace and O'Donal sat by the door. There was no way to stop the final act in the disaster that had begun the night of the ball.

What a fool I've been, his mind cried out for the hundredth time. *What an unconscionable, bloody-minded fool.* With an oath, he pounded his fist against the wall in frustration. All his efforts to reach the Fox at the townhouse or on his ship had been in vain, and now it was too late. Far too late.

Hurriedly, he tried to organize his thoughts and make plans. For a moment he considered fleeing, riding away from Williamsburg, across the mountains toward the land of which he dreamed. At least there he would have a chance, while here—

When he heard the frantic knocking at his door,

Hastings fully expected to find O'Donal standing there with a detail of men set to arrest him for high treason. Instead, when he opened the door he looked into the agitated features of Lady Charlotte Parkington.

"There's no time to waste," she said quickly. "You must ride to Shadowood at once and warn Phillip that the governor and his troops are on the way."

"Damn it, woman. It is just as I feared. You have betrayed us."

With a gesture of irritation, Charlotte grabbed his arm. "Listen to me, you silly boy. They know nothing of the Fox—not yet. They suspect only that Phillip is hiding contraband in his warehouses, but if you continue to argue with me instead of riding with a warning, then indeed Dunmore may learn everything."

Hastings did not move. Instead he looked down at Charlotte with wonder in his eyes. "You would risk danger yourself to warn me of this—even after our last evening together?"

"You mean our argument? Oh, Hastings, dear one, don't you know that all lovers argue, and I'm sure we shall again." Even at this moment when every second counted, she could not resist giving him a long, seductive look from the depths of her wonderful dark eyes. "And just imagine the pleasure we shall have in making up." Then she stood on tiptoe and placed an ardent kiss upon his lips. "Go quickly, my love and, above all, return safely to me."

At the barracks, O'Donal routed his men, shouting out orders and making the preparations, all the while cursing the governor for sending them off on a wild-goose chase and cursing even more roundly the Fox for setting off the chain of events that caused Lord Dunmore's aggravated temper and the need for this foolish foray to redeem his reputation.

Meanwhile, Hastings quietly saddled his horse around the side of the building, out of sight of the others. He would meet them later at Shadowood and blend into the company as though he had ridden with them all the way.

But now everything depended on him, and he must ride and ride hard.

Chapter XXV

The two men rode homeward across the broken fields of stubble, the ground dry and hard and cracking beneath their horses' hooves. Withered and abandoned stalks of tobacco, tilted at crazy angles or half ground into the dirt, littered the landscape as far as the eye could see, trailing ragged brown leaves that caught occasionally in a random gust of wind and waved like flags. The crop was harvested, safely hung to dry in the river warehouses, and now came the long season of rest.

Phillip paused before rounding the final curve that would put the river out of sight and looked back upon the warehouses. William, drawing up beside him, knew his thoughts.

"I don't like it either," William said, his brow growing troubled as he followed the direction of his friend's gaze. "But with luck it will only be for a few days, and what choice did we have?"

It made Phillip uneasy, it was true, to store such a great quantity of goods in the very warehouses of Shadowood. It was one risk he had always before made it a point to avoid. But until safer ground could be found there was no choice. Yet that was not the primary problem that was troubling him this late winter's afternoon. He said abruptly, without looking at William, "My wife knows."

William stared at him for the longest moment with a stunned astonishment in his eyes that was very close to incomprehension. When he regained his breath, however, he burst into such a stream of profanity that Phillip winced and his head, already throbbing from too little sleep and too much worry, ached with increased ferocity. "By all that is holy," William concluded at last, his face dark with an angry suffusion of blood and tight with the overwhelming implications of this revelation, "I knew it would happen! You wouldn't heed my warnings, would you? And now we're all fodder for the king's stable! You couldn't find your pleasure with a tavern-girl, could you? Or some nice, wholesome farmer's daughter. No, you had to plant yourself inside a chit fresh from the shores of England, a peer of the damned *realm,* for heaven's sake! She'll have the troops upon you like gulls over a single fish. There won't be a stone left unturned on this place—"

"No," Phillip said abruptly, perhaps a bit too harshly, as he straightened. He drew a deep breath, trying to relax, to normalize his tone. He kept his eyes firmly fixed upon the silent fields of Shadowood, which were bathed in the glow of the day's last rays. "No, Arabella will not betray me."

William stared at him as though he expected him at any moment to sprout wings and fly. "Have you gone mad, man?" he demanded at last. "Has she so bewitched you that you've taken final leave of what little senses you had left? Her brother is a bloody traitor! Scarcely a week ago we almost lost all because of his machinations! And how do we know that she was not in league with him all along? She has ambition to be the governor's next consort, I'll wager that, and what better weapon to further her cause than to put the Fox in his waiting hands? Can't you see what a trap she has woven for you?"

"No," Phillip said mildly. "I believe she means no treachery, for there is yet more." He took another breath. "Lady Arabella is also known as the Flame of Liberty."

Nothing but stunned, completely deflated silence met this announcement, and finally Phillip turned to look at William. His face was taut, yet resigned and Phillip continued, "It was she who had the wits—and the courage—to warn my ship away." He lifted his shoulders gracefully. "For the fact that I sit here with you today, you may thank my wife."

At last, in a voice low and strained, William managed, "My Lord. The Flame . . . How . . . ?"

Phillip's lips curled into a mirthless smile. "Strangely enough, I think she got the idea from me. She thought she was being helpful, I believe, by writing those stirring pamphlets to incite the people and distract the governor." Again he shrugged briefly. "Perhaps she was, to a point. But what we have now"—he met William's eyes with nothing but the frank acknowledgment of the inevitable truth in his own, and that truth was very bad—"is two criminals under the roof of Shadowood and twice the chance of capture. The apprehension of one means the destruction of it all. And for that most undeniable fact I'm afraid I can see no help."

A gust of wind blew up around them, rattling the dried tobacco leaves on the stalks and abruptly dying once again into silence. The silence went on a long time. Finally William said very quietly, "What are we to do?"

Phillip leaned forward, his arms crossed upon the pommel, his shoulders sagging, his face bleak. He did not speak immediately. "Ah, William," he said at last and so softly that his friend had to strain to hear over another restless breeze, "I am so very weary of it all. Will the day ever come, I wonder, when we might fight for our rights like men rather than like gutter rats who sneak to take the cheese and then run for their lives?"

"Perhaps," William answered thoughtfully. "When more Virginians come to believe as we do, when the word of our cause spreads far enough and wide enough . . ." And he looked at Phillip, hardly daring to comprehend the meaning of his own words. "Perhaps, if there were more like the Flame of Liberty to spread that word . . ."

The implication hung between them heavily for a long moment. Then Phillip straightened, taking the reins again. His voice was casual, his seat strong. "Your son . . . he thrives?"

William grinned with the barely suppressed pride of fatherhood. "That he does. Looks like a young goat but as strong as an ox."

Phillip cast him a sideways glance. "A family resemblance, I perceive." He clucked to his horse, urging him carefully through the broken fields. "I shall be down to see him on the morrow, and I won't keep you from your supper tonight. Come up to the house with me for a moment and we'll drink the lad's health."

"Aye," replied William glumly, for he knew the invitation was not made from pure cordiality. They had much to discuss this day, and much to decide. "And our own."

Phillip gave him a mild yet unreadable look. "We're not done for yet, William. We must merely rethink our position somewhat."

William wanted to agree, but it was plain he could not bring himself to do so. They rode a time with unspoken doubts and fears thickening the air between

450

them, then William had to speak. "Phillip," he said and reluctance clouded his face and darkened the eyes that darted quickly to his friend's face, then away again, "if she is not in league with the governor, how did she know about the trap?"

He saw Phillip's shoulders stiffen and the muscle in his jaw grow tight. He replied simply after a time, "I don't know." And then he nudged his horse, quickening the pace toward the house.

Sam burst into the library without a knock, something he had never done before, nor had even considered doing. Phillip had just lifted his glass to the youngest Hampton's health and had sunk, with great relief to his aching muscles, into the welcoming chair behind the desk. Sam's unexpected entrance galvanized both men, and they did not need the words that followed for confirmation.

Sam stood in the doorway with the look of a man who had ridden hard; his clothing was disheveled, his face sheened with perspiration. His expression was grim and his voice was harsh. He said, "We've got trouble, Master Phillip."

Instantly Phillip was on his feet, his fingers flattening against the desk surface, his color darkening. "Where is she?" he demanded. "Damn it, I told you not to let her out of your sight—"

Sam dismissed Arabella with a curt twist of his wrist. "The lady is with Mistress Hampton. I had to leave her. Hastings rode to warn Master William—"

"Hastings?" William took an alarmed step forward. "What—"

"The governor has learned of the goods stored in the warehouses," Sam concluded, oblivious to the interruption and without further delay. "Troops are on their

451

way to Shadowood at this moment."

The clock ticked off a brief, sharp silence and Phillip felt his world heave and lose anchor as everything seemed to drop away at once beneath his feet. His eyes inadvertently met William's and he saw in them only a reflection of his own thoughts: *Is it Arabella? Is it Arabella who has betrayed us to the governor?* Within Phillip, turmoil, disbelief, and horror whirled and jostled and canceled out one another. *How? When?* And most importantly, most incredibly, *why . . . ?*

Dimly he heard William demand, "Does he know of the Fox?"

And Sam, shaking his head, replied, "I don't know. He didn't have time to give me the details. All I know is that they intend to search the warehouses."

With a snap, Phillip felt the world right itself, his wits align themselves once more, and abruptly he was jolted into action again. He demanded sharply, "How far away are they?"

Sam took a breath. "Less than a league."

Phillip thought for a brief moment. "Then there's no time to lose." He came around the desk in swift, efficient strides. "William, every hand to the warehouses—house slaves, field hands, everyone." William was already on his way out the door. "Get the goods off my property and onto the barges and then sink them if you have to—I want no evidence remaining!"

The slamming of the front door was followed by William's running footsteps and Phillip's long strides in the hallway echoed them. "Sam, my horse!" he commanded over his shoulder on his way up the stairs. "You and I will meet the troops and do our best to buy William some time."

It was deep twilight when Arabella said a fond good

night to Caroline and mounted her horse for the short ride back to Shadowood. The first thing that struck her as odd was that her guard had disappeared. As she had been beginning her prolonged farewells to Caroline and the baby she had heard a rider approach the overseer's cottage, but he had not stopped to call. There had been murmured male voices in the yard, and now Sam was gone. Had that rider been Phillip, come to call his servant away on some more pressing task? She could not think of any other reason Sam would have disobeyed orders so blatantly and deserted her.

At first there was relief, and then amusement, for Phillip was already beginning to see how difficult it would be to keep her under guard every minute of the day. But as she rode along the dark, shrub-lined path that led from the overseer's cottage toward the back entrance to Shadowood, an uneasiness began to steal upon her that had as much to do with the eerily shadowed time of day as with Sam's inexplicable behavior.

How silent everything was at dusk. The only things that seemed to be stirring were the forest creatures, and even they, preparing for nightfall, were subdued. A muffled twitter here, a distant chirp, the rustle of a branch disturbed by a squirrel, and the crunching sound of her own horse's plodding hoofbeats were the only disturbances in the darkling silence. Not even kitchen sounds, which should have been clearly audible as she approached the outbuildings, or stable sounds or the cheerful chatter and singing of slaves from the family cabins reached her on the secluded path.

A prickling of her scalp registered nervousness she could not define, and she clucked to her horse, urging a quicker pace.

No stable boy came out to greet her, and when she led her mount into the dark barn, no one answered her imperious shout for assistance. Not even the lanterns had been lit, and with annoyance now underlying her uneasiness, she hurried to the house.

The front hall was dark and silent, and the entire house bore the unmistakable stamp of emptiness. Quickly she passed into the parlor, where not even the lamps had been lit, and called for a servant. Her voice echoed, and there was no reply.

Trying to keep her limbs from trembling, assuring herself over and over again that there must be a perfectly rational explanation for this unprecedented phenomenon, she went to the warming kitchen, where at least there would be a taper with which to light the lamps. Every room she passed was empty. In the warming kitchen she found the buffet was empty; the silver had been laid out in the midst of polishing and platters were awaiting the transfer of food for supper. The dining table had been half-covered with the linen cloth, then the task had been mysteriously abandoned.

She touched the taper to the candles in the sconces in the entrance hall, and lit the lamp in the parlor, taking another candle to guide her way up the stairs. Her heart was thudding now. The feeling of doom was like a breathing thing closing its tentacles around her. On the landing she called out as calmly as she could, "Phillip? Phillip, are you home?"

No reply.

She caught up the skirts of her riding habit and took the remaining stairs as quickly as her choking chest would allow, the candle streaming its smoky glow behind her and casting giant, menacing shadows on the wall. Without preamble, she flung open the door to Phillip's room. "Phillip? Sam?"

The room was empty and no one answered.

Methodically, she opened every door on the floor, ending at last with her own chamber. Not even her maid was present, and her change of clothes had not been laid out for supper.

Arabella set the candle on her washstand, taking a breath, unconsciously smoothing damp palms on her skirts. *It is nothing,* she assured herself. *Phillip has called the servants together for some reason; he has been known to do so before. A birthday celebration, a slave wedding, an impromptu party to reward a good harvest . . .*

There were no birthdays or weddings, and no party would have accounted for the stillness of the deserted house.

The fire burned low in the grate, and the draperies were still open, letting in the cold of the rapidly diminishing twilight. Arabella went automatically to close them, and there she stopped. Faintly, through the gathering grayness and the rising mist from the river, she thought she saw activity—the faint flicker of a torch, the movement of figures near the warehouses. In overwhelming relief and mounting curiosity, she bent to tug open the window, hoping to catch a clearer glimpse or even the sound of voices on the night air. And that was when she heard the front door open.

Releasing a long, pent-up breath, she turned toward the sound, expecting Phillip's commanding stride, the sound of his voice in the hallway, his step upon the stair. There was nothing but the muffled sound of movement below her, as though something were being carried, or dragged, with great stealth.

Her chest had begun to tighten again, but curiosity mitigated the sensation. Something was afoot and it boded no good, but if Phillip were at home at least the mystery's solution was close at hand.

She took up her candle and made her way downstairs again as some instinct, perhaps motivated by the deathly silence that still pervaded the house, urged caution.

The candles in the sconces gave off a flickering yellow glow and showed the entrance hall once again deserted. She paused at the foot of the stairs, seized by a sudden and horrible thought that made her heart slam against her ribs with a weakening force. What if it had not been Phillip who had entered the house? For why would he do so without announcing himself? What if it were some intruder . . . ?

She stood uncertainly in the hall, half turned toward the parlor, her pulses pumping with heavy, agonizing slowness, trying to think what to do. And then in the waving glow of the candles, something caught her eyes. There were droplets of something dark and glistening on the freshly polished floor.

She bent and touched a hesitant fingertip to one of the drops on the floor. It came away wet and stained.

Blood.

Arabella's head roared. Her breath stopped and she was not aware of the motion that propelled her to her feet again or made her cross the hall, following that deadly trail of gleaming drops toward the parlor, but only that the journey seemed to take forever, each step a separate moment, a separate action disconnected from the other and allowing no thought except the growing horror of what might lie at the end.

The scene that met her as she stood paralyzed at the parlor door would remain imprinted on Arabella's mind forever. Phillip was slumped back in the wing chair near the fireplace, his head thrown back, his eyes closed. He was wrapped in the dark cape upon which they had so recently lain wrapped in passion, and from the fingers of one hand trailed the telltale woolen mask of Le Renard. His face was tight and drawn and as white as death.

Sam was bending over him, gray faced with fear,

trying to press a glass of brandy to Phillip's lips. At the small, choked sound Arabella made he started and moved away, and that was when she saw that the entire front of Phillip's shirt was a vivid red.

He was covered with blood.

The candle jerked spasmodically in her hand, almost falling to the floor, casting crazily tilted shadows over the room. The stifled cry that emanated from her own lips sounded like a scream in the still-life silence of the room, but it was barely more than a murmur. It was enough, however, to snatch her back to reality, to galvanize her into action.

She placed the candle on a table and flew across the room, kneeling by her husband's side. Everything inside her was screaming, writhing, praying that it should not be so as she whispered, "He is dead!"

Phillip's eyes opened slowly, painfully, and met her own. They were fever bright, terrifyingly dark, and held within them the kind of contempt—and sorrow— that had the power to chill her bones. And he said hoarsely, raspingly, "No, my wife . . . I must disappoint you . . . for I am not dead . . ."

Those few words seemed to exhaust his capacity for speech, even for consciousness, and his head fell back again and his eyes closed. Sam moved quickly toward him, trying to lift his head, spilling brandy on his face and his blood-soaked shirt, and Arabella had no time to contemplate the significance of Phillip's words, or even to care. She could hear his labored breathing, see the stain on his shirt spreading even as the seconds passed, and she was on her feet.

Skirts flying, her own breath a series of choked, terrified sobs in her throat, she crossed the room for her sewing basket, scrambling frantically through its contents until she came upon a lawn nightgown the lace edging of which had begun to unravel and needed

457

mending. She caught it at the seam and tore off the front panel, wadding the material around her hand as she rushed back to Phillip.

She pushed Sam out of the way, demanding, "What happened?" as she grasped the edges of Phillip's shirt, wrestling with the blood-soaked material to tear it away from the wound.

"The troops . . ." Sam began to babble, his dark eyes constricted with shock and fear. "He thought he could lead them on a chase away from Shadowood as the Fox . . ."

The jagged wound Arabella uncovered in Phillip's shoulder was blackened with gunpowder and seeping blood at an alarming rate, and for a moment she reeled. Phillip's beautiful, perfect flesh marred in such a manner, torn and invaded by the signs of hatred and violence; Phillip, whom such a short time ago she had caressed with her fingers and her lips, now bleeding and broken before her . . . But she could not afford such feminine vapors, and with courage born of desperation she snatched up the wad of cloth she had torn from her nightgown and pressed it against the wound.

Breathing hard and sweating profusely, Sam said, "It's a clean wound, thank God. The ball went through—"

And Arabella demanded frantically, "What troops? Where?"

The ruthless pressure she applied to stanch the flow of blood shocked a moan from Phillip and his eyes flickered open, dazed and pained. Sam urged the brandy again on Phillip, and, his tongue loosened with fear and desperation, he replied, "The governor found out about the warehouses. We stored the goods from the ship there—all contraband. Tried to buy time . . . led a chase; almost made it too . . ."

Phillip, weakly rousing himself, tried to swallow the

brandy, choked, and began pushing Sam's hand away, trying to speak.

"No, Master Phillip, drink . . ."

"Phillip, be still . . ." Arabella tried to hold the bandaging firm against his futile movements, her mind racing frantically. Of Sam she demanded, "Troops? Here at Shadowood?"

And Phillip, knocking Sam's hand away with an enormous mustering of strength, gasped, "Let me up, you fool! Must warn . . . William—"

"Phillip, stop. You're bleeding—"

"Be still, Master Phillip," Sam pleaded.

"Damn you, they'll be here . . . any moment." Phillip rose to a sitting position, trying to push Arabella away. His face drained another shade with the effort, his pupils dilating and his mouth tightening against the pain. "We have yet . . . a chance to get away with this . . . but not if William is found at the warehouses."

He seemed stronger now, though whether from real strength or sheer determination Arabella could not be sure. Her eyes flew to the window, seeing nothing but darkness, remembering the activity by the river. If the governor knew, or suspected what was stored there, and if he rode to find the entire populace of Shadowood trying to remove it . . .

"You can't sit a horse," Sam was protesting almost incoherently, trying to push Phillip down. "Master William has the sense to take care of himself. The thing we must do now is take care of this shoulder and hide you—"

"He won't see the troops," Phillip protested through clenched teeth, desperately grabbing Sam's arm. "He can't *see* them from the river! I must go—"

"You wouldn't make it to the door."

"Then *you* go, for God's sake."

"I won't leave you, Master Phillip," Sam asserted stubbornly.

"*Damn* you. We're all finished if—" Phillip's words were cut off in a gasp as an unwise movement brought a new slice of pain running through him.

Arabella's head whirled as the two men argued over her head, almost having forgotten her presence. She thought of Phillip, bleeding and weak, and of Sam, who had no power without the man to whom he had pledged his life, and of the troops approaching steadily, determinedly, on Shadowood.

Arabella said sharply, "Sam. Hold this pressure firm against the wound. Keep him still."

She was gone and both men hardly registered her absence. She did not slow her pace as she stooped to scoop up Phillip's mask from the floor or as she grabbed her cloak from the hall tree. Phillip's horse, still saddled and restless, stood beside Sam's in the stable yard and she flung herself astride it, not bothering with her own mount and the clumsy sidesaddle.

The thunder of hooves alerted the two men inside the house. Phillip, strengthened now by the shock of what he could hardly believe, pushed himself to his feet as Arabella streaked past the window, her dark cloak billowing behind her, her figure bent low and intent upon the saddle. And all he could whisper weakly was, "Sweet Jesus."

The night air cut across her face, stinging her eyes, burning her dry and gasping lungs. She hugged the saddle, willing herself to become part of the beast that bore her, slapping the sweaty flanks of her mount into greater and greater speed as branches swept past her, brambles tugged at her skirts, and turf flew in her wake.

460

Her head roared, her frosted breath mingled with the steamy stream from the stallion's nostrils, and in the distance she imagined—she was certain—she could hear the storm of other hoofbeats, dozens of them.

The riverfront was aswarm with bodies and movement. A heavily laden barge slipped silently down the murky river as another, drawn up close to the bank, waited to receive remaining goods which were being passed by human chain from one of the warehouses above. Dark, sweaty bodies, yellowed by the hellish glow of flickering torches, rushed back and forth, voices shouting, arms lifted, eyes darting with confused terror through the night. Arabella drew up her mount so sharply that it reared and pawed the night, letting out an alarmed whinny. She snatched a torch from the startled hands of a passing slave and rose up in the stirrups, shouting, "Enough!"

Her preemptive arrival attracted some attention, her shout more. Some of the slaves paused in awkward, frightened confusion, turning to her; others, further away, went about their business unaware. "Go home!" She struggled to make her voice heard above the confusion, waving the torch through the night for attention. "Abandon it! Troops are approaching! Leave it, I say!"

She nudged her mount into a gallop and, throwing back her arm, released the torch into the open door of the nearest warehouse, where it caught instantly upon a sheaf of dried tobacco leaves that had been used to disguise more valuable cargo. The slaves began to scatter before her horse's hooves, and she grabbed another torch from its crude stand on the riverbank.

"Mistress Arabella!" It was William, grabbing for her bridle, his face gleaming in the orange glow, his eyes dark with alarm. "What—"

"Phillip has been shot!" She jerked her horse away,

461

riding toward the next warehouse. "Push the barge out! Disperse the slaves! The troops are upon us!"

She drew back her arm and let the torch sail. It caught, as did the next, and the next. Behind her, William was shouting orders; slaves were running for safety. When Arabella was satisfied that nothing of an incriminating nature would remain for the governor to find, she paused in the midst of the semicircle of lapping, rising flames to take out the mask. Quickly, holding her dancing, frightened horse steady with her knees, she tied it on. She lifted her reins and made for the woods as though all the demons of hell were upon her.

It had almost worked for Phillip; she prayed it would work for her.

"Lord forgive me, what have I done?" Sam's words were almost a whisper as he bound Phillip's wound with clumsy, shaking fingers. "I've told her everything—I didn't stop to think. She will destroy us all . . ."

Phillip, strangely calm now, winced against the renewed pain inflicted by Sam's ministrations, then lifted the brandy glass, downing its medicinal contents in a single fortifying gulp. His eyes narrowed on the window, from which the tendrils of flame licking the horizon were clearly visible. And then slowly, so unexpectedly that Sam began to suspect he was delirious, he began to smile. "I think not," he said softly, thoughtfully. In his pain-darkened eyes there was a flicker of something. Whether it was relief, admiration, or simply joy, Sam could not be sure. But it made him wary.

"We have too often made the mistake of underestimating the Flame of Liberty," Phillip said, and when he looked back at Sam there was new strength in his gaze, the determination for the future that had led his men through many a harrowing escape. And his voice was firm. "We shall not do so again. Hurry with that; we haven't much time."

Sam tied the last strip of bandaging taut and, satisfied, he rose to his feet. Both men froze as they heard the crackle of gravel, the muted approach of a dozen determined riders. Phillip got to his feet, drawing in his breath once, sharply, then releasing it, as though with that gesture dismissing for all time both pain and weakness. He could afford neither for the performance that yet lay before him.

"Quickly," he commanded, "my wig. Then go to the stables and bring around a horse. Hurry!"

Reginald rode forward, between the lord governor and the captain of the troops, his fury churning. If not for that foray into the woods, that cursed insanity over Le Renard, they would have been here in time. Now it was too late. Everett had somehow gotten wind of them and the warehouses were afire; the villain himself had probably fled the colony, leaving only Reginald to deal with the governor's wrath and make some kind of explanation for this expedition into the countryside in search of ashes.

His only hope was that Phillip had not yet had time to flee, that he had been careless enough to leave some evidence of his crime behind, and that none of that evidence bore the name of the Earl of Chatley. After that unexpected nonsense over Le Renard, it had taken all of Reginald's powers of persuasion to convince the governor to call off the search for the Fox and proceed to Shadowood. And even then His Lordship had agreed only in the slight hope that someone at

Shadowood might have encountered the brigand, for it was obvious the slim case against Phillip Everett had been overpowered this night by a renewed surge of Fox fever.

And, Reginald thought with some slight resurgence of hope as they drew to a halt upon the lawn of Shadowood and prepared to dismount, such concern for the Fox might yet work to his advantage. The governor could hardly accuse Reginald of leading him on a merry chase if, in fact, the chase had caused his path to cross that of the most notorious criminal in the Colonies. Perhaps it was best, after all, to work on this distraction, for it might cause the governor to forget the folly of finding no evidence against Everett in his excitement over almost having caught the Fox.

And, in fact, the governor had almost forgotten the original purpose of this journey. The encounter with Le Renard had thrown all their plans into chaos, and once again it appeared that the charms of Lady Arabella would have to be deferred in the face of more pressing concerns. He was in a foul temper as he gave the nod to O'Donal that would initiate the order to dismount, for once again he had lost Le Renard and Lady Arabella in a matter of a few moments. The only thing that brought him any comfort at all was the thought of the warmth of Everett's fire, the taste of his brandy, and the very small hope that the troops, while searching the grounds, might yet turn up something.

Neither he nor Reginald expected what happened next. And once again, the plans of both were set awry.

The front door to Shadowood was thrown open and Phillip Everett came lurching out, his coat torn and bloodied, his wig askew, his arm bandaged tightly to his chest, his face white and shiny with distress. He cried, "Thank God, thank God you're here! My prayers have been answered!"

Immediately, the lord governor was off his horse, staying the order to dismount as he hurried forward. "My Lord, Everett, you look the very devil! What has happened here?"

Phillip staggered down the steps, waving his good hand distractedly, obviously very much overwrought. "I can't believe it! The villain, the fiend—he's set my warehouses afire, can't you see that? We'll lose everything, everything! I am ruined!" And then, swaying dangerously as he turned, he shouted like a madman into the night, "My horse! My horse!" He turned back to the governor, his eyes wild, his voice high. "I saw the flames—my wife and I—and when I rode out to see what was amiss the cur shot me. Shot me in the shoulder, I say—a near mortal wound. Then he abducted my lovely Arabella!"

"Lady Arabella?" demanded the governor sharply, taking a stride forward. "Abducted, you say?"

"I am wounded, shot!" bemoaned Phillip. "Shot by the beast, that dastardly coward, Le Renard! He was here, I tell you! He has committed this infamy! He has taken my wife!" He threw his head around again, shouting, "My horse! Where is my horse?"

"Where did this occur?" demanded the governor, gripping Phillip's arm. "Which way did he go? I vow we passed the bastard in the woods, got off a shot at him too—"

O'Donal commanded, "Search the grounds! He may yet be about!"

"No time, no time!" shrilled Phillip. "He has my beloved! We must ride!"

"God's teeth, man, you're wounded! You can't ride!" The governor turned sharply to O'Donal. "Comb the area! He can't have gotten far with a woman on his saddle!"

"My Lord," objected Reginald, "let us not be hasty.

It was a lone rider we passed. This could be a trick."

The lord governor turned to him, scowling fiercely, as Sam appeared around the corner, leading his own saddled horse. "By damn, Chatley, you are the most pompous fool I've ever had the displeasure to know! This is your *sister* we speak of! Who knows what vile acts the beast may be committing upon her person at this very moment? O'Donal," he barked, "dispatch the troops!"

"No, wait!" Phillip, with a very great show of effort, pulled himself into the saddle. "You can't know where he overtook us. I'll lead! I need every man behind me if we're to find him! Come. Hurry. There's not a moment to waste!"

Phillip pulled his horse around and took off at a fast canter, and the governor hesitated only another moment before seeking his own mount. "You heard the man!" he shouted to O'Donal. "Let us be off!"

Chapter XXVI

The path was seldom used, for it was known only to the members of the Shadowood household as the shortcut through the woods from the wharf to the overseer's cottage. Arabella dismounted in a copse of dense evergreens well concealed from the path. Her frantic flight from the warehouses had gone undetected, but she dared not return to the house lest the troops had already arrived there and were asking questions.

She gentled her horse, for it was skittish from the smoke that drifted from the river, and lifted her hand to untie Phillip's mask. She froze at the sound of hoofbeats along the path.

The approach was sure and steady; the rider knew the way as well as she. The horse rounded a curve and came into view so that Arabella caught a glimpse of the rider's face. When she saw that face, her heart leapt.

Tossing aside the mask, Arabella dropped her reins and stepped into the path. "Phillip!"

Sharply he reined in and, without speaking, slid from the saddle. Arabella held out her arms in an ingenuous welcome, only to have her embrace brushed aside. Phillip's face was grim and pale and his eyes glittered dangerously, but whether it was from pain or anger she could not tell. But she could see the staining of his coat, the bright seepage of blood from his shoulder wound.

"Phillip," she gasped, "you should not be here. You are far too weak—" But her words were abruptly cut off by Phillip's swift and unexpected action. Deliberately he grabbed her arm and pushed her to the ground, his face ravaged by a grimace of anguish as he used his weight to hold her down.

Arabella fell hard, her skirts billowing about her knees, and her face became livid with shock as she stared up into the grim and determined face of her husband. "Phillip, have you gone mad?" She struggled to regain her feet. "What—"

"Lie still, Arabella, for heaven's sake, and do as I tell you." His voice was hoarse and strained and as breathless as hers. "Now is not the time for your endless questions." The words were spoken through clenched teeth as his hands reached for the lace trim along the edge of her exposed petticoat.

Outraged, incredulous protestations sprang to Arabella's lips, and then she saw his face, drawn and desperate, his eyes intent upon his trembling hands that tore at the lace of her garment. She knew then that his behavior was no aberration, no whim; this was not Phillip who had come to her tonight but Le Renard, and he was carrying out a deadly and dangerous plan upon which all their lives might depend.

Finally the material ripped and Phillip began to bind her ankles tightly together. He saw the look of sheer disbelief in Arabella's eyes. Of all the madness that had befallen them, of all the wild and improbable schemes upon which they had embarked together—willingly or unwillingly—this was by far the most bizarre, and the most uncertain. He was moved by the urge to sweep her into his arms, to hold her and reassure her, but there was no time, and he had taken chances enough already.

He took her chin lightly in his fingers and with his eyes he begged her to understand. "I haven't time to explain to you, Arabella," he said breathlessly, "but if ever you have loved me . . . if ever I have needed your trust . . . let it be now. Endure this, and ask no questions. Please."

There was much that she wanted to say: that he should not be there; that he should be at Shadowood taking care of his wound; that it was far too dangerous for him with the king's men about, that the warehouses were safe but the woods were filled with soldiers and he must not be found here. But the only words she spoke were simple and came not only from her heart but from her soul. "I love you more than life, Phillip. What must I do?"

Was it the shine of tears that she saw in his eyes or merely a glint of reflected moonlight? When he answered, his voice was low and gruff with pain. "Lie still and let me bind your hands."

Arabella lay still as he tied her hands and bound a swath of lace around her mouth. And then, with her tied and bound and lying helpless before him on the ground, he drew a knife, a long, wicked-looking blade that glimmered in the moonlight. She could only communicate with him with her eyes—wide, luminous eyes that looked into his and spoke without words. He hesitated for just a moment, then, as the knife moved toward her breasts, she closed her eyes.

She heard the rip of the cloth and felt the cool night air upon her chest. When she opened her eyes Phillip was cutting a bit of lace from her camisole.

"Trust me," he whispered. He looked once more into

her frightened eyes before he made his way back to his horse and rode into the night.

Phillip waited at the edge of the path until the last rider was a few steps ahead of him, then he urged his horse to blend in with the flank of red-coated riders that was fanning out through the woods. He had been right; in the confusion of half a squadron trampling through the unfamiliar woods, his brief absence had not even been noticed. Abruptly he pulled up, made a soft exclamation that attracted the rider next to him, and bent from the saddle.

"Look!" he cried. He lifted himself in the saddle, waving aloft a scrap of lace. "This way, this way! They have passed this way!"

The riders, each one eager to make the kill, barely escaped trampling one another in turning to follow his lead. Phillip made a show of rushing to the front but easily allowed himself to fall back once the direction was clear so that it was the governor himself who first arrived at the small clearing where Arabella lay beneath the tree just as Phillip had left her, bound and gagged and affecting a terror he could not be certain was entirely feigned.

The governor, gasping curses and exclamations of alarm, was off his horse and striding toward her when Phillip drew his horse to a sliding halt amidst the slick foliage of the forest floor and flung himself off.

"My lady! My lady!" he exclaimed, pushing past the governor as he flew to Arabella's side. "What has he done to you? What has the villain done!"

He sank to the ground beside her, and the governor clearly seeing himself bested by the ardent bridegroom, hesitated somewhat uncertainly, clearing his throat and casting a wary glance over his shoulder. The renegade might yet be around, he realized nervously.

Phillip wrested the bit of linen from her mouth and, upon her indrawn breath, covered her lips with his before she could utter a sound. He could feel the frantic pulsing of her heart against his chest, the warmth of lips that even through his pain and throbbing weakness had the power to infuse him with strength. He felt her uncertain struggles, her pounding questions, and he murmured into her mouth, holding her still with a caress that enabled him to wind his fingers into her hair, "My love . . . trust me once more as you have done so often before. . . . Follow my lead."

The governor sank down beside them to assist Phillip with loosening Arabella's bonds, and Phillip demanded frantically, "Did you see him, my wife? Was it Le Renard?"

Arabella, her wide eyes looking deep into his, her throat convulsing on all she would have liked to have said, nodded.

"Aha!" exclaimed the governor. He had freed Arabella's feet and now took the liberty of one caress of her shapely ankles on the pretext of restoring circulation. "Then we are upon him at last!"

"My lord!" O'Donal had dismounted and now held up a piece of dark wool in his hand. "His mask! He was here!"

"Of course he was here, you idiot!" shouted back the governor. "Who else do you think performed this infamy!" Then, turning to the woman before him, he asked with concern, "My dear Lady Arabella, are you all right?"

Phillip tore away the strip that bound Arabella's wrists, then wrapped her cloak more securely around her, holding her close with his free arm. "Which way did he go, my love? Did you see?"

Arabella shivered uncontrollably, though it was

471

more from excitement than fear or cold. She did not remove her eyes from Phillip's, for it was as though his thoughts were written there and, within his thoughts, the words she was supposed to say. "N—North," she managed. "He—He heard the troops and—and bound me . . . and rode n—north . . ." And then, as though overcome by the horror of her ordeal, she buried her face in her husband's chest, wrapping her arms around him, clinging to him as though for dear life. Only he could guess that the shudders that shook her shoulders were not sobs but hysterical laughter—the laughter of triumph, and incredulity, and of love so overwhelming she thought she would burst with it.

Phillip turned back to the troops, his face grim, his voice ringing. "I will have his hide stripped and mounted above my mantel! I shall have him boiled in oil! I hereby double the bounty on the Fox! *Two* thousand guineas to the man who can bring me the renegade's pelt!"

The troops, high with the excitement of the chase and the lure of the prize, wasted no time. They turned in all directions at once, shouting boasts of victory and fanning through the woods.

The governor hung back for a moment, bending solicitously over Arabella. "I say, my lady, are you sure you're all right? Everett, do you need any assistance?"

Phillip, looking greatly pained, pressed a tender kiss upon his wife's tangled hair before replying, "Thank you, my lord, but I beg of you a moment alone with my wife. After her terrible ordeal . . ."

"Of course." With much hrrumphing and creaking of leather boots, the governor got to his feet. "My men will need my guidance, at any rate. We will stop by Shadowood to report our findings. I hope you didn't lose too much to the fire."

"Your concern is too gracious," Phillip assured him

472

sincerely. "I'm sure by now my overseer has organized the slaves to put out the fire."

Again the governor cleared his throat, scowling down at the two of them, obviously uncomfortable yet obviously reluctant to leave. "Damned shame. But we'll get him, Everett. This time we will. I vow to you this gracious colony will no longer be plagued by vermin such as this. We will not stand for it!"

Phillip, his expression earnest and grateful, agreed gravely. "I have the utmost confidence in the King's Army. I for one will never feel safe under my roof until the Fox and all like him are utterly swept from our shores. And as soon as I am healed, you may count on my sword for your efforts!"

"Er . . . yes, well . . ." The governor shifted his eyes uncomfortably. "One can only hope it doesn't come to that." Then he quickly added, "I must catch up to my guard. I'll see you back at Shadowood, Everett. Lady Arabella, your most humble servant . . ." But Arabella, holding fast to her husband, did not reply. He swung around for his horse, barking, "Well, Chatley, do you stay or go? You're the one who brought us here, after all. I thought you would have wanted a taste of the kill!"

Arabella felt her husband stiffen beneath her hands and her own sweeping relief and joy were mitigated by alarm as she heard her brother's voice respond warily, "With your permission, my lord, I will see to my sister's safety first."

"As you will." Lord Dunmore nudged his horse around, and soon his mount's hoofbeats, like the rest, became muffled by the forest floor.

Arabella lifted her face and released her grip from about her husband as he got slowly to his feet. She could see the dangerous darkening in his eyes as Reginald, still on horseback, slowly approached. But otherwise Phillip's face, still alarmingly white, was perfectly blank, and neither his expression nor his stance revealed the thoughts that were in his mind.

Reginald drew up a few feet before them, letting Phillip close the rest of the distance on his own. His hands were sweaty on the reins and his courage had long since fled. One look into those devilish gray eyes would have taken the starch out of any man, and only now was Reginald beginning to suspect what a true demon was this man with whom he had gone into partnership.

Phillip walked close to him and laid a hand upon the bridle of Reginald's horse. His voice, mild and matter-of-fact, rang through the forest. "I think, Chatley, that the Virginia climate does not agree with you. Perhaps a lengthy sojourn in your homeland would be the best course for you at present."

Reginald looked at him for a long time. There was no doubt of the answer; it was merely a matter of finding the voice to speak it. He managed at last, "I think you must be right."

Phillip nodded amicably, but his eyes were as hard as steel as he continued, "And on the voyage home you might think on three things. First, I have in my possession—in my very safe possession—certain documents regarding His Majesty's Decree on Free Shipping and Trade, which would prove most embarrassing to you should they ever reach the wrong hands. I see no reason for that to happen at present, and, due to the great regard in which I hold your sister, I have no wish to bring misfortune upon the name of Chatley, but I do hope this is not a matter upon which you will merely think lightly.

"Second," he continued pleasantly, "you have brought me one gift"—his eyes left Reginald's to rest briefly, gently, upon Arabella—"for which I am

474

grateful. And for that reason, and that alone, all other transactions between us may be forgotten."

He brought his eyes back to Reginald. "And third"—Phillip smiled now, a cold, mirthless smile that had the power to chill the very soul—"if you ever set foot upon Virginia soil again," he said simply, flatly, "I will kill you." He released the bridle and stepped backward. "Good night, Chatley. And good-bye."

Reginald did not hesitate. He did not look at Arabella; he did not look at Phillip. He simply pulled his horse around and fled through the woods.

Through the speech, Arabella's hand had been at her throat, for now she knew the full truth of it and the horror and the shame was almost more than she could bear. "It was Reginald?" she asked shakily needing confirmation. "It was ... my brother who betrayed you?" Yet it had been she, however inadvertently, who had brought this disaster upon Phillip; she, who had the misfortune to be related to a man bereft of morals or loyalty.

Phillip's face was grim as he turned to her, and in his eyes she read the confirmation she sought. Sorrow and regret overwhelmed her so that she could barely speak. "Oh, Phillip ..."

His hand came out to touch her hair, very lightly, then to curve around her neck and gently pull her close to him. His lips touched hers, played upon hers with the softness of caresses, and she felt in the sweetness, in the glory of his touch, forgiveness for all her crimes—those she had committed and those she had not, and those of a lifetime yet to be lived.

He lifted his face and his eyes searched hers with such tenderness, such wonder, that her whole heart swelled to enfold it. As his hand stroked her hair, anxiously, adoringly, he whispered, "Arabella ... my dear love. So many things to say to you, and so few words ...

Know only this, my wife"—his voice was husky as his hand tightened warmly upon the back of her neck—"I have doubted you, I have feared you, I have been angered with you. But I have always loved you. And I love you still."

With a little cry, she swayed toward him, meeting his lips with a kiss that too soon turned greedy, for she was bursting with a joy no mere caress could contain. But too soon he broke away.

His hand was tight upon her shoulder now, his weight heavy against her, and his breathing rapid. His face suddenly seemed very white in the inconstant moonlight, and damp. He smiled at her faintly, shakily, as he moved his hand to caress her face one last time. "And now, my wife," he said weakly, "I must ask one more favor of the many you have done for me. Take me to my horse if you will, for I am not certain how much longer I can stand . . ."

Arabella moved quickly to support his sagging weight, wrapping her arm around his waist as he did hers. Slowly, carefully, they made their way back to their waiting mounts, and home.

Chapter XXVII

For three days, Arabella had not been alone with Phillip except for her lonely predawn visits. The first night of Phillip's injury, Sam had sat by his master's bed, tending him devotedly and single-mindedly throughout the night. He had hovered over Phillip all the next day along with the Granny nurse from the slave quarters, who claimed more curative powers in her potions and elixirs than Arabella could ever think of providing. The cook made numerous trips up the back stairs carrying bowls of broth and soup to build up the master's strength, but for the first day and most of the next Phillip slept, tossing feverishly, waking only when his bandages were changed.

Though her heart bade her otherwise, Arabella left him whenever he slept quietly, for while a band of devoted servants looked after their master, it was up to Arabella to manage all else that was besieging the plantation. The damage to the warehouses had to be assessed, the debris from the fire carted away, and repairs begun. A small portion of the tobacco stored in the adjacent warehouses had been lost, but most of the precious crop had been saved, thanks to Sam's diligence in putting out the fire. William had been invaluable in these last few days, working at Arabella's side as she supervised the moving and storing of the crop in other buildings.

The fire and the arrival of the governor's troops had been greatly disruptive, as had Phillip's injury, and Arabella was continually being barraged on all sides by slaves and servants who wanted reassurances and promises that nothing would happen to the quiet haven of Shadowood, to the familiar ritual of their lives. Of that Arabella could assure them, and to each her answer was always the same. "It will take more than a fire or the governor's troops or even Le Renard to drive us away from Shadowood. This is our home—a place for all of us—and here we shall stay."

They had, of course, quartered the governor and his troops overnight at the plantation, and he, being bitterly disgruntled over once again losing the Fox and over the horror Arabella had endured, spent most of his time muttering apologies and imprecations. He did not linger in the morning, possibly due to embarrassment over the fact that he was taking advantage of the hospitality of a man who lay injured because of his own negligence, and possibly because Arabella was too distraught and too distracted to bestow much of her attention upon him. With his departure, at least half of the burden was lifted from Arabella's shoulders.

What the governor did not know was that, in the early hours before dawn, one of his men had paid a visit to the bedside of Phillip Everett.

Phillip's eyelids had fluttered open tiredly, and when he saw the face of the young man above him, he managed a half-smile. "You have proven yourself again, Hastings. You did not fail me."

Remembering what had almost been, Hastings

forced an expression of casual nonchalance as he gazed down at his leader. Someday he would tell the Fox about his slip with Charlotte, but not now. Now he needed to bask in the glow of the Fox's compliments, though honesty made him add, "I cannot take all the credit. We have another friend who aided me." At Phillip's quizzical look, he went on to explain, "An old friend of yours, in fact. It was Charlotte Parkington who warned me of the raid on Shadowood. I think we have a convert to our cause."

"It is gratifying to know that one has placed his trust in the right quarters. Be certain to express my gratitude to the lady."

"Nothing will give me greater pleasure," Hastings assured him, "than to thank her in a very special way."

A tired smile played around Phillip's lips. The young lieutenant was like a knight of old, filled with the excitement of victory and now ready to enjoy the spoils. "You have done well, Hastings, but our work has not yet ended. William will be contacting you within a few days. Meanwhile, the Fox is going into retirement. Just long enough," he added, seeing the look of consternation on Hastings's face, "for our friend the governor to grow fat and complacent. And then, when he believes all is well—"

"The Fox and his men will be back at his throat." Hastings's lips curved in pleasure. "I shall be awaiting my instructions."

Phillip nodded, his eyes closing in exhaustion as he spoke. "But for now, Lieutenant, I believe you have some personal matters to attend to."

Hastings straightened imperceptibly and placed his hat squarely upon his head. "I am sure the lady is waiting for me, even now."

*   *   *

There was still an hour before sunrise. Quietly Arabella entered Phillip's room and stood by his bed. Outside the window the sky was streaked with mauve and purple fingers of dawn, which cast a warm glow across the room. She reached out a hand and touched his forehead. It was cool now; the fever had finally broken.

Now Arabella checked the fire in the grate, making certain that it still burned brightly enough to warm the room, then she returned to the bed. Phillip stirred, and when she leaned forward to straighten the covers that had slipped during the night, a hand reached up to grasp her wrist.

"Phillip." Her voice was gentle, soft with welcome. "Did I wake you?"

"I've been awake for awhile . . . thinking."

She sat down on the bed beside him and stroked his forehead, pushing his thick hair away from his face. "Your fever has lessened; I'm pleased." Suddenly she was shy, remembering all that had passed between them and all that was yet to be resolved. Her fingers touched his cheek and she smiled at the two days' growth of beard she found there. "I've never known your face not to be clean shaven." And this, she knew, was only one of the many new things she would be learning about Phillip, now that the mask was gone.

He took her hand and pressed it to his lips. "Then I shall have Sam shave me as soon as I've breakfasted. I'm hungry, Arabella, a sure sign my strength is returning."

His hand still held hers and he kissed the tip of each finger lightly as his eyes meshed with hers. Both knew what was happening; both could feel the need that had been within them rising and curling like a great wave unleashed from a deep, secret place in the sea. Yet Arabella tried to forestall the coming of the inevitable.

Withdrawing her hand slightly she said, "The governor departed—empty-handed—two days hence, and we did not lose much crop—"

His eyes never leaving hers, Phillip recaptured her hand, laying it against the silky stubble of his face. "Sam has kept me informed. My compliments, wife, for you have managed admirably in my place. And now"—his voice grew husky as his eyes searched hers— "I would beg of you only a kiss, to welcome me home . . ."

Arabella sighed a sigh of welcome and release, and she leaned forward to press her lips against Phillip's. For the first time she could kiss him unashamedly, unabashedly, with no masks between them, their secrets and mysteries all cast aside. It was as if in the flames of the warehouses she had been born again and her life with Phillip given a second chance. Phillip's lips opened beneath hers, warm and sweet and, as she melted into the kiss, his arms lifted and closed tightly around her.

Arabella drank from his lips as if they held all the sweet nectar of the gardens of heaven. She kissed him again and again, greedily slipping her tongue into the slippery cavern of his mouth, caressing and exploring. She drew him into her mouth then, wanting the sweet ravishment, shivering as his tongue invaded the dark secrets of her mouth.

She could feel the pounding of his heart through her thin gown, hear his ragged breathing, feel the taut muscles of his chest, the strength of the body that yearned toward her own. Some innate sense of propriety tried to warn her that this was not the time or place and that she should pull away, but she could not. The great wave of passion bore her along toward its inevitable end. She had waited so long—an eternity, it seemed—to lie beside her husband beneath the roof

481

of Shadowood.

When the kiss ended and Arabella's lips nestled against Phillip's cheek, she grasped at the last vestiges of reason. "We should not, Phillip . . . your shoulder . . ."

Phillip's arms only held her more tightly and the voice that answered was hoarse with desire. "Oh, my dear Arabella, I have never felt more fit in my life."

His right hand reached up to untie the ribbons at the neck of her gown. "But you will have to help me," he whispered. "Come, Arabella, come under the covers, away from the chill of the night. Come to bed with your husband."

She hesitated but a moment before she slipped the gown from her head and dropped it on the floor, where it lay like a pale splash of white in the coming light. She slid under the covers next to him, and for a time they both lay still, struck with the wonder of their long-awaited union.

Phillip stirred and pulled her tightly against him so that he could explore the sweetness of her body with his eager hand. It moved along her smooth, supple back, her wonderfully rounded buttocks, the line of her hipbone, the swell of her breasts. His hand lingered there and cupped one soft orb, caressing the rosebud of her nipple, rubbing his palm across its aching tenderness until he felt Arabella tremble in his arms.

"Oh, Phillip," she whispered against his chest, her voice throaty and broken, "my love . . . my love . . ."

He thought of all he wanted to do with her, the ways he wanted to make love to her. He wanted to kiss every inch of her lithe, sensual body, her full, pink-tipped breasts, the curve of her abdomen, the silkiness of her thighs. He wanted to plunge deep within her and unleash the pent-up longings that knotted and coiled within him. He wanted to love her at last as his wife, the

482

woman he loved more than all the world. Phillip silently cursed his wounded shoulder; he cursed the British and Lord Dunmore and King George as his desire grew like a swelling, aching thundercloud.

Arabella shifted so that she could look down at the face of the man she loved. It was a beautiful face, a strong, masculine face, and just to look upon it filled her with immense pleasure. She kissed him softly at first and then again, greedily, hungrily, not just his lips but the curve of his eyebrow, the line of his cheek, his chin, the hollow of his neck. She tasted him with her lips and tongue and smelled his musky masculine scent. Arabella's tender, aching nipples rubbed against the hardness of his chest, her arms wrapped around his neck, and she gave herself up to the desire that unfurled within the deepest parts of her.

Phillip returned her kisses with fierce abandon; he buried his hand in her thick hair and held her tightly against him, the length of her body molded against his. His kisses made her feel as though she were made of molten silver, for she was dissolving under a white-hot flame, flowing and merging into the body of the man beneath her. The skin of each was hot and slippery now, and their passion-damp flesh melded them together. The hard thrust of his manhood pushed against the softness of her abdomen, and she longed to touch him there.

Slowly and deliberately her hands began to explore him, touching his flat, hard nipples, feeling the light feathering of hair on his broad chest, tracing the edge of the bandage, willing herself to be gentle. She could feel Phillip's skin growing pliant beneath her ministrations and noted his rapidly labored breathing and the unsteadiness of his hand that caressed her back and hip as she made love to him with her touch.

Her fingers slid down across his flat abdomen,

skimmed the line of his hips, and found his hot arousal. Tentatively at first, and then with increasing boldness, her hand curved around him, stroking the length of him, feeling him grow even as her hand caressed him. She felt Phillip tremble, and her own desire heightened and surged, building, building . . .

"Sweet Jesus, Arabella, you will drive me mad . . . !" Phillip's words were husky, a groan torn from the depths of his need. He lifted his head and took one of her ripe pink nipples in his mouth, suckling with lips and tongue and teeth. She felt tiny shocks dance through her as she dug her fingers into the hard muscles of his back, unable to speak, unable to do more than moan and whimper as his fingers found the secret place between her thighs and worked their magic there. His fingers moved within her, playing her like a beloved instrument, bringing her to the edge of release, and all the while his mouth sucked upon her tender, swollen nipple. There was no way to describe the pleasures he gave her, no way to put into words the feelings that she held for this man, her husband, who was all the world to her. She wanted nothing more than to please him, to give him the ecstasy he gave to her, for he was her beloved Phillip—past, present, and future.

When he spoke to her, she was not at first sure of his words, but he repeated them. "Get astride me, Arabella, a knee on either side of my hips."

She was not certain yet what he meant to do, but as she slipped across his passion-damp flesh, a smile of eager anticipation crossed her face. She needed no explanation now, no instruction to raise herself and then slide down upon the delight that awaited her. When Phillip entered her she cried out in rapture, for he was home where he belonged, at last.

They moved together, slowly at first, a little unsure, until Phillip placed his hand at her waist to guide her movements. Then the rhythm of their bodies became as one, and the mighty wave that had been cresting within each could no longer be held at bay. Faster and faster they moved. Arabella's hair seemed a wild blanket of flame, whipping about her head in the uncontrollable fury of their coupling. She cried aloud at the wonder of their union, the power of their love as man and wife. With all masks cast aside, they gave freely of their passions and all barriers between them were forever swept away.

Then the great wave of desire broke, crashing against the shore and carrying them with it, leaving them trembling and shaken, weak and fulfilled, locked in each other's arms, renewed. Arabella felt tears dampening her face as she lay across Phillip, holding on to him for dear life, for indeed he was her life.

They lay together for a long while, lost in the wonder of what had happened between them, awed by the power of their love. As strength and reason slowly returned, Arabella slid carefully away from him, mindful of his injury, then snuggled close again as his arm drew her to him. There would be no distance between them ever again. Her head rested against his uninjured shoulder, one arm was flung over his chest and one leg hooked across his, as if she were determined not to break the contact between them. Phillip's hand played lovingly with her thick curls as their heartbeats slowed to a more normal tempo and their breathing eased so that they could speak.

"How long have you known?" Phillip asked softly after a time. "How long have you known that I am the Fox?"

She turned her head to look up at him soberly. "I knew you were Phillip the night that we made love on your boat. Did you think you could hide your eyes, the shape of your mouth, the strength of your hands, from

485

a woman who had loved you so long? When I made love to you, you were my Phillip from Devon, not the prattling, prancing fool that I had married. But then I was angry because I thought that you were playing some kind of mocking trick on me, pretending to be the Fox . . ."

Laughter rumbled in his chest. "You could not believe that your prattling fop of a husband could indeed be the infamous Fox?"

"Not at first; not at all. It wasn't until that night at the ball, when I followed you—"

Phillip's head turned sharply. "My God, Arabella, you followed me? Do you know the danger—?"

Now it was Arabella's turn to laugh. "Phillip, my love, you must stop that annoying habit of underestimating me. Of course I knew the danger—and if I had not, you made it clear when I met you in the churchyard."

"And the more I threatened you, the more determined you became. I should have known that you were the Flame, Arabella—stubborn and impossible to frighten away."

"I was only trying to help you, Phillip," she said softly.

His arm tightened briefly on her shoulders. "I know that, love."

"I thought my writings would distract the governor from his pursuit of you. It did not work as well as I had planned," she confessed, "so I had to take other measures. And if I had not decided to present the front of the perfect Tory wife, I would not have been in the lord governor's confidence when he planned the raid on Shelton's Cove."

Phillip released a soft breath. "So *that's* how you knew."

She nodded soberly. "A woman can go unsuspected

into many places a man cannot. There are advantages to being the Flame of Liberty . . . and a female."

He smiled at her. "And I am only just beginning to learn of them." But then the smile swiftly disappeared into an expression of fierce intensity as he pressed a long, gentle kiss upon her temple. "Ah, Arabella, so many games between us. I never meant to hurt you with my deception but only to protect you from the consequences of knowledge. The fewer who know my secret, the better chance we all have for survival."

Arabella nodded soberly. "And what would you have done if I had confessed to you my knowledge of your secret, before you had come to know me as the Flame?"

"I do not know," he answered honestly after a time. "Locked you up perhaps; sent you to the Indies . . . I truly do not know, Arabella, but I could not have left you roaming free with knowledge that could have meant death to so many, for I had no way of knowing what you would do with it."

"Then isn't it for the best that I kept my secret? You see, Phillip, I am becoming good at this game—"

"It is no game, Arabella. That is what you must understand, and that is why the Flame's career, spectacular though it has been"—he took a breath—"must now end. This masquerade is far too dangerous for you to continue. I must forbid it."

"Arabella's head rose sharply and she stared at him. "Forbid? Phillip, I am your wife, not your chattel or your slave." At these words, she could see the lines of stubbornness forming about his eyes.

"It is not enough then for you to be my wife, to live here at Shadowood, to bear my children and share my life?"

"There is nothing that I want more, Phillip," Arabella said distinctly, "than to truly be your wife—

487

not that mock creature I portrayed in Williamsburg. But don't you see, I can never go back to the way I was before. I can never forget what I have seen."

Her small fist tightened against his shoulder, and her emerald eyes took on an intensity that drew upon his very soul. "I confess that at first it was a game, a masquerade to protect my husband, and the truth of it I did not fully understand. But now I have seen the truth, and, Phillip, it is one I cannot abide." Her eyes fastened upon him with horror and outrage mounting in their fiery green depths. "Look at what they have done to you—you could have died! They have come into my home, they have threatened all that I love, they have brought their soldiers onto Shadowood, and they have spilled blood here. This I cannot allow. I will not stand idly by while my home and my husband and my livelihood are snatched from me by those who are yet strangers in this land!"

Phillip, watching her, felt a surge of love and pride so intense that it took his breath away and left him weak. *Yes, by God,* he thought, *that was the truth of it.* First one man—or woman—and then another, and another, joining in the fight, not for principles or noble words, but to protect what was theirs, because it *was theirs.* She did understand. She had joined him completely.

But she was his wife, the life more precious to him than any other in the world, and he had to protest, and firmly. "It is too dangerous. You serve best by staying behind."

"Would you quit?" she challenged him. "It is you who lie there with a musket hole in your shoulder, not I. But would you give up the fight? Forget the Fox?"

He took a breath. "I am in too deep, Arabella; there are too many people dependent on me; too much to be done." His voice had a bitter twist. "Too many who do not yet understand the importance of our fight—"

"And that is precisely why the Flame of Liberty must not die." She sat up, her eyes gleaming now with a new, excited fire. "Phillip, if I but had a printing press here at Shadowood my pamphlets could reach a whole new readership—people who have borne separately the oppressive burdens of the king. If they could be rallied together—if all the information could be disseminated to them . . . In knowledge there is strength; in numbers there will be victory. If I but had a press—"

"Absolutely not, Arabella." His voice was firm, slightly alarmed. "Surely you see it is not possible to have a press here—"

"Sam showed me a building that would be perfect for it."

"Lack of space is not the reason, Arabella; it is the danger. No."

She was quiet. She lay back down beside him thoughtfully. When she spoke, her voice was calm and certain. "I shall have a press somehow, Phillip. I still have friends in England, literary friends, writers, publishers—even printers—who understand the value of the written word. If I ask—no, if I beseech—they will somehow get me a printing press. Of course, such an undertaking would doubtlessly involve a great deal of notoriety. . . ."

"Are you blackmailing me, Arabella?"

She turned to him with a smile and her forefinger lightly traced the shape of his chin as she answered, "Of course I am, my darling. Did you for a moment think otherwise?"

Phillip laughed, his free arm tightening about her, and Arabella knew the argument was over. There would be more, many more, for she and Phillip were both too headstrong not to clash, but at least she had won this battle.

"I have a ship sailing for England next week," he

said. "On its return, it shall carry your printing press, but I still do not like it, Arabella."

"Of course, my love, I understand, and there will be many times when I shall not like what you do . . . but I shall never forbid you, Phillip. Entice you, perhaps . . ." She kissed his neck. "Wheedle you . . ." She kissed his chin. "Cajole you . . ." Her voice fell to a whisper as her lips touched his cheek. "Even seduce you . . . but never forbid you."

They kissed again, a deep and long and abiding kiss, and when it was over far more than a bargain had been sealed. They had made the commitment of a lifetime.

"Ah, Arabella." With a sigh, Phillip leaned back against the pillows, wrapping her hand in his, holding it against his throat. "My dear Arabella. You are more than my wife; you are my equal in every way—in courage and cunning and skill and wit. How can I exist without you?"

She kissed him again. "I shall see to it that you shan't. Oh, Phillip, I love you so; I cannot imagine life without you."

"Nor I without you." His eyes were penetrating and sober and filled with adoration as he lightly pushed away a strand of hair from her face with their entwined hands. "You have brought more than love into my life, Arabella, and more than desire, which I have known before. You have brought me trust, without which, I fear, nothing else can survive. I shall always be grateful to you for that."

"And I to you, Phillip," she whispered, "for much, much more than you can ever know."

Through the window the morning sun's first rays were just beginning to appear, their golden fingers awakening the fields and rivers of Tidewater Virginia and reaching beyond to the rolling foothills, the mountains, and across to touch the plains of this new and vital land. That same sun had sunk hours before on the British Isles and had left them in twilight, fading, while its colony now basked in the glory of the new day that would be.

They lay in each other's arms, the Fox and the Flame, their eyes turned toward a horizon that was not untroubled, understanding that for each battle that was behind them more lay ahead. Even now forces were gathering in the distance that would threaten their happiness, shatter their peace, and ultimately change the course of history. But together they would face each dawning day, doing what must be done, fighting for what was right, and knowing that, hand in hand, their love would shelter them and they would emerge victorious.

Each month you'll receive 4 brand new Zebra Historical Romance novels as soon as they are published. Look them over *Free* for 10 days. If you're not delighted simply return them and owe nothing. But if you enjoy them as much as we think you will, you'll pay *only* $3.50 each and save 45¢ over the cover price. (You save a total of $1.80 each month.) *There is no shipping and handling charge or other hidden charges.*

——— *Fill Out the Coupon* ———

Start your subscription now and start saving. Fill out the coupon and mail it *today.* You'll get your FREE book along with your first month's books to preview.

CAPTIVATING ROMANCE
by Penelope Neri

CRIMSON ANGEL   (1783, $3.95)
No man had any right to fluster lovely Heather simply because he was so impossibly handsome! But before she could slap the arrogant captain for his impudence, she was a captive of his powerful embrace, his one and only *Crimson Angel*.

PASSION'S BETRAYAL   (1568, $3.95)
Sensuous Promise O'Rourke had two choices: to spend her life behind bars — or endure one night in the prison of her captor's embrace. She soon found herself fettered by the chains of love, forever a victim of *Passion's Betrayal*.

HEARTS ENCHANTED   (1432, $3.75)
Lord Brian Fitzwarren vowed that somehow he would claim the irresistible beauty as his own. Maegan instinctively knew that from that moment their paths would forever be entwined, their lives entangled, their *Hearts Enchanted*.

BELOVED SCOUNDREL   (1799, $3.95)
Instead of a street urchin, the enraged captain found curvaceous Christianne in his arms. The golden-haired beauty fought off her captor with all her strength — until her blows become caresses, her struggles an embrace, and her muttered oaths moans of pleasure.